Praise for *Twelve*

"A wonderful and inventive nove...
measure. It was a true pleasure to...
—Miranda Cowley Heller, author of ...

"Not many people can pull off a story where two ghosts try to bring the partners they left behind together, but Louisa Young apparently can and did. More than a novel, this is a treatise on love, death, and grief that utterly blew me away. One of the freshest love stories I've read in years."

—Colleen Oakley, author of *The Invisible Husband of Frick Island*

"Equal parts tender, sparkling, and authentic, Louisa Young's prose is like watching a flower open, each moment beautiful, mesmerizing, and better than the last. *Twelve Months and a Day* will have readers captivated from beginning to end."

—Amy E. Reichert, author of *Once Upon a December*

"A tale of two love stories with a supernatural twist, *Twelve Months and a Day* is poignant and sad as well as funny and beautifully written and imagined. What if our beloveds lived on as ghosts and watched us grieve, what if they never really leave us, and what if some of these ghosts even meet? You will fall in love again as you read this clever book by a writer who understands grief. Hugely engaging and readable. A bittersweet pang in my heart as it ended. A page-turner."

—Monique Roffey, author of *The Mermaid of Black Conch*

"What a writer. A raw and beautiful exposition on grief and loss but so beautifully earthed in the everyday. Terrific."

—Elizabeth Buchan, author of *Revenge of the Middle-Aged Woman*

"The words 'emotional roller coaster' seem coined for Louisa Young's beautiful, bittersweet novel, as heart-stoppingly romantic as it's heartbreakingly sad.... Young has a playfully light touch, delighting in the absurdity of the supernatural situation and the unusual romantic complications, even as she explores the heavy emotional burden that death brings. A lovely, moving, ultimately hopeful read."

—The *Express* (UK)

"A modern-day *Truly Madly Deeply* ... Rasmus and Roisin both lose their partners, but the ghosts of Nico and Jay stay, unable to leave their loved ones alone as the brokenhearted pair find comfort in each other. Beautifully written, this is a haunting love story—literally."

—*Best* magazine (UK)

"Delicately balanced between wry and tender, *Twelve Months and a Day* is both an exorcism of the most brutal pain of final separation and a way of managing the stubborn refusal of the mind to accept absolute absence. Thoughtful, philosophical, and clever, it is also funny, and full of poetry, and powered by an unflagging and irresistible belief in the redemptive power of love."

—*Perspective* magazine (UK)

"Louisa Young is the great chronicler of romantic love and the pain of its loss."   —Linda Grant, author of *The Clothes on Their Backs*

"Left me happily in bits. A skillfully calibrated love-after-death tale, it's a four-course feast of hearts broken, hearts mended, of songs, laughter, old regrets, and fresh desire that demands a major film deal."

—Patrick Gale, author of *A Place Called Winter*

"A beautiful book. Insanely romantic and utterly convincing."

—Julie Myerson, author of *The Stopped Heart*

Praise for *My Dear I Wanted to Tell You*

"Inspires the kind of devotion among its readers not seen since David Nicholls's *One Day*."
—*The Times* (UK)

"This masterly storyteller fervently believes that the healing process begins with a decision to share your stories . . . with those you love."
—*The Washington Post*

"An epic love story."
—*Kirkus Reviews*

"Powerful."
—*The Sunday Times* (UK)

"Singular in quality . . . an unsensationalized and thoughtful story of . . . that universal constant—love."
—*Publishers Weekly*

"One of those books that doesn't leave you, and probably never will."
—Jacqueline Winspear, author of *Maisie Dobbs*

"Uplifting and emotional."
—*Tatler*

"Compelling and deeply moving."
—*The Observer*

"The lives of loved ones left behind are masterfully conveyed."
—*Woman & Home*

Twelve

Months

and a

Day

Also by Louisa Young

FICTION
Baby Love
Desiring Cairo
Tree of Pearls
My Dear I Wanted to Tell You
The Heroes' Welcome
Devotion

NONFICTION
A Great Task of Happiness
The Book of the Heart
You Left Early: A True Story of Love and Alcohol

CHILDREN'S
(with Isabel Adomakoh Young as Zizou Corder)
The Lionboy Trilogy
Lee Raven, Boy Thief
Halo

Twelve Months and a Day

LOUISA YOUNG

G. P. Putnam's Sons
New York

PUTNAM
— EST. 1838 —

G. P. PUTNAM'S SONS
Publishers Since 1838
An imprint of Penguin Random House LLC
penguinrandomhouse.com

First published in the United Kingdom in 2022 by The Borough Press,
an imprint of HarperCollins Publishers Ltd.
Copyright © 2022 by Louisa Young
Penguin Random House supports copyright. Copyright fuels creativity,
encourages diverse voices, promotes free speech, and creates a vibrant culture.
Thank you for buying an authorized edition of this book and for complying with
copyright laws by not reproducing, scanning, or distributing any part of it in any
form without permission. You are supporting writers and allowing
Penguin Random House to continue to publish books for every reader.

Library of Congress Cataloging-in-Publication Data

Names: Young, Louisa, author.
Title: Twelve months and a day / Louisa Young.
Description: New York : G. P. Putnam's Sons, 2023.
Identifiers: LCCN 2022047433 (print) | LCCN 2022047434 (ebook) |
ISBN 9780593542651 (trade paperback) | ISBN 9780593542644 (ebook)
Classification: LCC PR6125.O9415 T94 2023 (print) |
LCC PR6125.O9415 (ebook) | DDC 823/.92—dc23
LC record available at https://lccn.loc.gov/2022047433
LC ebook record available at https://lccn.loc.gov/2022047434

p.   cm.

Printed in the United States of America
1st Printing

Title page art: Cloud background © Ratchat / Shutterstock
Book design by Alison Cnockaert

To Michel Faber, with love and thanks.

Of old age, in our sleep

It seems ridiculous to suppose the dead miss anything.

—Marilynne Robinson, *Gilead*

Twelve

Months

and a

Day

1

Bloody Boats

FEBRUARY
London

RÓISÍN KENNEDY—THIRTY-THREE, observant, clever, a slight rockabilly look to her (blue-tipped hair, at the moment, and a little fringe)—was feeling good in the pale sunshine of the gastropub garden. She and her fiancé, Nico Triandafilides—thirty-six, nicely shaved, clean white shirt, quite the lad even on a Saturday lunchtime—hadn't seen much of each other that week. He'd been working nights and she'd had a deadline in the editing suite. They hadn't been getting on that well: for three months they'd been on a promise to discuss whether or not they wanted to have a child, though it was something neither of them actually *wanted* to talk about. They each thought that the other felt differently about it to them and was secretly upset. They were both wrong, and therefore they were both, secretly, upset. So this long-weekend morning of unexpectedly hot sex and breakfast out was bloody lovely.

It was the first sunny morning of springtime: too early for the crocuses, but the unmistakable secret sign had gone out. The light was a breath lighter; even London's sooty black walls and spit-raddled gray curbstones had an air of imminence. When the breeze lifted your hair, the sun was almost warm on your skin. The swans in the park had started with the neck-coiling; there was mimosa on the flower stalls. She was having avocados and stuff; he was going the full English, with triple espressos and extra black pudding.

"Funniest thing this week?" she cued him, their old habit, a guaranteed mood-enhancer—mood-changer if need be—and that started up the run of stupid jokes. One of her many sisters, Nell, had pointed out that the term "Leider-hosen"—like Lederhosen, the well-known and arguably regrettable dungaree-style Alpine leather shorts, only with an extra *i*—meant, in German, literally, "regrettable trousers." This alone provoked some hilarity. "Yeah, I've had a few pairs of them in my time," Nico said, and they remembered one brown tweed suit that had made him look like a confused sheep farmer.

"Or an Irish intellectual," Róisín had said kindly.

"Irish!" Nico squawked, which was fair enough as he really couldn't have looked more Greek, from his brown eyes and hairy chest to his quizzical mouth and not-very-secret desire to have a mustache like his granddad's.

"So does that make Lieder-hosen trousers for singing classic German folk songs in?" Nico said, and it went downhill.

Lido-hosen, she suggested, for urban swimming.

"You could wear them when you go to Crouch End," he said. "With Lilo-hosen to change into, for wearing on your lilo. Inflatable, maybe."

Lipo-hosen, she suggested, which make you thinner.

"We don't need *them*," he said. "Lager-hosen, for drinking beer in! Indistinguishable from the original Lederhosen."

"Luger-hosen," she said, "with a built-in holster."

Wader-hosen, with long wellies attached for fishing. Yoda-hosen,

Data-hosen, Gator-hosen, and make it snappy. Hater-hosen, for Twitter trolls; Mater- and Pater-hosen for Latin teenagers to address their parents; Straighter-hosen, if you're going for the skinny-leg look. They were in such hysterics by then that people turned to look. All those couples with nothing to say to each other after fifteen years, glancing across at the couple in fits of giggles. It wasn't because the jokes were that funny, because obviously they weren't. It was just that they were having such a lovely time. He'd even rolled up his sleeves, pretending they were by some sunlit blue bay in Ithaca, at Frikes in the morning sun, with bitter coffee and baklava—God, summer, so far away—and then something in the sound of his laughter changed and she was calling out.

Twenty-one minutes while she and the barmaid took turns giving him CPR, till the ambulance came. Paramedics who didn't know that he was one of them. But everybody knew that it was too long. Her eyes were still full of the tears of laughter he'd reduced her to. She didn't feel it was right for him to die while her hair was this stupid blue. She wanted to kiss him but once the pros arrived, she couldn't get near him for equipment. *CPR, our last kiss.*

After a while, alone and almost furtive by the trolley in A&E, she took her father's wedding ring from her forefinger and put it on his finger, third finger, left hand. And she took his stupid rock 'n' roll silver skull ring and put it on her own.

"I do," she tried to say. "You do too."

They'd been going to. He'd actually proposed the day they met: in the mudbath of a Glastonbury crowd bouncing around to the Fratellis. Nico had intervened when a drunk stranger was being difficult during "Chelsea Dagger" ("Listen," he'd said. "Go away."), and the resultant joshing ended up with him proposing to her. A year later he'd given her a diamond. No mud. But they'd never got round to the actual wedding. It seemed absurd, actually getting married. But a romantic revelation had crept up on them. *This* was love. This every day. This supporting each other. *Me supporting him, mostly*, she often thought, *but you know*. The diamond fitted snugly now with the skull, like a tiny flower behind its ear. Holding it on.

SHE STOOD ON the deck of the launch in the black-and-white Dalmatian-print fake-fur coat she had decided was just the thing for the occasion. *Well, what the hell do you wear?* she thought. *To denote courage, devil-may-care desperation, determination, I'm going to make it through today, I am, it's required.*

She'd cut her hair, because she didn't know what to do: slaughtered the peroxide strands with the blue tips and the little tumbling fringe; sent it to the cancer charity for children. Her head now wore a soft fuzz of its natural dark brown and she'd a feeling she looked like Sinéad O'Connor back in the day. Sinéad was a lovely-looking woman, but it wasn't what she wanted people to be thinking about when they were shouldering his coffin to the boat. Still, she'd done it now, so.

To the northeast she saw the red-and-white lighthouse of the Needles standing proud against blue sky. Southwest was the wide horizon down to the Atlantic. Behind her, a hundred people on a bright, terrible, unseasonably sunny morning out on the Solent in boats, all saying "I had no idea he wanted to be buried at sea!" But that's the good thing about dying young. Lots of friends still around to come to your funeral. *Look, darling, they all came! And they're all in bloody boats!*

Who knew!

She'd let his mum arrange it all. She was hardly going to make a fuss when Marina was ringing her wanting to know if she thought it would be all right, as there was no grave in the earth, to ask the sea-burial people if they could throw the grains of wheat into the sea, or should they just do it without saying anything? Róisín had no opinion about that.

Nobody knew where his will was.

Lots of his family were there, lighting candles in loaves of bread, and keening. Twenty-three of hers. Declan with the good voice sang "The Parting Glass"; Dmitri with the even better voice sang the one about how he gave her rosewater and she gave him poison . . . The works. He died. *Damn you, you utter bastard, darling*—Cavafy was recited, of course: "Ithaka." Kind of compulsory. *Don't hurry the journey at all, better if it lasts for years* . . . She hardly heard it; there was nothing in her to consider how inappropriate that was. And Tennyson: *Sunset and evening star, And one clear call for me! And may there be no moaning of the bar, When I put out to sea* . . . . The kind men in uniform put the lilies aside and flicked the flag away. Nico's coffin—plain new wood, heavily weighted—had been drilled through with more holes than she had expected. It was so quick! The men tipped it into the sea, green and choppy here, mercury-silver in the distance, *bloody sea, you can't trust it,* and it sank. She wasn't crying, because she didn't want to set people off, to raise the water level. She watched the bubbles swaying as they rose. *Goodbye. Αντίο φίλε μου. Slán.*

Everyone else cried anyway, friends and relations, throwing flowers on the water. Gulls appeared from nowhere and wheeled beautifully among them. The boat circled, and for a moment she thought she felt a hand on the back of her neck. She jumped—but there was nobody.

Someone put a glass of whiskey in her hand. She hurled it overboard, toward him.

Why did you die? But she knew why he died. Dying is what people do, who drink and smoke and argue and work all the hours God sends and, it turns out, have an undiagnosed heart condition. And anyway it was her fault. Making him laugh so much.

Even she realized that was stupid. *It's normal to think it's your fault but that really is stupid.*

◆   ◆   ◆

RÓISÍN LAY IN bed on her back. No position comfortable. Her body had knotted itself up in response to the absence of his. "Where are you?" she cried. "For God's sake, Nico, where are you?"

She did the usual human things. She lit candles, so his spirit if it was wandering about would have a light to see by. She went to Mass! Which wasn't like her, but there's nothing like death to turn you to religion. The Hail Mary hadn't looked so attractive for decades. *Pray for us now and at the hour of our . . .* She stood in the aisle of Sainsbury's on Fortis Green Road, staring at the bottles of San Pellegrino she used to get for him when he was cutting down on booze, and at bottles of ketchup she needn't buy anymore because it was him that liked ketchup. Supermarkets were comforting. She came out with three kinds of cream cheese and no washing-up liquid.

She went over to the Ladies' Pond on Hampstead Heath for her usual Sunday swim, *no Nico at the Men's Pond, no coffee together afterwards,* put on her little neoprene socks and gloves and her woolly hat, all so black against her white, white skin, and prepared to slip into the cold, forgiving water. *But the ponds drain to the river which goes to the sea . . .* She dived in off the steps and thought about staying there, underwater, in the murk; the natural animal feeling of it, and the strange gleams of Old Testament light.

As she came up, a robin made a side-head special-face at her from the fence.

In the changing room she stared at herself in the mirror. Her face so round and pale, her eyes so round and blue, her little mouth. Everything was normal, except for everything.

Her friends were being fantastic. Her sister Nell rang five times a day. "You can't live on alcohol and marzipan," she said. "You've to eat vegetables. Vegetables. In soup or something." Vegetable soup made Róisín cry.

"How are you doing?" Nell asked. "What's going on?"

"Dame Helena Handcart has introduced Monsieur Shit to Madame Fan," Róisín said.

"Ohhhh," said Nell.

"I looked up what happens without the will and guess what it said? It said: 'The following people have *no* right to inherit where someone dies without leaving a will: unmarried partners.'"

"It'll turn up," said Nell.

"Maybe," Róisín said faintly.

She didn't do anything about it. It was surprisingly easy. For a bit. Then at four in the morning she'd wake up terrified.

At work, her kind colleagues made sympathetic side-head at her like the robin. There'd been white envelopes on her desk, like for a birthday or when you leave. One card at home had a mauve iris on it, and glitter. At first she'd opened them, because she wanted to read the nice things people had to say about him. She'd laughed at how they'd found nice things to say even though he could be a difficult sod. "Nico was one of a kind"; "Such a character"; "I never knew anybody quite like him." *Just as well, in some ways*, she'd thought.

It turned out lots of people had suffered heartbreaking loss. The most surprising people! The very nerdiest of the IT boys who worked downstairs came shyly to her with a small book of so-called poems to save your life, and told her about his boyfriend Anwar at school. She'd had no idea there was so much death around. *You too, huh.* Her boss, Ayesha, brought her a cup of tea and said, "You take your time." Róisín remembered the cup of tea the nurse had brought her. She went home.

"NELL," RÓISÍN SAID on the phone. "You know how he'd always text me, all day, whatever was going on, and now he doesn't—so I think something's happened to him, even though something *has* happened to him, I know that perfectly well, but my thoughts are just . . . are just . . . so am I being an eejit?"

Nell said, "You're in bits still. Have you had something to eat yet today?"

"Marzipan . . ." Róisín murmured. She felt she was boring her friends and her family with her grief; that they would like her to start getting over it. "Mam wants me to come home for a bit."

"Do you want to?"

"NO!" Róisín yelped.

"Don't, so."

It wasn't that she didn't love them. But at least five of her siblings would talk in front of her about how terrible it was, their beloved Nico dying. She wanted peace. Nell would come up from Hastings at the drop of a hat. Already had done. Several times.

"What you need to do," said Nell, "is—"

"I don't want a counselor," Róisín said.

"A counselor would be good for you," said Nell. "But I won't be dragging you. No, what you want is to meet people in the same boat as you. Have you looked up those bereavement support groups?"

"Fuck off, Nell," she said. "Would you kindly."

SHE HAD A sense that he was looking over her shoulder, was just in the other room. There were dreams: one where he'd been putting a small child in the boot of a car. One where they had a glorious adventure running around in ruined cities, jumping off things on lianas, dancing, ending up in a dive bar with Johnny Cash; one where they were kissing on a shining cloud while tiny fish darted around like dragonflies over their heads, and just before she woke, he shrank, tiny, and ran toward her just at the level of her heart, and opened a door in her chest, and walked inside, waving up to her cheerily as he went.

She bunked off work one day because she heard, she swore she heard, his voice saying "Come here to me now, I want you," so she'd jumped on a train and taken the ferry to the Isle of Wight with an armful of hyacinths, in the rain, and she'd thrown them overboard mid-Channel, thinking about him, waving in the weeds, *those are pearls that were his eyes*—they'd make terrible pearls, an awful color for a pearl, worse than those shiny purplish ones you'd see on stalls at a craft market that looked like blood blisters, or buboes from the plague. She wanted to think of him being dead because she couldn't *stop* thinking about him and the aliveness of him in these thoughts was unbearable. So—physical. She'd smelled his jumper randomly on a bus—a waft of wool and vetiver and the way he had of *always* smelling of suntan oil. She'd found his T-shirt in her bed, when it had no business being there, though true, she hadn't yet changed the sheets, and yes of course she knew she should, but he had slept in these sheets. One evening, dancing alone to the radio, drunk in the tiny kitchen they had shared in presumptuous ignorance of what fate had lined up for them, she felt so strongly that he had just slipped into her arms that she hugged him back. Cyndi Lauper was singing, time after time, and on some level—what level? It confused her even now— she was holding him and crying and he was holding her, his arms round her shoulders, the weight of them. She danced with him, a slow rock 'n' roll, hands stretched out to invisible hands, to and fro, to and fro. Holding her arm up and out to be twirled, spinning lazily back into his nonexistent embrace, stars rolling round her head and a moonshine mood pervading her. Then she'd gone in to bed, muttering prayers from her childhood—*Now I lay me down to sleep—If you're lost—pray for us sinners now and at the hour—I will be there.* She tripped over a shoe—one of his, a black Chelsea boot—*what was it doing there?*—stubbing her toe, and then again there he was, the weight of him on the side of the bed, lying down beside her. She felt his hand on her shoulder, and half asleep she reached up to hold it, and that was so sweet but then she woke, shaking, and ran and hid in the bathroom, and cried. Knowing grief is going to be strange doesn't stop it being strange.

The following night she sat up late watching YouTube clips of elephants. People were playing Debussy to them on a piano in Thailand. It was very nice, but she was concerned. One elephant was rocking and she wasn't sure if it was really-digging-this-Debussy rocking, or I-am-going-mad-with-stress-would-you-get-this-piano-playing-twat-out-of-here-with-his-turn-of-the-century-melodic-noodlings rocking. She wasn't sleeping anyway. She kept remembering the touch on her neck during his funeral, and telling herself she was imagining it, *please, brain, could you not*. She'd read a book about hallucination and ghosts once. Maybe it was *her* going mad with the stress. To be honest, her brain was floating on a string a lot of the time.

Elephants do grieve, don't they? Rationalism's just another -ism. Who died and made reason king? We're animals.

2

❧

This Is Natural

MARCH
Glasgow

RASMUS, A MUSICIAN; a mystery; long, scruffy, and running on empty, was asleep in the chair by his wife Justina's hospital bed, at the moment she chose—did she choose?—to go. He'd hardly slept those last few days, wide-eyed, watching for it coming.

Chose! What kind of choice was it? She's thirty-eight.

Was thirty-eight.

They had fought it with every power they had and some they didn't; they'd spent most of their money and used up all their favors. Every time he and Jay made love they agreed it was probably the third-last time. To avoid the inevitable. Did hearing its hollow footsteps on the path make it any easier? Observing as slow-motion dying takes a young woman in installments; sharing the intense and astonishing closeness given them by the imminence of death. Every marriage needs a project, after all. Theirs: dying.

He would never know. There was nothing to compare it with.

You don't get two deaths like this in your life. You don't get two loves like this. Seventeen years together, from their youth; two kids who'd put themselves together out of trouble and loss, and in the course of it sacrificed for each other and saved each other. Life doesn't allow that to come again. Time doesn't allow it.

She must have chosen. He hoped she'd chosen. If she hadn't, he'd let her down.

After all that, he thought, *I let you down.*

HE KNEW FROM experience that Ghanaians do funerals properly, and he knew he wasn't capable of it. What, put Jay's body on ice and fly her back to Accra? Coordinate the timing around when fifty different people could come from forty different parts of the world? Lay on what they'd done for her mum for three hundred people he hardly knew, who would all be talking about how he was getting it wrong? Of course he would get it wrong. It was part of his job as *obroni* husband to get things wrong, so the Aunties would have something to affectionately josh him about. Or, invite everybody here to the island, put the Aunties in the youth hostel and the shielings and the bird hides, and give them fish and chips every day?

Here he was in their home of seven years, looking at the toaster and feeling puzzled. Before her illness, he'd spent his life in his head, in his studio, in music, whereas Jay had been the local GP. She'd been the one who knew what to do. She'd left instructions. Of course she had. But he was too paralyzed even to take them in—until her brother, Kwame, said: "Just do what you want and need. With Mum and Dad gone, don't even think about trying to go the full Ashanti."

Rasmus and Kwame and Efua and Jay had sat together side by side through both those funerals: days and days in gardens and receiving lines and churches. Rows and rows of chairs. Drummers and gifts and choirs and buffets and Jay surreptitiously pouring a bottle of ice-cold mineral water down her cleavage under a gazebo in the punishing heat. "Justina," observed Auntie Dolores sternly, "can't take

it. She left home and moved to Scotland FOR THE WEATHER!"
Kwame and Jay had got him out of wearing cloth like a son-in-law
should, and looking a prat with his scrawny shoulders bare. They all
knew there was no way he could wrap and wear and carry off a full
length of woven kente cloth. There was technique involved, and Rasmus did not have it. "Kente waistcoat," Kwame had said, and got the
Aunties to agree. "*Obroni* privilege," Jay had called it, ordering three
from her tailor, in all the correct reds and blacks and whites for the
different days of the commemorations.

Rasmus blinked as he remembered how Auntie Dolores had
kissed her teeth and said: "You know *you* are *obroni* now?" and Jay had
been hurt.

Seeing himself in the photos later, lined up with his glowing, mus-
cular brothers-in-law, doctors and musicians and IT guys gathered
back home from Ontario and Lagos and Bermuda and London, Rasmus kind of wished he'd been bolder, and just stood there white and
nerdy, shoulder to shoulder.

She lived in the Outer Hebrides but she still had a tailor in Accra.
She belonged everywhere. He—Danish and Argentine by blood,
brought up in too many small English towns to count—had only ever
belonged deep in music, and by her side.

Jay liked to do things right, and he would have liked to do that for
her. But in reality the best he could do was to acknowledge the in-
competence that came with grief. Loss was leaving him almost coma-
tose. He knew a little cremation in a Glasgow suburb seemed so
small, so cold, for a woman so alive, but he hadn't even been able to
do that himself, and if Kwame hadn't taken over . . . well, he was
grateful. More people came than he'd expected: friends, cousins, patients who came down from the island. Kwame had found an Ashanti
drummer in Edinburgh. Rasmus had agreed to stand, in the Ghanaian manner: let everybody queue up to look at him and shake his
hand and share their loving strength. Auntie Dolores had sent prayer

cards, with an out-of-focus oval photo of Jay in her graduation outfit. Someone laid them out individually on the seats. All day Rasmus had to turn his eyes away from the sweet smile. It was a radiantly sunny day, Scotland at its unpredictable loveliest, the sky wide, blue and magnificent. Everything he saw shimmered with rainbows refracting in half-shed tears.

The function room at the Victorian pub loomed grand with etched glass and paneling. There was singing, from the Scots, and fried crunchy plantain alongside the pints of heavy and glasses of Chardonnay. He'd worn one of the kente waistcoats—*but which one would be correct?* Without her to tell him, he didn't know. *Black for the sorrow, red for the red eyes of weeping, white for the clarity of spirit which comes after the burial . . .* He chose the black and red.

On the little plane back to the island, his heart rhythm went wrong, because for the first time they weren't on the same land mass. In Dougie's car back down from Stornoway, he was unable to say a word. Then he was at home in their stone house by the sea, crying in the shower about the drums, and the cat was standing there looking at him like "What have you done with her, you bastard?"

So he lay in bed, curled up and knotted, gasping, weeping, calling her name. "Where are you?" he whispered. "Jay, where are you?"

For a moment he thought he heard her voice, and he slapped his own head in fury.

HER ASHES CAME back from the crematorium in a cardboard tube as if she were a bottle of whiskey in a duty-free shop. It had a print of a sunset into the sea on it. When Rasmus turned it round, the horizon seemed to go on forever, round and round, a kind of infinity. He turned it upside down to see if it looked like a sunrise. It didn't.

He couldn't stand the fucking tube. A woman should not end up in a fucking tube. She shouldn't end up in—well, she shouldn't end. That was all.

Later, in their bedroom, he found the carved wooden box they'd bought together at the handicraft market in Accra. Perhaps a woman should end up in a box like this? He hadn't taken it out before. He'd looked at none of her things. Now he opened it. Earrings, hair clips, combs. He closed it again. *The scent of her.*

No, not in there.

You're meant to scatter them, aren't you?

She'd said, "Put me on the compost heap" but she hadn't meant it. She'd meant just "don't make a fuss." But funerals are for the living, and the living wanted a fuss.

He went outside to stare at the compost heap, slung there low and overgrown, *more of a nettle heap.* Every job and chore had been flung down when the demon guest had settled in with them. He turned back to the vegetable patch, on the old lazy beds, where he should be planting things out and sowing seeds. Gruesome handfuls he would be sowing now. *Perhaps warriors would spring up, like they did from the dragon's teeth. Or tulips—or was that from drops of blood? Yes. Scarlet tulips.*

What would spring up? Nothing. Nothing would spring up.

In the end he just walked out of the stone-walled yard and down the soft green field and the machair to the wide white beach. The tide was coming in. Near him the sea glowed like pale cold emeralds, further stripes of amethyst and blue streaked the horizon, the headlands were lapping each other in layers, and the sky was eternity. Only Taransay between him and Hudson Bay. But the tide should be going out. The ashes shouldn't be coming back to him. So he returned to the house, until the water was high. It seemed as right as such a thing could ever be, i.e., extremely and deeply wrong. But Rasmus had had time to think about these things, and knew that however much he yelled her name, she was not coming back, and this was natural, and happened every day, and to everyone.

When he took himself out on the rocks again, the setting sun had thrown a dazzle on the sea. The tide was at its highest, circling listlessly on the sands like a restless dog, and about to decide on its retreat. He stood boldly to take the stupid lid off the stupid tube, but as the breakers committed to leaving the shore the wicked wind changed; suddenly it gusted in, and her ashes were on his coat and on his hands, clinging to him, and he thought, *she doesn't want to go . . .*

So he stopped, and wished he hadn't tried to throw them at all, how could he throw her into the sea, however beautiful it was and however soft and fragrant the air, however much he thought he understood, logically, about the nature of death—and then the rain started, so he walked back up, his limbs chilling, and in track pants and hoodie he went into his studio to the piano and tried to write a song about the wind's direction. It didn't work. His head and heart were too full, too empty. Jay had had a way of finding the exact word or line that perfected his lyrics, and he could hear the harmonies in her voice. And he had another tune on his mind, an old island tune, about a woman waiting for a boatman who hadn't returned. Sometimes a song can just sit in your head for days. Like a mourner at a wake, or an unsatisfied ghost.

He lay awake, night after night, in his clothes, unable to sleep because of what had happened while he was asleep. He made himself shower. He made himself cycle into town for food: five vacuum-packed haggis, half price, lasted him ten days. When he had to go to Glasgow, he bought £42 worth of Indian takeaway, packaged up so it wouldn't leak on the plane. Back on the island it lasted him thirteen days. He ignored emails and the post, let the plants die. Their lives here had always been a bit of a madness, together in the house with nothing around but the rocks and the sheep and the quicksand and the sea. But deciding to leave would be deciding to live, and he hadn't made that decision.

◆   ◆   ◆

EARLY ONE SEA-FRETTED morning as he was cycling up the A859 he was knocked from his bicycle by a dead deer. Even lying on the roadside after it had happened, he was thinking, *how can that be?*

He'd noticed it running alongside him as he went. He was glancing sideways at it, its strength and grace, coppery and poetic in the mist, when the creature suddenly turned like a lunatic and leaped into the road in front of him. Rasmus braked and swerved as swiftly as he could, and managed to miss it, but a car was coming toward them on the other side of the road—and in a weird, impossible moment the car and the deer collided, the deer flew up high into the air, and when it fell, it hit Rasmus, knocking him in turn to the ground. It was so quick and surreal that though the pain and the shock were absolute, it seemed almost absurd.

The car stopped; the deer was dead, and the driver wanted to take Rasmus down to Leverburgh—or up to Stornoway, even—to be looked at.

"I'm all right," Rasmus said.

He'd landed mostly on the turfy verge. He hadn't hit his head. He spread the fingers of his large hands, gingerly peeled up his long body, trod his feet, and didn't think anything was broken. *It's not like last time. What could they do in the hospital anyway?* He did not say to the perturbed driver that he never wanted to go into a hospital again, not in Stornoway, not in Glasgow, not in London, not anywhere. And if his body was knocked sideways, well, perhaps that would counteract the other occasion on which it had been knocked sideways: the universe's previous big swipe at him, New York, 2001.

No, it was not like last time.

He left the bike where it was and walked the seven miles home and after that he stopped leaving the house. But he was writing songs. Kind of. It would keep him going for another week or two. They seemed to be about the process, not the result. He wouldn't ask for more.

THEY USED TO talk about his future love life. He'd shake his head, smiling down at his knees, and she'd say "Sweetheart, sweetheart," and once she had yelled at him: "Don't stop me thinking about the future. Don't stop me from helping you." She'd given him not so much permission as an order: in due course, when he felt ready, he was to go on out there and . . . Her sentence drifted to a stop. She could want it, in theory, but she couldn't say it.

They'd talked about who it might be. She said he would leave the island, move to Glasgow, and meet a musical girl, younger, and he was to make sure she was kind, because for an isolated, misanthropic hermit he was really quite naive and trusting sometimes.

"Are you going to put that in my profile?" he'd said.

"Could do, if you like," she'd said. "Might attract some dashing adventuresses . . ."

The profile she'd written went like this:

> Skinny musician,
> lovely husband, handsome in an odd way,
> can't cook except pancakes,
> uxorious, badly dressed, clean, clever, solvent, widowed,
> romantic,
> antisocial,
> good kisser,
> will write songs about you,
> seeks encouragement.

"What a catch!" he'd said, and she'd said, "You better believe it. There's some terrible specimens out there."

Terrible specimens. It made him smile now to think of her saying that.

"I've written something else for you," she'd said. "Well—not for you. For you to give to a . . . to the . . . when you find someone."

"Stop it," he'd said.

She'd leave it with her will, she'd said, relentless.

DAY AND NIGHT slid together. It rained and rained. There may have been knocking on the door but there was nobody he wanted to speak to. No speaking to be had, anyway. A dismal constant half sleep. Putting the kettle on sometimes. The number of times it burned dry, he stopped doing it. He didn't want tea. He probably was hungry, but it didn't seem to matter.

He was on the sofa, or on the bed. On the other bed. The dreams . . . she might be there in a dream at any time. Best to be ready.

She said to him, in a dream, "It's all so much more complex than you might think . . ."

The cat howled for food, so there was that.

His jeans were loose on him.

He flung himself from the bed toward the bathroom and got it wrong. Not so much he was unbalanced as there was no balance. So he collapsed. Flat on the floor in his loose jeans, splayed like a frog on the road. So he went back to sleep there:

If sleep is what this is.

Well, it must be, look, here are dreams . . .

"Sweetheart," she was saying, and she was holding on to him. "This is what I remember. Your hand on my bed, always ready waiting to take mine if I reached across for you. Your head on the curve of my shoulder . . ."

He thought about that, dreaming.

He didn't reply to her. Or did he?

It was so quiet he could hear the waves outside, rustling on the shore. A door slamming. The rain still falling and falling. Voices. Her voice.

Then a transformation: a sudden sweep, and a change of focus. Activity, faces, businesslike around him. Cheerful calling. Something in his mouth. Coughing. Not waking. He was being bundled and rolled, and whatever there was had slipped away. And then he was in fucking hospital anyway, on a fucking drip, as if he were her the month before.

"You need to eat and drink, Rasmus," they said. It wasn't because they were right that he did as they asked. It was because it was the only way out of that place.

WHEN HE CAME back, Dougie had got food in: packets all over the surface in the kitchen. Crumpets and sausage rolls and potatoes; a box of Tunnock's, bless him. The kitchen cloth was damp: he'll have wiped. A bunch of kale from their patch. *I'll have to go and pay him back*, he thought. *Can't die now.*

So that meant shaving. There were deep slants under his cheekbones. He looked like a saint. He screwed up his face into a frown. *You look older*, he thought.

My three tragedies, he thought. *My mother, the band, Jay.* And shook his head fiercely. *My three glories: the suffering that made me strong and sympathetic; my music; the love of my darling wife.*

It was Dougie who'd called the ambulance, apparently. Rasmus had had no idea. It didn't matter. He'd been caught up in some kind of hunger-induced . . . what . . . magical thinking? *Some gift beyond my understanding. Mine not to question why. Blake saw angels in the treetops in Peckham. I felt her with me.*

Outside, time had continued to pass, the bastard, and it was becoming spring. The sky seemed higher, and tiny pale green tufts had appeared on the larches. Pistachio tinged with rose. *Like a poem*, he thought. But not a lyric. He wasn't going to be writing a song about pistachios and roses. He took out a song he'd been writing before he'd ended up in hospital: "Sorrow Follows," about lying beside your beloved, about sickness and deathbeds. He'd knock that one into shape for her. Sorrow follows everywhere you go.

This is what I remember, she'd said.

But he felt riddled with strange happiness. *Sorrow may follow me, but I won't invite it in.*

He'd get the Vincent out soon, now it was a little warmer. Nothing like a motorbike on a cold sunny morning.

He wasn't short of time, after all.

Best to do things.

He cleared a space on the kitchen table, and set out a knife and fork, salt and pepper. He fried two eggs and ate them, with toast and shito sauce. Kwame had brought up some of Auntie Dolores's when he came to the funeral. "You'll be needing that," he'd said.

He ate his eggs. *That's for you, my love. No more falling behind with the eating.* He wrapped his hand round his second cup of tea and took it to his desk. Glanced to Jay's laptop, sitting there, pretty dusty now . . . he opened it but—nope, not today. No point looking at her messages. It would only be eternal spam. Charities. A message about a pair of leggings some algorithm was convinced she wanted. *One day when we're all dead the algorithms will still be spamming away, sending their junk out eternally across the universe, trying to flog each other control leggings and online guitar courses . . .*

The cat twined round his legs as he logged in on his own machine, to find emails from the bank and the lawyer. He replied blindly: *whatever you think best*. One from PRS: royalty payments from songs from long ago, keeping the ship afloat. A handful from girls with Russian names wanting to make him happy. And one from George, lead singer of the Capos.

3

Are Ghosts Allowed?

IT WAS JUST an ICU, and Nico had seen them before.

A chair drawn up behind a blue curtain; wires connecting from the instruments, an empty mug on the stand. And a body, laid out, unplugged. A dead body. He'd seen those before, too.

It was him.

But I'm here . . .

He stepped forward.

He was dead all right.

Whoa.

I was in the pub—

Where's Róisín?

He'd been at the pub having breakfast and everyone had suddenly gone crazy running around. Róisín at the heart of it, staring. She'd been holding him. *Then what?*

I died?

Jeez, is that what I was doing?

She wasn't there now.

He couldn't remember what had happened! *Christ, all that fuss and then you don't remember.*

Fuck!

Nico was a logical man, trained, professional. *I'm having an electrochemical brain incident*, he thought. *I'm undergoing a near-death experience—fugue—*

But that body is dead. Unresponsive, no chest movement . . . not long dead, not yet cold, with that waxy, pulled-in look . . .

He put his hand to his wrist, thinking to take his own pulse. It settled like snow: hardly touching, feeling nothing.

Neither of him was breathing.

Okay then, yeah, that's it. I just need to slip back in now. That's what they say, isn't it? Float around the ceiling, see everyone crying, someone calls you toward the light, you say no thanks, mate, not yet, check if some researcher's hidden something on top of a cupboard, and then you slip back into your body.

He sat down suddenly on the plastic chair by his mortal remains. He found himself smiling at the body. At himself. "All right," he murmured. He'd seen it happen—the sudden ragged swoosh of an independent breath, the relief and the laughter, when you thought you'd lost someone. *But how do you do it? You kind of . . . swoop?* How often had he been on the other side of this, talking people back into their bodies, hold on now, come on, don't leave us . . . breathing his breath into their lungs, CPR, defibrillators and AEDs, stand back!

Restarting their hearts.

Nobody was doing this for him.

He didn't seem to be swooping or slipping.

He lay down, gingerly, alongside himself, and put his mind to it. *It's psychological.*

Oddly hard to focus when you can't breathe.

Róisín'd told him years ago about an Irish thing: if a person dies without the last rites, you must kiss them to take in their last breath, then when the priest arrives you give it back to them in another kiss, so he can absolve them of their sins while there's breath in them.

No breath here.

Nothing.

He wondered if she'd kissed him as he died. If she'd had a breath for him.

He noticed, as he lay there, that her father's ring, the one she always wore, was on his body's finger.

Surely even in that no-man's-land of the process of dying, you are at any given point either alive, or dead? Surely he'd have noticed that ring getting on his finger?

Third finger left hand, that's wedding-ring finger.

Róisín! You did it? You little diamond—you did it without me!

Fuck, I hope I was alive for that . . .

I mean, I wouldn't miss that.

After a while he laid his hand on his shoulder. He looked at it: there was something unphysical about it. For a moment, it rested on the flesh of his body, then it started to drift slowly through, like honey falling through still water. Nothing linked them, or held them together. They didn't meld. He put his forehead to the back of his skull; felt it glide on the meniscus of it. Pulled back, in horror, at the emptiness.

There was no denying it. He was dead.

What, it's over?

He sat up and stared for a while at the wonder of it.

So what am I doing here then?

No two ways about it, mate—you're a ghost. He held his arm out in front of him.

It was kind of translucent.

But I don't believe in ghosts.

Well, go back and tell that to a scientific survey.

Panic began to rise in him. *I'm not equipped to be a ghost! I mean, why? Where? Am I to haunt somewhere? Here?*

He looked around. *What, haunt the strip lighting and the hand-sanitizer dispensers? Ghosts need fog and lamplight, creaks and glimpses. Unfinished business, desperate vengefulness.*

Unfinished business! Well, yes. Obviously. Like, my entire life.

Will I be seen? Or not? Which is worse? What am I meant to do? He'd arranged his life so that he always knew what to do: save lives. *Oh, the fucking irony.*

Even as he thought it, Róisín appeared. There she was at the end of the ward, in the same striped trousers and little jumper, walking up toward him, white as linen, her eyes big under her blue fringe. And as he thought: *I'm not alone!* he hurtled to her—and stopped himself. Could she see him?

No.

Okay. So there's that.

So he flung his arm around her, his thigh alongside hers, holding her so close that had he been real he'd have tripped both of them over.

His arm slipped through her and he cried out.

Róisín moved on and sat down by his body. She took its hand. Swiftly Nico knelt by her, and laid his ghost hand on hers and his own, cradling them both as a preacher might at a wedding. *Feel me. Feel me. I'm here . . . feel me, for God's sake, I'm here . . .* He focused all right. And his hand did not slip through.

Ah, thank God, he thought, and he smiled as it rested, as he held it there in place where it should be—and then suddenly she flinched, and shook herself, jerked her head—and he found he had pulled his hand away.

If she *could* feel him, then that was . . . He didn't know.

He watched her, bent forward in her blue chair like a mourning Madonna in the still light.

HOURS LATER, WHEN the men came and rolled his body over and rattled it off down the corridor, he walked in procession behind her. One of them tapped in a code on the metallic box by the door;

they walked on through. The door swung back in his face. And straight through him, a slam of wind.

Whoa!

He yelled.

Nobody looked round.

He threw himself through the door after her.

Can I still love her? he thought. *Are ghosts allowed?* He did love her. His heart might be dead and stopped in that cold body—

Whatever, it loved her. *Whatever I am now loves you.* That he knew, at least.

HE FOLLOWED HER home, walking beside her in the street. He watched as she lit a candle for him. He saw her standing in the aisle of Sainsbury's on Fortis Green Road, staring at the bottles of San Pellegrino, and at bottles of ketchup, and at the middle distance. He saw her finding supermarkets comforting. He sat on her bed; lounged at her feet, lay with his head by her knee as she sat on the sofa. Watched her shower, watched her sleep. He didn't touch her again, not once. He was scared of frightening her.

Each night he lay beside her in their bed, but sleeping didn't seem to be a thing ghosts did. The first night, he stared at the closed bedroom door: the panels he'd painted, his white towel still hanging on the hook. *Slipping through*, he thought. He put his hand to the handle. And across to the panel. And followed it through, his hand, his arm, his shoulder, and the rest of him, and he was standing in the hallway, in shock.

How can I do this, but I don't fall through the furniture or the floor or the surface of the planet?

HE'D NEVER BEEN to the hairdresser with her before. She seemed to know the woman well, and greeted several others by name.

It was touching to see her in a part of her life that he would never have seen otherwise. He wouldn't ever have been here. *Maybe that makes it an easier place for her to be*, he thought.

She was always changing hair color—with the season, with her mood, pink, dark orange, platinum—and then putting pictures on bloody Instagram. An interesting period when it was a pewter gray, which was gorgeous with her magnolia skin and her dark blue eyes. The little fine lines around them. Then the time she did her hair fading from one color to another, which she called ombré, and another time a *balayage*, in a comic French accent. He still didn't know how to spell it, whatever it was. He called it Baileyidge to make her laugh. "You get your hair painted," she'd said. But how can anyone paint a head of curls like hers? "Freehand," she'd said. *Freehand!* He'd imagined them doing it with Sharpies, like when you do a freehand tattoo, drawn direct onto skin.

"Show me that," she'd said. "Do it on me," and he'd drawn a clambering rose all over her, circling her waist, reaching up her shoulders, embracing her, while she giggled at the tickling, her curls falling this way and that on her skin as she tried to look.

"Shall I ink it for you then?" he'd asked, and she'd said, "Get away. Don't you come near me with your horrible needles."

Rosaki-mou, he thought. *My little rose.*

He was amazed now by her grief; by how much she loved him. It wasn't that she hadn't said, or that he hadn't believed her. But—to see it.

The hairdresser, Cara, had tears in her eyes as Róisín explained what she wanted.

How much longer her curls were, stretched out and wet. He thought of her rising from swimming, coming out of the shower, wet hair plastered on flesh. He thought the turquoise-tipped curls would just be cut and fall damp and dead to the floor, but instead Cara dried them carefully, half an hour of long strokes of the brush and

the dryer loosening them into strands, before she tied them in a ponytail, top and bottom. And cut it, neatly, with a crunch. She and
Róisín smiled at each other as it was laid to one side in a Jiffy bag, to
be made into a wig for children with no hair. Children having cancer
treatment. *It's like she's donating her organs*, he thought, *only she's not
the dead one. She's lost me, and now here she is giving bits of herself away.*

And then Cara called one of the men over: a quarter of an inch
all over was not one of her skills. They seemed to share a fundamental
understanding that this was a right thing to do. The razor buzzed
smoothly over Róisín's now-dark head. A number two. It looked
beautiful. Her sacrificial expression; her mourning made positive.
Even her grief was kind.

Mum won't like it though.

Oh God, Mum.

HE HADN'T MEANT it when he said he wanted a sea burial. He
never thought anyone would take it seriously—it was just, you know,
like a Christmas jumper or something, you don't mean it, you're just
having a laugh. So he loved sailing and swimming and was proud of
his family roots in Ithaca but now, watching Mum trying to put together the bits of tradition she'd salvaged from the religion she'd
given up and make that work with him being chucked off a boat in
the English Channel because that's the only place you can do it, except there's another spot off Northumberland but she'd thought that
would be too cold—*Christ, Mum, neither of them are the South Ionian,
are they?*

Anyway, now she was making koliva for the funeral: boiling up
farro, the nearest thing she could find to ancient wheat, toasting
cumin and aniseed and coriander seeds, stirring in honey and handfuls of blood-red jewels of pomegranate seeds, and parsley and nut-
meg and salt. Koliva was okay because, Mum said, it predated the

church: it was about Demeter (the grain) and Persephone (the pomegranate) and Hades (the parsley). Church services were not okay because everyone in the church was a money-grubbing jackal. Graves,
yes, because you can visit and how else can the priest break the plate
on the third day to release your soul? Consistency? Don't be ridiculous, I'm a grieving mother. Sea burial, yes, because her island-loving
nautical boy must have everything exactly as he would want it; if they
don't have what they want, they stick around until they get it. She
herself would take another boat out three days later and break the
plate over the stern. She would scatter corn in the wake. Nico never
felt as free as when he was sailing. He used to say the concentration
on the wind and the tide and the current and the sails meant no
other thing could possibly bother him when he was sailing. That was
what he would have, for eternity. Nothing bothering him. What
mother would want less for her beautiful boy, taken before his time?

They'd laid him out at the undertakers'. Everyone had come and
kissed him. *All right, Mum.*

Róisín was helping her. The pair of them crying into the koliva.
My big fat not-entirely-Greek funeral.

HE COULD SEE Róisín clearly on the deck of the boat, windswept
and bold under the high blue sky, her Dalmatian coat flying in the
breeze. He knew why she wore that coat. He knew how angry she
was. He knew she was shaking very slightly as the man held out the
white lilies for her to cast onto the face of the water. The works indeed! *Thank you, darling, for looking after my mortal remains.* He'd never
seen her look so strong and so weak. Her neck was so naked. Her and
Mum arm in arm, holding each other steady.

As she stood back to let others come forward to throw their flowers, he couldn't quite stop himself. *Maybe she won't notice, it'll just be
like the touch of the wind, what kind of man, of ghost, wouldn't . . . at his*

own funeral . . . Nico went up and put his hand lightly at her nape, just under where her hair would have been, that spot where she always felt the cold. She turned quickly, jumped almost. "Jesus!" she said— but there was nothing there, and then someone gave her a glass of whiskey, and she sort of shook herself, but her eyes flickered back to where he was. Alarmed.

For a moment it was magnificent: he had touched her, and she had felt him. And then terrible. *I must not do that.*

She threw the whiskey. *Is that for me?* he thought. *Ancestral libation or something? My parting glass.* He wondered if he wanted it. He didn't know the word for how he felt about it. Because he kind of did . . . *but no.*

CAN I EAT? he thought.

You're dead, Nico. I know, but—

In the pub at the wake, he found himself gazing at the crispy golden fried fish they served up. The crackle round the edge. *Squeeze of lemon,* he thought. He couldn't smell them. But he could want them all right. Like a shoplifter, he moved swiftly and discreetly to pinch one. He didn't want to give anyone else a heart attack, fried fish floating about at the funeral tea. *Is that how it works? Would they be able to see it?* He didn't think so. Though it would be funny. He'd held back from trying, but, *Well, now's the time . . . special occasion after all . . .*

He looked, focused, and touched a little fish. His fingers slipped through it. He concentrated. She'd felt his touch, after all. *This isn't logical, so what is it? Emotional? How much I want it?*

He said softly, *I really want you, little fish.* Touched it again. Felt it. Pushed at it. *Come on.* For a moment, he felt its presence—but that was it. No flow of hunger, no need to eat.

Fair enough. Food is for the living.

So what is for me?

He went back inside. The Greeks were all singing "S'agapo" now, in the corner, drinking brandy and eating the koliva: *I love you because you are you, I love the world because you're in it. Your window is closed, open a wing of your window, so I can see you.*

Mum and Róisín sitting together like a pair of queens in shock. *Oh Mum.*

S'a . . . ga . . . po . . .

Nell looks bloody miserable. Their mum, too.

HE WENT HOME in the car with Róisín and Nell, invisible and half-existent, folded up in the back of her Fiat 500. No discomfort, except when his legs went through the front seat on a speed bump, and he saw his feet on Nell's lap, and had to whip them back in horror. He practiced, gently: pressing his feet through the door of the car; resting them against it. Did it with his hands on the seat beside him.

HE LEANED, IN the kitchen, as kettles boiled; sat on the sofa as phones rang.

She lay in bed on her back, exhausted, calling his name. He found that he could lie on the air above her. She sat up suddenly and was in his nonexistent arms.

He saw her fear that she was boring her friends now. He noticed that she couldn't bear to have music on, unless she was dancing. Many times he restrained himself from stroking her forehead: *don't touch her.* He whispered words of comfort, though he wasn't feeling any comfort. What he was feeling was the loss of everything: what he'd had, what he'd obliviously assumed he would have in the future. "I thought maybe the Lake District," he said, as she put the kettle on. "For our holiday. Or a wedding. Kids, maybe, after all—why didn't we talk that through properly?—what do you think? Or Venice?" There'd been all the time in the world for the things he might have been going to get round to. *Unfinished business*. Now he didn't know what there was.

"Yes, babe?" he called from the sofa. She was in the kitchen. She had been talking to him all evening, and he heard his name again. She talked to him, yes. But she didn't *respond* to him. And when he responded to her: bam, brick wall. It really wasn't what you'd call a conversation.

And then, bloody Cyndi Lauper on the radio. He jumped up, went in. Oh, she had musical cues all right: and sure enough, there she was, standing on the red lino, kettle boiling, tears streaming down her face and her hips swaying slowly. He stood in front of her, so close, and he felt that the veil between them was so thin that she must have felt him. Even if it was just a tiny feeling. Like when you do Qigong and you get that little tremor when you're bringing your hands together, that kind of silent buzz. Did she feel that?

He couldn't bear it. He put his hand out, laid it on hers in the strong, conscious way that made sure it didn't just fall through her flesh, he slipped his arm round her waist, took the risk of alarming her if she felt it because surely she'd know it was him, here to comfort her? He lifted his arm to spin her, and maybe it was just coincidence that she moved at the same time, but when she twirled back in, it was so much like she was dancing into his arms that really, what was the difference? For a moment, his chin was resting on the top of her head. He used to rest his drink there sometimes. She was little. It made her laugh.

Or perhaps he just wanted it to be true, so much. So much so that, to get away from the feeling, he did his funny Greek Zorba dancing, there in the kitchen. If in doubt, take the piss. That *always* made her laugh. She didn't laugh. Of course not. She didn't know.

4

Floating Witchery

JAY DID CHOOSE.

She'd been planning it for a while, lying so sad and quiet in her medical bed, almost all the joys of life already gone from her, holding tight to the remnants. *You lack the guts for the final commitment,* she told herself. *You can't even make it happen. You can't lie to yourself convincingly enough.* Because she did know that nobody really wants to die. *In the moment, maybe, if the other options are so . . . unacceptable . . . but no.* She didn't think you could do it for wanting.

I'm procrastinating. Which means I don't want to do it. I want to carry on lying here making his life a misery and waiting for a nonexistent miracle.

There's no miracle coming.

I know there's no miracle.

But I'm human. I don't want to die.

Then when Rasmus fell asleep in the chair that night, she thought, *it's so restful to hear his breath as he sleeps.* She'd heard him so often over the years sleeping badly, turning over, turning his pillow over. Her own nights of sweat and fever, her own insomnia. So when he was asleep, in the chair, she thought, *wouldn't it be lovely if just for a while we were both resting, together, side by side like we should be.*

That was her choice. That thought was enough to carry her across. Perhaps it was just a giving-up. She just stopped doing whatever it was that kept her there. Or maybe it just was the right moment. *Take ye heed, watch and pray, for ye know not when the hour is.*

Either way, she wasn't aware of it. Until she woke up, and realized that not all of her had woken. Her body had not woken.

And yet here she was, still here. Sort of.

Am I?

She lay still and quiet. Something was very different.

She stood up.

Well, this was new. She hadn't stood up for weeks. Dizzying!

She moved her arms. No cannulas. No pain! *It is a miracle!*

No labored breath. No breath at all! No nothing. No cramped swell of the ribs on the inhale, no slide of the shoulders on the out. No rattling, disorganized heartbeat. A ripple of realization ran through her: *this thought should wind me*—but there was no such winding. *This is appalling*—but she did not feel appalled. She was almost relieved. She was dead. *But then why am I still here? Shouldn't I have gone somewhere?*

And she looked back at the bed.

Of course it hadn't occurred to Jay, in the time she'd had to watch her death approaching, to wonder whether the dead feel grief and loss. She'd expected nothing: a definite, particular nothing. The choices were, what—heaven, hell, oblivion? So oblivion, of course. *Brief period of consciousness as an individual done; window shut; self no more,* and if she'd looked forward to anything, it was a bit of peace and quiet. She'd assumed her death would be, in reality, something that happened to other people. Specifically, to Rasmus. *He* would feel.

But look—*it's not over.* Her heart leaped. *Ras!* she cried, and he stirred in his sleep in the chair, his long legs stuck out, his long back slumped—*that's going to ache when he tries to stand*—and his throat bare.

How vulnerable he looks.

Oh God, how does this work?

Ras? It's not over!

She looked at her poor body, a wave of pity washing over her. *Poor dear body.* Very gently, she touched the tip of her nose. *Not really touching at all. More of a gesture.* She sat down, thoughtfully, on the edge of the bed. It did not dip under her.

She watched him breathe. *We have never been so far apart. Even before we met, we were not so far apart. Because we were moving toward each other.*

She stood up again, gingerly, and turned to lower and curl herself gently on his lap. Stopped herself for a moment: *What if I can't touch him either? What if . . . ?*

What if what? She slipped her arms easily round him, and bent her head to his. It was not like flesh to flesh, but it was not like nothing. She'd read once about two rivers in Latin America, or she'd seen a film: they meet, and you see their waters meeting, at speed and rushing, and they don't combine. Instead, the two streams, one brown, one blue, flow side by side, twisting, merging of course, yet demonstrably not merging, connected and yet quite separate. It wasn't like that, either. Rasmus didn't—did he?—respond to her presence.

She laid her hand on his chest, where it looked like a sea creature: not all there, otherworldly. She let it rest on the soft cotton of the sleeve on his arm. On the hair sticking up off his head. On his tired face. She felt as if suspended in the love and care they had for each other. Held in their closeness.

Was she going to have to watch him suffer?

Yes she was.

Even if she *had* expected anything, it would not have been this. Not *feeling*.

◆   ◆   ◆

SHE WENT BACK to the island with him, learning, as she went, how she worked. Ground was solid. Benches and beds and chairs and airplane seats were solid; things were solid, unless she didn't want them to be. He was solid. She, her hand spread out in front of her, was not solid. The walls and partitions of Glasgow Airport were not solid if she needed to pass through them. It just took will and intention. Security gates didn't care about her. And gravity paid her much less attention than it used to. In the middle of the concourse, she was struck with sudden mad joy. She was still here! And she was stronger and freer than she had been in years. She jumped in the air, throwing her arms up, grinning like a fool. She flipped herself over: once, twice, three times. Landed like dandelion fluff. Shot herself off again: a string of cartwheels down the grubby floor; a flick up onto the back of a rank of seats, skip skip skip, then a mere leap to tippy-tiptoeing on the moving handrail of the escalator, balanced like the tiny plastic ballerina in a music box. And flying back into his arms the moment he sat.

Can you feel me? Do you know I'm here?

Safe as she felt there, huddled inside his greatcoat, she knew that while for the living the world might remain reliably itself, for her it did not.

CHRIST, BUT THE crematorium was grim. *Thank you, Kwame, for coming; thank you so much for reassuring Ras he didn't have to do the whole Ghana thing. Thank you for keeping the Aunties happy. Thank you for the Zoom and not making Ras join in.* She was glad Mum and Dad weren't there to have to go through it.

Do I see them again? It was a passing thought. Too much.

She'd told Ras to chuck her on the compost. A girl has to keep her frailties somewhere, and for her it was that she hated to think of her body being dead. She loved her body. She'd taken such care of it. How many coconuts had given up their good oil for her bounteous hair and rich skin? She didn't want it thrown away. She wanted to say to him, *Keep my hair. Keep my bones. Keep my fingers maybe—you could dry them out. Keep my heart; pickle it in wine. It was always yours anyway.* She remembered her arms when she was young. Sleek and dark on the beach at Labadi, frosted with salt crystals from the sea. Sweet soft mango juice dripping from hands to elbows as she slurped on the fruit from Grandpa's garden. The giant black butterflies that fluttered on the trees, drinking the ripeness. Glossy. And the same Atlantic Ocean washes the shore at Labadi as at Luskentyre. *The bloody sea. Uniting and dividing.*

Go on, she said to herself. *Say goodbye to your mortal remains.*

She wondered if she could.

Only one way to find out.

So she stood at the head of her coffin on its gurney, waiting to be trundled into the incinerator, and reached her nebulous hand out to the polished wood. Slipped inside. She looked at her face, and kissed her cold gray forehead. She recalled the gleaming, limber child she had been, and the queenly woman, and she sorrowed for how painful and misshapen her body had ended up. *Look at her now: packed in a box to be sent away.*

It's just a thing. She knew that now. *Thank you, old thing.*

Not even real flames.

She certainly hadn't wanted anything religious. She'd slid naturally away from religion as she moved toward science. Not since childhood had she foreseen judgment, and the judgment she had foreseen then was Old Testament, fed by Renaissance paintings where forked demons cackled and murmurations of dangling naked souls were flung this way or that across cerulean skies by the whim of God. *Maybe Dad was right after all, and only 144,000 human souls get to heaven.* She knew she wasn't one of the 144,000 best humans who had ever existed. *Or maybe it's just that you only go to heaven if you believe*—which she didn't, not even in the darkest times of her sickness. She did think about Jesus, her childhood friend, the blue-eyed child she'd been given at church. *Well, Jesus, I tried to do the important things. I didn't make much headway sheltering the homeless, but let's face it, I definitely healed the sick, and I fed the hungry, and I'm fairly sure I comforted the troubled.*

But religion? No.

She trailed a hand over the sorrowing shoulders of Kwame, Dougie, the Aunties and cousins who had been able to come, and then attached herself to Rasmus for the ceremony. Afterward he sat for a long while on the low wall outside, twelve noon on a Friday, overcast, might rain later. She sat beside him, her hand on his knee. The others had gone to the pub; he would join them. *Where you go,* she thought, *there I will be.*

DOUGIE DROVE RASMUS back to the cottage from Stornoway; the road a blacktop ribbon laid across green and gold velvet slopes amid the tracery of silvered lochs and inlets. Jay lay on her back on the roof rack all the way, feeling the light and the cloud shadows and the sea slipping in and out of view, watching for eagles. This so-familiar road.

Back at their stone house, their home, she sat drumming her legs on the windscreen as Rasmus didn't invite Dougie in for a cuppa. *How long have I been dead? Only a week. I suppose my ashes will be back, to sit on the mantelpiece. Hanging out with you.*

And here I am anyway!

Her home was empty of her. The dust lay differently; the wood had lost its shine; the plants were dying and the log pile was low. No one had plumped the cushions on the sofa. Post lay unopened on the floor. The kitchen tap was still dripping. She wondered how much of this mess had been there during her illness, and she just hadn't noticed. The place was half-dead itself. Except the cat: it raised its head, looked at her, and curled back down again.

She sat on the loo seat while Rasmus cried in the shower, and stood behind the piano stool while he hummed a curious simple melody, tried out chords, and scribbled. She caught his tiny smile and sigh as he slipped in an F7. He called F7 Hermione. All chords had names, for him. G was James; straight and noble. G minor was Luther. D minor was Joachim. A was Claire. Bb minor was Herb. C was Nelson. Their real names annoyed him. Hermione was the magic chord that could lift any song.

She saw his tousled hair, uncombed by her affectionate fingers. He looked like a parsnip, really; a long tall parsnip with tufty leaves sprouting on top. And his pale face like a gnarly parsnip, too. So beautiful. She put her head close to his, her chin on his shoulder. The melody was settling as he repeated it. It was lovely: sad, open-ended. She crooned a soft and melancholy harmony, and he glanced up, startled.

SHE WAS UP on the hill beyond the road when the wind changed at Luskentyre, purple rocks under her feet running out to the sea, to the Sound of Taransay, and a tiny golden eagle arching like a fallen eyelash in the great blue above. She couldn't feel the cold the brightness spoke of. Her eyes filled up with the beauty of this beloved place, and she reeled. *I still don't want to die.* She jumped off the rock and felt her feet take their time on the air; landed on the gleaming water like a swallow dipping, and found herself backflipping, because she could. *I can do all the things I used to do in my dreams*, she thought. *I am weightless yet I am strong. I can fly.* A brilliant everyday miracle. A new reality.

She saw Rasmus out on the sands there at high tide. *Look at him! Look!* He was walking toward the rocks, the absurd tube of her ashes under his arm, reaching out to steady himself as he scrambled out on the headland. Up on top, he stood like a tiny colossus, the sea on three sides of him. He held the tube high above his head and with his back to the wind he tried to pour out her mortal remains for the tide and the crabs and the black weed to have their way with. She saw her ashes blowing back as the cats' paws rippled this way and that, silver lamé on the surface of the pale emerald water, out in the bay; saw him staggering very slightly at the sudden mess and indignity at the water's edge. She saw him give up, and step down to the surf to rinse his hands and splash his unmoving face. Saw his wet salty hands.

SHE SAT BY him. He had the photos out. Real printed ones, and the digital ghosts on the screen. Scraps of film of her that he watched over and over, then slammed the laptop lid down on. There she is in that burnt-orange satin dress, '60s style, on the roof in Williamsburg the night they met. He'd said she looked like she should be singing with Ray Charles. And he was right! Clips from the Capos' tour, singing beside him, every night for months, from Brooklyn to New Orleans, Austin to Monterey. See them at the shared microphone, smiling. See them outside Al Green's church in Memphis, after an all-nighter in the blues clubs on Beale Street: leaning against the stone sign reading FULL GOSPEL TABERNACLE CHURCH. There were no pictures of the best moments. The moment she let herself fall in love with him, on the tour bus somewhere between some poetically named Southern city or another, not that the South was a poetry she could enjoy. Her thighs had been sticking to the leatherette, so she'd folded a T-shirt to sit on, and she was looking at him, and he glanced up. That was it! Their eyes met, and she knew. A slight movement of the head. A shift of expression. And something changed. How right she had been to do that, to choose Rasmus, despite what happened and what everybody said.

Him unconscious in the ER at the hospital on DeKalb in Brooklyn; the cherry trees blossoming outside and him a fallen soldier. She hadn't been with him when it happened. She cut off there and held the memory still in her mind for a moment, before sending it away again in favor of a happier one: *you and me here on the island, soon after we moved here, on the road out beyond Scarista, the first time we found the wild raspberries, the poignant scent of them in the rain, and we just stood there together eating them all, the sweet dusty tang of them, the huge Hebridean sky above us like we were on the edge of the world, and the raindrops scattering and the blackbird singing . . .*

RASMUS LAY IN the small bed, curled up, calling her name. "Where are you?" he whispered. "Jay, where are you?"

"I'm here," Jay said quietly, sitting by him, and he slapped his own head in fury.

She laid herself carefully down. Lowered her head onto his chest. He shifted a little, as he might have if he'd felt her weight. She lay all night by him, for many nights, sleepless. *I am here, where I always was. I don't know where I am.*

Days slipped by, dawn or dusk out the window, she often didn't know which. The familiar sounds came of the wind playing round the chimneys, its hoots and creakings; its groans and mumblings. Remembering when Rasmus tried to record them: the music of the wind; *ceòl na gaoithe.* First he put mics up the chimneys, then he became obsessed with setting up a Hebridean aeolian harp, and had one built, and it was out there day and night moaning and sighing as the wind breathed its angelic tunes—*such a soft floating witchery of sound . . .* though it could be maddening, it really carries—and then he hung pipes out by the lazybeds, and they just blew right away one tempestuous evening, and he was so happy: "The whole island's an instrument," he said. "Listen to it, to the wind playing it"—and he was right; the sea and the turf, the pebbles and the harebells ... Time slid around in her mind. Storms in Ghana when she was little, when it seemed the world would be washed away. Huge green palms with black-and-white-striped trunks, thrashing, illuminated by sudden flashes of lightning, then gone again, while invisible rivers of rain thundered down the red road. She and her mother in the car, drawn over on the verge, sitting it out. The curve of Mum's cheek and of her eyelashes, looking down at her, *it's all right, baby, just a thunderstorm.* Her modesty and formality. That English boarding school they'd sent her to, God forgive them—they'd thought it best and maybe it was— netball, dear Lord, and the kind young teacher who gave her a moment of sunshine when she taught her to make daisy chains. Twelve-year-old her in bed at night dreaming of Ghana food: kontomire and kelewele, fufu and soup. Her first period and nobody to tell. *Small madam is a lady now!* when she finally returned to Accra. Getting in trouble for running round Jamestown eating kenkey off the stalls, making friends with the fisherboys, that time she went out in a bright blue pirogue, *To Yet Not* painted on the prow, a piece of advice that had stood her well: "Head TO your goal though as YET you have NOT reached it." The waves so tall and cloudy, the boys so skillful. The hot sweet smell of smoking fish everywhere ... Oh, but Grandma was angry. So much of her fear and love came through in anger ... Then older her, studying: the joy of learning and being graded and making people proud (and surprising some people, let's face it). Proud princess, her at eighteen, free at last, disappointing them all by running away to be a singer in America, and to fall in love with an *obroni* man. And not just *obroni*, but white. *What did you expect? You sent me to a white-girl school in a white country!*

Why am I still having these fights with them in my own mind? she thought. *Anyway. I've had my chance. I had some kinds of heaven on earth, here, with him. And then I had to accept hell on earth.*

She drifted and dreamed: she and Rasmus were on a London bus, much younger, and dressed in leaves. Dreaming, all she wanted was physical closeness. Dreaming, she went with the simple joy of being in the same place with the person you love, at the same time.

So ordinary, so priceless. Sitting on a bus.

WHEN HE CYCLED into the village, she stood on the mudguard behind him like a Valkyrie. She was growing accustomed to moving like an imaginary friend, a parkour queen.

On the day he was knocked off his bicycle, she saw the deer's spirit rise away from its body, spiraling up and up like a synchronized aerial dance, a circus act. She saw its dark eyes bemused as the carcass crashed into Rasmus, and the ghost drifted away toward a copse of larches. Saw Rasmus on the road, his long back bent, saw the metal in his spine and the scar with the pinpricks where they had sewn him up the last time. She saw his skeleton, crooked within his skin, and saw him stand and shake hands with the driver of the little red car. She yelled at him that he was *not* all right, and then laughed with relief because he was not dead, and at the fact that he'd never listened to her when she'd told him to look after himself when she was alive, so why would he listen now?

Only later, sitting in her old seat by the fire in the cottage, did she think: *if he had died, when that deer hit him, he could be with me now. We could be dead together.*

She howled. *Dear God,* she thought, *could that work? Could that work?*

And later still: *where has the deer's spirit gone?*

Why hasn't mine gone somewhere?

◆   ◆   ◆

TIME WAS UNRELIABLE. Bendy. Without sleep or meals, there was no way of knowing how days passed. It reminded her of Las Vegas casinos without clocks, where day and night dissolve into an unmeasured eternity. And of long drugged nights in hospital. She judged time by how and when *he* slept. But that had always been erratic, and was worse now. She watched him get up before dawn one morning, and get the plane to Glasgow to meet the lawyer. Here there were people: they moved round and past and through her, a stream, circling. People with the purpose and papers she did not have. And bodies.

She'd already stopped missing her body. Being out of pain was miraculous. She remembered the ragged pain of breathing. What a relief it was, not lugging that poor thing around anymore. Giving up on it. *It's the greatest relief of my, well, of my life. Of my afterlife?*

She saw him eking out the Indian food he brought back, and she saw his hip bones emerging. *Look at him, feeding the cat but not himself.* She saw the neighbors knocking on the door, Dougie and Sandy and—oh! Suki, Rasmus's ex, what was she doing here? She lives in Manchester. That's . . . *premature.* And not okay. *Go away, you vulture. You're the last thing he needs.* When he didn't answer, they left saucepans on the doorstep, and he did not bring them in. She saw that he hadn't made that decision yet, about whether to live or die.

As soon as her illness had made its intentions clear, she had written him a careful and loving letter of instructions about how to survive this, both practical and emotional: her passwords and bank account details, where things were, how to live again. She'd told him about it, and they had sort of joked about it. She hadn't put *Eat.* She hadn't thought it necessary. She hadn't thought he'd fall apart so physically. They'd been in it together. Until they weren't.

Don't do this, she said. *This isn't the way.*

Sometimes it seemed as if he could hear her. A moment when he'd look up, or when they'd smile at the same thing—when the cat fell off the wall in the yard, landed ungracefully, and then looked round embarrassed before walking off with that expression declaring that it had never happened. But she didn't really know if anything from her was reaching him. There was a disconnect. Years ago she had broken her arm, and this disconnect now reminded her of the weird nauseous dangly feeling, the misbegotten lurch that happens if you lean without thinking on a hand or an elbow not decently connected to the other bones and the skeleton. A sense that the abyss was right there.

But I should be in the abyss.

If someone had come into her surgery looking like he looked now, she'd have thought *malnutrition, anorexia, social services* . . . It wasn't logical. It was grief. They say that grief is love that has lost its object, and here she was staring at what she had lost, as he stared at the loss of her.

He hadn't even looked at her list of instructions. How could she remind him? How could it be, after all these years, that she couldn't remind him of something?

She went in to where he lay sleeping. He was pale, yellow. When had he last eaten? She felt his forehead, took his pulse. When had he last drunk? He was the only person she'd ever met who measured what he drank in milliliters. "Oh, I had two hundred milliliters of water at breakfast," he'd say, as if he had picked up her medical precision. As she sat on the edge of the bed, he shifted in his sleep, as though to make room for her. She whispered into his ear: "You, Rasmus, are to go to the doctor. You are to eat and drink and get help. You're to open the door to your friends and neighbors. Not Suki, though. You don't like her. But those saucepans have gone moldy."

She felt him wake.

"You seem to have forgotten your plans . . ." she said.

He swallowed dryly. She looked clearly at him, with her doctor's eyes.

In the kitchen she lifted her hands and wondered. She hadn't, so far, been able to lift things. She'd tried. And failed. But the kitchen tap was still dripping.

She held her cupped hands out, under it, like the basin of a Baroque fountain, like imploring. *Stay*, she whispered. *Please*, and the water dripped. Not even through her fingers, but through *her*, altogether.

She felt his listlessness from the other room.

Please.

It seemed to her a little water gathered. She glanced at the sugar in its heavy-lidded glass pot, and the salt imprisoned in its clear Perspex tube.

Please.

A tiny puddle lingered in her palm. She carried it like a blessing to where he lay, and tipped it into his mouth. It dribbled from the corner.

Wake up, she thought.

He hasn't looked after himself for a long time. He was looking after me and it slipped and he's slipping. I haven't looked after him.

He shouldn't be here alone.

Her medical bag—did she have a feeding syringe in it? It lived on the box freezer by the back door.

It wasn't there. She couldn't have used it anyway.

No point going to the clinic in Leverburgh. It's only an hour to Stornoway.

Can't I take him in my arms and carry him? She had an image suddenly of them flying through the sky like a Chagall painting. *With a goat. Playing the violin. Which film was that? Julia Roberts and Hugh Grant . . .*

She couldn't.

There was a noise from the bed: Rasmus was pulling himself up, and lurching toward the bathroom. And collapsing.

Her professional reaction kicked in. External danger: none. Response: she couldn't check if he was responsive. Airway: *looked* clear. Breathing: shallow, but consistent. And circulation. She looked at his wrist. Put her ear close to his neck. But she couldn't check anything for sure. Couldn't put him in the recovery position. Couldn't help him.

He was breathing; he was facedown. Okay.

She looked for the phone, and concentrated herself. Could she knock the receiver, concentrate, drop her fingertips onto the buttons?

She couldn't.

He wasn't injured. Just weak. If she could only raise his feet, pull a blanket over him, drip him sugar water. *The* Stornoway Gazette *and* Dè tha Dol? *could publish stories about the ghost doctor who came back from the dead to save her husband . . .*

If I can't give help, I must get help.

She wasn't sure quite how she got to Dougie's. He was standing in front of his big-screen telly, doing his weights in a T-shirt. Cranking himself up and down under a set of barbells, red in the face, sweat shining on his stocky-man muscles.

She stood in front of him and said, "Dougie, Dougie, Dougie. Dougie, I need you. Dougie. Dougie. DOUGIE."

He huffed and puffed.

"DOUGIE, FOR GOD'S SAKE!"

Nothing.

Dougie's cat was there. She remembered their own cat. She stared at it. Approached it. It gave her a mild, distrustful glance.

She snarled at it, jumped at it, sat on it.

It jumped off the couch, skedaddled. Dougie dropped his weights and swore. His trance was broken.

"GO TO RASMUS! HE NEEDS YOU!" Jay shouted. "GO TO

YOUR FRIEND." She swept her arms around. "GO TO HIM." There was a crash—

A mug had fallen from the shelf. *It must have been me . . .*

"Go over to Ras's," she said. "Go to Ras's. Go. Go. Go."

Dougie looked at the mug, the puddle of cold tea on the carpet. He glanced out the window, over his shoulder, then suddenly grabbed his hoodie and his car keys.

"Rasmus," she chanted after him. "Rasmus."

She had *no* idea how she got back to the house, to lying beside Rasmus on the floor. But there she was. He was somewhere between coma and consciousness.

"I dreamed about you this morning," he said. "Or was it last night?"

"You'll dream about me again," she said.

"I'll dream about you always," he said.

"You're to find another girl," she said. "One who's alive."

"Aren't you alive?"

"No, my love," she said. "No, I'm not."

"But your tears are wet?" he said. His hand was at her cheek.

"I'm not breathing," she said.

"Oh," he said, on a long, living breath of his own.

She just said, "It's all so much more complex than you might think . . ."

And then, "Sweetheart," she said. "This is what I remember. Your hand on my bed, always ready waiting to take mine if I reached across for you. Your head on the curve of my shoulder . . . Ras, I did choose. It was so restful to hear your breath as you slept. I remember you creeping out of bed with insomnia, trying not to wake me. Trying to sigh quietly . . ."

He was silent for a while. She could hear the waves outside, rain and the waves coming over and over on the shore. A door slamming in the wind.

The kitchen tap dripping.

The sound of Dougie's car pulling up.

"IT WAS MY wife," he said to the paramedics, though everyone knew his poor wee wife the doctor was dead.

"She was here, wasn't she?" he said to Dougie. "Wasn't she?"

Was he a drinker? the paramedics wondered. Psychosis, maybe? All the more reason to look after him, the poor sod.

RASMUS, IN HIS hospital bed, was sleeping. Jay was watching him. Then he was in his hospital chair, eating, and Jay was watching him still, happier every moment. Starry-eyed. *I was so scared that you would stop entirely, and just fade away. And be dead like me. But I want you to live. Is that strange?* It seemed strange.

Jay'd always liked seeing people eat: plates on the table, hot food together, and "How's your day been?" When they had first got together, during the tour with the Capos, she was cooking for him in a friend's apartment, one of their first nights together, and she'd called out, "Can you lay the table?" And he had frozen. "No," he'd said. She had a sizzling frying pan on the stove, a dripping colander of steaming pasta in the sink, plates warming in the oven, and had just closed the fridge door with her bum. She'd looked across at him, astonished.

"I can't," he'd said.

She had been too busy to address the issue right then, but the astonishment had stayed. He wasn't an entitled person. He had fewer ingrained ideas about the roles of men and women than any man she'd ever met—which was one of the reasons why she loved him. She'd talked to Kwame about it. WTAF, he'd said.

A few days later she'd returned to it. "Why on earth?" she'd asked. "It was clear I was up to my ears—what was that about?"

When Rasmus had said he couldn't, that was what he'd meant. He couldn't. He didn't know how to. In his childhood, it turned out, a meal was a plate with some oven chips your mother chucked onto it and then you took it to your room, if you had a room. "Laying the table" was something servants in Victorian dramas on TV did, or, later, when record companies started taking them out, staff in fancy restaurants. It was hard for him even to sit at a laid table, especially if there were forks and knives of different sizes, napkins and various shapes of spoons, ranks of glasses with different duties, all laid out specifically to reveal ignorance, flagrant nonmembership of the clan that had designed and developed this torment, over centuries, purely to winkle out the likes of him, and to exclude them.

Jay knew what it was not to be considered a member of the clan. She'd felt out of place all over the world: in Europe she was Black, in Ghana she was *bintu*—bin to London, bin to America, *obroni* white-person manners. In the US she was some kind of weird foreigner who spoke English like *she* was from one of those Victorian dramas. But this response of Ras's she had found extreme.

"I just meant," she'd said, "my hands are full, so could you put some knives and forks on the table. And maybe the salt and pepper and shito and whatever we're going to have to drink."

He'd said, "Well, I can do *that*."

"Like normal," she'd said.

He'd grimaced.

"Not normal for you," she'd said, realization dawning.

He'd said, "I've worked out that my childhood was quite different to a lot of other people's."

"We'd probably better talk about that," she'd said, and his gaze had drifted again off into the corner.

That had been before the accident. Before New York bit him

in half, and laid him out for months, and the band sailed on without him.

She missed food. She wasn't hungry. But she felt the echo of a yearning.

JAY WATCHED HIM shave.

He looks okay.

I suppose, she thought. *I mean . . .*

Actually no, not okay. Some people just aren't okay alone. Often it's the ones who look as if they are okay, because they can cope, but being able to cope doesn't mean things are right. It can just mean that the stress is high and constant. Some people's relationship with reality just isn't very stable. No judgment on them—it's just a human thing. The human ingredients are not quite . . . balanced . . . And if he wasn't before, he's certainly not now. Dougie's not enough. The saucepan people—Suki! Oh God. He wouldn't. But would he?

She sucked her teeth.

But he's writing songs. An unexpected miracle. If he's working, at some base level he's all right. It'll keep him alive till he's over the worst. I think.

5

I'm Okay

MARCH–APRIL
London

HALF A BOTTLE of cooking brandy down, Róisín googled the bereavement support groups. A lot of old people. Hot Young Widows Club, online, and in Minneapolis. Jesus Christ, was that a niche porno thing? No, it was clever Americans. She didn't know any other widows. Certainly not hot young ones. Not even old ones. *And God forgive me, but it's got to be different when you're old.*

She sat for a while and felt bad for the old ones.

Widowed And Young, groups everywhere. Facebook. There was one for widows with children and her heart started to burn. *Lucky, lucky widows with children. To see your darling's eyes in your little child.*

Then she sat for a while feeling bad for the ones with children. *To see your darling's eyes in your little child! To see your child growing up fatherless. To have to find a way to be the both of you. I can't even find a way to be the one of me.*

And then sat feeling bad for the children.

She didn't want to go anyway. *Nico is dead and I'm going to be sad forever. Why go and talk to other sad people who are also going to be sad forever?*

There was a meetup in a room above a pub in Camden. A mixer, they called it, as if it were a squirt of tonic. *Well, maybe I could do with a squirt of tonic.* She told Nell, who said, "Would you like for me to go along with you?"

"No," Róisín said. "It's me the widow. I've to go alone."

SHE LIKED THOSE tall first-floor rooms above Victorian pubs: the high windows with the yellowing gloss woodwork, and the curly plaster friezes round the ceiling. The foxed mirrors. This one looked more or less untouched since 1975, brown patterned carpet, Watneys ashtrays and all, but then maybe they'd had it done just so as a style statement. *Who'd have an ashtray?* There was a door with a push bar on it leading to an iron fire escape, for the smokers. She could hear them out there, guttering and lead tiles all around them, talking about pleurisy.

She wasn't the youngest there. She saw an embarrassed-looking Indian woman; a long-haired man in cycling Lycra, looking oddly medieval—his leggings had a sort of codpiece and she thought his hair might be dyed; a plump blonde with very red eyes and a bag she kept digging around in. For none of them did she feel that instant pull like you had sometimes at primary school—*I want to sit next to you; I want you for my friend.* Rather she felt the great push—to go the fuck home and cry in peace. *Why are you here with strangers?*

Any minute now someone was going to come up and be kind to her.

They came up behind her. "I like your hair," they said. "D'you want a gin and tonic?"

Yes, she did.

"Alex," said the person, with a little gesture to their heart. "You're new?"

"I am," she said.

"Cherry's about to start her little pep talk," said Alex. "Then we mingle."

A swishy-haired Pilates kind of a woman in her forties stood up. *I'm leaving*, Róisín thought, but she had the gin now and she didn't want to be rude to Alex. A lot of the people seemed to know each other.

It's too soon for me to be here, she was thinking. *It'll always be too soon. I don't want new people anyway—they don't know him. I'll go when this one's stopped talking.*

"We all know that grief is the price we pay for love," Cherry was saying. She was Canadian, by the sound of it.

It's not that I hate you, Róisín was thinking, picking at her fingernails. How raggedy they were. *Has grief destroyed my vitamins?* The skull ring was heavy on her hand. The ashtrays had her thinking about cigarettes. She'd really like one. *Great result—take up smoking again!* There were some people out on the fire escape still. *But I can do what I want now . . . I can do whatever the fuck I want . . .*

But I don't want anything.

I just want to talk to Nico.

"Everybody knows that," Cherry went on, "since the Queen quoted it. We're all only in grief because we loved. No love, no grief. That's the math. It's that simple! But there's another side to this, which it took me much longer to get my head around. And it's this: *no grief, no love*. Let me enlighten you about this second meaning . . ."

You're going to anyway . . .

"Grief is also the price we pay, in advance, for the love to come." She paused, as if to see whether this idea was familiar to them. It didn't seem to be. "If we don't grieve and, in time, let them go, we'll never be able to love again. We pay in solid grief and healthy mourning, we have to—we *have* to do that before we can move on and love again . . ."

Love again?

Róisín didn't mean to let out the little snort of derision. She knew everyone had their own way through. She had been told, and no doubt it was true, that things would change. Yeah, yeah.

SHE DROVE HOME down South Terrace past the Alexandra Palace, rain glimmering, lights refracting, windscreen wipers splashing time with "If You Leave Me Now" by Chicago.

Well, thanks, radio, she thought. Though it wasn't the radio, it was her phone. She and Nell used to play a thing they called iPod I-Ching—you ask a significant question, press shuffle, and see what the god of iPod gave you. "Should I go out with such and such who's asked me?" and you'd get "Stop! In the Name of Love." Or that Dusty Springfield one about wearing her hair just for him . . .

Well, she certainly didn't want to listen to bloody "If You Leave Me Now."

She reached out to tap the phone in its little holder on the dash, peering still into the dark night ahead. Chicago's mellow trumpets and maracas faded out and—

Just because you're strong don't mean it's easy . . .

Róisín burst into tears. She slammed the brakes on, and the phone flew. With a muffled whump, the car behind slammed into her rear end. Without a thought she flung open the car door, jumped out, and ran to the curb, where she sat in the rain and cried while the car sat, lights on, engine running, doors open, George Vechten's voice singing so beautifully, so tenderly, *Just because you cry don't mean you're weak,* carrying from within.

The other driver came over: a young man, perturbed. He'd been shouting, but now he said, "You all right, mate?"

"Not really," said Róisín. "I'm sorry . . ." She fumbled for a tissue.

"You want a glass of water?" he said, absurdly.

"No thank you," Róisín said. "I'm okay." She smiled up at him, weakly, and rubbed the back of her head. There was a curious smell on the air, of lily of the valley and cigarette smoke. Reminded her of her mother. She hiccupped and stood up. "How's your car?" she said.

"Was me rear-ended you, mate," he said. "How's yours?"

Their cars seemed fine. They were both really sorry. The boy made Róisín take his number, in case she felt bad later on, and needed his details.

"Well," said Róisín. "If you're okay—"

"Yeah," the boy said. "Cheers." He kind of smiled and went back to his car.

She sat, breathing, swallowing, allowing all the physicality of her human emotion, before driving off down the hill into the sliding colliding miasma of lights and rain and darkness.

6

❧

Opening Chords

APRIL
The island

GEORGE WAS WRITING to say that he and the band had heard about Jay's death. They were really sorry. She was a lovely woman and a lovely singer, but Raz didn't need George to tell him that. Cancer is the worst but Raz didn't need George to tell him that either.

Rasmus closed his eyes. She didn't die of cancer.

Now, it might be too soon for Raz to think about anything, but George wanted to run it by him anyway because it might be—well, let it speak for itself. This is it: they were planning something for the band's twentieth anniversary; he understood if Raz didn't want to get involved, but they'd really like to get him on board . . .

You feel guilty, Rasmus thought. Finally. For dumping me, for getting the other guy in, and all the other other guys, for not asking me back when I was better, for leaving me and my talent out in the wilderness while you made your ever-worse albums on the back of the great songs I wrote for the first one . . .

There was going to be a tour, in particular a show in London—not stadium, they wanted it to be something more intimate, and really special: the Albert Hall—

Which was where they'd played their first London gig bigger than a dance hall or a matte-black room behind a pub—

They'd be playing stuff from throughout the band's career, including from *Strong*, including his songs—

Still some of your biggest hits, as I recall—

And they would like for him to play with them again—

That stopped him.

Or if he had work of his own, and wanted to do some solo numbers as part of the set—

Oh.

Maybe with the band—

Oh . . .

Or a separate set, a support slot if he liked that better—and George really did understand that the timing might be all wrong on this but maybe it might be right? But anyway, they all really wanted to offer it and really hoped there might be a way Raz felt he could do it, and how about he and George meet up? And George would come to the island, or to Glasgow, if that made it easier—

George, who never went anywhere or did anything to make things easier? George, who hadn't even visited him in hospital when he lay there with his back broken and a bill the size of Manhattan looming? George, who'd convinced himself, and tried to convince the others, that Rasmus hadn't really written the songs he had most definitely written? George, who he should've sued, and would've if he hadn't been awash with opiates and flat on his back for nine months after surgery. George, who didn't even mention him when he went up onstage to accept the Mercury Prize for the album Rasmus had written . . .

No fucking way.

It made his bones ache just to think of it. *Pain flares. Stress.*

He reached into his drawer for painkillers. *I know work is at least part of the answer. It's the only thing of value. We talked about that. I'm going to do the things she wanted me to do. I am. But not this.*

The reality that she was not coming back floated around him in wisps. He knew it, of course. Well, his brain knew it. His heart not so much. It still seemed to feel there was a chance.

She would probably like me to seize this day.

But onstage?

He couldn't play with the band again, that he knew.

Could he go out there, now? Onstage, in front of everybody?

Even at the thought of it, his body started shaking a little.

No. Fuck George.

But. Well. He had questioned his ability to look after a sick wife, too. And he'd done it. He'd bloody done it. And he hadn't let her down.

He ambled back to the piano, shooing the cat off the stool, and let his fingers drift to the opening chords of another new song. Or possibly the opening chords of a potential middle eight. He had a snatch of lyric for it: *One goodbye too many, one hello too few, something something something, tum tum tu-u-um, I love you . . .* an old-school ballad. Something Dusty Springfield might have sung, or Amy Winehouse, or Adele.

"What d'you think, darling?" he said.

7

Delusion

APRIL
The island

JAY JUMPED. "I like it," she replied. "A singer could fly with that one."

He made a fire in the evening; there was always damp lurking round the edges, even after a sunny day. He'd fallen asleep now, reading, the little cat in his lap. Lying back with his book open, his bare throat and his cheekbones. He shivered, suddenly and violently. The cat stood up, affronted. In his sleep, Rasmus smiled.

The fire was going out, but she couldn't give it a breath from the bellows, or put a log on. Physically she couldn't, but also she didn't want to confuse him. A ghost could so easily gaslight someone without any intention to, just by being careless. And a ghost, it turned out, could still be house-proud, could long to wash up and polish surfaces. The state of the vegetable patch was upsetting to her. She did try, a few times, to throw away crumpled tissues, which bestrewed the house like tumbleweed on a Western highway. But her limp, unreliable fingers couldn't manage it, and that was just as well. Reason told her she was not the person to fix this. But then reason also told her she didn't exist, so, really, what reason had she to listen to reason? And Jay was a great fixer of bad situations, and other people . . .

He can't stay here, in this isolation, alone and brokenhearted, staring backward. The damp will crawl up his trouser legs, and the moss cover him over. He'll rot away and start to smell. He must leave the island. And he must find a woman.

At some stage.

She trailed her hand over his hair as she drifted across the room.

His laptop was open. In life she'd never look at his work or his emails uninvited. *But he can't invite me.* She wasn't going to look. But she glanced. And saw George's name, there on the screen, on an email.

Fuck it, I'm a ghost. Different rules.

She paused.

She read.

Well.

It was perfectly clear to her that he must do it. *What an opportunity! Ideal!* Then perfectly clear that he must not. The sticking point was George: sneaky, out-for-himself George.

So she thought about George, and the past, and change, and opportunity. How one person has to give, or receive, in order to start the process of giving and receiving. It was necessary. She sat for a while, head bowed, in the dark, and then she began to draft a reply in her head. *Dear George*, Jay would write.

I'm not against it. Tell me more.

If Rasmus had woken, and looked up, would he have made out the dim shape of her, silhouetted against the window when the cold dawn began to creep in? She glanced across at him, folded awkwardly on the sofa, like a camel, or a parallel ruler. *Dear man.* She drifted over and lay down, very gently, resting her head on his, and whispered in his ear: "Say yes to George. Say yes. I want you to do it. Say yes."

And then doubts started swirling. *I should check George out,* she thought, *before I get Rasmus into this.*

I should go and find him, and see for myself.

Rasmus stirred, and sighed, and stood, and walked to the kitchen, idly reaching out to shut his laptop as he passed.

She laid a ghostly kiss on his cheekbone and left.

SHE TOOK PUBLIC transport: the walk to the bus; the bus to Leverburgh; the other bus to Stornoway, the ferry to Ullapool, the coach to Inverness, the train to Edinburgh, where she sat on top of a bus shelter on Princes Street, waiting for the night train, legs swinging, contemplating members of her sex. There were very young women, very drunk women, very tired women. A skinny woman in a parka, arguing in a doorway. A bus driver, huge-eyed and patient. In a bar behind the bus stop, a group of women had gathered: Jay watched them arrive, alone and nervous, and drifted in, curious. One wore a T-shirt: WIDOWS GET TOGETHER: YOU CAN TALK TO ME. She laughed: *coincidence! Well, no doubt the world is full of widows, you just don't notice.* Their jackets lay on the banquettes, their handbags on the table among the tapas, and their Chardonnay warming as they clutched their balloon glasses. *Hold it by the stem, for God's sake. It stays cold for longer.* Their feelings flowed out as the wine flowed down. She loved when their laughter got raucous, and blinked when it turned to tears. One spoke about his curry spices being still in the kitchen cupboard, and she didn't cook curry. One told of trying, on the first anniversary, to climb a mountain they had climbed together on honeymoon, and turning back, and now she felt a failure. No, they all said, you're a success, for trying. One said she wasn't sure she should be there because they hadn't been married as such.

Am I a widow? Jay wondered. *Who can I talk to?*

She watched them leave arm in arm, telling each other not to worry about their mascara, they looked lovely. She pressed her back against the plate-glass windows and wasn't certain she was still human.

None of them would be right for him.

Outside, a woman who looked like Cleopatra, her skin deep bronze and apparently made-up all over, was vaping tetchily behind a twisted velvet rope. Black straps crisscrossed her narrow shoulders; a black skirt, shorter than her heels were high, wrapped tight around her tiny backside. It was clear from her every movement that she did not consider being delayed by this rope appropriate.

Of course they're not right. You don't want them to be. She didn't want to see Rasmus tumbling with Cleopatra, biting her made-up flesh, breathing her heavy artificial perfume, or with any of these perfectly nice women, indulging some desire he'd never manifested in life, to go off with a woman entirely different to his wife.

Perhaps he would want *to go mad. Perhaps he wants to be alone. Perhaps he doesn't need protecting. Perhaps it's not my business.*

No. It is.

In the station, drifting past people and through things came into its own. *A strange kind of senior rail card*, she thought. *Now that you're dead, you travel for free.* And it was nice to have her own sleeper berth, with the tartan rug and the little ladder.

He would probably leave the island, and at some stage another woman would be a good thing. They'd played about, drawing up that ad . . . joking, of course. A love letter from her to him, really. At that time she'd run through friends in her mind, past and current, for whom he might have had a soft spot. But that game he wouldn't play. He just said no. Wouldn't see any comfort in it for *her*, to know that he would be on the right road to restitution as a man who was loved by a good woman, a man who was not alone with his grief. The nearest they'd come to fighting was over that. Well, she had shouted at him. Not her proudest moment.

She didn't want someone who was looking for a new partner. She didn't want him scared away. She didn't want to accidentally introduce him to a gold-digger or a stalker. There'd been some before: one who'd seen a photograph of him and sent him a pair of boxers and a white T-shirt, thinking he looked as if he didn't have good underwear. Her mouth tightened at the memory. *As if!* He'd opened it—and there was a scarlet lipstick kiss right over the heart on the T-shirt. "Jesus," Rasmus had said, and dropped it as if he'd touched a slug. Jay'd said: "It's like one of those Restoration tragedies where they send a poisoned wedding dress." He'd said, "At least it wasn't the boxers." They'd used the fire tongs to put the things in the bin, laughing at themselves, yet in no doubt that it was the only thing to do. So no, nobody who might vampire on his odd celebrity.

But none of that had stopped her running through women in her mind: *the poet with the hair who lived out toward Hushinish? Too neurotic. The viola player with the boat? She was lovely. The pink-cheeked Edinburgh publisher with the sense of humor and the brother on Uig? Edinburgh would be good. He needs to be free of my illness and away from the scenes of loss. Away from memory.*

Free of me.

Would Edinburgh be far enough?

Real life would be best. Someone wrapped into the web of acquaintance; somebody who was already part of it . . .

Traveling threw into focus the shiftiness of time. There were periods when she didn't seem to exist. She'd come to, and know only that time or place had changed since she had previously been aware of herself. Like sleep but not sleep. She didn't know where she went at those times. Or if there was a where. It didn't seem to take very long at all to get to London.

At King's Cross, she smiled and just stepped up onto the roof of a bus, and sailed off into town. She liked this physical freedom she had now. Yes, she couldn't really affect material objects, but affecting herself was so easy.

I could go home to Ghana, she thought. *I could fly around the forests at Kakum with the black butterflies, sneak up on the elephants . . . see Kwame . . .*

Not yet.

The train had got in early, so at Marble Arch she jumped up to the flat roof of the arch itself, surveyed Park Lane, then hopped and skipped from statue to statue into Hyde Park, backflipping high into leafless treetops, her feet and hands faultlessly finding a grip on each branch. She wandered: around the muddy bird-built island in the Serpentine, all twigs and guano, with nowhere for a human foot to tread, where the cormorants and geese lived their own lives of claws and feathers. *Where are the ghosts of their dead?* In South Kensington, in the basements of museums, fragile manuscripts and moth-eaten stuffed bears—*bear ghosts!*—vied for her attention.

He's not going to want a stuffed bear, Jay.

No, he wants me. And he can't have me.

She cartwheeled along Birdcage Walk, bounced up onto the Queen's balcony, and took her time in the private apartments at Buckingham Palace. *Surely there would be ghosts here, of all places?* She stood in the bow of a Thames Clipper going down to Greenwich; she lay on London's most expensive lawns. She examined Tower Bridge from below, Big Ben from above, and 10 Downing Street from inside.

Maybe you're deluding yourself with these notions of generosity, of handing him over, wanting him to be loved. Maybe you just like this image of yourself as this perfect loving woman, faithful and generous even beyond the grave. God, what was that song? "The Unquiet Grave."

> *And if you kiss my cold clay lips*
> *Your days they won't be long.*

So romantic! So self-sacrificial!

So unevolved and desperate and medieval . . .

Such great songs, though. A lyric swam into her mind like a glittery fish, trailing a possibility of a melody behind it:

> *Down by the Thames sweet Mistress Jay, Mistress Jay,*
> *sweet Mistress Jay*
> *She only had but one true love and she gave him*
> *away . . .*

She'd never heard of a ghost writing songs. *It must happen, though.* Oh, how she wanted to play at playlists with Ras. She'd bring the folk and the country—"Phantom 309" by Red Sovine. Dwight Yoakam's "Johnson's Love." "The Long Black Veil"! *Of course—now, there's a ghost singing. That stunning Nick Cave album,* Ghosteen. *And he'd bring*—well, she never knew what he would bring. That was the joy of him. One of the joys of him.

Ah, Jay, be a proper ghost, and haunt the fuck out of any woman who comes near him. Go on. It'd be fun. Suki's hair standing on end—

She stopped in the street and stamped.

Come on, she told herself. *I'm here for a purpose. In life, you choose your purpose. I chose music, then I chose medicine. I chose Rasmus, and I couldn't choose some other things I would have chosen, if things had been different . . . but here I am and I can choose again. Who gets that opportunity?*

Our story didn't end right.

The sun climbed the sky and she drifted up to Soho, to her destination: the offices of the Capos' record company. In reception, she lay back on an orange plastic sofa and stared at a huge screen showing projections of the current bands, waiting for Carola to come in. The sound was off. The loop played. There were a few women among the parade of men. A very young, very pouty blonde with wide black eyebrows like two halves of a dashing mustache, looking up, framed like a selfie. An athletic-looking light-skinned Black superheroine of a girl, so airbrushed and photoshopped she might as well have been CGI. A moonfaced, moody-eyed Goth, painted even paler than she naturally was, drooping over an acoustic guitar, in what was presumably intended to be some kind of charismatic sulk. *It's like online profiles*, Jay thought. *So much presentation that you have no idea of the humanity beneath. No idea who these people are.*

The receptionist was beautiful: bleached blond, gray eyes, a noble profile, nice muscles under his T-shirt, and being courteous and kind to someone on the phone who was clearly upset. Jay didn't think Rasmus had a bisexual side he'd want to explore. She didn't think he'd want to explore much new ground at all. He'd rather be with one person a hundred times than a hundred different people. His exploration went deep, not wide. You wouldn't think, to listen to the world go on, that there are men like that.

Anyway, she was looking for Carola. In any situation there's always someone who knows what and when and where, and it's never a musician, and it's usually a woman, and in this company it was and always had been Carola. And here she was, pushing through the rotating door, phone in hand. Aged a bit, of course. Wearing big laser-cut earrings: a mistake, really. Same smiling face and eyeliner. Good old Carola.

Jay followed her to her desk, and for a moment wished, desperately, that they could just go for a coffee, have a chat, catch up. Just be normal. She'd always really liked Carola. But *all that stuff is the business of mortals*, she told herself. *I have other business. Find out where the Capos are; find George.* She perched, eavesdropping and spying and scouting the wide room.

Carola put her earbuds in, about to go into a Zoom. Jay couldn't hear, but her eyes swept the screen. The meeting was with a woman called Ayesha@ConstantEyeFilms, who seemed to be making Carola laugh a lot. Jay took advantage of Carola's engrossment to check the large diary lying open on her desk. *Here we go*: Capos in the studio, the TrackShed. She knew the TrackShed. Mile End. *Excellent.*

Her eyes flicked back to the screen. Emails, contacts, *ah—* Constant Eye.

Ah. They were to film the Capos' gigs.

Jay glanced at the address, and back at the amusing woman. Black hair, strong nose, loquacious, nobody's fool. *Hm.*

GEORGE WASN'T HARD to find. There he was, in the booth at the TrackShed, all in black, skinny legs, a bit of a potbelly, ponytail with a little thinning spot just above it. A *very* nice coat. *Pregnant pencil*, she thought. *Middle-aged rock star style.* He looked healthy. He stood with a producer and a couple of others, staring meaningfully through the glass at a guitarist, who was cradling a handsome Gretsch Country Gentleman twelve-string (*mm*, she thought) and looking bemused by something George was saying. Jay smiled. Many times in the past had she been bemused by George.

She leaned against the back wall of the booth, listened, and waited. The guitarist was good. Not as good as Rasmus. People slipped in and out; George and the producer murmured and smiled and frowned. There were no women present. *Plus ça change.* But George was polite, and sober, and the atmosphere was constructive. Convivial. Nobody had come out of the gents sniffing and wiping their nose. *Good so far.*

The producer called a break; the guitarist headed outside with a packet of cigarettes, and George pulled his phone from his expensive pocket. She watched on, interested.

George cracked a big smile. "Guys!" he yelped, real excitement in his voice. "Raz is on! He says he'll do it!"

What?

Had Rasmus heard her, even? Had he made his decision so quickly? Under her influence, or of his own accord?

Delusion! To think you can control anything at all.

George was tapping out a reply. She peered over his shoulder.

Christ, well, OK, we're on. One way or another.

Instinct said: *go home.* But instinct then interrupted itself to say: *But go and look at that woman first.*

THE AMUSING WOMAN from the Zoom call didn't seem to be at the Constant Eye office when Jay slipped in. The room—small, mid-century furniture, classy—appeared empty at first. But there was someone. Jay could hear her crying in the bathroom.

It was unbearable. *Wait for her to come out,* she told herself, leaning sympathetically against the cubicle door, full of concern, *God, poor woman.* She couldn't even say *Come out, what is it, how can I help?*

And thus it was that when Jay first met her, Róisín was in floods on the seat-down loo, and Jay had slipped through the door and landed practically in her lap.

Róisín hiccupped.

Jay was apologizing, and realizing she really didn't need to. She pulled herself up and away and looked at her.

The woman had short-cropped duckling hair, a white shirt, a high forehead. Her eyes were intelligent and red with tears. She was ankle deep in bits of screwed-up loo paper. She was looking so directly at Jay that for a moment Jay thought, *she can see me.*

But it wasn't that.

"Hello?" the woman said, as if she'd heard a noise. An Irish voice.

Jay was transfixed. She couldn't take her eyes off her. She was just adorable. Her weeping face, her soft-shadowed eyes. She saw the hollow cheeks, the bitten nails, and the skull ring. Of course it was silly to think you could tell at a glance. *Oh, darling,* Jay thought, and didn't know why. It was just automatic. She knew, like you know at primary school: *this girl's for me.*

Come on, she said. *Wash your face, and a cup of tea.*

Róisín stood up, unlocked the cubicle door, went to the sink, and splashed cold water on herself in that useless way. Patted it dry, didn't check the mirror. A phone was ringing back in the office, and she went and answered it.

"Of course," she said. "Yes," and proceeded to be both astonishingly patient and quietly effective with someone who didn't seem to understand that money was a real thing.

Jay watched her intently. There was an ID on a lanyard lying on her desk. A photo of her with a grand, confident smile, and a head of dark curls bouncing around all over the place.

Why are you so sad? Jay said. *You're as sad as me. As sad as Rasmus.*

At the end of the working day, she followed her.

8

Boiled Egg

APRIL
The island

THE SUN WAS shining that morning, and he'd boiled an egg without it going hard. Insofar as it went, it was not the worst day.

He was curiously certain that he wanted to do this thing with George. Strange, as he'd been quite against it yesterday. Unconvinced.

Dear George,

he wrote, without really thinking.

I'm not against it. Tell me more.

He squinted at it. He leaned back in his chair. *Grief, eh. The great confuser.*

Is that what I think, though? Do I want to know more? I suppose I must do, on some level.

He added his name and pressed send.

Hey Raz,

So great to hear from you. Let's talk! I don't have a number for you?

George

Dear George,

There's no need to talk about it. I'll do it. Albert Hall only, no touring. I'll support, solo, new songs. Half an hour max. No press, no fuss. What's the date?

Rasmus.

Raz,

I can't tell you how delighted we all are to hear this. I'm not going to push you on doing more than you're willing to do, man, I really appreciate you doing it at all, but the option is there and can stay open if you might wanna change your mind. Can I give Carola your details for arrangements?

One thing, though: there's an industry warm-up gig at Bush Hall, in June. Remember the old Carlton Club in Shepherd's Bush? That place! I have to ask you—would you do that too? It's gonna be filmed and your comeback performance has got to be recorded for posterity, for sure. I totally understand though if you don't feel up to it. Don't wanna push you because this is just so great that you're on for it. We're all really chuffed.

All the best mate,
George

Dear George,

Being filmed is borderline Press and Fuss.

But OK. Just don't tell anyone I'll talk to them because I won't.

Rasmus.

Hey Raz,

I seem to recall you loved the Carlton Club back in the day. It's just the same now only with bands. Fancy plasterwork still there and the big chandeliers and stuff, really evocative. It's a great little venue. I think you'll really like it. Capacity about 300, think we're gonna have little tables and stuff for the bigwigs. Pool tables all gone, though. Long long time ago, hey?

George

I can see that working.

Rasmus.

Listen, Raz, how are you doing?

George

Dear George,

Give Carola my email then and let me have the dates.

All the best,
Rasmus.

9

Strong

APRIL
London

NICO STAYED IN the flat. There, though he continued to have no idea why or how, at least he knew where he was. Loosely, he was in shock, and only beginning to learn how to control what he was now. It went against everything he'd known in life; everything he had learned and taught himself. He'd been a fiery boy: he'd trained himself out of it through sheer dignity. When his dad had said being a tattooist ("Tattoo *artist*," Nico had said, for the umpteenth time) was "no job for a grown man, clever kid like you," well, in the end, yes, he'd put the guns away and trained as a paramedic. He'd been "popular with the ladies," as his mother put it. "You are Latin lover," she'd say, giggling at him. Though she didn't know the half of it. He'd trained himself out of that, too. Or rather, the existence of Róisín had pulled him out of it. If that's what it took to have her, cheers, no problem. Done. He was a science-and-evidence-based person. He was accustomed to knowing what to do. At work: do your job. At home: look after Róisín and make her happy as best you can. But now . . .

How can you spend your adult life saving lives, fighting to save lives, suffering when you fail to save a life, training yourself out of suffering when you fail to save a life, understanding that we live and then we die, okay, electric meat in a cage of bones, that's the deal, fair enough, get on with it—and then, when you lose your own life, you're still here?

It felt to him like some kind of bad joke. Or personal insult. Though of course it wasn't personal. But, if it happened to his mum, say, Marina, she wouldn't be troubled by it—*well, okay,* he thought, *she would be, but not in the same way. She'd be well chuffed, she'd go round everybody's houses to tell them she was right and they were wrong, ha ha. Because she believes in ghosts.* It seemed clear to Nico that the people who believe in ghosts would be the ones to see them. She said she saw her father on the balcony of the old flat in Athens, sitting in the wicker chair. She said she smelled his cheroot. Dad said probably Mr. Katsoukakis next door smoked the same ones, on his balcony. She said Mr. Katsoukakis smoked Karelia and this was no Karelia she smelled. Mrs. Katsoukakis then, Dad said, with one of his sly looks from behind the newspaper. And everybody laughed because Mrs. Katsoukakis spent her whole time spraying air freshener on Mr. Katsoukakis and opening windows and turning up the air-conditioning and fanning her face on the balcony because she couldn't abide the smell of tobacco.

So where did that leave him? If he went to see Mum, she'd smell him—*of course she would! You know Mums—and she'd've driven Dad mad going on about it, if he hadn't gone first. And she felt Dad all over the place, in London, in Athens, on Ithaca, everywhere . . .* He could picture her now, sipping her coffee, saying "Not now, *Nico-mou,* Yiannis is with me."

Or maybe I wouldn't be able to get near her, past all the blue mataki eyes she has hidden everywhere. She'd sewn one inside every piece of his uniform, because she didn't trust him not to take off the one on the leather thong that she'd sewn on round his neck when he was sixteen. God, she loved a superstition.

It was still there. *Ghosts wear jewelry; who knew?* He could touch it and feel it.

So he sat in the flat, nervous, twiddling his bloody mataki.

Sometimes he thought Róisín *could* hear him. Sometimes there was just a little echo, a glimmer of a response—not now. But she might be feeling him. Or he might as well not be there at all. It was all out of kilter, the communication between them. There seemed no rhythm to it. However he called to her, there was no adequate response. *That's what's unbearable. She doesn't bloody know!*

He didn't mind touching an inanimate object like his necklace.

He watched her. He counted her drinks. He lay down beside her over and over. He sat in her cupboard for a while. What if he suddenly became visible? He could see himself, faintly, in the mirror. He looked like him, only less so. His mustache was there. His nice brown eyes. His hair still plenteous, swept back, his widow's peak . . . but—ghostly. If real living him was a plain thick sheet of paper, now he was more of a Rizla. Not enough ink in the printer. Copy of a faded copy. *She'd have conniptions, if she saw me.*

I should go out, he thought, over and over, but he didn't. Outside had too many loose ends and unknown rules; God knows what's going on out there for a guy like him. He remembered coming to London with no English, aged six. Outside now was what the school playground had been then.

And April was a fucking insult. Just looking out the window. *Fucking blossoms. Fucking blackbirds.*

Then one evening she came home from work red-eyed and a bit early, and changed her shirt, and headed out to the car. He didn't know where she was going.

Fuck it. How much trouble can you cause in a car? He went with her.

HE WAS BEHIND her as she sat on the uncomfortable upright chair she'd chosen over one of the low-slung leather armchairs that he knew would make her feel vulnerable. He'd checked out the person who'd bought her the gin and tonic. A place like this would be full of chancers. Well, she'd be okay. He was with her.

He didn't like her being here. He didn't like other living people and her being one thing, and him being another, one they didn't even know about. He wanted Róisín to meet *his* eyes. Drink a gin and tonic *he* had bought her. To touch him, to look up and smile at *him*. He wanted this as much as he had ever wanted anything in his life. More, because in life he had been good at getting what he wanted, and now he was powerless.

There was one woman standing back from the group, like him. She was tall, her hair a black dandelion halo, her cheekbones broad, her mouth sculpted. *Beautiful.* Maybe Róisín might like the look of her. Same kind of age, bit older probably, anyway, too bloody young to be here. He smiled at her before he even noticed that she too had been printed out too many times, and was hazy round the edges.

Her face turned to absolute shock and she gasped aloud.

No one turned their head. No one looked up.

Shit!

What?

"You can see me?" she cried out, across the group of the unnoticing living. She was checking the room, eyes flickering swiftly. Nobody was taking the slightest notice of them. Her eyes came back to him.

"Yes," he said, before he could stop himself.

"I can see you," she said.

They stared at each other.

"Bloody hell," he said.

"Yes," she said. "Are you?"

"What, dead?" he said. "Yeah. I am."

It was just a little sympathetic smile, but when her face opened up, it lit the room. She moved toward him. "I know nobody can hear us, but it seems bad-mannered to be calling across," she said. "I've been wondering where everyone was. Because I once read there are fifteen dead people for every living person and I couldn't be the only one, why would I be the only one?"

"Yes," he said.

They looked at each other a bit. "This is peculiar," she said.

"Yes," he said again.

"Have you been . . . here . . . long?"

"I don't know," he said. "I'm bad at time. Or time is different. A few months?"

"I don't know either," she said. "Not long. I haven't seen anyone else . . . like us."

"Same," he said. "But I haven't really been out."

"You'd think there'd be more," she said. "I mean, given there are *any*."

"You'd think there'd be some here, looking out for their . . ."

"Their widows, I suppose."

"Weird to talk about your own widow," he said.

"Not the weirdest thing going on, though," she said. "Is it?"

"No," Nico said, comforted by her words. And also freaked out. All around them the bereaved, like them, were conversing, or failing to converse: bright chat, frozen courtesies, warm attempts, involuntary rebuffs.

"Do you—know anything?" the woman asked. "About why?"

"Why we're here?"

"Yes."

"No."

She seemed resigned. "Is *your* widow here?" she asked.

Nico looked down and gestured at Róisín, whose eyes were a little clearer, and whose expression was skeptical, distraught, accepting.

"Oh!" said the woman. "Right. Of course."

"What?" he said. "Why of course?" and the woman looked back at him, smiled, and put out her hand.

"I'm Jay," she said. "I was a GP. Lived in the Hebrides. Family from Ghana."

"Nico," he said. "Paramedic, as it happens. North London. Family from Greece. Hi."

"I like Greece," said Jay. Their hands glided straight through each other, and they each gave a rueful little laugh.

"We—" he said, and stopped. He didn't know how to put it.

"We ought to talk," said Jay.

"Yeah," he said. "D'you want to come back to ours after?"

"I do," said Jay.

The Canadian woman stood up to speak.

NICO WAS IN the seat beside her, watching, as Róisín drove home, Chicago's "If You Leave Me Now" crooning from the car's speakers. Passing headlights moved over her face, her duck-fluff head. In the back seat sat this new person—this new ghost. This beautiful and rather grand doctor, who did not seem scared like him. He twisted round to glance at her, composed in the back seat, looking out of the window like a lady in a cab.

The wind has changed, he thought. *What might she know? Now what?*

"You all right back there?" he called.

"I am," she said. "Thank you."

A cool customer, he thought, and smiled at the old-fashioned term. One of the collection of English colloquialisms his mother had armed herself with when they first came over. Róisín's mother, Clare, when she came from Dublin, had brought a stock of the hardest-core Dublin slang she could get her hands on. She wanted it very clear to all that she wasn't English.

He and Jay didn't seem able to talk in the car in front of Róisín. That too seemed rude.

She drove on. There were tears in her eyes.

God, he wanted to comfort her. To kiss her. Not much to ask. To affect her. To . . . *something*.

He'd like this cool customer to see, as well, that he had things in hand here. That he was competent.

Music always gets through, he thought.

"*Just Because You're Strong*," he thought. *The Capos.* The one he'd mimed to and it made Róisín laugh; the one they'd made love to and it made her cry. Their song.

Her phone was on the dash in front of her. Unlocked—she'd just checked her messages coming out of the meeting. How he wished he could just tap it, bring the song up. Play it for her. How he wished . . .

And it worked. Chicago's mellow trumpets and maracas faded out and—

Just because you're strong don't mean it's easy . . .

Nico crowed with delight—*bull's-eye!*

Róisín burst into tears.

Sweetheart! Oh God . . .

And then someone rear-ended the car, and Róisín jumped out, the engine running, the doors open, *Just because you cry don't mean you're weak* carrying from within.

He leaped out after her, calling, and stood helpless under the lamplight like Lili Marlene.

10

Monstera

APRIL
London – the island

JAY, IN THE back, flexed. The collision, George's voice. Rasmus's words and guitar; her own harmonies, all those years ago. Though she thought often about that period of her life, it had been a long time since she'd listened to that album. Too much of what went wrong for Ras, and for her, was caught up in it. The chords it struck in her . . .

She saw the phone, on Nico's seat where it had fallen. *Stop that.* To her surprise, it did. The silence rang for a moment, and she wondered.

She drifted out of the car.

The other driver came over: a young man, perturbed. "You all right, mate?" he said.

Nico sat invisibly by Róisín now, his hand on her arm, trying to bring her back to earth, to stop her shaking.

He glanced up at Jay. "Are you okay?" he asked.

"Were you afraid I might have been killed?" she asked. He did laugh.

"It's one of her favorite songs," he said. "I never thought . . ."

"Mine too," she murmured.

Jay came and squatted on the other side of Róisín, the three of them in a row between rain-slicked car bumpers, a bin, and the speckly concrete base of a bus stop. Above them the new leaves of ash trees waved acid green against the night sky; beyond, traffic lights changing inexorably: crimson, amber, petrol green, reflecting on the black road and dripping rain. Jay leaned against her. Beyond the grief, inside it, behind it, was strength, humor, a possibility of joy. *There will be sunshine after this storm*, she thought. *In the midst of all this cold and dark, there's an indomitable spring . . .*

"What would comfort her?" she asked.

"Me not being dead," he said.

"What achievable thing?"

Nico didn't answer. Just laid his arm round Róisín's shoulder, an invisible blanket. "I don't know—her mum?"

After a moment, Róisín hiccupped and took some long, shuddering breaths. She gave a soft small smile. She stood up and asked the other driver if his car was okay, and took his number when he offered it. Jay liked how she was being: undramatic, straight, kind.

Nico's face had gone a little tight. Jay couldn't tell if it was anger or pain. "Bloody ambulance-chaser," he said. "Hitting on her when he's just driven into her."

"He didn't mean to," said Jay. "Poor boy."

The poor boy was smiling politely at Róisín. "Better get on then," she was saying.

"You keep away from her," Nico was muttering.

"But really," Jay said, "it's good of him. He's not filled with road rage. And he's not being nice just because she's good-looking. I mean, she's also bright red and covered in snot."

"She's beautiful," Nico said. "She's always beautiful." He stopped wanting to hit the boy.

"Yes, she is," said Jay.

"I can't bear it," Nico said.

"Not being able to help her?" said Jay.

"Not being able to do anything."

"We *can* help them," Jay said. They both smiled at the word "we."

"No I can't. Don't think I haven't tried."

They slipped back into the car. Róisín spent a moment breathing, swallowing, before driving off down the hill.

Jay whispered: "Why's it so hard to talk in front of her, when she can't hear us?"

Nico glanced up at her, a funny look on his face: part gratitude, part relief. "That's yet another thing," he said, "that I have had nobody to talk to about."

I T   W A S   A very nice flat. Raised ground floor in a '30s block, small but good proportions, parquet floors, and they'd done it up well. Nice little sofa, side lights, monstera plant climbing up beside the window. If it hadn't been for the empty mugs lying around and the fruit rotting uneaten in the bowl and the shiny look to the sheets and the scruffs of tissue littering the floor like confetti at a wedding, it would have been charming.

Róisín went to the bathroom.

Jay said, "I know it's absurd. But it seems so rude."

"You get used to it," said Nico. "At least—I talk *to* her quite a lot."

"Well, you know her."

"Shall I introduce you?" he said, and that idea was quietly pleasing to both of them.

"Kinda," said Jay. "Only that's even more absurd."

Nico was sitting on the sofa, arms along the back, fully at home.

"I feel I should offer you something," he said, looking about, as if a cup of tea or a glass of wine might materialize.

"Can you *eat*?" she asked eagerly.

"No," he said. "Why, can you?"

"No such luck," she said. "What can you do?"

"Nothing," he said. "How about you?"

"I can run up buildings," she said. "And move through walls. I can whirl up trees."

"I can go through walls," he said doubtfully.

"I bet you can run up buildings then," she said. "Wanna try?"

"Sure," he said. "Not now."

They spoke at the same time: "What do you—" she said, and he said, "Have you been anywhere else?"

"Scotland," Jay replied. "That's where my—"

"Your widower?" he said.

"Yes. Where he lives."

"But have you been anywhere, any—ah—afterlife kind of place?"

"No," she said.

"Me neither," he said. And that was a disappointment.

The sound of flushing came from the bathroom. A tap. The sound of hands squelching as they washed. She'd left the door open. Jay glanced at her own hands. *No eating, lifting forks, going to the loo, wiping arses. No washing. How little we think about our bodies, really, when we have them. We're only taught to find fault with them, and to take them for granted.*

"Why not?" Jay asked. "Why are we still here?"

"I have no idea," he said.

Róisín came out of the bathroom, in a T-shirt and knickers. She went into the kitchen and flicked the kettle on.

"Róisín, love, this is Jay," Nico said, turning, as she passed. Jay smiled. "She's another ghost! I hope you don't mind me bringing her home with us. I'm kind of excited because I never met a ghost before. I'm hoping she knows stuff I don't know, might be able to steer me right. In the being-a-ghost department . . ."

"I do have an idea," said Jay, and then shut herself down. *It's too soon. In various ways.* She looked at him carefully. All very well to study Róisín; what about him? His look is frank; his leather thong necklace, which could so easily be the sign of a twat, suits him, as does his longish hair and his well-worn linen shirt. She'd spotted a photo of him in his hospital kit on the mantelpiece: his hair pulled back in what looked like a hairnet. *Well, that takes a certain kind of confidence. He's handsome.* He looked like quite a sure-minded person who has received a massive shock. *Bit like me, then,* she thought. *He looks scared. He looks all right.*

Róisín's phone, on the table between the two of them, rang. Jay had to scoot over to avoid being sat on as Róisín, mug in hand, picked it up and settled on the sofa.

"Hi, Nell," she said. "No, sorry—just going to bed. Yeah. All right . . . No," she said. "Not yet. Yes, I know. I know . . . Yes, I will—oh honey, please. He told me he had, so he did, and I *will* find it. Maybe he lodged it with a different solicitor . . . yes, I'm goi— Oh God would you . . ."

Jay fixed Nico with a look.

"You didn't," she said. "Tell me you didn't."

"Didn't what?"

Foreseeing a torrent of double negatives, Jay cut to the chase.

"You didn't make a will."

"Of course I made a will," he said. "I just didn't tell her where it is."

Jay stared at him. "Forgive my asking," she said, "but why would you not?"

"I was going to," he said.

"Did you not know you were going to die? Had you not noticed people drop dead out of the blue?"

"Of course I had," he said. "I'm—was—pretty practical. But I was young. And it was sudden."

"Young enough to still be immortal," she said. "You thought you were going to live forever? *We know not when the hour is*, Nico! Look at her!"

The call over, Róisín had got up from the sofa again, and was drooping toward the bedroom. Nico's gaze followed her.

"Is she going to lose this flat?" Jay asked. "At every step while she tries to sort out the remains of your mortal existence, people are saying, 'And can you send a copy of the *will*, and are you the executor of the *will*,' and she's going to have to say no and they will sigh and every little thing will be difficult."

Nico had his head in his hands. "I thought she'd have found it," he mumbled.

"Where is it?" Jay said. Then, "Do you have children?" Though it was clear from the flat that they didn't.

Róisín came back through, wrapped in a towel. Even her white arms looked sad. The sound of the shower running came across the hall.

"No," he said, eyes following Róisín.

"Are your parents alive?"

"My mum."

"If the will's not found, everything'll go to her then. Will she share it?"

"She doesn't need it," he said. "At least I don't think she does. And she adores Róisín."

"Oh dear," said Jay. "Because *that's* a recipe for harmony."

"Some's in a joint account," he said. "Building society."

"For Róisín to be safe she must find it. Who's the executor?"

"She is," he said. "I mean, I did the right thing, I just didn't—"

"You just needed to tell her."

"Didn't want to upset her."

"How much more upset is she now?" Jay said mercilessly.

They sat in silence.

"Your death was expected, then?" he asked.

"Yes," she said. "As is everybody's. But yes, I was given notice. Anyway."

Róisín passed back through, her flesh pink now. They heard the soft creak of the bed as she lay down and the soft, labored breathing of someone trying to be still, desperate to sleep.

"Fuck," said Nico. "What can I do?"

"You must tell her where it is," Jay said. "Where is it?"

"How can I tell her? She can't hear me! I can't write her a note or send her a"—he stopped himself from swearing—"an email."

"Can't you get in her dreams?"

"What?" he said.

"Haven't you tried?"

"How?" he said. "Can you?"

"I have done," she said.

She told Nico about it. Not all of it, not in great detail. But the salient bits: getting Dougie. Making herself felt. Talking to him.

"Did he hear you? Did you—was it, talking to *each other*?"

She couldn't swear to it.

"Come on," he cried, and would have taken her by the hand, to pull her up and through to the bedroom, only his hand fell through hers, and they both just stared for a moment at their limp, useless limbs. And they went through, and stood at the foot of the bed where Róisín lay.

"How do you do it?" he said urgently. "I lie down by her. Often. I try not to touch her because I don't want to scare her, but one time we danced—I mean, she cried—but how was it when you—"

Jay perched herself on the small bedroom chair, and raised her hand. "Wait," she said.

He waited.

"It's emotional," she said. "I think. He was very ill."

"I have to wait for her to be very ill?"

"I don't know," she said. "I don't know how it worked. But it's worked a few times. It worked mostly . . . clearly . . . when he was

unconscious. No, I'm not suggesting it can't work under other condi-
tions. I'm new to this."

"If I got in her dreams, I could tell her?"

"I think so. I told him things."

"Like what?"

She glanced up at him: a smile, a reproof.

"Sorry," he said. "Carried away."

"Don't worry," she said. Then, "So when you were dancing, you felt
her? Did you feel she felt you?"

"Could be wishful thinking," he said.

"Well," she said.

Nico stretched himself out, carefully, beside Róisín. She was still
staring at the ceiling. "I'll wait till she sleeps. I'll think about it, and
I'll try."

Jay wasn't sure what to do. "Shall I wait next door?" she said.

"Make yourself at home!" he replied, and she smiled at that. *Funny
guy. Nice guy?* She would lie on the sofa and try to think about how it
had worked.

HE EMERGED TOWARD dawn, looking hangdog.

"Nothing," he said. "For a start she hardly slept, and I felt I was
keeping her awake, and then I was in some kind of trance, I don't
know—but we weren't in the same place, not for a moment."

"I'm sorry," she said.

Róisín came out, in pajama trousers and a T-shirt, her eye sockets
darker than ever, her shoulders slumped. She crashed the kettle on,
and collapsed onto the kitchen stool.

"Do you really think she'd sleep better if you weren't around?"

"I have no idea," Nico said.

Róisín was rubbing her hands up her face, and down again, sighing. She rested the heels of her hands on her eyes.

"Come to Scotland with me," said Jay unexpectedly. "Change of scene. Meet *my* widow. Why not?"

"I can't just leave her!" Nico said.

Jay looked kindly at him. "You already have," she said.

"I want to carry on with this dreaming thing," he said. "Vicious circle, isn't it? She'll sleep better when she knows about the will; I can't tell her about the will till she's asleep. And I don't even know if I can then."

"Maybe a break would make a difference. Come back refreshed," Jay said.

"A break?" he said. "It's not like, 'Oh I'm a bit knackered, lots of overtime, need a holiday,'" he said. "'Weekend in fucking Prague.'"

Then he was sorry. Jay knew. He knew she knew.

"Yeah," he said.

SOMETHING ABOUT THEIR snug bunks on the Caledonian Sleeper, Jay above and him below in the dark, encouraged confidences. England hurtling along outside; the train thundering on the rails; deserted stations flashing up in brief moments of Hopperesque illumination. Neither of them slept, of course.

"So how did you two meet?" Nico asked.

"Hm," she said. "How did *you* two meet?"

"At Glastonbury," he said. "Love at first sight. Though I did fall in love at first sight a lot in those days. Your turn."

"Through the band we were in, in New York," she said. "I was one of the singers. Then he was knocked down by that godforsaken yellow cab."

"New York, eh?" Nico said. "A singer! But you're not American . . ."

"I'm a Ghanaian Brit," she said. "My father was sent all over. But being African in America when you're not African American was . . . odd. People assume that you are, and that you all have a similar story.

After Rasmus's accident we came back to the UK and I went to medical school. I became a GP, he . . . it was a long recovery for him. Still not fully recovered, really. I mean he's been working, but not putting it—or himself—out there."

"So we both stepped back from the fun work to do the serious work," he said.

She thought for a moment about that. About the serious work she had done, and the more serious work she had not done, because she had given up on it. About what an ambitious young woman doctor gives up when they choose being a small rural town GP over specializing in obstetrics; what a Black doctor gives up when she leaves where Black people live. It wasn't that being a GP wasn't serious, or Scotland wasn't serious, or the country wasn't serious. And what was to say she would have achieved anything much in obstetrics anyway. *Oh, be quiet. You made your choices, for good reasons. It's over.*

She'd never talked about it anyway. Not even to Kwame—though he knew.

"Did you?" she asked. "Give up a fun job?"

"I was going to be a tattooist," he said.

She smiled, and said then well, she supposed so.

"Do you ever think," he said, his voice drifting up from below, "about all that work we do, saving the bodies, and it comes down to this?"

"Yes," she said. "I do. It's humanity's great gift, isn't it? That we can ignore the fact we're going to die."

He laughed.

Jay asked, "Were you going to get married?"

Nico froze. Then, "Yeah," he said. "Very much so. Just, you know, didn't."

Jay didn't answer. She couldn't imagine not getting round to something, if it was something that mattered. She was considering the little packet of shortbread, and the goodie bag laid out on the bunks. She remembered lines from a poem from school: *There's a funny little basin you're supposed to wash your face in, and a crank to shut the window if you sneeze.*

No shortbread. No sneezing.

No wedding.

"NO CHILDREN?" NICO asked, later.

"We were still thinking about it," Jay lied, kind of, "when I got ill. But I loved my work. The island was my family. You?"

"She wanted to. I put it off. What did you die of?"

His abruptness did not dismay her. In life it would have, but now it was like opening a window or taking off a tight shoe. *Anyway, in life of course you can't ask people what they died of.*

"Sarcoidosis," she said. "You?"

"Stupid massive heart attack," he said. "It's almost funny."

"Almost," said Jay.

"Not the worst way to go," he said. "I'm just sorry she had to be there."

"Well," said Jay.

"We were having such a laugh," he said. "You know it takes two to be funny?" Jay did. "Well, we were both being really funny together, and then I just kind of lost track. In all the excitement. I don't know what she's taken away from it all."

"I'm sorry for your loss," Jay said finally.

THEY WALKED FROM Stornoway to Luskentyre; they leaped, and spun, and cartwheeled. By the time they arrived, sunrise was rinsing the distance out over the sea to Taransay, the water glowing. The tide was coming in, taking its time over the pale flat sands, lapping up around their feet. It was a ragingly beautiful morning: mist burning off to reveal all, bright and clean and magical.

Rasmus was playing as they crossed the sandy turf to the house. They heard him before they saw him, sitting on a bench with his guitar in the morning sun by the shed. He was working out a riff and humming quietly to himself; his back against the yard wall and his feet resting on the battered saddle of an old black motorbike. Abandoned on the flagstones stood its battery, at which the little cat was sniffing.

"*It's a happy song, the bird is singing,*" Rasmus crooned softly, to D and A minor, as sad a pairing of chords as you can get. "*It's a happy song . . .*"

"No, it's not," said Nico, puzzled. But Jay was smiling.

"*The pale moon is rising now across the open field,*" Rasmus sang. "*I'm thinking of you, how we were, and how it really feels, to be alone, to be alone . . .*"

The song had a dying fall.

She couldn't smell the salty land on a spring morning, or the tang of WD-40 that accompanied every foray into trying to sort out the Vincent. She couldn't feel the cool dew on her feet or the promise of warmth in the early sun. She couldn't go and kiss his cheekbone just in front of his ear, and offer him a fresh coffee in place of the one he'd let get cold beside him, and something to eat because Lord, he was still so thin. But she could see him, and she could hear him, and *look, he's got the bike out. And written a new song.*

"That's really pretty," said Nico, nodding along.

"Isn't it?" she said.

They sat down on the stones, and eased against the wall, listening to Rasmus.

"Lovely guitar playing," Nico said. "Is that his thing—like, what he does?"

"Yes," she said, and her ghost heart cramped. "He was in a band," she said. "Wrote the songs, sang, played guitar. He did one album with them, and one tour, then broke his back. Couldn't play, couldn't tour."

"That's harsh," said Nico.

"Yes."

"Did they make it?" he asked.

"Yes," she said. "Without him."

"Anyone I'd have heard of?"

"Yes," said Jay again, and jumped up, and did ten backflips down toward the wet strand, flip flop flip flop. *Lost opportunities. Potential former futures that never came to pass. The possibility of people thinking I'm showing off.* Upset.

But the thrill of backflips!

"I could never do this kind of thing when I was alive," she said, walking back. "Not a sporty girl at all. Not bendy."

Nico drifted to his feet, and looked over the wall at the tide as it crept up. "Tell me in detail how you did it," he said. "How you managed it."

She knew what he was talking about. She told him, as best she could. It didn't seem very good. The right words didn't seem to exist.

"I'm going back," he said, when she'd run dry. "I've got to try."

"Can I come?" she said.

"Why?"

"I don't know."

SO MANY OF Róisín's sleepless nights Jay and Nico sat through. So many nights she slept a bit, and he tried, but it didn't work. He grew disheartened. Jay grew disheartened. Her theories seemed wrong. Night after night the three of them sat at the kitchen table: Jay and Nico trying and failing to pick up a Sharpie (Could they write her a note? They could not); Róisín listening to the World Service and boiling the kettle dry.

Perhaps she was sleeping at work? They went to her office.

She was not sleeping at work.

He was desperate.

"Concentrate," said Jay.

One morning, as Róisín was dressing and trying to make tea, she went back into the bedroom. A moment later, they heard a soft, heavy breath. One might almost call it a snore.

Jay looked at Nico. His eyebrows were up.

"It's about need," she said. "Feeling."

He rushed in, straight through the wall. Threw himself onto her, so that his ghostly self filled her as if she were a rock pool and he the rising tide. He felt her skin from the inside, her blood in his heart, her thoughts in his mind. *Be calm*, he murmured, to himself, to her. He paused. He held her. "Hey," he said. She moved. "I love you," he said. He was speaking Greek. He could feel her smile.

Don't linger. Or, linger later.

"My will," he said. "It's in my *History of Ancient Greek Navigation*. The Greek-language one. Tucked in the back. I'm so sorry. I'm sorry. I'm so fucking sorry, darling, I can't begin to tell you how . . ." He was crying.

She woke with a shriek.

He found himself squatting on the end of the bed, staring at her.

"What the fuck!" she shouted. Sat bolt upright, yelling.

"Fuck!" Panting. Staring wildly around. "Jesus fucking Christ, Nico, what the—"

She flung herself off the bed as he cowered. Tears pouring down her face. Chest rising and falling. She stalked into the other room, to the bookshelf. Right at the bottom; far corner. Pulled out his school prize from when he was eight: *Ιστορία της Πλοήγησης της Ελλάδας.*

All Greek to her, he thought, that old and vastly overused joke.

The long white envelope fell out the back.

She sat on the floor, cross-legged in her little T-shirt, tears falling, shivering.

NELL MADE RÓISÍN take another week off work and go to stay with her. "We'll start the probate together," she said. "Come on."

Jay made Nico come back to Scotland. "You haven't rested either," she said. You couldn't exactly say a ghost looked peely-wally, but peely-wally is what he looked.

"OKAY," SAID NICO, sitting on Rasmus's bench the next morning. "Thank you. I couldn't have done it if you hadn't told me it was possible." His face was both embarrassed and humble, making her want to cry, or hug him. "Ghost solidarity!" he said. "I owe you one."

"That's okay," she said. "I like helping. And she's nice, Róisín."

"Isn't she?" said Nico.

Jay smiled.

"So's Rasmus," Nico said, turning back to look at him. He was in the vegetable patch, weeding and softly singing. Jay hummed along.

"I worry about him," she said after a while. "I mean I know he's all right now, physically. But he wasn't, when he was in hospital, and he hated it, because it's where I died. But what could I do about that?"

"Yeah," said Nico. "I worry about her."

Jay wondered how she was going to put this. She stood and stared out to sea. The waves lapped closer now; to and fro, to and fro, curling lace, the shifting skin of the world.

"Nico," she said, in what she intended to be a mild and enquiring tone.

"What?" he said.

"I think they might really get on."

Even as she said it, she heard it drop with a thud.

He said nothing.

"They have a lot in common. Not just being widowed, but creativity, and commitment, and not being English, in Britain, and they're both funny . . . I just feel they might . . . what if . . ." And she paused.

"No," he said.

"No what?"

"What you were going to say."

"What was I going to say?"

"You know what you were going to say."

"I don't know that *you* know what I was going to say."

"*I* know that I know what you were going to say."

"What was I going to say?"

"You were going to say, why don't we get them together, it would all be so neat and nice."

Silence.

"Weren't you?" he said, leaning back, with a dangerous look in his eye.

"Yes."

"Over my dead body," he said.

"Well, actually," she said, but the pain on his face stopped her. "Don't you think . . . I know it's too soon for them. But they could take their time."

"No," he said. "Don't even think about that."

LATER, JAY WAS staring at Rasmus, who was in the kitchen, making soup, in other words, pouring it from a tin into the pan, and burning some toast.

"What are you doing?" Nico asked her.

"Just thinking," she said.

"You can't interfere," he said. "It's like time travel. The grandfather paradox. You can't go round changing things."

"I'm not," she said. "Just making a suggestion."

"By staring at him?"

"The last time it was very easy."

"Well, bully for you," said Nico, remembering Róisín in her little T-shirt, her shoulders shuddering. "Suggesting what?"

You should take a look at the film company's website, Jay was thinking. *See who you might be working with. See if there's anyone you like the look of.*

"Nothing really," Jay said, but she couldn't lie, and Nico wasn't an idiot.

"I said no," he said.

"They can be friends," she said. "Don't we all need friends who're going through the same thing? Solidarity?"

"No," he said.

"You didn't mind me interfering when it helped you," she said. And then wished she hadn't.

"Just because you helped doesn't mean you can have her," he said. "What do you think this is? Some kind of swapsies? Or, what, now she's got my money you'll set them up? Is that it?"

"Nico!" she said. "No."

"Stop it," he said.

The look he shot her was miserable.

It didn't stop her, though, from following Rasmus when he next went to his laptop, and murmuring, *The film company—Constant Eye, they're called. Go on, take a look, I heard Róisín Kennedy's good. Have a look at Róisín Kennedy. There! Her! Look at her!*

11

Into the Sea

APRIL–MAY
The island–London

NICO WALKED STRAIGHT into the sea, on and out, till the water was deep and his head covered, and he swam down in the icy, mobile murk, so dark that to a mortal body it would have seemed solid. *My body is out there somewhere*, he thought. *Down here.*

He watched himself upside down on the raucous underside of the surface of the water, mirrored and surreal, shattered and reforming like mercury. *Over my dead body.* It was funny. After a while—it was dark when he emerged—he let the surf throw him back to land, and crawled up the beach like an ancient life form. He lay dry as a bone on the white sand, and watched the stars come into focus. *But you're not a life form, Nico. You're not even out of breath. You've no breath to be out of. You're dead.*

He was lonely. So absolutely lonely.

He wandered on the shore. Anger was pervading him, and he didn't like it. He almost felt drunk with it. Uncontrolled. He stomped along for a bit, frowning. He stepped aside, pointlessly but instinctively, to avoid a puddle; leaped over a dune or two. Nearly landed on a little crab, which scuttled, then froze, as if immobility were invisibility.

Put your head in the sand, why don't you, he thought.

He watched it for a while, wondering how long it could keep up its act, then the thought struck him that he'd like to do something nice for the crab. He didn't know what a crab would want. To be put in the sea? To be put somewhere else? To be honest, all he could do with the crab was put it somewhere (which he couldn't anyway because he couldn't bloody pick things up) or, well, not.

He decided to put himself somewhere else instead. That might be nicest for the crab.

So what if he and Jay were the only dead people walking the earth tonight. He didn't care. About any of it. *Fuck Jay. Fuck Rasmus.* He was going home. He was just going to go home and get in bed with his girl.

But he didn't. He returned to Rasmus's cottage and lay on the roof beam all night, thinking, and wishing he could smoke, because now, waiting, would be a perfect time to smoke, and as he was dead, in theory he should be able to smoke to his heart's content without it harming him, if only he *could* smoke, which he couldn't. He stopped a moment to think about the odd definition of contentment his heart had achieved from smoking all those fags, back in the day. He thought: *my smoking was not an act of love. Giving up: that was an act of love.* He thought about his mother and Mr. Katsoukakis's cheroot; about Athens and terrazzo floors and souvlaki rolled up in paper and jasmine on dusty railings and ouzo and his dear old dad and the blue, blue, salty Ionian sea rolling and lifting under the bow of a little boat.

He thought about loss for a while. So much he had lost.

He came to in the early light of the rising sun. The astonishing beauty of the dawn crept around him: the gray and rose and lilac over the waters; the promontories and the sea and the sky in interlocking stripes of light and dark, gleam and shadow. He'd never been to Scotland before this. He'd had no idea. *Róisín, babe, what a world you live in! What a world . . .*

The small gray cat was staring at him from beside the chimney.

"Hello," he said.

The cat blinked.

"Can you see me?" Nico asked.

The cat blinked again, turned its back, and slithered away.

"You can, can't you?" Nico murmured. "Bloody cats."

Soon he dropped down to the yard, surprised still at his own agility. *I wonder if I could run up a wall like Jay talked about.* He sat himself on the black Vincent, hands on the bars as if he were about to take off. He was waiting for the sounds of waking, the flush, the clatter of a coffeepot. He didn't want to disturb them. They deserved privacy. "Vroom," he whispered sadly.

The coffee noise came, and he lingered with it, trying to remember the smell.

A cascade of piano notes rippled from within, and it stopped him for a moment. He knew that melody. As Rasmus started singing, his voice croaky and morningish, Nico recognized the song: "Love Ain't Listening"! *Róisín loved that song. The Capos!* It had come out just when he and Róisín had first got together. He hummed along. Such a sweet, merry love song, with these sad undertones. From their first album, *Strong.* Rasmus was singing it slower and sadder—singing the woman's part as well—

Oohhhh . . .

Christ, I'm an idiot. Rasmus, full name for Ras, as in, Raz Sartorius. He remembered that story. One of those Richey Edwards, Syd Barrett kind of stories, but without the drugs and self-harm and the—or no, maybe there *were* some mental health issues. The musician who disappeared just when he was about to be loved the most; "troubled rocker" Raz Sartorius, who either got stabbed in the back by his un-grateful band, or fled the limelight pursued by his demons and became a hermit. Take your pick.

Nico lay back on the bike, put his feet up on the handlebars, and listened. Inside, Rasmus moved on to another melody, humming, murmuring, stopping for a moment, adjusting a chord, going back over. The morning sun came round the corner of the roof, and shone gently on the tiny dandelions sprouting in the cracks in the concrete.

So this is the guy Jay wants Róisín to be with, Nico was thinking. *Bloody Orpheus, who can't follow his wife into Hades.*

He can play and sing, though . . .

And then:

And me making cracks about her being after my money.

Shit.

"Jay?"

Jay wasn't around.

He looked; he searched. All around the house, the yard, the beach, the road. She just wasn't there.

He watched Rasmus some more.

Fuck, he thought.

Then he gave up, and went home to his girl.

12

A Really Crap Quality

MAY–JUNE
London

MAYBE IT WAS the car crash, maybe it was time, maybe it was going into work yet again wondering what she was doing there. Maybe it was finding the will. After all the searching, pulling drawers out, finding all kinds of things she didn't need and couldn't bear to look at but not the thing which, above all, would make her life easier, after conceding that she really was going to have to admit (to herself, to his mum, to all those authority figures) that he hadn't even left her his half of the stuff they shared—there it was. Where it might well be. Where she'd looked a hundred times before: in the bookshelf. *By search five you've been down the back of everywhere*—but she hadn't actually opened each and every book in the place. They had quite a few books. Why the hell had he put it there? And how the hell had she woken up knowing that's where it was?

But there it was, just where it was meant to be, dated eighteen months earlier. Written, it said, "in expectation of marriage." And his letter.

Dear Róisín,

*Signed, witnessed and all, for the unlikely possibility that I
might at some point kick the bucket. Which I won't because
how could I, with you to love and adore? S'agapo my babe. Σε
λατρεύω, Τριανταφυλλακι μου.*

Your Nico
PS Now make your own will, OK?

She hadn't expected such a gift. Such sweetness. They'd just been
so kind of ordinary together for so long. To get that declaration . . .
and that reminder, that kick in the guts: "the unlikely possibility that
I might at some point kick the bucket."

Anyway, somewhere between grief and mortality, a moment of
enlightenment came to Róisín. She had been behaving as if it were
she who were dead. As if she were cut off from life and the living;
from her own life. And this was unnecessary, wasteful, and dog-in-
the-manger of her. *Róisín, he is dead, but you are not. You are alive. You
are grief-stricken and broken apart, but you are also adult, healthy,
solvent—thank God—and alone. You are a free woman in the twenty-first
century. You are thirty-three, widowed, stuck. Róisín, nobody cares what
you do. You need no permission. Everybody wants you to be okay.*

Róisín, you may—and indeed you must—do what you want.

What do you want?

Four months. No time. A lifetime.

She'd managed to read a bit of a book by someone whose husband
had died. It said: "For a year and a day, don't do anything you can't
undo." But she wanted to. She really wanted to do something massive,
and massively not undoable. She really, really wanted to—in retalia-
tion against this massive thing that had been done to her, and which
couldn't be undone.

"Maybe I've to leave my job," she said, aloud, on the bus going down Regent Street.

"Good call," said the girl beside her, with feeling, and a grin. "Good luck!"

"Sorry!" Róisín said. "My boyfriend—fiancé—died. I've gone a bit bonkers."

"I went bonkers when my mum died," said the girl, but then it was her stop, so just the shreds of two sympathetic smiles linked them as she wriggled her way down the bus. Róisín gathered that glow into herself as she pondered, yet again, what the hell she was meant to do without him.

Anything!

Everything!

Oh, shut up.

I've to take hold of everything I've ever denied myself, she thought. *New Life's Resolutions. No more waiting about, assuming that one day I'll have a child who will validate me and give me meaning. No more skittering on surfaces. No more doing myself down and not committing. No more diminishing what I've achieved because it's not—or doesn't look—as good as what other people have achieved. No more judging my life by what other people put up on Instagram. No more lecturing myself about what I should do or be . . .*

The irony did not escape her.

It's a simple fact that living with someone who saves lives daily doesn't make you feel completely great about your own contribution to the world. Her major contribution, she knew it, hadn't been the fine footage she produced that time for those sweet Hungarian death-metal guys. It had been looking after Nico: protecting him, bollocking him, soothing him, reassuring him, loving him. Sending him in each day fit and cool to do his amazing work. How many hearts had he restarted? How many throats had he cut open for emergency tracheostomy tubes? How much blood had he stemmed in its flow? How many dreadful situations had he assessed, arriving with no clue as to what would meet him? How many shattered bones had he held in place, how many horrific burns had he bandaged with cling film? How many vulnerable bodies had he lifted; how many terrified people had he calmed? How many drips inserted, how many reports written, instruments cleaned and put away, ambulances decontaminated? How many crimes attended, how many hands held in how many helicopters, how many times had he been too late to do any good?

She was so angry at the waste. All his skill and experience, primed and ready to be used at any moment by human need, was now gone from the bank of human usefulness.

Shut up, Róisín, you're not going to train as a paramedic to make up for him. You'd be a crap paramedic. You'd cry all the time. You can hardly even clean up sick.

She'd meant to do more with her work—be more ambitious, more creative; get into features; go freelance . . . but so many ambitious men had marched ever forward on the back of her reliability, and so many hungrier and mouthier girls had snapped up the pathways of ambition before she had got herself into focus. And with every one that glided onward she, Róisín, found herself less and less fit and hungry and mouthy and pushy. She was out of the running, really. She hadn't paid attention.

Maybe the domestic habit of looking after vulnerable, volatile Nico had shown, at work. *Maybe I had "bring me your flawed man and I will back him up" tattooed on my forehead. Allow me to pick up the pieces and do the legwork.*

No, he wasn't flawed. Obviously he wasn't perfect, but.

Well, loving someone uses a lot of energy. A lot of time. Whoever you love.

My Big Fat Greek, she used to call him, when he was on a porky bender, i.e., eating full English for breakfast, and ice cream before bed. Comfort food. My Little Colleen, my Oirish Rose, he'd call her back, in the world's worst and most embarrassing attempt at a Dublin accent, and God knows there'd been plenty of those.

You're not to think of him all the time. Go on, think of something else. See if you can.

She reached for her phone, to check Instagram. Caught herself doing it. She laughed. God, how he had hated that. "Get off that bloody thing and talk to *me*," he'd say. *And he was right. Squandering my talents and the precious minutes of my life—but come on, who uses every precious minute of their one-and-only God-given precious life constructively? No one, is who. And I love my work. It's just . . .*

I want to be an artist, Róisín thought, *but I don't want to be some woman who wants to be an artist. I'm not going to move to Wales and make bad shorts based on poetry. I'm not going to put quotations up on Insta like that's a magnificent contribution to human civilization.*

But I want. I want.

She had once promised—threatened?—Nico that she was going to read one of her poems at a local group. *I bloody will,* she thought now. *Or I'll write a novel. Two novels! I could join a writers' group?*

Or—CAKES! I could go on a TV show. I could start a company. Audition for Bake Off! *I could . . .*

Give up the flat and move to Berlin!

Throw out all my clothes—total Marie Kondo!

So many possibilities. Squashed by choice.

Enough faffing—but I don't know how not to faff. Surely death would've taught me not to waste time? Didn't I used to be hungry and mouthy?

She decided to go and live in Prague.

Or New York.

Or 1957.

That night she rang Nell and said, "I'm going to be a rom-com—what's that one in Greece? Not the Abba one. The other one. Wanna come?"

"Are you drunk?" Nell asked. "The Winner Takes It All" was wailing at full volume.

"Yes," said Róisín. "I'm dancing in the kitchen. I'm thinking of maybe training to be a sailor, then I could be like ship's cook on round-the-world yachts? Or doing something with anorexic children."

"Shall I come up?" Nell said.

"Yes," Róisín said distantly. "I'm so fucking sad and lonely and I don't know what to do."

RÓISÍN HAD FALLEN asleep before Nell arrived—a late train, an overpriced ticket: necessary expense. Nell let herself in and gently shoved Róisín's bedroom door open to check on her. Róisín rolled over, fast asleep. She sighed. Nell sighed. The sighing in these days could have blown away the house.

Róisín looked very beautiful to her sister. "You were too good for him," Nell murmured. "But I do miss the old bastard."

She sat down on the bed and lightly stroked her sister's damp forehead. "You just don't know what to do without someone to love, do you, darling?" she murmured. "And being dead, that's a really crap quality in a boyfriend."

NICO BLINKED.
It's true, though.
Everyone's right and I'm wrong.

RÓISÍN, IN THE office, gazing at a commission to film an interesting and important avant-garde band for an interesting and important and 100 percent unfinanceable documentary about them, was wondering how Nico would have taken it if it had been she who had died.

He'd have drunk, at a guess. If it had been sudden, like his. But perhaps he wouldn't have. Perhaps he'd have thrown himself into his work like a dog off the pier in a heat wave. Perhaps she could throw herself into working out how to get finance for interesting and important documentary projects. She could work on working out why she was still working here when it was so hard to get anything done. She'd hope his colleagues would have tied his hands behind his back if he'd wanted to get straight back on the job—but then again, maybe not. There was that way the emergency teams had of cutting off (ha ha) their emotional, human, responsive selves, when they were dealing with a crisis. Because an emotional person, one whose hands shook or brow dripped at the notion of responsibility for life and death, could not do what they do. And perhaps Nico being grief-stricken, even about her, would come under that part of him. Perhaps even her death would have been just another everyday trauma for him, from which he could hold himself apart, leaving him to continue to do the work. His hands, restarting human hearts. His hands, on her face or her waist.

His letter said he was never going to die. Said: I love you, I adore you. In expectation of marriage. Τριανταφυλλάκι μου. *Triandaphillaki mou*—my little rose.

Yeah, grief comes in waves. Tidal, sometimes. Tsunamis.

Thank you, Nico, she was murmuring to herself. *I'm so sorry for all the rude things I've said about you,* when Ayesha, her boss-cum-partner, perimenopausal, and in a one-woman battle with the world to prove that women can do everything all at the same time, called her into her office.

Róisín sat down expectantly on the olive velvet sofa under the multipaned Crittall windows, in front of the Danish teak coffee table with the mother-in-law's tongue in a rough yet fancy ceramic planter, and the latest issue of the *Hollywood Reporter*. Her hair had reached a number four, and her neck felt easily naked enough for her to be beheaded. Maybe Ayesha was going to sack her. She wouldn't even mind, really. Only the wise words from the book hung around her mind: "do nothing you can't undo."

Ayesha put down her phone, and Róisín wondered if she had just been on Tinder. Last week she had been helpfully offering to set up a profile for Róisín, "Now that . . . you know . . . ," as she had put it. Astonishingly, Róisín hadn't headbutted her. She'd been in a very bad mood last week, with the lawyer pressing for the will again.

I'd never deck Ayesha. Ayesha's great. Now, though, she had her sheepish I-want-you-to-do-something-for-me-you're-not-gonna-like look on. Róisín used the carte blanche of recent widowhood to not have to smile at her.

"Well, okay," said Ayesha. "I wanted to have a little chat. Got this job coming up, actually, pret-ty nice, actually—soooo—the Capos!"

The Capos?

So it wasn't the sheepish I-want-you-to-do-something-for-me-you're-not-gonna-like look. It was a sheepish I'm-gonna-do-something-really-nice-for-you-because-your-fiancé-died-but-I'm-too-embarrassed-to-admit-that's-why-I'm-doing-this look.

I must have lost my touch, getting that wrong, Róisín thought.

"Opening their anniversary tour with a little industry do at Bush Hall," Ayesha went on. "Private, very small, ex-clu-sive! And, support act—well, feature appearance more like—you'll never guess . . ."

"Who?" Róisín asked politely.

"I remember you and Nico," Ayesha said. "Ah, Christmas party, years back. Dancing to 'Love Ain't Listening.'" She made a curious sentimental shape with her mouth, and Róisín gave her side-eye.

"Very cute. Sweet," Ayesha said, and got a little confused with her cup of coffee. "Sooo, yeah—it's Raz Sartorius."

The name hung there.

"But he's a recluse," Róisín said.

"Not on July the 17th he's not. He's opening the show at the Albert Hall. And we've been asked to film it, and the warm-up gig. And you're doing the shoots."

Something inside Róisín woke up. Whatever it was felt nineteen.

"You're having me on," she said. (She clearly wasn't.)

"Nope," Ayesha said. "Carola asked for you. Apparently he's heard you're good!"

Róisín was stunned. *Raz Sartorius has heard I'm good? In what world can that be true?*

"All on the level," Ayesha was saying. "Okay? Are you up for it?"

"So okay," Róisín said. Her face crumpled a little. "So up for it," she said. And she was. She could feel it, like slipping into water. Slipping into competence and energy. *Jesus, Mary, and Joseph, yes, I'm up for it.*

"Thank you," she said. *I can do what Nico would have done. I can throw myself into work. I love this. I can do this.*

"Go and start your homework then!" Ayesha said softly. "Anything you need, I'm here."

Róisín was so touched, and so amazed at the energy inside her, that she kind of patted the plant as she went out.

SHE WAS GOOGLING him, a cup of tea and a bar of plain chocolate marzipan beside her. She found a lot of speculative pieces in various languages, all wondering where he was, and what a loss, and what had happened after the accident. And she found a local paper from the Outer Hebrides reporting the death of the popular local GP, Dr. Justina Akufo Sartorius, aged thirty-eight, of sarcoidosis, and that Dr. Sartorius is survived by her husband, Rasmus Sartorius, who readers will no doubt remember as the former choirmaster of the

South Island Community Choir, as well as a founding member of the well-known group the Capos. There was a photograph of the doctor: low-res and out of focus, but you could see the cheekbones.

She checked the date.

Jesus, it's no time ago! What's he even doing trying to get up onstage so soon! The man's a lunatic! And where are his friends? He should hardly even be leaving the house.

And here I am wondering if I'm up to the job of just filming him.

The pictures of him were all from when he was young, so tall and narrow in the black coat, with a figure like overcooked spaghetti and those pale eyes the size of soup spoons, with a kind of silver ring, a gleam, round the pupil. *Frightening-looking fella. Or frightened. Same thing, really. Beautiful.* She knew those eyes well. She'd actually had a picture of the Capos on her pinboard many years ago, and though her friends all liked George, Raz Sartorius was always her favorite. Something she would *not* be mentioning.

He's heard of me?

She really couldn't see him running a choir.

But running a choir! How great is that!

Actually, what was best about it was that there hadn't been a TV series about it. *Just a matter of time, probably.*

Men like him seemed like an endangered species.

Hi Ayesha,

Briefly, what's the brief?

Róisín

―――――――――――――――――――

Posterity! So far. But obv there's more to it. The record company's commissioned this; it'll be for a doco or retrospective of some kind down the line. So lots of live; lots of ambient, and

an interview—liaise with Carola about that. They're super
excited for it, doing a separate sound recording as well. They
haven't said so but I get the feeling they're thinking in terms of
an album from Sartorius, but unless there's something I don't
know, he's not under contract. So we'll see where it leads.

BTW he's insisting no press.

xA

Róisín had filmed enough musicians to know they were 50 percent professional, 50 percent arsehole, interested only in their kit,
their status, and their intoxicants, and, if interested in her, then
purely in a shag-me-now-and-never-hear-from-me-again kind of way.
The music itself, in her experience, was 99 percent of the best part of
musicians. Music is like sausages: delicious, but you don't want to
look too closely at how it's made. And Róisín had visited the sausage
factory before.

The Capos would be as arsey as anybody, no doubt. If it were just
them, the main lineup, she would still have been thrilled to get out
there and get the footage, but no more thrilled than for any band, for
any opportunity to get out of the office and make something. Anyway, she wasn't directing that segment. Just Sartorius. And he was a
mystery. And there was something pure about him, that she had
liked even all those years ago. He'd written all their best songs, and
sang quite a few of them on the first album. She had an earworm now
of "Love Ain't Listening." *Doo doo, d'doo doo doo, Doo doo, d'doo doo doo.*
The duet with the woman—what was her name? Made you want to dance
around in a twirly way on a spring morning.

At Bush Hall, Róisín had it all in place before the soundcheck
started, so they could get extra atmosphere-setting material. It was a
simple enough setup: one guy onstage under a high ornamental ceiling

in a Victorian dance hall. Chandeliers and a beer-stained carpet. Lovely.

Oh, and there he was. She saw him across the room and couldn't stop a little smile. She glanced at her shoes and stood up straight to go and introduce herself.

"Hi, I'm Róisín," she said. "Róisín Kennedy. I'm directing the filming today."

"Hello," he said. He was pale, hollow-looking: hollow-eyed, hollow-cheeked. It was a look she was familiar with from the mirror. Just ligaments holding him together, the frame of his shoulders, his lanky legs. He didn't look safe.

"Anything in particular you want from me?" he said, politely.

I wouldn't ask a thing of you, she thought. *You look like you'll fall apart if I even breathe too hard.*

"Are you all right with being filmed just around the place during the soundcheck?" she asked. Grief burned off him. He was incandescent with it.

"I am," he said.

"Thank you," she said. Shireen and the guys were getting plenty already—Rasmus and George Vechten greeting each other (Rasmus unearthly quiet; George somewhere between bouncy and chastised, like a dog that knows it's been bad); him sitting and reading as he waited; a brief but firm discussion with the young man who seemed to be setting up some kind of multitrack recording kit. "That's great," Róisín said cautiously. "And, as I'm to interview you today—"

"Are you?" he said. "Do I know about that?"

Nee naw; lurch inside.

"Oh fuck, do you not?" she asked. "I . . ."

He looked at her doubtfully, and said, "I might do. I haven't been reading my emails properly."

Unlurch. Up to a point.

"It was certainly all set up," she said, falling into a similar quiet tone. "Between us and somebody. I should maybe have been in touch with you directly—"

"No, don't worry—"

"I didn't want to disturb you; I thought—"

"This is one reason why I'd make a terrible pop star," he said, glancing away. "I can't abide things like this."

She thought he meant interviews.

"Let's forget it for now," she said. "Absolutely, forget it. Can't have anything you can't abide going on, not when you're about to perform."

"So true," he said. "Thank you," and then something called him away, and with a little nod he was gone.

RÓISÍN WAS AT the desk as Rasmus started tuning up for the performance a few hours later, watching on the monitors as he sat there on his tall stool, black speakers piled high behind him. His hands were astonishingly big as they sorted the guitar out, fingers spidering, tuning it, calibrating its various needs. "Camera two, you're on, that's lovely, close in on the hands." Her hands were tiny; it took her whole arm to get anywhere on a musical instrument. His palm could cover the sound hole.

The move as his long fingers graduated from tuning and strumming to picking and playing took her by surprise. "Cut to camera three . . ." she said. It was like looking over their shoulders. "Camera two, you're on again," and even as the frame arrived on him, Rasmus was turning gently to camera, a dry look on his haggard face. His pale, silver-rimmed eyes were looking right at her as he said, with considerable grace and sadness: "I wrote this song for my wife. She's just died. It's a hard time. Some of you may know about that . . ."

And with that his face changed, he glanced down, swallowed, glanced back to camera, and said, ruefully, to the future audience, to the world, to whatever stranger it meant something to, "And if you do, sweetheart, I feel for you."

Róisín blinked.

She glanced up at the stage: his eyes were closed now, his fingers walking the strings. He started to sing: a low, midnight, sleepless voice, cross-hatched with suffering. Something conversational about it. He was just telling them how it was.

> *I always knew that I'd be safe within your arms*
> *I've always known the devil gets his due*
> *But when today it seems you're gone forever*
> *I don't know what to do,*
> *I don't know what to do.*

Róisín froze in her movement. She couldn't—

> *If it don't kill you it'll only make you strong*
> *That's what all the people say, but oh, they're wrong*
> *It makes you sad, it makes you mad, it makes*
>   *you gone*
> *I don't know where I am,*
> *I don't know where I am.*

She wanted to go to the back of the room and sit as small as she could against the wall in the corner, behind a pile of chairs, her head against a plaster frieze.

"Camera two, you're on . . . hold that . . . lovely," she said.

> *One goodbye too many,*
> *One hello too few*
> *Not enough I'm sorrys,*
> *and missing one I love you*

> *Missing one I love you*
> *How can this be true?*

It is possible, Róisín learned, to cry very quietly. "Hold that," she said, swallowing and blinking.

> *I always knew that I'd be safe within your heart*
> *I never wanted anyone but you*
> *I'm lost in time; this isn't getting better.*

She couldn't not: she stood up, raising her eyes again from the monitors to look at him in the flesh. How could he *sing* these words? This plaintive melody? Why wasn't he in floods?

He had that little smile on. *He's strumming my fate with his fingers.*

She sat down again. "Camera four," she said. Bit of distance on the instrumental. *Though his face—the concentration . . .*

> *I don't know what to do*
> *I don't know what to do*
> *One goodbye too many,*
> *One hello too few*
> *Not enough I'm sorrys,*
> *and missing one I love you*
> *Missing one I love you.*

He drifted to a halt. His hand stopped moving, he blinked and looked up.

Silence across the room.

Róisín was sitting on the floor behind the desk, her head in her arms.

THE NEXT DAY, Róisín sent Rasmus an email.

13

Cuban Heels Under a
Disco Ball

JUNE
London

RASMUS CONDUCTED THE whole thing ice-clad. He'd refused to tell anybody what he'd be playing, other than that it was new material. And he hadn't come to any of the band's rehearsals. Hadn't even met up with them. So curiosity must have been piquing people, because when he pitched up for his soundcheck at around two on the day, thinking to get it done quickly before anyone much turned up, and leave them plenty of time to do the full band setup, the little hall was not empty. The current Capos were all there, sitting about in their skinny black jeans, looking just the same, but older, tireder. He nodded to them politely, let them greet him, and moved on by. Then George—*oh God*—came up, backslapping away, a lot of manly hugs, so happy to see him. *Do you think yourself forgiven?* Ras thought, and he felt the little flinch in the hug as George realized *oh yes, maybe you shouldn't backslap and bearhug a man who has so much metal holding his spine together . . .*

So much time hung between them. Ras thought he could even see it: a silvery curtain, with indigo, shimmery. *I'm not going to be your friend again. But I'm not going to be so unkind as to tell you that.*

He didn't know who the other people there were. Record-company faces no doubt, curious staff from the hall. The film crew—apparently they needed eight cameras, two sound people, and a desk feed, even for this documentary unplugged kind of affair. A woman who seemed to be in charge of them—beautiful, shaven-headed, dark circles under her eyes. *Like they were put in with a sooty finger—where was that from?* He didn't immediately recognize her as the woman from the website, the one he'd liked the look of, and rather inexplicably emailed Carola about. It was the lack of the curls. He was looking at her when a keen, plump-faced lad, so young, red beard, bare ankles, came up earnestly to be introduced and discuss mic placement for the multitrack recording.

What multitrack recording?

The place was already festooned with microphones; a team of black-clad bouncy-trainered techs were obeying the lad's directions and sneaking glances at Rasmus.

"No," he said, and closed his eyes. Nobody had mentioned this. He wasn't signed with this company. This wasn't for them.

"Aw, man!" cried George. Rasmus just turned and looked at him. It was clear to Rasmus that filming was all right: the music was at an easier level in its existence, it was part of a whole, and could be flawed and imperfect, just playing its role, a record of an occasion. Filmed, music was just one of the gang. Recorded uniquely, it would have had to be king or hero, with finality and completeness. And then that evil jealous old vizier, perfectionism, would sidle in, undermining and sabotaging and trying to take control. Anyway, what did they want it for? Nobody was going to be releasing this as audio.

He moved away from them, admiring the ceiling. He half thought that he'd only agreed to do this warm-up gig because of the venue. It was so small and nice, and he'd spent so many evenings here—well, and days—when he and Jay had come to London, back when it was the snooker club. Wasting time, shooting pool, trying to hide from her how little he could lean now; her comprehending hand on the small of his back. He felt he could just sit up there and sing as if he were in his own room at home. Piano and him; guitar and him; a few hundred people and him. Like in the old days, when he was young. Open mics and tiny festivals. Fields in Suffolk; beaches on islands. Nothing fancy. There'd be one in the audience, there always was, whose eye he would catch, who would become the human heart into which he poured his songs.

He was fully aware of his own curiosity value—perhaps all these people had just wangled a way in to see the man who had, as it were, come back from the dead. Bearing his own dead with him. But he had no feelings or fears whatsoever about grief affecting his performance. It didn't occur to him. He hadn't been doing nothing all those years; he felt entirely at home in his music.

The shaven-headed woman came over shyly. She had manners and an Irish remnant in her voice, and was under the impression she was going to interview him. It was momentarily awkward. But she was cool about not interviewing, though he could see it mattered to her. Once people had melted back from their demands, the soundcheck was cool. The techs were cool. The kit was good.

He paused; glanced over at her again. He wished he'd just said yes.

The look on her face when he'd said no. Her eyes were blue. Real blue.

Why's she shaved her head?

He didn't like to let anyone down.

RASMUS ROSE TO the gig like a raptor to a thermal. The handsome room was all his, dim and waiting for him; the audience primed and feeling lucky to be there. His breath came deep and steady just as he liked it, and he was no longer rewriting the lyrics as he went. Professionalism held his voice up, where emotion cracked it. He hadn't been sure he'd be able to do "One Goodbye Too Many," but he was. From the stage he glimpsed the spark of tears in other people's eyes, the lights picking it up, and he felt a bitter kind of pride.

Three numbers, eyes closed, Jay on his mind. *Are you proud of me, sweetheart?*

He reminded himself: *all these people are just people. Don't hate them for being Londoners, for having survived the industry, for being fashionable. They're just little human animals.* The chandeliers hung above, each one as tall as the ceilings in his home. The light was beautiful, flickering and refracting with the mirrors and the disco ball spinning slowly in the middle. *A disco ball.* He smiled fondly. Here he was again, in Cuban heels under a disco ball. Giving what he had.

At the end he nodded and said, "Thanks"—sheepish again, and shy. He put his guitar on its stand, and stepped off the stage.

"Yeah!" shouted one of the techs, and a flurry of applause broke out as he walked up the hall toward the bar at the back. Someone might be able to do him a cup of tea.

The crowd was applauding so much he had to go back up onstage, and was a little embarrassed for the band having to come on after him. But not much.

The Capos did four; two new and two old. None by him. He stayed, alone, in what passed for the wings, interested to hear. They had become, as bands can, a fossilized version of their best self, a perfect 3D printout of the magic they had created when they were twenty-three. Like a middle-aged woman still wearing the clothes and makeup of her heyday, a messy blonde in her fifties with a Marianne Faithfull fringe and *history* and smoker's wrinkles round her sexy red-lipsticked mouth. And what Jay called "been-around legs." Shapely, sun-scarred, muscled calves, high heels. He loved those women, though. There were worse ways to face age. The band . . . it was more like embalming. *Guys*, he was thinking. *Have you not thought anything new over the past fifteen years?* The audience were now, if anything, hyperattentive and respectful—admittedly they all had an interest.

He slipped away as quickly as he could. He didn't want to be rude or hurt anyone's feelings, but people wanted to talk to him and he felt like maybe he was the buffet.

THE FOLLOWING DAY this arrived:

Dear Rasmus,

I'm sorry to have headed off last night without having seen you again to thank you for your beautiful performance and for being patient with us about the filming, and to apologize for the interview misunderstanding. Shireen tells me the rushes are great, and we'll have something to show you soon.

The truth is I am one of few people who have been in a similar situation to you last night. Don't laugh. When my fiancé's dad died, I stood up at a poetry night in Muswell Hill and read aloud two poems I'd written about it. That was hard enough. Nothing to compare though. When my fiancé died, in February—even to type those words I still find hard—I could not stand, let alone stand in public, let alone onstage.

Now you are an accustomed and practiced creator and performer, and I'm a rank amateur, but to stand up, because you know you have to, because life must go on, because you said you would or you feel you should, or feel that they would want you to—it's not nothing. Just because you're strong don't mean it's easy, as a wise songwriter once wrote. Anyway so, the beautiful gorgeous songs undid me, I'm afraid, and the performance itself melted me into a puddle, and so what with the weeping and the puddling I wasn't up to saying much to anybody. But I wanted to say something to you, which with the six weeks of experience I have on you I can pass on as if I were some kind of a wise woman. It is this: this is not the time to be hard on yourself, nor to do anything you can't undo. Also: God, she must have been a lovely woman to inspire those songs.

With all good wishes,
Róisín Kennedy

14

Machinations

JUNE
London

I SHOULDN'T GO, Jay had been thinking. *I should leave them to it. It's up to them. I shouldn't go.*

But I want to go. How could I not go? To Rasmus's comeback gig? Of course I'm going.

She went.

Legs dangling from the chandelier, dark streaks among the crystal drops, she saw all that happened. She saw the young woman undone by him. *How powerful you are, my husband*, she whispered. *How beautifully you speak for us.*

But she was pleased. She was right. She could always tell when he liked a woman. A softness in his glance. He'd had a tendresse the size of Mars for Rita Hayworth. If that scene came up with the dance and the slinky gloves—*Put the blame on Mame, boys*—he'd get all . . . she thought of an English phrase that made her laugh: *he came over all unnecessary*. To be said in a comedy Northern accent. He was transparent, and she knew him so well.

The other thing she saw was Nico, behind Róisín at the desk, noticing every reaction. And tears rolling down his pale, unfocused face.

At the end, as the crowd dispersed, exclaiming and chattering, toward the bar and the smoking balcony, she slipped down.

"Hi," Jay said.

"Hi," said Nico. "I wasn't going to come."

"Me neither," she said.

"So is your work here done?"

"Not in the least," she replied. "They've met, but they're neither of them the forward type, or even looking. They're so full of grief and they're both working too. They're not going to fall into each other's arms . . ." She looked around. Rasmus had disappeared; Róisín was talking to Shireen and clearing kit away.

"I don't like it," Nico said again.

The living flocked past them; their flesh and their warmth, their breath and their voices.

"I know, love," she said. "But *they* might. Let them like each other. Let them. Please."

"I don't know what to do," he said.

"Me neither," she said. "We should go somewhere else. Shall we pretend to get drunk? Wanna mess about on the cables of Tower Bridge? Or shall we see if we can fly? Or, I don't know, take an unguided tour of wherever we bloody well like?"

He smiled a little. "Don't you need to be here to machinate?" he murmured. "While they're still in the same building?"

"No I don't," she said. "If it's to be, then I want them to do it themselves. I really do. If they want to."

He shrugged.

"Let's take the Orient Express," he said.

"Really?" she said.

"Christ, I don't know," he said. "I feel like she's dumping me for another man. My cold dead heart is breaking."

"They've exchanged five sentences," she said. "But yes. Mine too. Kinda."

15

Have You Exploded?

JUNE

Dear Róisín,

Thank you for your email.

I've found a number of people are scared to talk to me since she died. Have you found that?

With all good wishes,
Rasmus.

Dear Rasmus,

Yes I have. I think it's because they're afraid talking about it might serve to remind us. As if you know we might have forgotten. I try to bear it in mind that they're not being nasty, they're just being useless. Are you having trouble with that?

With best wishes
Róisín

Dear Róisín,

I forgot this morning, for about eight seconds. I knew there was *something* wrong, but by the time it occurred to me that I wasn't sure what it was, it had come back to me.

Is it any better, six weeks ahead?

With best wishes,
Rasmus.

Dear Rasmus,

No.

It's not worse, either. It's not different, even, though I gather it does change. I'm told it changes. And of course it must, because who could keep going at this level? We'd explode.

With best wishes,
Róisín

Dear Róisín,

Have you exploded? I have, several times.

With best wishes,
Rasmus.

Dear Rasmus,

I exploded when a fella drove into the back of my car. And once when I was dancing in the kitchen to the radio. Turns out I am dead susceptible to Cyndi Lauper. Another time I was in Sainsbury's and overcome by the San Pellegrino. When were yours?

With best wishes,
Róisín

PS Can I just thank you for using the accents in my name? It's a rare courtesy and I appreciate it. People mispronounce it all the time of course (it's RO-sheeen, for the record) but spelling it right just takes a moment of attention which a lot of people never bother to give, so thank you.

Dear Róisín,

I don't need to tell *you*, but the holding down the letter on the keyboard till the accents appear and then tapping the number for the right one was a revelation for me.

Explosions: I was knocked off my bicycle by a dead deer, and I wondered if I had in some way invited it.

And, in a way, agreeing to do these gigs after fifteen years without performing. But what you said is pertinent. I do feel that Jay would want me to say yes.

Also I feel bad about letting her plants die.

With best wishes
Rasmus.

Dear Rasmus,

That is hilarious, but also—Jesus, were you hurt, and how did that happen? I mean it's not a normal thing, a dead deer assaulting a cyclist. Don't worry about the plants. Everybody knows their boyfriend is going to let their plants die at some stage.

With best wishes
Róisín

Dear Róisín,

I was cycling to the shop near where I live on the Island,* and admiring the deer, a lovely youngster, which was running alongside me, and it turned suddenly into the road and was hit by a car coming the other way, and landed on me. I wasn't hurt but my ankle is still a little sore, so maybe I should have had it looked at.

Thank you, regarding the plants.

With best wishes,
Rasmus.

*The shop is not near where I live. I was cycling near to home.

Dear Rasmus,

Were you not tempted to take it home and skin it and live off it
and so forth? Venison is fine meat.

With best wishes
Róisín

Dear Róisín,

Yes I was, but towing it behind the bent-up bicycle would have
been a problem, and I think dealing with a dead thing might
have been beyond me. Jay was ill for a long time and that meant
I had to move into territories of tending to the flesh that I hadn't
visited before. The deer wasn't there the next time I passed,
though, so somebody else had the idea. Was it you?

With best wishes
Rasmus.

Dear Rasmus,

I've strangled a chicken before now when it was required but
the butchering of a stag would be too much for my capacities. I

think. I'd need to look at a clip on YouTube at least. I didn't have the experience of the long illness. My fiancé died very unexpectedly. Though of course we do know we're going to die.

With best wishes
Róisín

Róisín had a strange feeling about these emails. The two of them seemed to be mirroring each other. She kept with the slightly formal mode of address and sign-off with which she had started: Dear Rasmus, with best wishes. And so did he. Exactly the same each time. Why had neither of them relaxed? Particularly when the conversation itself came so easily. So suddenly. So immediately.

Dear Róisín,

Are you coming to the concert at the Albert Hall? I believe it's to be filmed by your lot. You, perhaps? Would you take me somewhere afterward to eat? Otherwise somebody else will try to. And do you have a spare room or a sofa? There are people I could stay with in London but it'd be nice to talk. I hate hotels.

With best wishes
Rasmus.

She was flattered by his correspondence—honored even, given his reputation for being antisocial—and she was astonished by his inviting himself to stay. But why not? His reasons were good.

Perhaps they could be friends. Even recluses need friends. Widow pals.

But he put a full stop after his name. Every time. Who puts a full stop after their name on an email?

She felt like a birdwatcher: no sudden movements or this rare creature will lift its wings and drag itself up and up, looking reluctant, actually determined. And fly away.

Dear Rasmus,

Yes, we'll be filming at the Albert Hall as well, and I'm directing your segment again. I'd be delighted to take you to eat. Are you a vegetarian or anything? I'm supposing not, what with the venison opportunity, but maybe you're one of these wild eaters who launch themselves at the roadkill with the happy life but wouldn't touch something farmed. And yes, I've a sofa, currently knee-deep in balled-up kleenexes (is that the plural? Sounds like there should be a special plural like in Greek or something), if you're sure you wouldn't prefer the fifty-carat top-of-the-range rock 'n' roll luxury lifestyle that I'm sure the company would lay on for you. Maybe we should swap. I love a hotel room. All those towels.

Maybe that's a bit much. Will he think I'm coming on to him, like I'm inviting myself? One of the best things about hotel rooms anyway is hotel sex. Nothing to break, nobody to overhear and if they do it doesn't matter, all those pillows and mirrors. And breakfast brought up on a tray . . .

She stopped and thought about sex for a while, and the fact that she wasn't ever going to be doing it again, there being no Nico to do it with. And she thought about his hands and his neck and his arms and the dear smell of him on the beach and how Greek he got the moment they were there, yelling in Greek to guys in cafés, wanting spanakopita and a backgammon board, off to the rocks looking for sea urchins and octopuses to feed her, not that she'd eat them—one too weird, the other too intelligent, *don't want them hating me when they become our overlords.*

How he got a suntan the moment he took his passport out. How without a trip home he would sort of dry up, physically. You had to put him in the sea and pour olive oil down him and he'd come up glossy and happy again.

They'd had sex up an olive tree once. That was bloody hilarious.

Anyway let me know your dates for that and I'll locate the spare duvet.

All the best
Róisín

Dear Róisín

I'm sitting here with the cat on my knees. It's a very blowy day—we get a lot of those, of course. I've put eighteen pegs on the duvet cover on the line, and it'll be dry in half an hour the way its ballooning. No ironing required.

I'm wondering whether to go out and try to do something about the vegetable patch. In the past year I've done nothing to it except a little weeding. It was Jay's really. I'd just do what she told me needed doing. Initially that was mainly collecting kelp to make the earth into earth in the first place. It's barren up here and the growing season is short but there's a few things we learned how to raise, at the mercy of the weather. A few years ago we'd just transplanted the cabbages and the wind got up and they actually took off in the gale, and whirled round and round like little green planets in crazy orbit. When I look up today in this wind I half expect to see them flying by the window.

The duvet cover might have caught them if the wind were in the right direction. But I planted nothing this year.

I'm not a vegetarian. It would be too much work to be one up here, interesting fresh vegetables not usually being an island priority. Plus it would be too much of a bother for whoever is preparing the food I'm going to be eating. (I've become a capable cook since Jay's illness but before that I hardly cooked, and there's no medal heading my way.) I daresay there are vegetarians in Scotland but they'd be the big jessies in Edinburgh, where they drink flat whites and everything. What I tend to like when I'm away from here is the food I can't get here: Vietnamese, Japanese, Middle Eastern.

I won't tell her about Ghana food. There's nobody I want to eat Ghana food with now anyway. Unless Kwame is around. He pondered the idea of spending an evening with Kwame and Efua and the girls, if they were around, while he was in London. He would do that. And not just because they would make kontomire for him, and check he had enough shito at home, and spoil him and just be really kind. But because it's so unfair to lose everything a person gave you or introduced you to, along with losing them themselves. He didn't want to lose her family. He was sad that without her he was somehow no longer a brother to Ghana, an adopted son. People would look at him and never know he was uncle to these little girls, brother to Kwame.

He and Jay had built a planet of two, and while that can be okay, a planet of one is probably not.

I'm getting lonely, he thought. *Not just missing-her lonely.* Lonely *lonely.*

I'm going to try to see my brother-in-law and his family when I come too.

Did you promise your fiancé that you would look after yourself? Or did you not get a chance? I promised Jay, and I've found it a hard promise to keep.

With best wishes,
Rasmus.

Dear Rasmus,

No, I didn't get that opportunity. I don't know if it would've made much difference, though, because as has been known to happen in the caring professions, he usually had very little caring left in him by the time he got home, so I was traditionally the one running the bath for him and getting the kale down him and wondering if he'd like a nice back rub which needless to say he would, every time, and who could blame him for that. I have so much time empty now. Are you finding that? Just he's not here to chat with. Watching the telly now I'm talking to myself— Oh look it's that fella that was in such and such—and nobody to tell me the fella's name or what it was he was in. Nobody to complain about the rubbish I'm watching, and could I turn it down. I'll be shouting at myself no doubt soon, just to try and keep things normal—

Best wishes
Róisín

Dear Róisín,

What was his line of work?
Rasmus.

Dear Rasmus,

He was a paramedic. 999 calls all day long. And paperwork.

Róisín

Dear Róisín,

Jay was a GP. Similar levels of involvement and responsibility, I would think, but operating in very different ways. Jay was a good friend to almost everybody in the community here. The way a priest might be. Because she'd always be there conducting the births and the deaths, she was always invited to the christenings and the funerals. Whereas Nico, I suppose, was just there for the crises (is that the kind of Greek-sounding plural you were thinking of?), which uses a different energy, and a different set of emotional skills. Had he been doing it long? I don't know how old he was.

Rasmus.

Dear Rasmus,

He was thirty-six. He'd been doing it for ten years, and was in that state of dilemma where he knew the value of his training and experience, but at the same time he *really* knew the stress and pressure the work put on him—and the rewards too of course. I've never delivered a baby in my life but he'd do a couple most months, and always come home with a special glow afterward. Equally though he'd lose people. After you're team leader you really feel that. So he kinda sorta wanted to leave, but also really didn't want to. He didn't want to squander his training, plus he knew nothing else would be so exciting, and also felt a bit ashamed of finding it exciting. But he loved being the hero, he really did. Loved his kit: Nico, coming through to save the day . . . Oh I shouldn't mock, I'm not mocking. I loved him and I love him still and I'll love him forever. God, he was just a funny man. Funny peculiar. Funny ha ha too, though. But a lot of contradiction in him, even though to meet him you'd think him a bit of a smoothy maybe. A charmer for sure. Good with the mums. Self-protection, of course, from the sad side of it all. And the stories were great, you can imagine. Every week a new "You'll never guess what this guy had his dick stuck in . . ." tale. Once there was a pet monkey up a tree; the woman had said on the call it was her baby . . . Anyway, you can imagine. Sorry, I'm going on. You're right, GP must be different, specially in a small place. You'd see the same people over and over; get to know them, there'd be fondness involved. The only people he saw over and over were the pub fighters and the alcoholics whose neighbors were calling 999 on them all the time. And one poor epileptic guy whose meds they could never get right. Ironic it seems to me that he saved a lot of lives and then when it came to it his own colleagues were not able to save his. I can't and don't hold it against them. How could I, knowing how they work, and knowing how they feel about it themselves? God, look at me blathering on.

How do we sign off, now? I can't really be dealing with the best wishes business as if you'd fitted a boiler, when I'm telling you stuff I don't tell my sister even.

Yours sincerely,
Róisín

Dear Sir or Madam,

All the best is a good one, I feel. Impossible to achieve, of course, but a nice sentiment.

All the best,
Rasmus.

PS How did you and Nico meet?

Dear Rasmus,

He was watching when a mad drunk guy skidded up to me in the mud at Glastonbury, flourishing a Coke can ring pull and asking would I marry him. It was sort of funny but also not. Nico just laughed and laughed though, and then the off-his-head guy wanted to fight him, and Nico was saying really philosophical things like "I think you'll find the strength of neither your emotions nor indeed the drugs you're on can negate the illogic of your response," which I found hilarious. Then the off-his-head guy's friends took him away, and Nico was just standing there looking cute, and he said, "You could always marry me" so I said, "Sure, why not." The Fratellis were playing and I thought—insofar as I thought at all—that it'd be a great story for the grandchildren: "I knew at first sight he was special" etc etc. I felt he'd protected me somehow. The ridiculous logic of women . . . so then he went and got me a Coke, and he gave me the ring of the can.

Anyway so, the following year he gave me a diamond, and I'm still wearing it. How did you and Jay meet?

All the best (aye aye sir),
Róisín

Dear Róisín,

In New York, 2001. I was there with the band, our first trip to the US, our first tour outside the UK just about to start, our first album just out and doing well. We were four very excited boys. There was a party on a roof, given by I don't even know who, and she was there silhouetted against the skyline. Someone said she was joining the tour and I thought oh thank God, I have time, I don't have to make her love me at a party, in one night. Which I would not have been able to do. She says I told her she looked like she should be singing with Ray Charles, but I hope I wouldn't have been so clichéd with a Black singer, though it was a very stylish dress she had on, with stitching like an art deco cinema, in a kind of sunburst shape, and panels very well fitted, quite '60s. She told me the color was burned orange. Her voice was made of equal parts laughter and music and I had from Brooklyn to San Francisco and back to impress her on the tour bus, via Nashville, New Orleans, West Texas, and Las Vegas.

All the best,
Rasmus.

PS What year? We played Glastonbury three times.

Dear Rasmus,

That is beautifully romantic. Silhouetted against the NY skyline!
Funnily enough I think I know that dress. Was it by Karen Millen
and did it have a matching coat?

All the best
Róisín

PS I know, I saw you. You were great.

Dear Róisín,

It did have a matching coat!

I gave it to a charity shop in Stornoway, in a moment of madness.
Then wanted to go and get it back. Spent two days thinking
myself round in circles—but why? What would I do with it? Why
does it matter? Every single thing I own evokes her, from my
own toenails to the roof over my head. It all scatters her dust.
Telling myself not to be ridiculous. Then I went and bought it
back. What can you do? We *are* ridiculous. At least, we're not
logical. Specially not now.

All the best,
Rasmus.

PS I have three bookshelves of her medical
journals.

Dear Rasmus,

For a while I couldn't find Nico's will, and I thought I was probably going to have to give up the flat. I tried to calculate the percentage of the mortgage I was paying on the cupboard space his clothes were taking up. How much of his stuff I could afford to take to a new, smaller, farther-out flat. Financially as well as emotionally. But all that is too soon, too soon. Now I know the flat is safe I won't even think about sorting his things for as long as I bloody want. I've given some to his mother though. She's a widow and she loved him to a degree you might call lunacy.

All the best
Róisín

PS Oh God, all right. The other day I bought him a pair of socks. Yes, I know. But he'd have loved them. They have Dolly Parton on them.

Dear Róisín,

I'm tempted to set fire to everything.

Rasmus.

(Not the Dolly Parton socks though. They sound excellent. I assume you were in the habit of borrowing his socks? I've been buying myself the chocolate Jay used to get me online. Am I pretending she's sending it? Maybe. Will I give myself a birthday present from her? Who bloody knows.)

Dear Rasmus,

I'm pretty sure setting fire to everything comes under Things You Can't Undo.

Róisín

Dear Róisín,

It does.

Rasmus.

Dear Rasmus,

It's good, I think, to hear that someone else is in as much pain as me.

I think.

Róisín

◆   ◆   ◆

Hi Róisín

FYI reports back are all good; I'm forwarding them. Well done!

They're wondering about the interview—is that set up now after the initial hitch?

Ayesha

Hi Ayesha

Did you want me to be in touch with him directly about this? Is it not going via you and Carola? I got the impression that he had classed it under "press," which he didn't want. Happy to approach him if that's the line we're taking.

Róisín

I'll talk to Carola. See if they can fit us in around his trip for the Albert Hall gig.

A x

Was it relieved she felt at this, or dishonest? Things had become suddenly double-pronged. *He's going to be sleeping on my sofa. And third parties are applying for permission for me to talk to him. That's a bit odd.*

◆　◆　◆

Dear Róisín,

Sorry it's taken me a few days to answer that. I was thinking.

I know exactly what you mean. Another person might think it a heartless comment, and I had to double-check with myself that I wasn't deluding myself in thinking that you meant it in the heartfelt way, i.e. that the broken heart needs company in sorrow, rather than in any heartless, trite way. But it's pretty clear that you're not a heartless, trite person.

Yes, it is always good to know that we are not alone. Especially when, as you and I, we really are so alone we can hardly bear it. And wouldn't be able to bear it, if we knew of any way to get rid of the fact that we have to.

Rasmus.

Ah Rasmus

The only ways out of this are time (which I'm not sure even works, no matter what they say) and topping ourselves, which I for one can't do, because family, also residual Catholicism and not much desire to go to Hell even though I don't believe in it (don't tell God I said that). And if you can see I'm not trite and heartless (for which, thank you?), I can see that you're not the topping-himself kind. You might dress like one but I've seen the way you cradle your guitar. And the way you carry pain. I'm sorry about your accident. Again.

Róisín

Dear Róisín,

Untrite, heartfelt, and clear-eyed too. I am not the topping-myself kind. It might not show but I can't stand a rock 'n' roll cliché. This is how rock 'n' roll I'm not: it was dark for about three hours last night, if you can call it dark: the astonishing pale dark of the northern summer midnight. I went for a walk on the sands beyond Scarista and found a sheep skull in a dune. It must have been there a very long time, as it is worn so thin and so smooth. It's like silk made solid. And it's a very silky color. I took this photograph of it in the perpetual gloaming. It seems to glow itself.

Rasmus.

Dear Rasmus,

Re not topping yourself: Good.

Re the photo: it's beautiful.

Re rock 'n' roll cliché: you don't need me to tell you the long-term employment prospects are shite.

My sister makes me go out. She thinks I need sympathy and company so she sent me to a widows' and widowers'—God but that's a mouthful, isn't it? Maybe if the words were easier it might be easier to talk about the things themselves—you can't really call a widower a widow, can you? Or vice versa—for all the gender-neutral language and proffering your pronouns I still see a staring-eyed woman with a black veil and suspect jewelry— anyway a social night for us lot in a room above a pub. In theory I can understand that having something as fucking horrible as this in your life in common might be enough to forge a friendship, but in practice I looked around at them and felt terribly sad for them all, including the ones who looked quite happy and had maybe been coming for years, and had forgotten about the dead partner they maybe never loved that much anyway, and just came for the gin and the jollies, I mean so many people are just lonely anyway—God, now I'm imagining they weren't widowed at all, they were just on the lookout, maybe it's a hot dating game at the Widows' and Widowers' Social Night—maybe some of them were chancers looking for a vulnerable meal ticket— anyway, there was nobody there I'd even want to sit next to on the school bus, let alone slop my grief onto, and vice versa. Then on the way home "Just Because You're Strong" came on the radio, and I've been a bit shy to tell you this but it's a song that's always broken my heart, and Nico's too, he said it reminded him of his mum after his dad died, and the one time I tried to break up with Nico (which I did, long story, not proud, infidelity-related, not on my part) it was the song that set him off. Anyway, previously playing had been Chicago, "If You Leave Me Now," so that was bad enough but when "Just Because You're Strong" came on I slammed the brakes and the poor fella behind me drove right into me, and then I had I don't know maybe what they'd call a panic attack or something, I was sitting there on the curb in bits and the poor fella trying to comfort me. And then the smell of my mam came to me through the rain. It was like when you're little and she leans over your bed and says there there love you're having a bad dream, all gone now. And in a moment it *was* all gone. So then when I got home I thought, shit what if Mam's died, so I rang but it was ten thirty by then so of course anyone ringing her after ten thirty she thought someone else must have died—long story short, no she wasn't dead, no she hadn't been thinking of me. Just a stray smell across north London, of lily of the valley and smoke from a Silk Cut.

All the best
Róisín

16

More Honestly

JULY
London

JAY WAS LYING on her back up on the roof of Alexandra Palace. Up in the wind and the sky on this endless midsummer day, resting on glass, she was fearless. Nothing she had to fear involved wind or glass or height.

Beware, for I am fearless and therefore powerful—where was that from? Someone had it on a lapel badge. Was it from *Frankenstein?*

She didn't feel powerful. She felt—

Leave them alone, she was thinking. *Leave them to it. Don't go and read their emails. Don't.*

He'd laughed at something, at his laptop, and she'd looked over his shoulder and seen the words "Dolly Parton" and "pair of socks." Clear evidence of a friendly exchange. That was all she needed to know.

A squadron of little green parakeets zapped by, squeaking. She was close enough to see the pink cheeks on their leaf-green faces, to sense the swift beating of their tiny wings. Along the edges of her eyeline the ash trees were still waving their frondy fingers in the evening sky. There had been a summer storm; it had cleared and now tiny clouds were scudding, swift and very high. Idly she wondered if she could go up there and bounce on them. *No, they're too small and quick. You'd need piles of proper cumulus for that, piles of whipped-cream clouds like in those paintings where the angels tumble around and Mary in her blue cloak is floating up to heaven . . .*

Hark at me! Holding forth on which clouds would be best for bouncing on.

Leave him be.

But I'm the only person who says I have to leave him be. And if I—What if—

Her eyes were full of ghostly anomalous tears.

She stared out over treetops and car parks and building sites and red-starred cranes and the first lights coming on and the river in the distance. Evening was beginning to draw in now, the color of the Virgin's cloak, and the sunset the color of a Negroni. She'd never had a Negroni. Negronis hadn't been a thing when she'd last been in the kind of place they had that kind of thing. That wasn't the kind of life they'd lived, these past years. Theirs had been a life of fog and tide, of wandering sheep and other people's snotty infants, mountains and moss and music, and holding on to suicidal patients. Depression. Not his anymore, thank God: the air and the sea and the light and the quiet and the healing had dispersed that, as they'd hoped it would. A beautiful life.

Come now, it's over, you can look at it more honestly. Nobody's listening.

Ours was a life of me studying and him suffering. Of pain and immobility and boredom and surgery and finally, finally, healing, for him. And decision, for me. We turned our back on a couple of possible lives, when we chose the one we chose. As people do. The shrinking of opportunity that comes naturally with growing up, and focusing. No to London; yes to the Outer Hebrides. No to bands; yes to composition. No to obstetrics and women's reproductive health; yes to local GP. No to living as a Black woman where other Black people are; yes to living where Rasmus needed to live, for his sake, because I love him.

She still didn't know if he ever *really* understood what that meant. It wasn't about the shito and the hairdresser, though that was part of it. It was about not hearing Kwame's ridiculously loud laugh, or any other laugh in the street that sounded like it. It was about not seeing little girls, any little girls, the curve of whose cheek reminded her of Kwame and Efua's daughters, Aph and Freddie. Of her mother. About not having a Black church to feel a bit awkward about walking past on a Sunday morning, when she for sure wasn't going to go in, and all the Aunties outside giving her side-eye as a godless hussy. It was about no longer living down the road from Evelyn and Taia, about there being the Tube at the end of the road to take her to Heathrow to take her to Accra, about no longer working with Justin and Sophia and Mahmoud and Tomiwa and Leticia. Never hearing the particular husky ring of West African voices. Never seeing big brown eyes. Only seeing out of them. It was about reading that recent report, that Black women are five times more likely to die in childbirth than white women, and not having a single Black patient.

Yes, he had felt bad about it. He was aware. And she, once the decision was made, had developed a habit of kind of hushing him about it. *Don't worry, no no no; Rasmus, are you telling me a Black girl can't pine for the Northern Lights?* She bloody loved the Northern Lights. It was built on the simplest of emotions: gratitude and false guilt.

She'd wanted to make up to him for the pain he'd suffered, for his not being able to do anything, while she went out every day to study and meet people and work and be a clever young living person in a glorious city. And he lay there and did his physio, and moved like an old man. And paid for her. He paid for her to study. So when he wanted to leave the city, yes, she damn well would live where he wanted to live, where he needed to live, for his mental recovery as much as his physical. They supported each other in sickness and in health, and, in the evenings, she read all she could find about how Black health and women's health have suffered for centuries, because the default human body was seen as white and male, and she wandered in those forbidden territories of the imagination: what might have been. It wasn't the lack of cocktails that she regretted.

Then Nico was there beside her, and she pulled herself up to sitting.

After a bit he started pointing things out to her: Róisín's office, their street, his old school, where the Woolworths used to be where he'd nicked a nail polish in 1996. And Jay pointed things out to him: the river, the sea, the curve of the horizon beyond the buildings. All human experience. The universe.

"How was your death, Jay?" he asked.

"I don't know," she said. "I just did it—let go of what I was holding on to. I'd been dying for a long time." She didn't feel it was a very satisfactory account.

"How was yours?" she asked.

"I don't know," he said. "I can't remember the moment. The circumstances were—like an explosion. Sudden, torn away, kicking and screaming, knocked out flat . . . What about your funeral? Did you go?"

"Yes," she said.

"Me too," he said, and smiled.

Below, people were beginning to turn for the gates, and going home; others settling into the summer evening like prides of lions, lounging, voices getting louder, music softly pounding. The rare beauty of a hot night in London. *There'll be shagging in the parks and squares tonight*, Jay thought, but she just wanted to go home. *It's me that's dead. It's me that feels mournful—about the life I didn't have, that I*

somehow thought I would be able to get back to, taking him with me, when
he was well enough. When it was my turn.

But now, she just wanted to go home. Toast and Marmite.

Something on the telly. Rasmus.

Marmite, Negronis, ambition. The life I had; the lives I didn't.

No regrets.

Oh, bollocks. No regrets is always a lie. What kind of a psycho has no
regrets?

"He's going to be staying at hers after the next gig," Nico was saying. His tone was carefully reserved and polite. "I gather."

"Are you reading their emails?" she asked.

"Aren't you?"

"No. I take the odd look is all, because I'm—" She'd been going to
say "influencing them" or "steering them," but the words didn't sound
right now they'd reached the tip of her tongue. "On their side," she
said finally.

"We're both on their side," Nico said. "It's just that one of us thinks
this is rather sordid."

"Listen," she said, "the inviting himself to stay isn't a come-on.
He's being literal. He needs somewhere to stay and he'd rather stay
with her."

Nico gave her a come-off-it look. An I-know-men look.

"Really," she said, with what she hoped would be clearly read as a
you-may-know-men-but-I-know-this-man look. "Believe me, this will
take time."

"Thing is," he said musingly, "it's very easy for me to see this as you
setting up a new widow with your charismatic honey-tongued rock
star ex, just because you can—"

"It's not like that," she said, stung. "I'm not providing some harem,
some groupies for him. Jesus—and by the way, I'm *NOT* after your
money."

"Yes, sorry about that," he said. "Unreasonable. Feelings a bit high."

"And he's not my *ex*," she said, only partially mollified. "We didn't break up. It's not the same—as you of all people should know."

This Nico also conceded. "Yeah," he said. "Sorry. Someone referred to me as her ex, to Róisín, and she was so hurt. I mean it's one comfort, isn't it—you may not have each other but at least you didn't get divorced. At least you still love each other."

They pondered that silently for a while. Because, you know, love. What use was their love now?

"Seriously," Jay resumed, after a while. "He doesn't want sex-because-sex. He never has. He only wants sex-because-the-woman-in-question. And he likes to know the woman in question. He's a slow mover."

"He's a mover all right," said Nico.

"If you genuinely think that, Nico," she said, "and it's not your grief and your jealousy and your possessiveness speaking, then you are a twat. I didn't think you were, but maybe I was wrong."

"You don't ever think you're wrong," he said. "That I've noticed."

It was not the first time someone had said this to her. It infuriated her.

"Well, if I thought I was wrong," she said, "I'd think something else, wouldn't I? Something right? Everybody thinks they're right, otherwise they wouldn't think it. Just like everybody thinks they're the good guy. The best we can do is acknowledge when we don't know, or when we find we were wrong after all . . . But I'll tell you one thing, about which I am *absolutely* right—evidence-based fact here—they *will* talk late, and he *will* sleep on the sofa. Not only will he not touch her, it wouldn't occur to him to touch her. Don't let popular culture fool you—not all men are sex-crazed louts."

Nico blinked. Lights were coming on across the city now, spread before them like a jeweled cloak over mud.

"I don't like it," he said.

"Right now," she said, "I don't like it either. To be honest, I don't like any of it and I wish I'd never been ill and I wish I hadn't died and I wish I was alive and well and doing all the things I ever took for granted."

"Me too," he whispered.

She leaned forward to him and looked right into his eyes. "I promise you, Nico," she said. "He'll be nice. And furthermore, even if I changed my mind, there's sod all we can do about it."

17

It's a Leap

JULY
London

WHOLE WEEKENDS RÓISÍN had lain in bed, through spring into summer, and why not. Over the weeks the multiple pale greens of the leaves of spring were blending and blurring outside and now they were all the same color. Tulips long gone, roses blaring. She could raise her head and look out at all this joy. Hey ho.

July it was. Mad long white nights, hardly any dark to speak of, a sense of untetheredness still. She'd lie awake at night running through her personal rosary of doubts and discomforts: the missing of his body beside her; the sense of tangledness with the duvet cover around her feet; the heat of the pillow (turn it over); the fretting as to whether hot feet denoted an ailment or condition of some kind; the wondering whether she, or he, or they, should or could or might have noticed some such clue to the condition he had; the midsummer four-in-the-morning light beyond the curtains, the cursing yourself for having opened your eyes, which made it all so much worse; the re-closing of the eyes, and the shifting of the consciousness into that dark world, refocusing your eyes on the inside of your forehead; the reminding yourself to breathe, deep breaths, not the shallow little lifting of the chest. The getting out of bed to pull the bottom sheet straighter and tighter, because who knows, that might be the magical detail that would make all the difference to whether or not she'd get any sleep at all tonight. The fantasies of travel. The wanting to be underwater. The what-about-the-money. The probate was taking its time; she would have to clear his stuff at some stage however boldly she'd spoken of it to Rasmus. All the things she would *have to have to have to.*

The shelves of medical journals! She thought about Jay: Hebridean GP, Ghanaian woman, coming back from the surgery and reading professional journals. *Why did they go there? They could have gone anywhere.*

I could go anywhere.

Sometimes in the mornings she felt she put Nico on like a garment.

Wrapped him round her. For safety, for company, for comfort.

She'd shaved her head again. Number two.

This summer would pass and the future would, as it always did, gradually, sneakily, become now. But who can see spring from December?

Things to do. Life kicking and needling her: *I'm still here. Come and live me. Work to be done, gigs to be filmed, this widowed rock star to be interviewed.*

THE DAY OF the Albert Hall gig, Róisín rippled with heightened feeling: for the coming evening, for the music, for the dinner, and for the overnight guest. For doing something that Nico would have loved but that did not involve Nico at all. It was not his business. The dead do not have business. It was, if you like, post-Nico.

Post-Nico. There's a punch in the belly.

And, for the interview. Which she hoped was properly confirmed with him this time. But also because whenever you interview some-one, it's exciting and a responsibility, but there's a double stir-up when it's someone you admire professionally. Plus there was this widow-pal thing. He'd told her a lot. Was she going to draw on that?

No, because she was not some sleazy tabloid scumbag.

What they wrote to each other was real and true and valid.

This double strand, the professional and the personal, and how to respect it, was so clearly going to be an issue that she didn't let her eyes settle on it. The desire for the having and the eating of the cake was not something she felt up to dealing with.

She'd had a few conversations with Nico about it—in her head, though, not in that intense way she'd had to start with, that sense of him actually being there with her. He was certainly farther away now. Or at least he was today. Sometimes he would suddenly charge back, trailing grief in his wake like a silver cloak, and upset the boat all over again. They say it ebbs and flows. Sometimes a lapping tide nibbling your toes; sometimes that bloody frothing overwhelming tsunami. Forty days is one of the traditional periods of mourning, one of those magic numbers. Seven nights, forty days, a hundred and one days, a year and a day. Like in the Irish songs and fairy tales. All those "I Am Stretched on Your Grave" songs that her mother used to sing in Irish. Laments. *Táim sínte ar do thuama . . . with you in your cold grave I cannot sleep warm.* But there's nothing regular about it. No steady development. Christ, one day she would get to a year, and there would be an anniversary. Even thinking about that made him more dead.

Every time I swim I'm literally stretched on your grave.

Onward, Róisín. To be going out and facing the world, it's a leap. It felt, in some weird way, a bit like a date. Not a date with Rasmus, of course, but a date with—the future? With the possibility of having a future? With life?

18

§

I Don't Know How

Dear Róisín,

I've explained to everybody that you are to be let in backstage. I only hope it will have sunk in. I do have a mobile phone: here is the number. I can't promise I'll answer it, because I've never answered it before and I don't know how to. Sending a text is better, in that it's easier for me to notice that it's happened. But of course you will be on the list anyway as the important film director that you are. Or if you let me know where we are to eat, I can meet you there, which might be simpler.

Also, and I don't know if you knew about this, it turns out I did agree to be interviewed by you and they—the great They— would like it to be done during this trip. So we'll need to find a way to do that.

with best wishes from Rasmus.

Dear Róisín,

Actually, can I come to yours before the gig, and leave my bag? I don't need to be there for their soundcheck.

with best wishes from Rasmus.

Dear Rasmus,

Of course you can, but I won't be there. The spare key is rather absurdly under the flowerpot, in full view of any villainous neighbors.

I knew they were trying to schedule an interview but thought it best to leave it to one channel rather than muddy things by setting up another.

Róisín

Dear Róisín,

OK. We can do it afterward, or the next day?

Rasmus.

19

Sandbags

JULY
London

IMPORTANT FILM DIRECTOR! Róisín was still thinking about that as she came out of the Tube. *It's readable in so many ways. Straightforward recognition of her role and her importance? Hardly. She wasn't D. A. Pennebaker, or Penelope Spheeris. Patronizing joke? Not that either— though it easily could be in some other man's mouth. Sarcasm? No.*

She did feel, though, that she could ask him. That's what she would do. After the interview was done. Something about him kept her on her best behavior. He might still flap away.

She'd spent the last few days watching all the footage she could find of the Capos, old and recent, with Rasmus and without. Naive interviews from the early days, out-of-focus snippets on YouTube, clips made on phones in dive bars, ultra-professional videos filmed on volcanos in Iceland and in cocktail joints in Hong Kong. Live performances on the radio. Snatches of meet 'n' greets in Idaho and Florida and Austin, Texas. George in a shirt and tie, flirting with fans who wanted a picture. Nigel the drummer, unsmiling in a Lurex tracksuit. Cole the bassist with a cigarette stuck between the strings just above the top fret. Twenty-one-year-old Rasmus grinning and stalking the stage, throwing his head back, playing like a demon. George Vechten watching him, laughing. *What is that? Admiration? Camaraderie? Envy?* Him watching George. The elegant, long-legged girl singer—*Oh! That's her! That must be her*—watching them both, eyes flashing, side to side. And when she sang, *oh wow.*

It fell into place. *This lioness—in that tiny leather dress—is the singer he married. This is who became a GP in the Hebrides. This is who died.*

Look at her!

Róisín watched that clip over and over. The exuberance of it; the fullness and energy bouncing off them all, so young, so bloody good-looking, firecrackers, all to play for. Literally. Eyeliner and skinny legs, and shaggy sticking-up hair. She bet they'd had some great after-parties.

There didn't seem to be much of a rule about who sang which songs: sometimes George; sometimes Rasmus. Often together. In the actual videos, made for the singles, George was the show-off; Rasmus hung back. George up a tree, skinny legs dangling; Rasmus lurking behind the trunk, a shy smile. She tried to remember the time she'd seen them live. Nigel in an animal head; Rasmus long and strange coming down the front, always watching, curious, as if the humans didn't quite make sense to him. Cradling his guitar like a beloved; singing in the way that draws you near, then letting loose with George: wildfire men.

Then there was another live clip: "Love Ain't Listening," which must have been from the US tour. Rasmus and Jay singing the duet— like a pair of cooing birds. Sharing the mic. Can't take their eyes off each other, except to glance away trying to stifle a grin. Like they can't believe their luck. The way he's smiling at her. She's got her head practically on his shoulder looking up at him; he leans in and their foreheads touch. Voices twining. *Fuck. Doo doo d'doo doo doo . . .*

That one she didn't watch again. Seemed a bit, you know, like walking in on them at their own private after party.

Watching later clips, the Capos without Rasmus, she couldn't put her finger on it. George was still George; the band was still the band, the new guitarist was a fine player (several different fine players, actually), the old songs were still the old songs. But the new songs were not interesting. It was as if an arty, funny, unusual, sexy band, which should have gone on to artier, funnier, more unusual, and even sexier things, had instead reversed into a niche of cliché. An oh-yeah-they're-that-kind-of-band band. A blokey band. What made the Capos' fortunes, after Rasmus, was the old popular and familiar blend of the macho and the melancholic, radio-friendly, with predictable melodies and lyrics as fatuous as most rock lyrics are. And live—the Capos without Rasmus were meat without salt.

They were damn fools to have lost Jay, too. They didn't take on another singer to replace her. No backing vocalists, either. It all went more straightforwardly rocky. The guys. "Love Ain't Listening" was the only duet, and it didn't reappear on the setlists after the first tour.

She really wanted to know what Rasmus had been doing up there in Scotland, all those years. And to hear it.

THE GREAT *THEY* had sent a list of questions they wanted asked, saying that Rasmus had approved them. *Well!* She was nervous nervous nervous, in a good way. Nerves as rocket fuel.

SHE'D COME OUT from the Albert Hall for a breath of air and decent reception, and was trying to get the definitive information on what volume the Capos would be going to that night, so as to decide whether she needed to bring in the sandbags for the tripods for cameras four and five at the top of the staircases, when there he was, ambling up the road, a guitar on his back. To avoid the excruciating moments of long-distance smiles of recognition/can they even see me/now they'll think I'm just watching them walk/should I wave or something, she pretended she hadn't spotted him.

Either he was pretending too, or he really was just gazing at his boots, deep in thought, as he drew nearer. Then he did look up, and wave she did, and got off the phone.

"It is you, isn't it?" he said. "I wasn't sure I'd find you in the crowd inside. Is there a crowd?"

"Yes," she said, and had an absolute sudden feeling that they *were* on some kind of first date, that he was wearing some kind of a shroud over a charisma so strong women would fall over, and that he was— not delicate, not weak, not even wounded—in peril, somehow.

They ended up almost embracing—her, light-headed anyway, swaying suddenly; him catching her elbow; her smiling her thanks as she steadied. They walked inside together, round to the desk where Shireen was double-checking everything. There he laid his guitar case down, opened it, and took out a slightly battered KitKat.

"Blood sugar," he said as he handed it to her, then ambled off backstage.

Sandbags, she thought. *For me, if not for the tripods.*

There was too much going on. *Wish me luck, Nico.*

Concentrate.

RASMUS'S HEART WAS big as he stepped out onstage that night: big with a potent flux of rightness and vulnerability, nerves and love, safety and fear. He'd had one nip of Dougie's homemade whisky, which worked for him. There was his gear all laid out: guitars on their stands with their various tunings; the Gretsch slung across his back, his audience before him in the dark. He sensed them in the great vault, rows of them in their velvet seats and rows more up the walls in gilt circles of balconies and boxes. Glimmers of gold and red in the cavernous space; so grand, so Victorian. He knew it well from long ago. She'd built it as a memorial to her handsome husband, father of her hundreds of children. Stylish move, he felt.

Oooohhhhh.

As he came on, facing them, so many, so expectant, the auditorium began to twinkle . . .

Photography? was his thought.

But it wasn't the aggressive flashes of stolen photos. It was . . .

Oh, it was what used to be lighters, swaying. It was five and a half thousand phones held up at arm's length, and glowing. A massed electric jellyfish; a mythical luminescent underwater millipede. The sweet sympathies of all those people, silently extended to him. Their welcome.

He stood before his mic, and bit a nail on his forefinger.

"Thank you," he murmured. "That's kind of you," to which there was a massive cheer, and he was so touched, so surprised, that it threw him, and for a moment it occurred to him that this might be difficult, this might after all be a difficult thing he was about to do.

He thought about that, till the waves of cheers and applause died down.

He leaned in again, close to the mic, close in their ears.

"My wife died," he said softly. "You probably know that. These songs are about—that. That death thing."

A great soft murmur from the crowd. "They're new," he said. "I hope you like them."

An audience is a huge beast, where many hearts come to beat as one, and many ears absorb into one consciousness. You can read its mood by the sound of its breath and the angle of its head: this was a calm and pensive beast, expectant. A beast ready to love. And it did. He gave them seven songs: four with guitar, three at the piano, no encore, the story told. While he played and sang, he looked up and out as if he expected to see Jay in one of the gold-encrusted boxes, or in the spandrels of the arches up in the gods, lounging on a girder or the lighting rig, or in the chandelier, leaning forward, the better to take him in. It was her he sang for, and he knew they knew it, his audience of eavesdroppers.

JAY AND NICO sat together on the front of the royal box, like a pair of unlikely quasi-caryatids. Jay sang quiet harmonies; Nico watched and listened, and decided he wouldn't watch Rasmus perform again. Not because he wasn't good. Far from it.

Jay was thinking, *maybe I should just stay and haunt him forever. Look at him. My beautiful husband.*

RÓISÍN TOOK HERSELF outside during the interval, when Rasmus's set was done. She stared across at the fantastical, outrageous Albert Memorial, swathed in stone-carved portraits of philosophers and with outriders of lush stone animals on plinths—the elephant of Asia, the bull for Europe, Africa's camel, and some kind of buffalo for the Americas—built by Queen Victoria for her darling husband on his death. She let the creak and murmur of Rasmus's memorial to *his* wife roll around her mind. *Not much I can do for you, Nico,* she thought. *Not even a gravestone. Fucking sea burial, you selfish arse . . . can't even plant a fucking rosebush . . . Oh stop,* she thought, and took out her phone to change the mood; go on, take a look at Instagram. And there they were. Her and Rasmus, papped and all over the web: The Capos' Lost Rocker with Shaven-Headed Mystery Woman, with many comments and many, many likes.

It hadn't occurred to her that it was going to be like that. But apparently appetites were now so niche that even Rasmus could be

offered up as a tasty mouthful on the internet's smorgasbord of celebrity, for the delectation of poetic-minded men of a certain age and
followers of Rock's Backpages. Someone had helpfully tagged her, so
she was not Shaven-Headed Mystery Woman for long. Hardly long
enough for her to enjoy the sensation. She giggled. She could hear
Nico in the back of her mind saying "Yeah, Shaven-Headed Mystery
Woman—didn't I see them supporting Grindmother at Glasto in
'98?" *Old jokes. Nearly as potent as cheap music.*

She posted underneath it: *Nothing to see here, folks. Shaven-Headed
Mystery Woman filming the gig with Capos' Lost Rocker, that's all.*

After the show was organized chaos. Milling crowds of excited
punters going this way and that, the techs in black jeans doing the
get-out, lugging giant stacks of matte-black gear. Shireen and the
guys packing up, looking happy. "I'll have the link to the rushes with
you by breakfast!" Shireen cried. Down some stairs, past security, and
along a corridor, the aftershow was letting off its hubbub in a distant
room. Róisín snuck through, stirred up, smiling, into the crowd of
laughter, cheekbones, swishy hair, clinking glasses. Famous faces. She
was pretty certain he wouldn't be here, and if he was he'd be being
mobbed.

She went to text him: *no signal.*

Attempted the dressing rooms. A security man, silent and the size
of a moose, made that impossible.

She spotted him at the end of a rammed corridor. He was in a
corner with his jacket on and a guitar case over his shoulder. A
woman with artful hair was telling him something she clearly found
very important. Five other people made an impressed audience. His
expression was between concerned and desperate, his eyes gleaming.
Róisín waved. Felt like an idiot. Waved some more.

He caught her eye, but couldn't move. She fought her way down.

"TERRIBLY SORRY!" she shouted, in a crowing posh voice she
used to amuse Nico with when he was hating the world. "TERRIBLY

SORRY, RASMUS IS NEEDED, AWFULLY SORRY! BE RIGHT BACK BUT IF YOU DON'T MIND, THIS WAY, RASMUS, PLEASE—"

For a moment he looked alarmed as she barged through. When she grabbed his arm and physically dragged him away, he tried to disguise his laughter as a coughing fit. They dodged through the crowd like naughty kids, ducking away from claims and attention and the call of his name.

"Stage door," he hissed, "this way," and turned her down a different corridor. Soon they were quite lost. They nipped up a little staircase and suddenly the warren disappeared behind them and the world opened up in front: they were onstage, breathless, looking out over the great auditorium, empty but for a couple of cleaners setting to at the back.

"Thank you!" he said. She was still giggling at her own audacity,

He looked up, and round, and back at her.

"What's your favorite?" he said, slipping the guitar from his shoulder.

Really?

"Not of the new ones," he said. "The old ones." Then he was struck by sudden embarrassment. "I assume you know them . . ." he said, and tailed off.

"I do actually know them," she said, like *obviously*. "Off by heart, actually. Had the special edition vinyl, and the lyric sheet insert pinned up on my bedroom wall." *Next to the picture of you*, she didn't say.

"Next to the picture of me?" he said, purely joking, but she went pale and said, "Er . . ." and he said, "No—" and she said, "Well, yes it was so—I mean, the band, not just you," and broke down laughing, and he was looking at her with his silvery eyes.

"That's either hilarious or very embarrassing," he said. "Though I'm not sure for which of us."

"Both, for both," she said, thinking *no way he'll be singing for me now, damn, damn!* But he said, "So?" and she blushed, and made a "no way" gesture. Then, "'Love Ain't Listening,'" she said.

And so, yes, he took out the guitar, tuned it, and played it—for her, and for the cleaners, who came down to the front, and laughed and clapped and sang along: *"And I am happy on the bus, and I am dancing on the doorstep . . . doo doo, d'doo doo doo, doo doo, d'doo doo doo . . ."* Everyone had their own memories flying round their own minds and hearts, and for those few minutes they were all happy, in the power of a song, and with the joy of being given something contraband, and unexpected, and more often reserved for people richer and luckier.

NICO, A FEW rows back in a red velvet seat too small for him, said quietly: "I knew she liked them but she never told me she had a picture of him up."

Jay's mouth was a bit tight. She wanted to say something reassuring but she'd done an awful lot of that, and it was hard to actually watch.

AFTER THE SONG, the cleaners showed Róisín and Rasmus a fire door that led out the back, so they could dodge the photographers and the crowd.

IN THE BLUE dusk, taxis roared by and the Albert Memorial loomed.

"We'll let 'em go, will we?" said Nico, watching them head off.

"Yup," she said.

It was like a second death, so they stood there, feeling suddenly irrelevant and pointless.

"We're a right pair of gooseberries," Nico said.

"We can't just stand here," Jay said. So they slipped into the park, and walked over scuffed summer grass up toward the Serpentine.

"They won't do anything tonight," Jay said, to comfort someone, it wasn't clear who.

"But they will one day," said Nico. "That's the whole point, isn't it?"

Jay ran on ahead, and started backflipping.

"Let's swim!" she yelled, pointing to where the willows hung shaggy and ghostly over the pale sleeping swans and the cool gleaming lake. "Last one in's a sack of potatoes!"

RÓISÍN AND RASMUS gave the restaurant a miss. The day had been full enough and the little studio was booked for the interview tomorrow. It was going to be strange, she thought, to switch back to professional when they'd been making friends, so much more open and personal than you'd expect people to be in an interview, and so quickly, on top of the oddness of the friend-making being all on email, so at a kind of distance. And them only really meeting properly today. And when he sang for her. Plus the oddness that none of it seemed odd to him at all. *I'm going to have to find a balance here.*

The Tube was crowded and conversation was stilted. Back at the flat, waiting for a Deliveroo (Thai green chicken curry, jasmine rice, stir-fried green vegetables), she showed him the Instagram post on her phone. He looked at it, and at the comments, and murmured, "Oh, Vienna," and she laughed, because her mum used to say that too, when things Meant Nothing to Her. He liked her bookshelves; she liked his jacket, but only to be polite really because it was a perfectly normal jacket, she just wanted to like something back and the best option was his clothes as she couldn't keep going on about how great the show had been. Of course there was his guitar, too, but that would look like fishing.

While they ate they talked about song lyrics; so without any fishing at all he sang her a new song he'd been working on; she was so pleased with this that she made him hot chocolate with real chocolate. He was so skinny. They talked about loss. How it messes with your concentration; how odd it is that really good jokes can appear while you're going crazy with grief; sleeplessness; madly realistic dreams; Chet Baker versus Ben Webster; Ella Fitzgerald versus Cosey Fanni Tutti; what would happen if you took alcohol out of Western culture; why Hemingway isn't all that; how confused the headline writers were about having to describe a woman without having a hair color to define her by; the way people often assume that if you don't hold one current polarized opinion then you must by default hold the polarized opinion which is currently held to be its opposite; and how Rasmus couldn't swim. He spoke of Jay fourteen times, she of Nico twelve.

Rasmus lay awake long into the night on the sofa, his feet dangling off the end. Róisín slept better than she had for months. In the morning he was up making pancakes, and Róisín was amazed to learn that you couldn't get maple syrup in the Outer Hebrides.

"I'm intrigued as to why you're doing this interview," she said to him. "And why they're paying for all this. Are you signing with them?"

He stared at the frying pan. "Is this the interview starting?" he said, with a little smile.

"No, no!" she said. "I'm not filming!" She held her hands up and out: innocent, unarmed.

"I don't know yet," he said. "They've approached me. But I mustn't do anything I can't undo. In theory this is all in support of the Capos' anniversary, from their point of view. You know—marketing, history, and so forth. And I suppose it's part of their courtship of me."

"Exciting?" she said.

He didn't know.

Then she went to work, and she went in a strange mood. Something had become apparent: *there are other men in the world, living men, and one at least of them is kind and interesting and handsome and lovely. And talented. And I can talk to him. That's just a fact, and I've just been given proof.* There was something very comforting about it.

RASMUS STAYED IN her flat awhile after she left. He saw by daylight and alone her pretty cushions, her colorful clothes hanging on the rack, the fruit in the bowl, the bin full of tissues. Fairy lights along the shelf, and a rubber duck in the kitchen sink. Photos. *That'll be him*, he thought, looking at a dark, smiling man beside a little Róisín with long curly hair and a jacket cinched in at the waist. There was something saucy about her figure. He blinked. They were in a garden of some kind; it looked formal. A wedding maybe. Another where Nico was in his paramedic uniform, with a hairnet. *Respect*, thought Rasmus.

Rasmus hadn't made a new friend for ten years. He hadn't needed friends. Friendship is serious. Once someone is your friend you have a responsibility.

He folded the duvet and straightened the cushions on the sofa, then lay back on them, and wondered what on earth he was going to do.

"What do you think, Jay?" he murmured. "Do you like her?" But Jay wasn't there.

20

Alchemy

JULY
London

"I WON'T BE in the film," Róisín said, as they went in through the swing doors, and along the gray corridor to the studio. "The way we do it, I'll be edited out, so could you phrase your answers in full sentences, as if you've not been asked the question?"

"No," he said.

Eh?

Then, "Sorry, that sounds abrupt. But no, I can't."

"Oh. Ah—why not? It's quite a normal way of—"

"Because I wouldn't be saying these things unless I'd been asked."

Fair enough. In a way . . .

"Everyone will know you've been asked," she said.

"Will they?"

"Most people who watch something like this will know, they're people who will—"

"I'm quite interested in the other people, the people who won't," he said.

She was perplexed.

"Anyway, you should be in it," he said. "It's better if it's a conversation, isn't it?"

Róisín said: "Is it?"

There was a pause. Quite a long one.

"Of course it is," he said. "It's more honest, I'll be more relaxed, it won't sound artificial. There's no camera on now, is there?"

"No," she said. "Of course not."

He was thinking. She watched him. She positioned him and arranged the lighting in a way that would catch the silver of his eyes without shining in them.

"It's lucky we didn't meet today for the first time," he said, "because you'd be thinking I'm very uncooperative and prickly. And you'd be right. I would be. Even pricklier, if I didn't trust you." He looked up at her.

Did he just say he trusts me? I think he did. He doesn't trust people much, but he trusts me.

"And I'm being bad enough as it is," he said. "Sorry about that. We just have to have different hats on, don't we? Professional hats. I was wondering if that would seem dishonest, but I think it'll be okay."

"Okay," she said. She did not want to make him jumpy. *Work with what you have.* "Professional hat," she said, and tip-tilted an imaginary brim so it came down over one eye.

"Suits you," he said. "I like the dashing feather."

THE LITTLE STUDIO was as anonymous as a place could be, from the gray carpet to the little water cooler to the ugly desktops to the low ceiling. The brief had said to keep the surroundings as non-specific as possible, so the footage could not clash with whatever in the end they wanted to do with it. It wasn't what she would have chosen.

"So," she asked, from just behind and just above the camera, two lists of questions on the table beside her, her own and the one sent from on high. "Give me some level. What did you have for breakfast?"

"Delicious pancakes," he said. "I stayed at a friend's last night, so that was my offering as a not-too-terrible guest."

"Great," she said. "I didn't think you'd be needing mic technique help. Ready to go?"

He was.

First question. "So, it's been a long time since you were last on-stage, or in the public eye. What have you been doing all this time?"

"Music!" he said. "Of course. Bands, composers, history, rabbit holes, Futurism, instruments. I've learned the pedal steel. A beautiful item. I was the local choirmaster for a bit, until . . . Last week I was talking to a violinist who is on a personal mission to achieve the longest, slowest bow stroke ever recorded. I've learned to read and write music; I've learned orchestration. I'm experimenting with replacing traditional instruments in classical music with electronically manipulated natural or mechanical sounds."

"Really?" she said. "How does that work?"

"Okay—ah, I haven't talked about this much. Bear with me."

He paused for thought. Quite a long pause, enlivened by the fact she could see thoughts chasing each other across his face. "I acquired a Fairlight a few years ago," he said. "Any sound, once it's recorded, is electronic noise, and can be manipulated. So, who decides what is a musical instrument, and what is just a thing making a noise? Do you know about Luigi Russolo, and his noise machines? Kind of clockwork techno geek, Italian, Futurist, 1910s and '20s—Fascist, which is a shame, but that's another story. He wrote a concerto for factory siren and steam whistles, and also made these Noise Machines, on wheels, and rolled them round the streets. They look like boxes with funnels sticking out. He called it 'expanded polyphony.' None have survived, though people have re-created them. But the point is, the question still stands: where's the line between music and noise?"

She watched him and thought, *no, I cannot stop him and ask him to reframe. The rate he's talking. It's fine. I'll be able to edit. Maybe.*

"Who decides?" he was saying. "What's the overlap? So, in order not to frighten people off—not that anyone's heard any—rather than compose my own weirdo music, for now, I've been taking pieces that people know, using their original orchestration, and re-performing them, on non-instrument noises. Cover versions, in a way. For example, take a solo piece: one of the Bach cello suites, for example, something very well-known and much loved. Instead of a cello, can I play it on the sounds of icebergs creaking and cracking, deep underwater? Yes, I can. It sounds pretty magical, actually. I use an underwater engine sound as the drone notes. Technically it's easy. Or, say, 'The Queen of the Night' from *The Magic Flute*. I've done it in birdsong. The whole thing. Because it's second cousin to a blackbird. I'll play it for you. I made the walking bass line for 'Dido's Lament' with the engine noise of my motorbike, and I'm using wineglasses for the vocal, at the moment, which works well because of the bell-like clarity, and the variety and richness of tone, though I'm going to try a few other options. Whalesong, actually—I mean, it's a lament . . . we'll see. Or, doesn't have to be classical. I did 'Always'—the Ink Spots—you know, *I'll be loving you, always* . . . in pigeon coos. Dove doo-wop. Yes, of course the whole idea sounds whimsical, and gimmicky, and that potential is absolutely there, I can't deny it. It could so easily be ridiculous. Some of the things I've tried *have* been completely ridiculous. My priority in doing it is the same, though, as with any music. To move people. To make it beautiful. If it doesn't make people want to cry or dance or fuck, if it's not working, *as music*, drop it."

She was staring at him. All she could think was *Christ, he's lonely. Only lonely people talk this much.*

Then, *I am totally unqualified to interview him about Italian Futurist music in the 1910s. And whalesong. Is he insane?*

"Does it sound insane?" he said.

"Er," she said, and he laughed.

"Yes," he said, "well, and also you'll have noticed that I haven't tried to put any of it out . . ."

"It's not what you were doing at the recent gigs," she said.

"No, no. It's not what people want from me at the moment. It wouldn't have been right, alongside the Capos. It's not ready for performance either. And to be honest, it hasn't been uppermost in my mind the past months. It's a very intellectual pursuit, although I intend the result to be emotional, and recently of course I have been a . . . an emotional person. Sometimes you just want to sing the blues, with a guitar."

She let that sit for a moment. She did not want to go into his grief here either. She did not want to do one thing which might smack of taking advantage of the fact they had been open with each other. *Let him speak for himself. Or not.*

Which he didn't.

"Tell me how you respond to stories of your disappearance," she said, picking another question from the list.

"I never disappeared," he said. "I just haven't been where people were looking."

She waited.

"I was always findable," he said. "Just not via music press or tabloid connections. People who matter knew where I was. Me. My wife. There's what you're doing, and then there's what you present. I was doing plenty, I just wasn't presenting for a while."

"Even though there were rumors that you were dead?"

"To be honest, I wasn't looking at the kind of places where people might have been saying that."

"You weren't googling yourself?" She meant it almost as a joke, but he didn't laugh.

"Like most people," he said, "I had some trouble earlier in life working out who I was. So I don't need strangers telling me things about myself, telling me who I am and what I'm doing and why. I need to hold on, if you know what I mean."

"Is that part of why you went away—retreated from public life?"

Long pause.

He was really very at home with silence.

"I retreated because I had no choice," he said after a while. "I couldn't stand up. I was for a while both broken, literally, my bones, and also broke. It took a long time to heal. Going to live far away from attention, and from other people achieving what was not available to me, was part of it, yes. Depression. That was part of it. Self-preservation."

Such a full stop after that word. Such a loud, silent "Don't ask more."

She took the hint. "So are you presenting now?" she asked. "I mean you speak so openly about awkwardness and difficulty in your life, and yet onstage you do seem so very competent and confident . . ."

"Onstage I know what I'm doing," he said mildly.

"So do you not offstage?" she said.

And bit her tongue.

He paused. Turned to camera. "Look at this beautiful woman," he said, gazing down the lens. "Asking me these things. What's a man to do?"

She looked pleadingly at him. *Sorry*, she mouthed. *Beautiful!* she thought.

"Tempted to turn the camera on *her*," he said, his eyes moving back to her.

She swallowed. Blinked. Realized she was blinking away a tear.

"So will you be—are you starting to present again, now?" she asked.

"Not yet," he said. "But I will. Those gigs were me telling myself that I will again."

The light seemed to have changed on his face, though it couldn't have. She wondered. Was it that the light had gone out of his face?

He's delicate, she thought. *It's been a long time. He's not . . . Safe? Steady? As tough as he looks?*

Or is that me?

"The next thing is going to be a fairly straightforward, old-school album," he said with a little smile. He seemed to have gathered himself. "Nothing too frightening. Proper instruments. Ones people have heard of."

"The songs you performed?"

"Yes. My late wife was very involved in my more old-school music. We wrote together. Shared credits. My more technical stuff, not so much. She was a *much* better singer than me. She had that gift of instantaneous harmonizing, that you learn in church, almost by instinct it seems, but it's practice and familiarity, from childhood. Not just parallel thirds." He stopped and smiled. "She loved to sing with other people. That was her thrill: where the harmony takes flight and the voices entwine and become more than the sum of their parts. Where the alchemy kicks in. Plus she was good at sharpening a lyric. So this next album is for her. To tell her ghost how fucking heartbroken I am. In case it hasn't noticed."

Róisín breathed carefully.

"Do you believe in ghosts?" she asked, as much to cover her own emotion as for any other reason.

"Is that on your list of questions?" he asked, looking up.

"No."

"Then it's for another time," he said, and paused. Then: "No, of course I don't believe in ghosts, but other people do and I believe in other people. So I'm not going to be making declarations."

Fair enough.

"Another from the list, then," she said. "How did you start out?"

"Really? Everybody knows where to find this if they're interested, don't they?"

She didn't say anything. It seemed to be going wrong again, and she didn't know why, and she was paddling, trying to find some way to steer it back. He gave a little huff of breath.

"George and I went to the same school," he said. "I was in care at the time. My mother wasn't an unkind woman but neither was she competent. George's dad was landlord of the pub, and they had a piano, an old upright left over from sing-along days, you know, 'Oh, no, what a rotten song, what a rotten song, what a rotten song . . .' I was a little chancer back then and if I saw an opportunity, I'd grab it. So George and I formed the band. Used the school kit as well. We had a malleable music teacher, back when there were music teachers in schools: Mr. Russell. Nice guy. Very much into the Grateful Dead and out-of-hours spliff-smoking."

"You don't mention your father," she said, and could've kicked herself, because he hadn't last night either, and he'd have his reasons. *Stop thinking about last night. He's a stranger; this is a job.*

Another pause.

Damn.

"All the clichés," he said eventually.

A beat of time.

She left it. *I mean, it says it all.* Then: "Do you recall your first gig?"

"George's sixteenth birthday party," he said. "We played in the pub car park, on extension leads out the window. Cole—the bass player—took all his clothes off. Someone called the police."

She smiled. He poured himself some water.

"So what's your next plan?"

"I need to move. Find a place to live. I've been made some offers, work offers, that I need to think about carefully. In this period of bereavement, apparently, I'm to do nothing I can't go back on." He glanced up at her again, and she felt rewarded. Forgiven, maybe. *Fuck, this is hard work.*

"But for myself, I want to do right by these songs for my wife. I don't want to hang around too long with them, over-polishing them and making them sweet for easy consumption. When things get honed too much they're not true anymore. If they come out a bit rough, that's good. Grief *is* rough. The past few years have been about suffering and striving and caring and learning and grieving; now it's time to produce. Like one of those ten-thousand-year-old cacti that flower once a century. That's me now."

"So will that be you done for another hundred years then?"

"Oh no. I do want some of the reorchestration project to end up releasable. What can I say—it's a long-term project. It's very solitary and studio based, though. I have a technical pal in Berlin who helps me out as my skills are not top of the range, and they really need to be—but he's even more antisocial than me. And yes, in the meantime I do find I want to work with actual musicians. I think it's just loneliness. My wife and I were the band. So there's professional loneliness, on top of the personal. So yeah, lots of plans. I'd like to do film scores, for art films by young people. Maybe Hollywood blockbusters, if they'd like me. I like the way sound design has developed in cinema. I just have a feeling I'm going to want to get out there and collaborate."

"And do you have any immediate plans for that?"

"Not yet. Perhaps in the new year. But you know, it just depends on what comes to you. I want to write songs for other people to sing. My singing is idiosyncratic rather than any 'good.' So much of singing is personality and style. I'd like to write songs for other characters than me to sing. Go with that storytelling aspect. For women, really. I love what female voices can do."

"Will the association with the Capos help you or hinder you, do you think?"

"Christ, is that you or the record company? What do they want me to say?" He stopped. Laughed.

"It's them," she said, and he gave an almost invisible little twist of the mouth.

"Yeah, um," he said. "Okay. For one, you wouldn't be interviewing me now if it wasn't for that association. Two, I cut my teeth with the Capos, learned to play, and to write, with and for them. Plus the success that we had has given me a financial buffer, which I have appreciated, and an automatic place in the public eye, which in these venal times is useful if you want to get anything out there."

He looked straight to camera, and his message to her was clear: *Less of that shit, please.* So the next question was a tricky development. She was pretty sure that he would not want to tell the truth, that he wouldn't lie, and that he wouldn't make up a sugarcoated version for posterity. She stopped the filming.

"This is not me," she said. "Feather hat or not. And I'm sorry if it's a scab you don't want to pick. But it's there."

"Fire away," he said.

Okay. She started filming again. Gave it a second, just on his face.

"What really happened when you left the band?"

He grinned, glanced down, and back up.

"I was knocked down by a yellow cab in New York," he said. "And my back broke. The band had commitments they had to fulfill, so they got another guitarist in and fulfilled them."

She left a gap to see if he had more to say.

He didn't.

"No hard feelings?" she prompted.

Pause.

"Hard feelings are not the point," he said.

She returned to her list. "How did you learn the guitar?"

"My father taught me. He was Argentine, so it was quite a specific style. Do you know *chamamé*? The Corrientes Polka?" She did not. "It's a northern Argentine folk music. Spanish guitar, accordion, and violin. I'll play you some. Oops, wrong hat. You may have to cut that as well."

She wondered what else he was going to want her to cut. Searched for an innocent question. Tried not to look as if she was searching for an innocent question.

"Also, most of it's really terrible. *Muy folklórico,*" he said.

"You speak Spanish?" she said, surprised, and then wondering why.

"Come on," he said. "That's not on your list. Back to the tonic. Back to C."

She blinked.

"The tonic," he said. "First note of the diatonic scale. Where it all starts, and to which it returns, after japesing around with your enharmonic semi-diminished Cb7ths, and your microtonal clusters."

Her next question seemed quite apposite after that.

"Would you call yourself a geek?" she blurted.

"Oh God, yes," he said. "I'm geeky about the purity of the Fairlight sounds—because of course a Fairlight is now itself a traditional or historic instrument, so I can be as purist about that as a violinist could be about their Stradivarius or their Tourte bows, or about vinyl over digital or whatever floats your boat. You can be geeky about anything if you want to be. Well, you must know that. Do you get geeky about cameras?"

"I do," she said with a smile down at her—or rather the company's—PXW-FS7 II 4K.

"I'm *very* geeky about my Mellotron." He glanced at her. "Mellotrons. I have an M4000D and an original MkII with the replaceable tape-frames. But you don't want to talk about that, do you? I mean, because if you do, you know there are entire online forums who would worship you as a goddess?"

"I don't qualify," she said. "Sorry."

"Oh well," he said. "How about Omnichords?"

She shook her head. "I don't know what that is."

"It's a very sweet thing," he said. "A kind of Japanese electronic autoharp from the early '80s. Makes a sound like feathery rainbows."

She smiled willingly.

"Where were we then?" he asked. "Oh yes, my father."

Another long pause.

"It takes your whole life," he said at last, "to work out what your parents gave you." His eyes flickered. "And what they didn't . . . Listen," he said, "are we done?"

"Sure," she said. "Not everything they wanted, no, but enough for now and I'll see if it'll satisfy them."

"Thank you," he said. "Listen, can we never do this again? I don't like having to be defended when I'm talking to you."

"Ah," she said. "Um."

Eggshells, she thought. *Minefields.*

Professional.

Right.

THE RUSHES OF the concert had come in. After he left, she set them up and watched: Rasmus from this angle; from that angle. The clarity in his face.

Then when she got home that night, she found a note:

That was the longest conversation I've had since she died.
Maybe even the only conversation. I refer to the conversation
last night; as I write this, we haven't yet had the conversation of
this afternoon, though by the time you read it, we will have.
Perhaps it was even longer. But with an audience, so, you know,
different.

21

Don't Remind Me

JULY
London

AFTER THE GIG, after the swim in the park, late in the evening, Nico pointed out that he couldn't go back to his flat.

"You don't have a flat," Jay said. "You're dead."

"Don't remind me," he said, and they laughed.

Home, they both thought, and the word didn't seem to belong to them.

"Well, I can't go to Róisín's," he went on. "With Rasmus staying there."

It was unspoken between them how much they needed somewhere to be. When you belong nowhere, or are stuck in between, when you're always in the wrong place, when nobody hears you, or sees you, you can get very tired.

"Some ghosts have buildings they never leave, don't they?" Jay said. "I mean, that's the classic thing. A haunted house."

"Scene of the death, usually," said Nico. "Where they were murdered, and their spirit is stuck."

"Do you believe in ghosts?" she said.

"No."

"Did you ever read up on ghosts?" she asked. "Were you into any of that?"

"Of course not," he said. "Why would I?"

"So do you know anything about what we are now? Because I don't."

"I know we're not tricks played by Victorian photographers, or ladies in fur collars in 1930s suburban villas."

"So what *are* we?"

"Big question," he said.

"We weren't murdered," she said. "Why can't we leave?"

"I have thought about this so much," he said. "Why I of all people have been given this blessing."

Jay said nothing. *Blessing?*

"What are ghosts for?" she asked, staring across the wide lawn toward the Round Pond.

"For vengeance?" he said. "To put something right that was wrong."

"Those murdered girls in ballads, who appear to their mothers and accuse their sweethearts," Jay said. "Maria Marten in the Red Barn. But we weren't murdered. Are you bent on ghoulish vengeance of some other kind?"

"Not an enemy in the world," he said.

"What else?" she said.

"There's a ghost army on horseback in Crete." They'd just come to *Physical Energy*, the huge bronze of the horse, high up on its pedestal, with the rider shading his eyes with his hand. "It's rather weather dependent," Nico said. "Gallops along under a mountain on the anniversary of some battle against the Turks."

"But why? To remind people?"

"I suppose. Not wanting what you died for to be forgotten. Fat chance!" he said. "In Greece, home of the long, long memory."

"What else?"

"Weird energies, psycho teenage girls—sorry, yeah, *troubled*—tormented maidservants, murdered travelers . . . because something is unfinished . . ." he said. "We do have zombie vampires in Greece—*vrykolakas*."

"What do they do?"

"They're just bastards, I think."

"It can be about protecting those left behind, too," she said. "Comforting them. Guiding them across quicksand . . ."

"Because they haven't been buried properly, or with the right rites, and they can't go where they're meant to go . . ." he said.

"Oh yes—and then if someone does do the rites for them, pays for the funeral or something, they come back as a ghost and help them. The grateful dead—"

"Is that where the band got their name?"

"I suppose," she said. They thought about that for a moment. Then:

"I really can't see Jerry Garcia and an army of Californian hippy musos leading a weary traveler through the treacherous bog with a mysterious lantern," Nico said, and Jay snorted with laughter.

In time they reached the Italian Gardens. Sleeping swans glowed like piles of snow at the edges of the formal pools; lights from the main road beyond reflecting on the dark waters, broken by foliage.

"On the island we didn't have ghosts so much as kelpies and sea monsters," she said. "A giant fairy hound on the beach of Luskentyre. We never saw it. And there's a mermaid's grave on Benbecula. She was tiny. Her body a child's, and her tail the size of a salmon's."

"Was she a ghost, though?"

They both smiled to think of a tiny mermaid ghost.

"But seriously, why aren't there more of them?" he asked. "There are so many dead people. They should be everywhere."

"Why are we calling them they?" she asked.

"Good point."

Bayswater Road glowed and rushed ahead of them.

"I think I'm saying we have to acknowledge that we can't be here," she said.

"Acknowledge reality?" he said.

"Something like that," she said.

"But we're nothing to do with reality," he said. "Scientifically we don't exist."

"Do you have times," she asked suddenly, just before they left the magic calm of the park, "when you're not here . . . when you're not really anywhere?"

"I do," he said, and stopped there on the path, the water of the fountains arching and falling, arching and falling behind them.

"Do you think that's maybe where we're meant to be?"

"Christ," he said. "No. But it might be a step on the way."

They moved onto the main road, watching cabs sail by, orange lights aglow, and couldn't think of anywhere to go. So Nico decided to visit his mother, and Jay to visit her brother.

It seemed to be morning already. Time was getting slidier.

22

Tá Mo Chroíse Briste Brúite

JULY
London

RÓISÍN DIDN'T NOTICE. You often don't notice what you
don't expect, unless it leaps out at you like a piglet on a cake stand.
Which this didn't.

The weekend after the gig, Nell came up to town, forcing her out
of bed, as usual, with mini croissants and a paper cup of café coffee.
She watched as Róisín hauled herself about, getting up. She said:
"You're strangely fat-looking, love, given how skinny you've got."

"Bog the fuck off, would you please?" Róisín responded, from
halfway into a T-shirt. Then, "What do you mean?"

"Have you taken a look at yourself?" Nell said.

Róisín looked. Down at her own body, and then in the bathroom
mirror. She saw herself overall skinnier than she'd ever been, with
none of the curvy, shapely, all-over plumpness that had been her
physicality since her teenage years. But with her waist thicker and her
stomach firmer and her breasts

hmm

different.

She thought about how tired she'd been, and how she'd felt faint at the Albert Hall. And she thought about her periods. She wasn't an especially organized person in that area.

Have I had a period since he died?

A double fan of sunlight and shade, of hope and fear, of possibility, was opening slowly across her mind. A cloud parting. Or maybe drawing in . . .

Could two such things happen on one day? Life and death?

They'd had sex that morning, that lazy, unexpectedly sunny, day-off morning. She counted back, thought about the days and weeks before his death. They'd been back to using condoms because she'd grown so bored with the fertility mapping and revolted against having her hormones messed with the whole time and *God, the IUD, no thanks.* She remembered the exact time. The last time. That morning.

Had she had a period since?

Actually, no. She'd read somewhere that shock could do that. Grief.

"Come on," Nell said. "Chemist."

"No," said Róisín. "I'll be needing a cup of tea first, and a sit-down." *Just a moment to stare this possibility in the eye.*

The thing I wanted so much. Now a possibility. And him not here for it.

Nell made the cup of tea. "Will I put sugar in it?" she asked, and Róisín laughed. "It's not that kind of shock," she said.

"You don't know what kind of shock it is yet," Nell pointed out.

"I do not," said Róisín.

THE WALKING DOWN the street to the chemist became a little unreal. She bought two tests, and back at the flat retreated into the bathroom. She peed on the first stick, and lo.

"What's going on in there?" Nell called from the other side of the door. "For God's sake, girl, you're driving me mad out here."

"You just hold your horses," said Róisín. "I'll be out in a bit."

"You must have finished the peeing bit at least."

"Shut up."

So she peed on the second, and oh. She looked at her belly.

As soon as the idea occurred, the reality became obvious. She put her hand to it and—there it was. *Jesus fuck, hello in there.*

Hi yourself, she felt the baby say, and she had to sit down on the loo.

Oh sweet Jesus, my little pal . . .

Nico. Nico.

When she came out Nell took one look at her face and yelled and shrieked like a banshee. "I knew it I knew it I didn't say a word but Holy Mary Mother of God I knew it!"

NELL WANTED TO stay over, to talk and marvel and be there.

"I love you," Róisín said. "Go home."

A RESTLESS DREAMING night, and she woke early, her heart shrunk, her strength gone, her mind dim.

I mean . . .

She didn't seem entirely able to get out of bed, so she stayed there. It wasn't a physical thing. It was a physical manifestation of a mental thing. Which was itself the result of a physical thing. She hadn't felt so terrified for . . .

Oh, not that long really.

Outdoors was too much. Company was too much. She kept her eyes closed and she curled her feet round each other for warmth in the bed. *What have I done what have I done what has been done to me?*

She lay in the tangled sheets and fretted about how to word her email to the office saying she wasn't coming in today *or ever, I mean why?* And about *what a sloven, to stay in bed. And not answer the phone.* And about a host of other things that couldn't matter less.

An old song was haunting her, one of her mother's: scraps of the words came back to her in Irish, with their heavy, heart-bruising, lilting melody, a waltz like waves lapping on a beach, the absolute inevitability of it all:

> *Tá mo chroíse*
> *briste brúite*
> *Is tric na deora*
> *Ó mo shúile . . .*
>
> *Fhir a' bháta*
> *'s ná hóró eile*
> *Fhir a' bháta*
> *'s ná hóró eile*
> *Fhir a' bháta*
> *'s ná hóró eile . . .*
> Ten thousand blessings where'er you be . . .
>
> Oh my boatman,
> and no other,
> oh my boatman

When she'd first sung it as a girl, the words had meant little to her: *Her belt is lifting, not for the fiddler, nor for the harp-player, but for her boatman, and no other . . . And if he doesn't return, it's sorry she'll be.*

Well, yes she will, because she loves him.

Because she's pregnant and they're not married and it was Then so she will be cast out and scorned and all alone. With her baby . . .

But Róisín, you're not living Then. You're not dependent on the gold ring that he promised you . . . you don't need the respectability . . . You're not a white swan, torn and bleeding, crying your death song in the lough meadow . . .

The melody washed on.

And the sun slid across the sky, all the noises of summer racketing away in the distance. Children going to school. Children coming back from school. Ice cream van chimes. "Greensleeves"—*another sad love song. But women don't die and leave men pregnant. Though we must have left plenty with babes in arms, dying in childbirth . . . if they were there to take them in arms.* Her mind wandered to the killeens, the little graveyards for the stillborn and the unbaptized. *That one by the bridge, on the marshy island surrounded by reeds, tiny headstones, and the whole place flooded in spring . . . little daffodils midstream, their heads bobbing . . . In Galway was it?*

Neighbors chatting. Traffic. Radios from open car windows.

Her windows were closed.

Oh my boatman, and no other . . .

Grief again, in all its insidious, invidious, inevitable, never-ending coolth. *Fall before me, humans. I'm your king.*

They'd bury shipwreck victims in the killeens too. And the suicides, and the insane.

Nico said that once: "Shipwrecked on your thighs . . ."

Who's shipwrecked now?

Around nine in the evening she realized something. She'd been dozing, and it arrived. *I'm feeling bereaved again because I am bereaved again. Something else has died, something I didn't know existed, and that never had an opportunity to exist—but it was there: Nico and me and our baby. That little family. It lived for a few hours. It lay that morning in our bed; it walked down the road in the February sun, and it sat round a pub table laughing its head off at stupid puns.*

She saw it, quickly and cruelly: that table, them, a buggy parked up, and a plump little dark-headed toddler on Nico's lap, clapping its fat hands on his cheeks.

That family has died. Nico's life as a father has died.

He was a father. That father died.

I didn't know that before.

In the small hours, another thought: a thought more bitter, more individual. This was not wife or girlfriend or mother thinking. This was her own lone self, a voice she didn't often hear, because there was rarely the silence to hear it.

If nothing else, it said, *I was to have been free. Freedom was one thing he left me that was of any use. A gift that men who leave can give women. A new start. A new life.*

And now I am not to be free after all. Here is this other new life, which I must now honor above my own. I am again and immediately pressed into service. My own new life has just shriveled on the branch.

Not my work. Not the fiddler, or the harp player.

Double bereavement.

By the following morning, the thoughts of the night were beginning to come to terms, inside her, because that is what happens with women. Let women sleep, and all will be dealt with. She woke like the sky after a storm: clear, clean, and ragged.

THE DOCTOR SAID, "Congratulations!" and "Here's your certificate," and "Just in time to go for your scan." And the scan was perfect, lovely, a sweet little typical healthy scan, about four and a half months, better late than never, your baby is the size of an avocado.

A little tiny baby the size of an avocado inside me. The size of an avocado. That's sweet. She imagined it curled up and snoozing in its leathery green coracle.

She tried out putting her hand to the upper slope of her buttock, the traditional pregnant-lady-supporting-my-back move. It felt good. She moved her hips from side to side. It made her giggle. It made her cry.

23

∎

Not Absolutely Biblical

JULY

Dear Róisín,

Thank you for letting me stay. It turned out to be exactly how I would have wanted it to be.

I'm back in Scotland now. George has been sending me reviews. Do you know any managers? It seems I might need one, or at least someone to tell people to go away.

with best wishes,
Rasmus.

———————————————————————

Dear Rasmus,

It was great to have you.

Something very strange and brilliant has happened. I almost
wrote "come to pass" but though it is a miracle it's not entirely
and absolutely biblical so I'd probably better be avoiding
terminology of that kind. Right. Well . . . much to my own
surprise, I'm pregnant. With a baby! I'm kind of speechless
(only of course I'm not, you know, you've met me) and I am
incredibly happy and in a state of shock, really, because first
your world gets turned upside down and then it gets turned
upside down again, but not back to where it was before, to
right side up, but to *another* upside down altogether, like
there's a new dimension of upside-down-ness been specially
invented, or you're in a Bourne movie or something . . . I don't
know why I said that as I've never seen a Bourne movie in my
life . . . is that even what they're called? Is it the Bourne
something . . . Strategy? Compendium? Or something?
Anyway I don't know why I'm asking you. So, this definitely
counts as something which can't be undone, doesn't it? I'll be
self-obsessed for a while, and then obsessed with the baby,
and I daresay I'll be no fun at all for about six or seven years,
maybe 25 . . . and you'll probably not want to be my friend
what with all the dullness. But I think I'll need you as a pal
because being hauled suddenly into motherland doesn't
mean I'm not still a widow; I'm hardly used to being a widow
at all, and now this.

Apparently it's the size of an avocado. Next week it'll be a
pomegranate, though that depends on the size of the
pomegranate. There's a website with a list. I'm kind of sad
that I missed it being a kumquat. And a pomegranate seed.
And a peppercorn! I don't suppose anybody knows when it's
the size of a poppyseed. Imagine, a peppercorn. Mostly

people are saying it's a miracle, and it is, but Rasmus, I feel strange.

Róisín

PS The rushes are looking great. I've not told them yet at work.

PPS I put that in a feathery font so you can see I've my feathered professional hat on for it. Might help with the boundaries?

_____

Dear Róisín,

This is the most wonderful strange good news! It gave me shivers.

Are you prepared to give it the middle name of Posthumus/ Posthuma as the ancient Romans would have? And indeed Ghanaians do. I can't recall the name they use but I'll look it up.

Babies aren't dull, I don't think. Just very young.

Are your hundreds of sisters on hand to help you and look after you?

This is really very magnificent. I'm going to think about it. What comes after pomegranate?

from Rasmus.

PS Thank you for the font. I appreciate it.

Dear Rasmus,

Yes, they are. Nell's here now and the rest are coming to London in shifts from all the places they live in order to boss me, comfort me, criticize me, congratulate me, find me wanting, and tell me how much they love me. It's going to be great and possibly more tiring than being pregnant itself. Do you have family? You didn't say much about that the other night.

All the best
Róisín

PS Artichoke. It's like an Ottolenghi recipe.

Dear Róisín,

I don't, no. Obviously I must have some, somewhere, and I've read that we can only look back four generations before we're all related to each other, but in practice no, not one. Two dead parents, each an only child. Your baby will have a thousand cousins. What do Nico's family say?

Rasmus.

Dear Rasmus

They don't know yet. I imagine they'll swamp me too, so I am trying to spread the height of the emotional tide at any given time, if you see what I mean. Marina, his mum, is away at the moment. I'll go and see her when she's back. Face-to-face is best. She'll want to steal the baby and I'll have to let her, a bit. I know I'll want and need all the help everybody has to offer but to be honest I just want to be alone now it turns out I have someone INSIDE ME. How is the island? How are you?

Róisín

Dear Róisín,

I too am swamped, in a way. Both swamped and drained. I can't stay here. Even I know that a man my age living alone up here in grief will just waste away and start smelling funny.

Did I tell you about when Jay saved my life? I know I didn't.

During a period soon after her death, when I wasn't eating and got quite unwell, she came to me in various dreams and appearances. There was a crisis when I ended up in hospital. She was there. She instructed me quite clearly to get a grip, and comforted me. That's explainable as mental and emotional aspects of me and my grief. My pal Dougie called the ambulance. He was absolutely certain that Jay told him to go to my aid. It's true there was no reason for him to come by. He'd been mid weightlifting, and was still in his gym kit. I can't explain why he'd say that, though. People respond so oddly to death. And Jay was popular.

That apart, I promised her I would live, and I cannot live here.

There is also a woman I used to know threatening to come and stay, to "look after" me, and that must not happen.

This is a long-winded way of telling you that the Capos' record
company want me to make an album of the new songs. They're
offering me various moons; I am making do with three months in
a rather beautiful recording studio in France, in a long golden
building with tall windows and gray shutters and ilex trees. It's
by the sea. They have a Mellotron.

So I'm going to France, taking a few days in London on my way
to sign things. May I stay with you? I will do my own sheets and
buy you dinner and make tea. I have a nice tweed cushion here
I could bring for you to put your feet on. What else would
you like?

I checked with my brother-in-law—well, with his wife—and
the Ghanaian name for a child born after their father's death
is Anto. Literally: they didn't meet. There's also a name
meaning "we don't want you," but you won't be needing
that.

Rasmus.

Dear Rasmus,

Re France: Lord that sounds like heaven. It's wonderful. New
territories are important. Places they never were. I'm so glad
you're saying yes and not no.

Re staying: Yes.

Re cushion: Thank you.

Re the woman: Oh dear.

Re Jay:

Listen.

I've heard Nico's voice. And I wasn't even sick. I've woken knowing for a fact I was in his arms. Forgive me, but tell me— was it real to you? I want to talk to you about this but I've weighed it up and I think I'm less embarrassed writing to you about it so . . . was the physicality of her like a real person? I mean, in a dream you usually know it's a dream, if you get to think about it at all. But, and this is the thing: I'd a night early on after his death when Nico was with me in such a real way I mean he absolutely was with me. Sorry I'm not being clear. I've had moments when he was there. He touched the back of my neck during the funeral. I was dancing one night in the kitchen and he took my hand, and twirled me, and held me tight. Grief makes lunatics of us, doesn't it? TBH I don't know or care if ghosts are real or if I was hysterical hallucinating or half asleep, or if love sets up some kind of memory-loop in the nervous system which feels things or feelings that we knew so well even after they are gone . . . or what. It's real on some level. Who knows? We just have to accept it and be glad of it and acknowledge that we don't know. It may not be real scientifically or rationally but isn't it a massive part of who and what we are?

Re we don't want you: correct.

Róisín

Dear Róisín,

Everything is real. Or nothing is. I can't tell. Genuinely can't.

I'm glad you're saying yes, too.

Yours,

Rasmus.

PS The weather is terrible, even for here.

Dear Rasmus,

I've knocked the footage into shape now and I have to say we have some really lovely stuff. I am itching to send you some of it but everybody's got a huge privacy/security thing going on at the moment because somebody hacked something and put it online and now it's the end of the world as we know it, so everything's numbered and locked away in ways beyond my ken, and I don't want to get either of us in trouble. You could always put in an application to see it if you'd like to, but it has to go through what my old dad used to call the Brass Hats.

Róisín

Dear Róisín,

I don't think I want to see it yet. There's something about being observed at your work by someone else which is all right, and can be quite fruitful, in that you're reminded that you exist in the real world, and that you're making something which other people will experience and hopefully find rewarding. Observing your own self while you work, though, would bring about quite a different kind of self-awareness—self-consciousness, rather, and not one I want. I feel it might stop me in my tracks. No pun intended. Do you like puns? I don't really get them, but I know they give a lot of people great joy.

Rasmus.

PS Also it would be me watching you at work on watching me at work . . . too meta.

Dear Rasmus,

I love puns. The worse the better. I said yes to a pre-natal yoga class. After the invisibility and ignorance I'm evolving into the galleon-of-magnificence-in-pregnancy kind, and Nell pointed out I'd missed several months' worth of planning and fussing, and she signed me up, but when I got there it turned out Nell can't read and it was actually a _parental_ yoga class, with all the dads and partners there, sitting back to back with the mothers, elbows linked and so forth, holding on to them like they were one benign creature. So I left. At every stage of the new pregnancy people are unadulteratedly delighted for me. It feels mean to rain on their parade. I've months' worth of experience of saying "he died," but it seems just rude to keep on saying it to innocent midwives and yoga teachers and girls working in baby-clothes shops. The look on their faces! So I'm thinking to hold back on preparations. After all, people can just drop dead.

So it may be wiser. But Holy Christ what a reason to stay
alive! What a glory clutched from the jaws of death! I can't
keep up . . . One moment I'm a normal gal with a boyfriend who's
not well organized in the marriage and baby department, the
next I'm a brave young widow in full grief, and now I'm a
single mother-to-be all of a sudden. Like God just up and
swapped Nico for a child. Like . . . like nothing I can imagine,
to tell the truth. Like nothing in this world I ever knew.
How can I carry death in one half of my heart and birth in
the other?

Róisín

Dear Róisín,

You're a human being and that's your job. Well done. Keep
it up.

Think about how we all know we're going to die, and yet we
manage to put the information away and carry on enjoying cups
of coffee, talking to our friends, bearing children, brushing our
teeth, buying premium bonds, as if Death weren't going to
extinguish every little pleasure, and might do it at any moment.
Jay was fond of a gloomy Bible quote: "Take ye heed, watch and
pray, for ye know not when the hour is." It's the kind of thing little
seventeenth-century girls might have been made to embroider
in crimson thread on a linen sampler, to scare them into
obedience and good behavior. (Those things frighten me, by the
way. Every little stitch made in training for a lifetime of servitude
and terror.) But we don't do it, do we? I've never taken heed or
watched and prayed in my life. At least not until Death was

already in the room, with his hand at Jay's throat, and then of course I couldn't stop.

You're just living as a fully formed human has to. Like a preacher with Love and Hate tattooed on his knuckles.

Yours,
Rasmus.

Dear Rasmus,

It's been a while since I was in touch, but I wanted to let you know that the footage from the Albert Hall came out really well, and that with that and the Bush Hall and interview footage, and archive film of the band, we have pulled together an excellent collection of material to be the basis of a documentary film. The next step will be the record company and of course you deciding the brief. Going by what you said earlier, I'm not sending you any links at the minute, but if you do change your mind there's plenty for you to see.

With best wishes,
Róisín Kennedy

Dear Róisín,

Thanks for the update about the filming. No doubt we'll hear news at some stage.

With best wishes,
Rasmus.

Dear Rasmus,

Nico was a tattooist. He was very good. Though personally I
can't stand the things. At least not on me. I like them on other
people. He said I'd the perfect skin for it, though, and we had
jokes enough about what I would have if I ever did have one,
which of course I never would. His name across my heart—he
didn't like that, said he didn't want to read his own name on me
as if I were a school sock. He only wanted to cover me with
flowers, basically. I said the only one I'd have would be the
knuckles, but with Love and Love. You're right about samplers.
Dead creepy. You could have them on a TV show with the young
ones singing ring-a-ring-a-rosie in creepy high voices.

I told my mother today. She cried and cried and cried and cried,
and said she's going to move in. She's not, but it was a kind
thought. So long as she doesn't do it. So only Nico's mum to go
now. Deep breaths for that. She's very clever, very superstitious,
and VERY emotional. I can see how torn in half I feel, but God, it's
hard to put into words how it will be for her. It'll be her own dead
son coming back, basically. Did I tell you he was an only child?

Róisín

Dear Róisín,

For once, the messenger really will be the message. She'll take
one look at you.

I love tattoos.

Rasmus.

24

~

Earthlings

AUGUST
Accra

WHAT ARE GHOSTS for what are ghosts for?
  Have I a duty to fulfill?

She needed to spend time with her life beyond Rasmus, before
Rasmus. Her flesh and blood. Her brother; her childhood, her lovely
little nieces.

At Heathrow she kept herself out of the way, hanging around in
the artificial ceilings; draped over displays in shops built like stage
sets, hanging from lighting rigs, which had become a place of safety
for her. Nobody can sit on you when you're on the ceiling. And after
all, she still had to wait for the flight to be called.

She slipped easily onto the plane; took an empty seat in first class.
Stared at the clouds, wondering again about bouncing. It took as
long to fly from London to Accra as it did to drive and boat from
Stornoway to Glasgow. But Ghanaian people were around her and
her spirits rose. Flesh of her former flesh. Voices and laughter. At
Kotoka Airport, Ghana rushed at her: pitch-dark at 7 p.m., hot,

bright, lush, familiar. For the first time in her existence, nobody was there to meet her. No gang of brothers, no bunches of flowers, nobody grabbing her luggage and dragging her to somebody's car to take her home.

No flesh to droop and complain about the heat, while simultaneously relaxing into it, slowing down, getting back the ease in the joints, the looseness of the lungs . . .

She didn't know the way to where Kwame was living now, so she just drifted to their parents' house. Nobody was there. A cousin was meant to be looking after it, but she seemed to be out. Jay lay on her mother's sofa in a manner she would never have been allowed to do in life, and stared at the fan; lay on the long chair in the garden and stared at the palms, put her feet in the pool and talked to the tricolored lizards on the white-washed concrete wall. Then on Sunday she went up early to Ridge Church: Efua would be there even if Kwame wasn't. And there she was, with the little girls. All three so chic and sweet; the girls in matching print outfits. How happily she would have swept them into her arms: one on each hip though they were much too big now, those long dangly legs in white socks, teasing them and cuddling them, pretending to eat them up.

She followed them home.

She stood behind their chairs as they ate, fufu and soup, frozen yogurt. Sat on their beds as they slept, sang to them and stroked their hair. Their little cheeks. Their insane sense of humor. The way they sang together: their lovely little-girl voices twining and climbing, finding the harmonies just as she and Kwame used to. One afternoon they were singing an old Ghanaian folk song: *Tuwe Tuwe, mamouna tuwe tuwe* . . . Then "Amazing Grace." Then new songs she didn't know.

Seeing Kwame sitting with them, playing with them, feeding them . . . Efua coming home, washing her hands, cuddling them . . .

Dance classes. Teddy bears. Nit combing. Little darlings. Her brother's future. Her photo on the shelf next to Mum and Dad and Grandma, and Efua's dead people whom she didn't know. *There I am with the dead where I belong.*

At the weekend—she assumed it was the weekend—the family went out to Mile 13 with some friends, where the beach stretched out gray-gold against the gray-gold Atlantic and the long, slow rollers curled in along the expanse, such a length, such distance, rolling in from South America. The adults set up their umbrellas and loungers and the girls played in the very shallowest waters, mere inches of ocean spreading and swirling and circling around their sprawled legs and upturned toes, and their parents' eyes returning constantly to them. The beach men were still there, moving up the sand in order: crayfish man, followed by the man with the little stove, who would cook the crayfish, followed by the sugar-bread man, and then the man with the sweet limes to squeeze over it all. Kwame in his cargo shorts, and the cold box full of Club beer, and minerals for the ladies. Lucky Dube crooning from someone's iPad. It should have been marvelous. It was marvelous. It was not marvelous. It broke her fucking heart. Right there, all of it. Unreachable.

She felt that her presence was unsettling the girls. A little hand brushed at her, in sleep, as if she were a trailing plant, or an annoying fly. A small frown on a watchful face. A shiver, as she looked over a small shoulder, admiring the untidy homework.

I'm pining, she thought. *For earthly things that are no longer mine. Earthlings.*

SHE FLEW BACK full of the faces of her nieces and thoughts of the babies she hadn't had. *Pining.*

I was busy. He wasn't well. I wasn't well.

Five times more likely to die—but no, that wasn't it. If she had been afraid, it hadn't been of that.

Of passing on sarcoidosis?

Stop it, it doesn't matter. It's done. Over.

Anyway, you don't not give someone a life just because they're going to die one day.

25

~

Don't Hurry the Journey

AUGUST
Ithaca

NICO'S MUM WASN'T at the flat in Camden Town. *Of course not. It's August.*

He found her in Ithaca, under a vine, outside Dmitri's bar on the beachside at Frikes. Dmitri was inside in the cool, giving the Wi-Fi password to some English people, including a soaking-wet woman who had apparently just swum across from a boat. The sun had already slid behind the island and the rough *ting tang ting* of distant goat bells told him they were wandering toward wherever they wanted to be when night fell. And there was his mother, drinking gin and reading the paper.

He went and sat by her.

She shot upright.

"Nico?" she said. *"Nico-mou?"*

He drew back.

"Agóri-mou, eísai edó?" She stood, her full five foot two, pushing the chair back. She was wearing one of her kaftans, and the Lalaounis ring his dad had given her. Her sandals had heels, and her hair was

perfect. *Widowed, bereaved of her son, in August, in a village, her hair is perfect.*

"My darling?" she said. *"Nico-mou?"*

She moved her head, looking.

"Here, Mama," he said, and he stepped toward her and hugged her. Hugged her and held her.

By the time Dmitri and the English people came out, she was sitting down again.

"I told you, Dmitri," she said. "I told you he wouldn't go without saying goodbye to his mother."

"Eh," Dmitri said. "Good boy. He was always a good boy."

He brought her another gin and tonic, and some little crackers on a saucer.

"I'm glad he came," he said as he returned.

"So am I," she said. "But I'm lonely again now. Come and sit with me." And Dmitri fetched himself a brandy, from the good bottle, and pulled up a chair in the last of the evening light, to drink to Nico, and to Yiannis of course, and to Marina.

Nico ran to the end of the jetty, dived in, and swam out to sea. *Salt water.*

26

Location

AUGUST
The island

THE HOUSE SAT there on its rocky knoll. No smoke. The bike
not there in the yard. Actually nothing was there. Anywhere.

Inside was empty. Proper empty, chilly with a hint of damp, even
though it was late summer, like a holiday cottage no one had opened
up that year. Empty drawers, empty bookshelves, cobwebs in the corner of the window. No piano.

Jay went through to his studio. No Mellotrons. No Omnichord.
No harmonium. No guitars.

She sat for a moment on the fireguard, the only thing in the sitting room there was to sit on.

*He's packed everything away. All that's here is the location, and sud-
denly it means nothing.*

It's not here anymore, to come back to.

Well, it's not the place that matters. It's who was in the place, at the time.

He's gone, he's taken it to bits. It's gone with him.

And where's the cat?

She knew he would have done the right thing with the cat. Dougie
would have the cat.

Maybe that's what we mean by the good old days. Back when everybody was there, the right people, all in the right place, together.

She stood and stared round at the empty walls and naked stone floor. *Well, you knew it was gonna happen . . .*

After a while, it started raining: sharp, piercing, diagonal. She knew that rain well. It could go on for days. She was about to start feeling properly dismal when Nico turned up. She was surprised to find herself so pleased to see him. *But then, he's my only friend now.*

"I wondered if you'd be here," he said.

"It's getting worse," she replied. "Isn't it?"

"Is it?" Nico said. "I don't know—"

"Moving on," she said sadly. "Look! All gone! It's so soon! Is it? I don't know *when* it is." There was a book she'd read once—no, more than once—with a castle, and at one stage there were kings and queens in the castle, and then at another it was in ruins, ivy-clad, tumbled, and had been for centuries. *What was that book . . . ?*

"Bloody lonely up here," said Nico, looking around. "Probably a bit . . . you know, haunted, for him? Memories and that?"

"Yes," she said. "I wonder what he did with my things."

She found out later that day, as they wandered round Stornoway, waiting for the flight to Glasgow, and ended up outside the charity shop. The rain was a little milder this side of the island. Dripping through them rather than piercing them.

"Oh," she said, peering in at the window. She wondered why he hadn't just taken things to the other one, which was much nearer, but then she knew why. He was respecting her privacy. He knew she wouldn't want their friends and neighbors seeing her stuff in the shop, going through it, recognizing it. There was her red raincoat. The blue silk shirt she'd never liked, but it was silk, so . . . And there—was it? Yes. Her Swiss cheese plant in the green pot.

Her Swiss cheese plant.

Well, at least he didn't kill that one . . .

Then, "My old earrings!" she squeaked. Two flat, open-centered disks made of pale blue Bakelite, hanging on a little stand. "I thought I'd lost them." She felt grounded by them, by their existence. She *had* lived. She had worn those earrings.

"Do you want them?" Nico asked.

"Sort of," she said. "But . . ."

She craned to see if she could see anything else of herself inside. She couldn't. He'd have put things into storage, she supposed. With the Mellotrons. Or perhaps he'd taken everything somewhere else. To France? Surely not. She could see the volunteer bobbing about inside, in her hairnet. *Janet, was she?*

She wondered what he'd chosen to keep. *He's allowed to get rid of things. He's gone away . . . He's not coming back.*

Or rather, he knows I'm not coming back.

Only I am back.

"I thought it would get easier," she said sadly. "Nico, how long do you think it's going to go on for?"

He stared at her sharply for a moment. "Sod this," he said, and went into the charity shop.

He returned. "I tried to nick them for you," he said. "Couldn't manage it. Obviously."

"Oh!" she said. "I mean—thank you." Then, "How was your mum?"

"Beautiful," he said. "How was your brother?"

"Alive," she said.

They stood for a while, the rain gushing down. God, there was so much of it, didn't it ever run out? And the sound of the sea, clear and rushing in the distance.

"Now what?" she said. "I'm wondering, if I just go and lie in a ditch might it all be over? If I stop doing things."

"You don't want that," he said.

"What do I want?"

"To find them?" he said.

27

❧

Tangerine
AUGUST
London

IN LONDON IT was not raining. In London there were hot ex-hausted days, worn and yellowing grass, cigarette butts, and empty crisp packets bowling down dry gutters. On the neat dried-out little lawn outside Róisín's building, in the late afternoon, Nico and Jay peered up toward the window of the flat.

"So, is she in?" Jay asked.

Nico couldn't tell. It upset him. He was longing to see her. He needed to know how she was. Jay had terrified him with her question "How long do you think it's going to go on for?" A vista was spread-ing before him: forever. Róisín living her life, her days and nights, for years. Róisín growing old, before his eyes. Him unable to be there, and unable to leave. Different types of ghost stories were entering his mind now. Tragic ones.

Or, this unnatural situation might end. Suddenly—now, *maybe!* Without him having put things in order. *Again.* The words "inexpli-cable" and "powerless" were bouncing around inside him.

And then Róisín appeared round the corner, carrying string

shopping bags, full of fruit and vegetables from the market. Apples and onions bulging.

She paused for a second, resting her hand on the back of her waist, easing herself. She was wearing a nice smocky kind of dress that Nico had always liked. Black and white, with a belt. She wasn't wearing the belt—oh yes, she was, but up under her bust. She was—

Nico stared. He frowned. A two-year-old's this-cannot-be frown. He lurched forward. Jay held up a hand to stay him.

"Hold on," she said.

"Hold on what, I mean what the—!" he exclaimed, and stood forward.

"Oh my Lord, she's pregnant," Jay murmured.

"Has she been sleeping with him?" he said.

"Nico, they've only just met."

"But she's pregnant."

"Looks like it," said Jay in wonder.

"Is it mine?" he asked idiotically.

"How could it be anyone else's?"

"I've been dead since February!"

"Nico, it takes time for a pregnancy to show."

"I know that! How pregnant is she?"

"I don't know the timing of your sex life, Nico . . ."

"Well, what does it look like? Oh my God, my mum's going to have a heart attack."

"Easily within however long it is," Jay was saying. "What, five, six months? Sure. Could be."

"Could be," he said, staring at Róisín as she struggled with the door key and the bags collapsing on the floor. He couldn't even help her in or pick up the shopping in those stupid bags, everything just rolls out the moment you put them down, and the handles don't even stick up, so you have to bend right down and she—

He couldn't do anything for her. He *mustn't* do anything. *No shocks, no loud noises.*

He raced into the road and stopped a runaway tangerine. He could at least stop a bloody piece of fruit. Couldn't take it back to her, but he could stop it. So he stopped it.

"Well, either you got her pregnant before you died, or she slept with another man during the weeks after your death," Jay said, "despite the fact she was in deep grief for you, and there is no evidence or suggestion of any man, and it would be absurdly out of character, and also you were at her side almost every moment. Yes?"

"Yes," he said.

"What she certainly isn't is pregnant by someone she's met in the past eight weeks because *it wouldn't show.* Listen, Nico. *Nico.*"

He stopped goggling.

"Let's just accept that your widow is pregnant, and let's step back to material reality. You had sex before you died, and now she's having a baby."

"She's having a baby," he repeated.

"Your baby."

"My baby," he said.

"Your baby."

"I'm going to be a dad," he said. "A father."

"You are. At least . . ."

He went very quiet. Gazed at Róisín, then turned his face very quickly to Jay, as if he were going to ask a question—but didn't.

"This changes—" he said. "I mean—"

But it didn't change anything, and he didn't know what he meant.

"She'll need money," he said.

"Nico, you're dead," Jay said carefully.

"Can I do that? Get money for her?"

"No. She has sisters and friends of her own, a bevy of living people who'll be only too happy to look after their own special widowed new young mother. Including, no doubt, your family."

"We've got to set ourselves up now, though," he said. "Her and me. It's all different now. There's a baby. We can't ignore a baby."

"Of course. Nico. Nico. But it's not your job anymore."

A strange energy was flowing through him. Rippling and glowing. "It is too," he said. "It's got to be. Or, something's got to be. Come on."

They slipped up the stairs after Róisín.

Nico started crying as they went into the flat.

"I'll leave you two together," Jay said.

JAY SAT IN the bus shelter across the way and swung her legs, thinking. *Poor guy.*

Fuck fuck fuck, she said to herself. About what, she wasn't sure. If she *had* had a baby, it would be motherless now. So.

NICO WATCHED RÓISÍN slip her shoes off, put the fruit away, flick the kettle on. He saw her glance at the washing-up, still in the sink from breakfast. Saw her check the fridge: six open jars of jam; vodka, gherkins, chutney (at least four years old), sad lettuce, a knob of butter still in its greasy gold paper, iridescent bacon which she threw in the bin. The bin was full. She glanced at the cupboard and by the look on her face he knew there were no bin bags.

He saw her glance at her laptop, choose to ignore it, and go into the bathroom. Heard her peeing, then washing her hands. Saw her come out, and sit, and close her eyes.

Can't even go and get her a curry. Can't.

Can't.

He could lie beside her though, and that night he did, and put his hand so very carefully on her belly.

It kicked him. Tiny foot or fist. Tiny elbow maybe. He saw the taut skin bulge suddenly under his hand. Did he feel it? He didn't know.

He shook. Had to turn away.

He got out of the bed and sat across from her. From them. Powerless and inexplicable. He sat all night, watching her every shift, hearing her every breath and murmur. *What are you if you're not mine? What am I if I'm not yours?*

So it was different with Róisín after that. He didn't go so close again. Something stopped him. He sat across instead of beside; watched instead of joining in. He marveled at her, at the physicality of it—which seemed ever farther away, no matter what he thought or what he wanted.

How gentle she was.

He was with her every moment. Loyal and continuous. At work, at home, in the studio, at the editing suite, to the shops, on the bus, at the Ponds and the Crouch End Lido, and into the snot-green sea at the Forty Foot swimming club when she went to Dublin to see her mum, and her mum stood on the side calling to Róisín to come on out of it, it wasn't safe, and the both of them laughing at how the gentlemen in the old days would have squawked at the idea of a big pregnant lady invading their exclusivity, and her mum telling Róisín about being in the Women's Lib demonstrations in the '70s, pregnant with Nell, when they got the club to change the rules.

He saw with clear eyes. He watched other mothers, with young children. He'd never looked at them before. He looked now.

In a smart little shop in Crouch End he looked at babygros and soft shawls. A silky little elephant. Pictured a little hand grabbing tight to the velvety trunk.

Why are we here without guidance, abandoned and alone?

There were facts here that seemed unavoidable. Truths about the reality of life. But nothing certain for him.

He felt farther away every day. Like life was squeezing him out.

28

Change Everything

AUGUST

Dear Rasmus,

I've been in Dublin with my mother. She is a lovely woman and I have no complaints about her. Can you hear the but? There's no but. But. I needed to see her because I'm pregnant and she's my mam and she gets that. She couldn't come over to see me, because I don't know. Too busy. And once I'm here, having taken the day off work to make the long weekend, and flown, and everything, she's still too busy. And busy with good important things, so I can't even have a moan about it. If she has a morning workshop with the Domestic Violence Survivors' Group, what decent daughter would complain about that? If she's the sick to visit on the Saturday afternoon, and the shopping to do, well no decent daughter would come between her and that either. On the Sunday there's Mass, and she has my sister Sorcha's children to look after, because Jim's done a bunk and Sorcha's working, so, fair enough, yup, I quite understand,

and it's lovely to see the kids, they're adorable, and learning Irish at school, and no doubt it's a great lesson for me to get to hang out with some actual children, and then she's actually arranged to see Jim on the Sunday evening, to see if there's anything to be done about getting him to come home again, which is a mighty virtuous, loving, and good thing for her to be investing her time in and I wouldn't deny that for a moment or have her not do it—although, talking of moments, she's found hardly a single one for me all weekend, despite the fact I've made a cup of tea every hour on the hour in the quiet hopes it might make her sit down for five minutes and utter the immortal words: "So how're you feeling, Róisín love?"—those immortal words so missing from my childhood and indeed the childhoods of all of us (with the right name inserted), and probably every child alive who was one of six or more. My friend Paul was one of fourteen and his father literally used to say to him "which one are you?" But what the hell, we're all grown up now and we've learned to stand on our own two feet and we don't need to be a massive pain in the hole about it any more—I mean who needs individual love and attention in life?—and anyway there's always Nell. Funny how my sisters shared out the mam duties to each other between us: Nell's my mam, Sorcha is Nell's mam, Kathleen is Sorcha's mam, and so on. The boys just slotted in wherever. There's always someone to ruffle your hair and let you cry on their shoulder. Anyway she did come swimming with me, but mostly so she could tell me I shouldn't be swimming and me in my condition. Anyway I love her. She's fine.

"So how're you feeling, Rasmus?"

Róisín

Dear Róisín,

I had to think about your question. It's not something I'm often asked. You might think it would be, given my situation, but I simply see so few people, and all these emails about the gig don't seem to be that concerned with how I am. Well, no, that's not fair. Carola is very motherly. Nice woman, and clever.

I'm physically well. I've thought long and hard about whether I'll be able to give them what they want. As you know I've been pondering your lines about "do nothing you can't undo" and "don't be hard on yourself"—and I do acknowledge that agreeing to do your first solo album months after your wife's death when you've done no official studio recordings with other people for some years might be seen as a big leap. Is signing the contract something I can't undo? Yes it is. But it's also an act of faith in myself. So, I'm asking myself how I am, too. And the answer comes: this is a great opportunity, and the work I have to do on these songs I'd rather do now than hold on to till later. We talked about this in the interview. I'm told grief calms down with time: I don't want to do this work calm. And I don't want to be manipulative—I don't want to hold it to me as something to milk for creativity. And I don't want it to last forever. My continued suffering is not, after all, a compliment to Jay, a declaration of her value in my eyes. So, I think this is the right time to do this work.

You, though—you are carrying out the most immense act of creativity known to humanity, and at a time which may not be of your choosing but is after all the only possible time.

Short answer: I've signed the contract. I got a lawyer to read it, and took Carola's advice too. She's read every contract since 1999, as I understand it. I'm feeling trepidatious but bold.

Another question is on my mind. Do you think we have to change everything about our lives because of this? I ask because we both seem to be doing it, each of us in our different way.

Rasmus.

───────────────────────────────

Dear Rasmus,

God well done with the boldness. Really, well done. You're carpe-ing the bloody diem and quite right too. I'm depleted in that department. I'd a bad night or two after I came back from Dublin, and I cried for three hours straight yesterday. I timed it. I've been too sad. Yes I know there's no "too," but you know what I mean. I don't think any fetus needs that amount of weeping going on all over it. Stress forms their little brains apparently even before they're born. I've to flood it with dopamine and serotonins and such, not salt tears. I know my family are great and I know Nico's family will be great but I've been fretting and fretting about whether I can even do this. Yes I know I'm already doing it and I've no choice. Just a sudden desertion of me by my courage. It'll come back, I know! That's my nature after all. Re the record company, now don't you know you get carte blanche in the first year of bereavement to refuse, refute, or deny anything at all? Make sure they know this. Or anyway, isn't it that if they value you as much as they obviously do, they'll bear all that in mind and take care of you? The creativity thing. Hm yes—it's different though isn't it? As you're doing your thing consciously with your brain and your heart, whereas my body has this whole project going on and it's kind of nothing to do with my conscious self—as evidenced pretty effectively let's face it by the fact that the body had actually half completed the project before I even became aware it was going on. I'd been thinking a lot in the past months too in between bouts of weeping about what the hell I was to do with my life now—work-wise, LIFE-wise—and had some thoughts, and ideas, about maybe leaving my job, going freelance, finding something more creative and less on the admin—I'm just so bloody conscientious and good at the organizing that Ayesha likes to keep me at it, and doesn't often let me do anything more interesting, and that's not going to change unless *I* change something . . . but of course that's all blown out of the water now, as young Anto will consume even more of me than Nico did and any requests to Ayesha will be about maternity leave not "please let me direct more." And no new employer would consider me for a year at least and then how long do I want off to be with him / her? I mean if the poor sod's only got one parent then they kind of should at least HAVE that parent, shouldn't they? So it's all about saving up now. Buying time, literally. When are you off to France? Gonna be strange leaving your island. Will you rent the house out? Keep it going for swift visits and downtime?

Róisín

Dear Róisín,

I've left. I'm in Edinburgh at the moment, and London on Tuesday. Is your sofa still free? One night only. I could take you for dinner perhaps? Or bring a takeaway?

The guys packed up the last things from the house last week. I did a bit more sorting, lost heart at the thought of letting go of her things, of throwing things away or giving them to charity; lost even more at the idea of putting them into storage, even *more* more at the thought of having to get them out again one day and go back into it all, at some distant and unimaginable future date when things will be different. Felt sad about things I'd already sent to charity; wished I'd kept them. But I can't stay here and I can't leave the house in aspic, a doll's house of our life that was—put in a pair of mannequins in our clothes to sit there like in a provincial museum, a dubious tableau getting dustier by the day. So after those initial half- and quarter-hearted efforts, yes, everything I'm not taking to France has gone. I managed to throw away some worn sheets, and greasy past-their-sell-by-date jars of spices. There were some tins within date which are going to the food bank. Friends have taken the cat and the open jars of jam and the curtains and such vegetables as self-seeded. Everything else has gone into storage in Stornoway except the piano, which is going to the school. The neighbors' cousin is apparently going to rent the place while it's on the market so it doesn't get damp. I now officially live nowhere.

Yours,
Rasmus.

PS You have a benevolent and optimistic view of the workings of the music business. Unless things have changed drastically I don't foresee huge amounts of sympathy coming from the institution, though individuals will undoubtedly be nice.

PPS I kept the orange dress and coat.

Dear Rasmus,

Tuesday night is booked in. Let's go out, as presumably I'll never go out again once it's born. I only just really realized I'll be a single mother.

Your activity is so drastic. I mean I get it. But it's so drastic. It brings us back to the other question you posed and I neglected to answer because it was a bit big, the changing everything question. Everything in me is yelling NEST NEST NEST, which means "don't change a thing because security" but also "change everything, there's a whole new person about to invade (well, already invading) and you need to prepare." But also I don't know what to do about work in the long run. I haven't been doing what I wanted for a long time and now I can't address that. And also I can't leave this flat because I need to be here in case he comes back.

I actually mean that.

Am I a hopeless case?

I'm full of admiration for you basically.

Róisín

29

For the Boatman

SEPTEMBER
London

IT WASN'T THE dinner they had, at the Korean place by the British Museum, the spicy bibimbap with the fried egg on top, that Nico minded. It wasn't that they were pleased to see each other, and laughing. It wasn't the patheticness of sitting beside them all evening amusing himself by trying to spill gochujang on Rasmus's trousers. He didn't take pleasure from the fact that Róisín was actually tired after the day's work, and that made her a bit absentminded. He forgave Rasmus for noticing, and calling a cab so that in fact they were home by nine thirty. It was the sight of Rasmus in the bathroom brushing his teeth, and Róisín saying something to him, and him coming to the bathroom door with his mouth full of toothpaste and trying to respond. The ordinariness undid him.

If I were a proper ghost I'd pull his toes all night. I'd make noises and knock things over and—

Well, you did—you spilled Korean hot sauce on him, you child. Is that what you want to be?

Yes, since you ask. I want to put glue in his beard and give him a heart attack.

No you don't.

Yes I do.

Anyway, he doesn't have a beard.

They were talking about language. He knows Danish and Spanish and French.

Well, bully for him.

She speaks Irish. Rasmus wanted to hear some.

"Do you know a poem or something?" he said. "I like to hear the music in the language."

"I know some of the words of songs," she said.

"Oh, won't you sing one?" he said, and Nico snorted, because if there was one thing she couldn't do it was sing.

For sure she was shy. She'd heard him sing. And Jay too. Who wouldn't be intimidated? Beyoncé maybe, or Adele. Well, she was no Adele. But he had sung for her, and she wouldn't be ungracious. So she sang it quietly, no breath to speak of, just as any girl would. And he sat so quietly, listening, that she sang as much of it as she could remember, in the wrong order probably, she wasn't good with songs.

> *Théid mé suas ar*
> *an chnoc is airde*
> *Féach a bhfeic mé*
> *an fhir a' bháta*
> *An dtig tú anocht nó*
> *an dtig tú amárach?*
> *Nó muna dtig tú idir*
> *is trua atá mé*
> *Tá mo chroíse*
> *briste brúite*

Is tric na deora
Ó mo shúile . . .
Fhir a' bháta
's ná hóró eile
Fhir a' bháta
's ná hóró eile
Fhir a' bháta
's ná hóró eile

A thousand blessings where'er you be . . .

"That's 'The Boatman,' isn't it?" Rasmus said. "She goes up the hill to look out across the sea for his return."

"She does," she said.

"That was written on my island," he said. "By a woman, Jean Finlayson. He did come back, and they got married."

"Did they. Lucky, as she was pregnant."

"Indeed," Rasmus said. "I like how you sang it. Poignant."

"Isn't it just," she said, and hauled herself up and went into the bathroom.

Nico just sat there, crying as best a ghost can cry.

"I'm sorry," said Rasmus, to the bathroom door. "I'm so sorry."

LATER, WHEN RÓISÍN was in bed, Nell rang.

"Why are you talking so quiet?"

"I'm not."

"You are. What's going on?"

"Nothing's going on."

"Then why aren't you speaking properly—is there someone there?"

"No—I mean—"

"Who's there?"

"There's a friend sleeping on the sofa."

"What friend?"

"You don't know them."

"I know all your friends."

"It's a new friend."

"You've no new friends. When did you make a friend?"

"We met through work."

"Why d'you call them 'them'? Is it a man? It's a man. You've got a man there!"

"Jesus, Nell."

"Jesus, you *have*."

"He's on the sofa."

"What's he doing there?"

"Spending the night before he goes to France."

"Why?"

"Because he lives in the Outer Hebrides."

"Now you're being silly. Nobody lives in the Outer Hebrides."

"He does. But he's moving."

"Onto your sofa?"

"To France, for now—Nell, what do you want?"

"To know why you've a strange man on your sofa at this time of night."

"That's not what you rang for—and he can't stay the night during the day, can he? What would be the point of that?"

"What's the point of him anyway?"

"You wanted me to make friends. He's a widower."

"Oh he is, is he?"

"Nell." Silence.

"Sorry."

"Okay."

"Protective."

"I know."

"Is he handsome?"

"Fuck off, Nell," she said kindly, and ended the call.

NICO, MEANWHILE, WAS staring at Rasmus as he slept. Not for the fiddler, or the harp-player. For the boatman, and no other.

RASMUS WAS DREAMING of himself and Jay in a barge, the rocking, creaking noises, echoing and slapping as they drifted into a dark, dripping cave. His mind clocked the sounds, noting them down, lining them up.

30

∾

A Red, Red Rose

SEPTEMBER

Dear Rasmus,

Are you there yet?

Róisín

Dear Róisín,

I am. I passed into France yesterday, my Mellotrons behind me in a truck, and I'm just looking round my new life as a prosperous French miller, maybe with three beautiful daughters. The house is old and golden, the gardens lush, and the studio facilities very impressive. There's a stout cook called Francine, a helpful youth called Eric (pronounced Erique), an excellent sound engineer, Pernille, and a producer I met in London last month. I have fifteen songs ready, i.e., with a very clear idea of how I want

them to sound, and an army of musicians lined up, from the
splendid to the unbearable, suggested by the record company,
who I am to indulge on this, apparently, because collaborating
with these people will introduce me to new markets and the
company likes that kind of stuff and I like this studio they're
paying for so here we are. It's going to be a lot of work. I wish
she was here.

What vegetable are you on now?

All the best,
Rasmus.

_____

Dear Róisín

Hard work is swamping me, but this doesn't mean you're not on
my mind. Don't not write to me. Both fonts welcome.

Rasmus.

_____

Dear Rasmus,

An aubergine?

I finally went to see Nico's mother. I didn't tell her in advance
what the situation is—they'd been on Ithaca which is their family
place for the summer and she'd wanted me to go out and have a
bit of sun and relaxation but I couldn't bring myself to. I wanted
to because I knew she wanted comfort from me as well as to
comfort me but it's just memories, memories, all the bloody time,
and Nico in Greece, being his Greek self in that beautiful place,

and the boats and the moon and the sea and the scent of the air
and fucking jasmine and cousins up from Athens and
everybody's grief and the cool of dusk and the fucking gorgeous
food and I just couldn't. So when she got back I just walked into
her flat, where they've lived all this time, where Nico was
brought up, and where his dad died, and she took one look at
me and she shrieked. With hindsight maybe it wasn't the best
way to do it—but how could I send a text or even a letter, or tell
her on the phone? It's a face-to-face thing if ever there was one,
isn't it? So she shrieked, and then she fainted. She's tiny, and
seventy-five years old, and always so smart, with the warmest
heart and the strictest rules which she's always breaking and
well anyway I thought I'd killed her. Next thing she's up and
weeping the place down and drinking and it's all Rosaki-mou
this and Rosaki-mou* that and laughing and weeping and the
hugging—dear God and she only reaches to my shoulder so
she's basically got her head in my cleavage and lipstick all over
my shirt—ah Rasmus, I've made her so happy. I will be lucky to
get away with my life if this kid isn't called Nicolas. Nicola might
do, just. Then she had to ring the entire family, every damn
Triandafilides* and Pappadopoulos from Ithaca New York to
Melbourne Australia, and I'd to sit and be put on the phone to
every one of them, and some of them not English speakers so
my terrible Greek was put on full display. Her love is like a week
of the weather in Galway—sunshine and tears, Jesus, Mary, and
Joseph. Then she sewed one of her mataki eyes on a leather
cord round my neck and made me swear on Nico's memory and
that of her late husband, Nico's dad, that I would never take it
off. Never! Not just until my baby (sorry—her grandchild, as it's
now known) is safely born, but never. So that's me. When Nico
and I first got together and he was a tattooist she wanted him to
tattoo us all with them. I digress.

Anyway so. That's done. I will never be alone in my life, will I? Is it possible to get work done, I mean real work like art and so forth, if you're never alone? This is a serious question. But I've noticed that you do take questions seriously so I probably don't need to mention that.

Róisín

PS *Rosaki-mou is My Little Rose in Greek. Róisín is Little Rose in Irish. Triandafilides is rose (literally, thirty leaves, or petals) in Greek. This has always been hilarious because I would, had I actually married him and taken his name, have become Rose Rose.

PPS He had great aunts and uncles called Olympia, Cleopatra, Afrodite, Achilles, Herakles, Efrosini, and—a favorite— Triandafilos. Like me. Rose of the Roses.

Dear Róisín,

All this family. I still don't know how many brothers and sisters you have. Is it not overwhelming? It's overwhelming for me just to read.

Rasmus.

Dear Rasmus,

I have lots. You still haven't really told me about your family?

Róisín

Dear Róisín,

I think I have. Really there's nothing.

Rasmus.

Dear Rasmus,

I don't see you as a liar, and I know you're not stupid, so I'll take that reply as level one self-protection, and respect it as such.

Róisín

Dear Rose of the Roses,

Thank you.

Rasmus.

Dear Rasmus,

I really wish he had a grave. The funeral was a fine and dramatic occasion and appropriate in every way, specially as it was what he asked for, so I could do nothing else even if I'd thought to at the time, but dear God I wish there was a place I could just go and sit and it be his. Somewhere with green grass and a bench and some evergreens. People say oh plant a tree or a lovely rosebush but what's that tree or rosebush got to do with him, if I just plant it and go oh, now you're Nico's tree? Because compared with a tree

that's grown out of the flesh and blood of a person's corpse it
hasn't got much to stand on (as it were) to be honest, as far as I
can see. I'm thinking more of the old song where from his heart
there grew a rose and so forth—trying to remember the words
now but you know the one I mean. Sweet William and Barbara
Allen. And from his heart a red, red rose, and from her heart a
briar—which I thought was a bramble, which isn't very nice—even
though I know she was meant to be hard-hearted, who wants
thorns and blackberries growing out of them?—but I googled it
and it's those wild pink hedgerow roses. Did you see that lovely
film *Volver*? It opens with all the Spanish ladies doing housework
on the graves, sweeping and changing the water and all that, all
in their housecoats and their hair done. Lovely. It's just I want to
sit down with him and tell him face-to-face. I have this stupid idea
about him finding out by accident, or someone else telling him.
Don't laugh, but I've been going down to the river some evenings
and sitting on the benches there, because the river's tidal so
when the tide comes in maybe he's there . . . I found myself
eyeing up a heron the other day, wondering if maybe he'd eaten a
fish that had some of Nico in him . . . Circle of life, eh? Anyway
there's an urge to lay flowers, what can I say, and an urge to talk.

Róisín

Dear Róisín,

Jay was very clear about wanting to be cremated. She became
quite antsy about the idea of being in a box, under the earth,
weighed down and shut in in the dark. She was concerned that
the undertakers might lay her out in a position that wasn't
comfortable for her. She didn't like lying on her back, which is of

course the classic position, unless her knees were up. She wanted me to find out for her if she could be put on her side, but realized in time that that was crazy. You'd need a wider coffin, and a different shape of grave.

And she'd still be under the ground in a box. So she chose what she called a chemical release, where all that she was could swiftly meld back into everything that existed. Dust to dust.

Rasmus.

PS I have half a memory of a culture where they throw flowers out onto the water, and candles floating on leaves. Puja?

_____

Dear Rasmus,

Have you scattered her ashes yet?

Róisín

_____

Dear Róisín,

I have not.

Rasmus.

_____

Dear Róisín,

Sorry, that was a little abrupt. I tried and failed and now I don't know what to do with them. Or when. I look at them and my heart falls like lead overboard. I put them away and I feel like a schmuck for not wanting them around. I can't touch them for weeks. They make me feel sick. Or, rather, I feel sick to think of them. They're doing nothing. They're not her. There's nothing of her, physically. They remind me daily that we didn't have a child and she would have liked to have a child, and a child would have had her smile or her eyes, her genes. This in itself was complicated because sarcoid, the condition which ultimately killed her, has a genetic component. She didn't want to pass it on. I didn't encourage her. I didn't feel qualified. I wish I had. Sometimes. But I was depressed. Deeply, clinically. I didn't feel I could help or support her. Her ashes remind me of everything I held her back from. She would not have chosen to live in the middle of nowhere, if I hadn't wanted to. She wanted to live in a tough city and be a good doctor all day to tough city families who needed a good doctor. She wanted to work in obstetrics, particularly with Black women, and then in the evening to go out to watch funny or beautiful films on big screens, and eat popcorn from the machine and sushi from a Japanese place. She wanted to raise her voice in glorious harmony with other glorious voices, in church or in a choir or in a band. She was a New York and London kind of girl. She could easily have been a Glasgow girl. A city kind of girl. I stopped her. She didn't mention it. She was decisive that way; she knew how to cast off what she couldn't have. She even did it with her life.

We were trying to get pregnant when her sarcoid flared up again and we found out how ill she was.

This is quite the opposite of abrupt. Though also abrupt in

its way. Is it? If it's upsetting, I apologize. It seems to
me there's no point talking about any of this unless we tell
the truth.

Rasmus.

PS Sarcoid is primarily pulmonary. She couldn't sing anymore.

PPS While I'm telling you everything, I'll tell you everything.
At the end of the first tour when I idiotically threw myself
under the taxi and broke myself, it took two or three years out
of my life, important ones at that age, health-wise, and
financially. The band sailed on, and, to my amazement, she
didn't sail with them. Which I thought mad of her, which is why
I spent so much of the rest of my life with her trying and
failing to make up for it. She told me she didn't want to be a
singer anymore anyway. I think she was only half lying. She'd
been doing it at least in part for the money. Touring, you get
per diems, and no expenses, so it's a cheap way to earn and
save, if you see what I mean. She was saving up to study. I
wanted to come back to the UK as soon as I could be moved.
There were insurance complications, bills and so forth. She
gave me her savings to get out of the US, so I funded her
medical training when my royalties started coming in. We
became our own project. Each time something got derailed
we made sure for each other that nothing else did. Mostly we
succeeded.

But whatever else, it is a huge thing for a girl at twenty-one to
take on a man who might never have been going to walk
again.

Dear Rasmus,

There's a company that makes little wooden Viking boats—you can put the ashes in the hull and light an oil lamp there on its deck and send them out to sea; the sail catches alight and off it goes. It only takes a certain amount though: 200 grams. For myself what makes me feel a bit ill is the separating out of the remains. Putting different bits of them in different places. There was a dreadful Catholic thing of burying actual body parts in a variety of places so you could get more prayers said over your body. So the richer and more powerful and more villainous you were, the more different monasteries you'd set up, to send your arms and legs and so forth to. You'd put your heart in the biggest. It seems sneaky, doesn't it? I'd be surprised if God didn't see right through it. Even with ashes I don't like it. Irrational, yes I know but there we are, humans. I'm so sorry you didn't get the baby you wanted. I am so sorry for what happened to you and Jay.

Róisín

Dear Róisín,

It wasn't me that wanted the baby. It was her. If I had the baby now I'd be a very poor father to it, because I would be staring at it all the time, looking for its likeness to its mother. Who wants a father who can't look at them without crying?

I read somewhere that that's where the term "stinking rich" comes from: rich enough to be buried inside the church, so everybody smells you during the service. Is it literally that the closer you are to the prayers and the services, the more likely you are to go to heaven?

Rasmus.

PS Are you the type to want to know the baby's sex before it's born?

Dear Rasmus,

I'm afraid it is so. Which is why the term God-botherer never bothers me. Always struck me as odd that God was so vain he just wanted to be praised all the time, and as for people just pulling his sleeve and begging for stuff day in and day out . . . tiring.

My mother was brought up very religious, as everyone was in those days, but she cast it off when all the pedophilia started coming out. She said she'd talk to God directly, thank you very much. My sister Nell pointed out that that made her a Protestant, that being exactly what the Protestants were about, and she said she'd be a Quaker then. She still goes to Mass though to see her friends and make sure the old people are OK, and to give the priest a hard stare to make sure he knows it's not forgotten. Nico's family were similar: Orthodox because that's what there was, but then there was a dreadful scene after his dad died, in Athens, where two policemen and a priest got in a terrible fight over his body—literally, across his body, on his deathbed—about which undertaker was to be called, because they all wanted the commission. His mother swore then: never again. Are you religious?

Róisín

PS No. It seems to me like reading its diary or something. Kind of disrespectful.

Dear Róisín,

No I'm not. I find it attractive sometimes, the theater and drama of it, the music and the incense and the high vaulting arches and high vaulting emotions, but going into that would just be self-indulgence for me. And the idea of comfort is, well, comforting. And it's clearly something human beings need. I don't mock it. It fulfills something, doesn't it? My mother sometimes belonged to a mealy-minded judgmental Low Protestant church with a tatty modern building and a lot of very bossy men running it, whose main obsession seemed to be the grinding down of innocent pleasures, particularly female ones. They spent so much time castigating women for being attractive that you couldn't help but think they spent the rest of it masturbating.

I don't care for the human habit of making yourself feel good by judging others to be somehow worse than you. It doesn't lead to anything helpful.

Rasmus.

Rasmus,

Tell me: do you want me to not write to you while you're doing this recording? Because I could understand if there was a creative thing that needed to be left alone. If I'm anything here, I belong to the new life and you're looking at the old; I don't want to roil things up.

Meanwhile: Jesus Christ the rain!

Róisín

Dear Róisín,

I'm sorry I haven't responded for a while. It's not that, no. I've just been working very . . . not so much hard, even, as full-time. Trying to settle into the mood in this place, which is VERY different to what I am used to.

Thank you for the delicacy of your offer. But please don't stop writing.

I was thinking that I may have hurt your feelings with the silence. I hope not.

Rasmus.

Dear Rasmus,

When things as bad as have happened to us happen to you, anything smaller is a fly on the windowpane. It takes a thing equally as bad to hurt you again. And let's face it, nothing as bad ever could happen again. There's not time, life-wise. I read somewhere once that scar tissue has no feeling, and took that as an emotional metaphor: if you're hurt enough, you become numb. I used to think about that when I was fifteen and in love with a different lad each week. I hate to laugh, because it hurt. So much. And people would say "One day you'll look back on this and laugh" and you'd want to kill them. I hate when people laugh at teenagers, like teenagers are ridiculous, and no grown-up ever was one. I've never had such strong feelings as when I was a kid. Well, almost never. Sometimes I wonder why our society disparages emotion so much. Reason and facts being so important, and how we feel about them being amateurish and childish and pathetic somehow. Think about it: "I feel ill" as opposed to "I am ill." "It doesn't feel right" against "It isn't right." Sometimes it just seems like a way to put down women and children and people who deal in nuance. Not that I'm against reason and fact, but they're not the only flowers in the bunch.

People love certainty, don't they? Even when the certainty is wrong wrong wrong. (She says with great certainty.)

Anyway work well.
Róisín

31

❧

What About Breathing?

SEPTEMBER
France

RASMUS WAS RESTLESS in his heaven. The music was all-encompassing; the joys of encountering the developments other people had discovered in the years since he'd last been in a modern studio; the effort he had to put into explaining that he really didn't want all of them, that indeed there were several he wished had never been invented. It was easy to sit all day and night with guitars and musicians and mixing desks, with the southern autumn outside, the lush harvests, and all your food prepared for you. The sea was not as intoxicatingly various here as it was in the Hebrides, but it was pretty good. Immersion in work with others was indeed a blessing. But being treated like a rock star was a mixed one. Above all, nobody responded naturally. They were tiptoeing around him, treating him like a delicate diva, and also a tragic figure of bereavement. It didn't make for closeness of any kind. For what you might call company. *I don't know how to put people at their ease. That, like so many things, was Jay's job.*

Jay would have loved it here. She'd have been in the kitchen, charming the cook, talking about organic vegetable-growing; next thing you knew she'd have joined in the olive harvest, up a tree with the silver leaves twinkling, nets laid around the trunks, evening shadows lying across the groves. That's if she'd ever have got out of the sea, which rippled and glinted in the sheltered bay as if someone had thrown golden sequins across it from the evening sky.

She was indeed out of reach of his two empty arms.

All the ways you can miss someone.

Seize the day.

It felt all right writing to Róisín, and getting her answers. Now, *she* knew how to be easy with people.

Hi Rasmus,

I know you're hardly combing social media for diversions, what with all the creativity and so on, but did you see in the news about the rat getting a medal for sniffing out land mines? It made me very happy to hear, though I'm concerned as to where they're going to pin it on her, unless she gets maybe a special little jacket for the occasion, which I think would be my preferred option for her, as nobody wants a pin through their fur when they're meeting the Queen. In other news, fruit-wise, having passed pineapple and cantaloupe, my child is now the size of a honeydew. This isn't exciting really, is it? Would you say a honeydew is actually any larger than a cantaloupe? Would it keep you awake at night? I'm afraid I googled it last night and learned that they are members of the same family—cousins, perhaps—and that honeydew is the green one, and a bit sweeter, and with a few more calories, whereas cantaloupe is the orange one, and has more vitamins. But not which is larger. Anyway, now they've run out of fruit and moved on to salad—last week: baby the size of a romaine lettuce. I'm rather concerned about the density here. I mean a little gem is quite solid, but a romaine? Too leafy! I realize I am sharing jokes with you that I would be sharing with Nico. I hope you don't mind. I do know you're not its dad. But it helps . . .

xx Róisín

Jeez I did kisses. Is that a bit forward? Or is it something you know that we could do? On the page, I mean. Oh FFS. You know what I mean. Sorry. Shambolic.

_____

Dear Róisín,

I don't mind at all. The joke-sharing, or the Xs. It makes my heart ache—your pregnancy, your jokes and ease, your sorrow; your courage. I like to see this flower blossoming from the darkness.

Rasmus.

Oh—yeah. X. Is that how you do it? Xx?

_____

Dear Rasmus,

Thank you. I'm a blossom. It's all compost, and I'm a blossom. No, hang on, I'm a tree surely? About to bear fruit . . . How's your French idyll at La Ficelle? How's the work? I mean what I said about that track you sent me last week, I've been playing it over and over, it puts the little one to sleep inside me when it's wriggling, so thanks for that. I'll try it as a lullaby after it's born. I don't see why you don't think it perfect as it stands. Are you the kind of perfectionist who never gets anything done because you

rewrite the same things over and over? I can't believe you are.
But what do I know? Got to go. Pee!*

xx Róisín

*As in, all the time. When am I ever not peeing?

_____

Dear Róisín,

What about breathing? Is there enough room in there for your
lungs to expand?

Rasmus.

PS Genuine question.

PPS XX

_____

Dear Rasmus,

I hope you are well, and that your recording time is proving fruitful.

I'm just writing to confirm what I hope you are already aware of.
The record company have requested more footage, to include you
working with the musicians in the studio. There's a suggestion that
this be done soon, as I will be on maternity leave from the end of
the month. We would of course come to you.

Under the circumstances, please be aware that the team would be
just me, and that I would keep the filming as unobtrusive as
possible. I don't want in any way to disturb your work.

I'm waiting for official confirmation but wanted to let you know directly as well.

With best wishes, Róisín
Róisín Kennedy

Dear Rasmus,

I wanted to say, though obviously with my feathered hat on I'm not meant to say it, don't feel obliged. You're putting out a lot after long periods of not putting out—I love that term, don't you? Like for teenagers having sex—well, not that that applies here but you know what I mean—you're offering yourself, having been very private, and though it would be GREAT to have studio footage, and lovely French location shots, it is NOT necessary and if you want to concentrate on your work or on sitting under a tree please just say no to them. People forget grief's a full-time job on top of whatever else is trying to go on in our minds and worlds and lives and hearts. But I know, and I'm saying don't forget.

xRóisín

Dear Róisín,

I'm sitting at the window, feet up, a cup of coffee and the autumn sun. The air smells beautiful.

It would be great to have you here. Are you and the lettuce up to traveling, though? It's not too late? It's sunny still and there's

loads of room and nice youngsters who cook and stuff. You
could stay for a bit. I won't be madly sociable but when you're
not filming you could lounge about in the sea. You like the
out-of-season swimming, don't you? They have antique linen
sheets with complex monograms embroidered onto them; it's a
bit like sleeping on sacking but in a luxurious way. I'll
commandeer a motor for you. There's plenty here they send to
airports and stations. If they can do it for my favorite Ukrainian
theremin player, they can do it for you.

xx Rasmus.

PS Here's Herbie Hancock for you: "Cantaloupe Island."

Róisín, reading it at home, laughed aloud.

"What is it?" asked Nell, looking up from the sofa where she was
knitting bootees. (They were very sweet. Pale yellow, against the pink-
or-blue of patriarchy. Róisín loved them and secretly hoped Nell
would knit a tiny cardigan to match—which she was certainly going
to. She was teaching Róisín to knit as well. "It's a great alternative to
wine," Róisín said. "Something to do with your hands.")

"A lovely invitation," said Róisín. "From, um, Rasmus. I told you
about Rasmus?"

"You have not . . ." said Nell, on row thirteen of knit two purl two,
looking down again.

"He's a musician. I met him when we were filming, and we've become kind of, well, widowy pen pals."

"Oh," said Nell, significantly. "Mr. Sofa. And?"

"He's recording in France and I'm to go and stay, to finish off filming," Róisín said. "It's perfect. Just for a week or so, before all this gets
too imminent . . ."

"Sweet," said Nell.

"You don't disapprove, so?" Róisín asked.

"Are you *shagging* him?" Nell shrieked.

"No I am not. What a suggestion. And Nico not cold in his . . . seabed . . ." Where he is undoubtedly cold. Laughter and tears, flipping like a coin through water.

Nico, in the kitchen doorway, closed his eyes. Pain and anger all over him, and no way to express it. He slid down the wall to sit on the floor, folding over his knees.

Róisín looked up. "What was that?" she said.

"What was what?" asked Nell.

"Nothing, I suppose," Róisín said, after a pause. Nell looked a query at her, and she changed the subject. It was just that odd feeling she had from time to time. That little lurch.

"I mean I suppose I should be saving up," she said. "I'm going to try to save his pension for the baby but to be honest I do believe that being with your mum when you're little is as valuable as uni anyway . . . Turns out money *can* buy happiness, in some ways."

"It can buy peace of mind, and time, for sure," said Nell. "When are you off?"

"The sooner, the better. Preg-wise."

32

It's Sweet to See

LATER THAT NIGHT, Róisín threw up.

Nico sat on the edge of the bath as she retched and spat and reached uselessly for the tap to rinse her mouth. He couldn't bring her a glass of water. The angle was bad and the tap stuck. He couldn't even reach across and release it for her. She turned back to the bowl and threw up again; back to the bath to try to rinse again.

He asked Jay straight out: "Do you think I'm upsetting her?"

"There do seem to be times," Jay said, in the doorway, "when we're closer to them. When they're almost aware of us. Life and death times. As if the veil between us is thinner."

"Pregnancy might do that, then?" he wondered.

"Yes, I think so." Jay moved aside to let Róisín through.

"I don't want to make her sick," he said.

"Of course you don't," she said. "Of *course* you don't. She's just being sick. Perfectly normal." The kindness in Jay's voice made him want to cry. *That and everything else*, he thought. Róisín's toothbrush there by the sink. The look on her face when she closed the door on her day and let her fears float out.

"But there's nowhere else for us, is there?" Jay said.

He wasn't thinking about that.

"How are they getting on, do you think?" he said. He hadn't looked at the emails. Too proud. He could . . . want to know, though. A pause. "Are there still emails?" he asked.

"There are," she said. "I don't read them. I watch him while he reads them. They're getting on well. It's sweet to see."

He was glad she didn't say anything more. Glad too that she wasn't eavesdropping on them.

Róisín went back through to the bedroom and lay down, clammy and exhausted. Restless on her sweaty sheets, she tried to find a comfortable position, tried to get to sleep.

"I can't stay here," he said.

He would just have to go and look at Rasmus again.

"You coming?" he asked Jay.

"God, I don't know," she said.

33

❦

A Big Beautiful

SEPTEMBER

Dear Rasmus,

Are you sure you're happy to have me being pregnant all over the place *and* filming? I mean obviously I won't be all over the place, I'll be exceptionally disciplined and well behaved and respectful of your work. I appreciate that you are being too, of mine. But I will also and undeniably be exceptionally pregnant.

Red cabbage, btw. Though it's absurd—I mean, the heaviest ever recorded was 27 kilos which is, what—four and a half stone? And vast though I am I don't believe there's a four-and-a-half-stone baby in there. Its tastebuds are now fully developed though. And it can hear all right. I've been playing it the Graeme Revell *Insect Musicians* CD you sent, for which thank you! It's quite bonkers and very soothing. Also pleasantly historical. And yes, I do have a CD player. Dusty, but scrubbed up nice.

Róisín

Dear Róisín,

It's all good. As long as you sit still and don't knock anything over. I've told them you can have three days for filming us. Feathered hat apart, as I said, come for as long as feels right. It'll be nice. For me, I mean. It might be quite boring for you. Though the sea's still warm and the sky very high and blue. Let me know when you're coming.

x Rasmus.

Dear Rasmus,

It'll be sooner rather than later. Will confirm.

Róisín

Dear Rasmus,

Listen, about the filming—my commission here is just to film you. (Dear God, spellcheck just gave me "fix" for "film." Don't worry! I'm no longer someone who goes round trying to fix people.) But no, what I'm thinking is this, and stop me if it's invasive. I don't want to take professional advantage of the fact that we get on. But. So far my career, such as it is, has been a lot of organizing and arranging, supporting the creativity of others, down to and including coffee-fetching and spreadsheet-wrangling; up to and including shooting (i.e., directing) footage which then goes off for grander folks to work their magic, produce the magnum opus and get their credit above the title. For a long time I've meant to change this and I never have. But. What I've got of you is really good. The interview is great. Your integrity jumps out of the screen, and the moments where we were prickly are—

She'd watched it over several times.

To be honest, it was so charged between them she wasn't sure it could be used in any straightforward documentary. It disturbed her.

—proper salt to the sandwich. If I'm coming out to film you at La Ficelle as well, there will be a lot more good stuff. But for any footage to make sense, really there has to be a theme and a tone to it, which so far I don't have, because that will start to come through in the editing . . . but this footage isn't for me. It's for someone else, I don't even know who, they haven't even decided. It's just raw material, news footage, if you like. I'm just . . . OK, fuck it, I want to direct the whole thing. I want to make a big beautiful feature documentary about all of—*this*. I want you to let me. I know it's a massive ask and at such a time when you're (a) in grief and (b) starting to turn that grief into something beautiful. I really, really don't want to be invasive and at the same time I really do. I just think you're the most amazing talent and this is such an extraordinary time and I want to make something beautiful from my grief too, beyond the baby, as well as the baby, and it could be this. It could be not just about music but about the love that fuels it and the sorrow and the vast fucking hole that has to be filled, about the past and the future— I want it to be about you and her and love and death and fruitfulness. I haven't mentioned it to anyone at this end as it's ridiculous because, well, baby; and it would take years and you would probably hate it and never want to talk to me again but I'm beyond dismissing dreams now. If I don't do it nothing will happen. There'd be no dreams.

She didn't send it.

Sometimes a person wants two things and doesn't even know it. Sometimes those things might be mutually exclusive, but a person might never find out if they are or not because they already feel so far out on a limb they don't feel they can stick their neck out as well.

Sometimes it might be a good idea to stick your neck out.

34

Love and Love

OCTOBER
France

IF RASMUS WANDERED out across the veranda and the neat clover lawns, past the rows of orange and lemon trees in terra-cotta tubs and the Range Rovers and Lexuses of the people he was working with, he could stroll up the dusty cypress-lined drive and turn left to the bus stop. The local bus, blue and juddery, full of cleaners and gardeners in baseball caps going home from maintaining perfect Riviera villas, would take him into Marseille. In Marseille, nobody knew him or wanted anything from him. He could take the air without being attended to. Nobody cared if he was a widower or a lost rocker. He wandered the Jardin du Pharo, where the leaves were heavy with the exhaustion of a long hot summer; gazed over to the Old Port; smiled at the statue of David, observed the drunk sailors on shore leave as they careered around the bars of Le Panier. One evening, in a picturesque little square lush with ornamental olive trees and special offers on bouillabaisse and salade Niçoise, he saw a group of bikers, young men and women, gathered round a big bike with a sound system. They were dancing. He couldn't imagine a sound system on a motorcycle—*how could you hear anything over the roar of your machine?*—but anyway here was a reason. A portable disco. Dancing wherever you wanted it. They were waltzing to what sounded like Moroccan hip-hop. They weren't French. Norwegian, perhaps, or Dutch: cold-blooded northerners who needed an excuse to touch each other. He wondered if he was like that.

He walked on. The air had a hint of chill but still smelled of the ghost of summer—rosemary, cigarettes, and petrol. He didn't know what he was hoping for. He should have given her more, or not let her give so much. He had made her life so small. *And now no South of France for Jay. No professorship; no life-saving research. No baby.*

Yes, I needed stuff, but so did you.

He walked a little faster. No regrets. But no regrets is for oneself. You can't claim it for someone else.

Outside a tattoo parlor sat a man in a gray suit and a tight T-shirt. Rasmus noticed him because he looked both shifty and sad; an unusual combination. He found himself giving the man a blokeish nod, which was unlike him, but he was still uncertain about how he wanted to behave in this big wide world full of other human beings. He had been so private for so long. He'd had all he wanted.

No more. No more. *You need to want something else*, he told himself. Go on. *Want other stuff. Want something completely new. Seize these days, the days you have and she doesn't.*

But it's been no time at all. I can't want anything new.

Love and *Love* on the knuckles. He smiled.

He strolled past the shifty sad man and into a bar festooned with fishing nets and rather beautiful globular glass floats. He thought about the sea far to the north, where one day he would scatter her ashes. Not yet. The bar's specialty seemed to be hot spiced rum. Well, the evenings were drawing in; the season was late. He ordered some.

It came in a white tin cup, enameled, with blue edges—and was delicious. He had four cups. Ha! Well, this was different. He'd never even tasted spiced rum before and now suddenly he was quite drunk on it.

Outside, the street was transformed; the figures walking were magic; every sailor was Gene Kelly; every girl Minnehaha.

Why Minnehaha? He had no idea.

He stared at the images in the vitrine of the tattoo shop.

35

He Hadn't Meant To

OCTOBER
Marseille

NICO HAD BEEN following Rasmus around.

Christ, he's drunk.

And now drunk Rasmus was leaning on the counter of this third-rate ink parlor, making enquiries.

Ohhhh...

Nico's tattoo hand was twitching. The worst in him began to laugh. *What a fucking gorgeous opportunity that would be. What a delicious chance to fuck up this guy who may well be about to set up with my woman and my child, and to live all the natural joys that I will never have.*

He imagined the letters manifesting on Rasmus's skin:

> *Nico loved you more than this bastard ever will*
> *Róisín, my darling, Never Forget*
> *Nico will never stop loving you*

Or a lovely death's head, dark roses in its eye sockets... That Irish song, "Róisín Dubh," "Dark Rose."

What a splendid opportunity.

And he stopped himself.

Lucky you can't do it then, isn't it? Ghost boy.

Rasmus was asking the tattooist if he spoke English. He did. He was a New Zealander, by his accent.

"I want something on my back," Rasmus was saying. "I've a scar. I'd like to . . . extrapolate from it. Use it to make something beautiful." His voice was low and polite.

Nico smiled.

"Absolutely!" said the tattooist. "No problemo. How long ago was the surgery?"

Don't ask him to take his shirt off. I don't need to actually LOOK at the scrawny chest that's going to be pressed against Róisín's beautiful soft breasts. If it hasn't been already. Which it hasn't, because she's in London. And she's a decent girl who, as she herself pointed out, wouldn't be shagging another man when pregnant. Oh God.

"Oh, yeah, that's quite long ago enough," the tattooist was saying. "So—my name's Matt, by the way—so, what are you thinking? Inspiring message of survival against the odds? Lyric from a favorite song? Rearing cobra like Kurt Russell in *Escape from New York*? Zips are popular . . . staples . . . internal bone structure . . ."

No, no, no, Nico murmured.

"A vine of some kind," Rasmus said, very polite, almost apologetic. "Or, just a bird, sitting on the scar? Holding it in its claws as if it were a small branch—what do you think?" he said, peeling off his shirt, which Nico recognized as quite a nice bit of linen, *probably not bought by him as he's not exactly the modish type . . . so are he and Róisín on shirt-buying terms now?* And here was Rasmus's naked back presented to him. Waxy white skin; slender corded muscles, vulnerable shoulder blades like the first sprouting of an angel's wings. The long, clean scar up the spine, like a row of stitching in an antique book, birds' footprints in snow. Skin like parchment. The vulnerability of this human body. Alive.

"What kind of bird are you thinking of?" Matt said, gesturing to various 1950s swallows, American eagles, and mystic owls that hung in smeary frames around the shop. He reached for a sheet of paper.

"Nightingale," said Rasmus. "Nothing special to look at, but symbolic."

Matt sketched a plain little bird on the translucent paper and held it up against Rasmus's scar, about a third of the way up his back. He held up a mirror. Nico and Rasmus both stared, and frowned. "Obviously I'll look up what a nightingale looks like," Matt said. "This is just for scale. To get the general idea."

It looked as if it had landed in a wild wind, and was holding on for dear life. As if it were being blown around. A decent drawing, though.

Rasmus said: "It doesn't look entirely comfortable, does it?"

Tell you what, said Nico. *How about a vine winding round the scar like it was three-dimensional? Like the scar was a pole?*

Rasmus pondered the bird. "Could you do a vine winding round the scar? As if it were three-dimensional? And the scar was a pole holding it up?"

"Sure," said Matt. "Were you thinking an actual grapevine? Or a climbing flower of some kind—morning glory's popular, trailing lilies, or roses, of course . . ."

Nico watched carefully for Rasmus's reaction. *He probably doesn't know that Róisín means rose . . . a conversation they haven't had yet. Or maybe they have.*

"Can you show me some examples?" Rasmus said, very carefully. *He really is drunk.*

Matt could indeed. "Here you go," he said, pointing at some more dusty-framed drawings on the walls. "Here's a Goth-looking style; I wouldn't do that myself, there's a Goth specialist who comes in Wednesdays. This one's a bit ladylike, maybe . . ." It looked like the bathroom of a cheap brothel run by a My Little Pony fanatic. Bubble gum and mauve.

Nico laid his hand carefully on a heavy old design catalog on the shelf behind the counter, and looked at Rasmus. Rasmus turned to it. "What's that?" he asked, pointing.

"Nineteenth-century botanicals," Matt said. "They're a bit classier?"

Nico smiled as Rasmus looked through the drawings: ferns and mushrooms, angelica and fir trees, shading, crosshatching, and tiny delicate roots. And a lovely vine.

"Okay, like that?" Matt said. "I can adjust it to have it coiling round . . ." He did another quick sketch to demonstrate. Nico put his hand on Matt's—so light, he wouldn't feel it.

Rasmus smiled.

"And how big?" Matt asked.

Rasmus made a sweep with his arm, up and over his head.

"Okaaaaay," said Matt.

"But musical," Rasmus said. "Not a big lump. It must ebb and flow. Like it's in the wind. Quite spare. Not . . . shrubbery."

"I reckon I can do that," said Matt. "Would you like to come through to the studio?"

"Yes," said Rasmus, and marched through. He sat.

Matt picked up a Sharpie and in a few swift movements sketched out a design on paper. Nico stood beside him, watching. Once or twice he reached out and guided Matt's hand.

"It's a bit vertical, still, for a bird to sit on," Matt said.

"I am on an experiment with newness," Rasmus said brightly.

"Would you like to come back tomorrow?" Matt asked.

"No," said Rasmus, and laid his long pale body down.

"I need to design this," said Matt. "You don't want freehand—"

"Freehand," said Rasmus dreamily. "Freehand sounds nice. Start. Let it grow."

"You're drunk," said Matt. "There are rules about that."

"Not that drunk," said Rasmus. "Please." He glanced at the paper. "Beautiful," he said. "As if my skin is the sky."

Matt looked at the sketch. It looked subtly different to his usual work. Better, to be honest.

"Um," he said.

No problem, said Nico, and touched Matt's hand, and his green pen, and led: marking the stem of the vine looping the stem of the scar, from the knotty landscape of the base of Rasmus's spine up toward the shoulders, where it spiraled off to wave in the wind. Arabesques trailed out; leaves and offshoots appeared.

Matt melted.

Grapes? Nico asked. *Or just leaves and tendrils?*

"Grapes and leaves and tendrils," said Rasmus, into the padded head of the treatment bed. "Dangly. Trailing. Do vines have flowers?"

Yeah, little spiky white ones, Nico said, thinking of his grandfather's stony vineyard on Ithaca. *But you can have what you want.* Nico already knew what to give him. Among the spiky vine flowers, and the small glossy grapes, Rasmus would carry a blowing red rose, like the one on Nico's own wrist. Dark red. Behind his heart. And a paler one, beside it; a bud maybe. A few strokes of the pen. *Look after them or I will come back and fucking haunt you to death and tattoo you with giant ghost spiders in your sleep . . . on your face . . . Hurt a hair on her head, raise one moment of sorrow in our child . . .* By the time Rasmus knew it was there it would be too late. And who would care, apart from Rasmus?

And Róisín. She'd know. People always know. When a song plays, a stair creaks, a butterfly settles on a cup or a coffin, when a robin looks at you or a feather falls or a droopy heron flaps away, tired, out of view.

The bird could be coming in to land. Feet forward, wings extended. Or taking off. How about that?

"Have the bird rising, and a leaf falling," said Rasmus, and softly he began to sing the song about birds and leaves, rising joyfully when they rise, and falling gracefully when they fall.

Matt's hand sketched in a curling leaf. Carefully, almost detached, he set up the gun, calibrated the machines, mixed the dark green ink and the crimson. Gently he wiped down the flesh he was to inscribe. Swiftly he applied Vaseline and started to etch the green loops around the scar. He gave just the irregularity that nature requires to look harmonious. No artificial perfection here. Wiping off blood, soothing the flesh, noting, dabbing, coloring, delineating. Taking care round the tender knobs of the spine, letting the vine grow as it would. Nico was very careful. *Sit up,* he'd say. *Look.* Not saying, *I'm making this beautiful for my widow to admire.* Not crying. Holding up the mirror. *I'm not blind.*

At various points Matt took a photo, warned of the redness, the swelling, offered admiration of how it was going.

Rasmus did not want to look.

Nico and Matt worked steadily and beautifully. The vine grew and blossomed under their hands, lines and shading and all so delicate that it wasn't taking long, even the more intricate sections. They worked on through the evening, giving it just the right amount of depth and movement.

"You do need to come back," Matt said. "It's too much for one session. You'll be pleased."

"I'm enjoying the pain," Rasmus said. "It makes a change from the usual pain."

Okay, Nico said.

"My wife died," Rasmus said.

Nico said, *So did I.*

There was quite a long silence.

"And you have to do something," Rasmus continued.

"Sorry to hear that, man," said Matt. "Man, that sucks."

Nico was quietly etching a tendril in the shape of a curly capital *J*. He hadn't meant to, but the falling leaf brought it out.

Yes, he said.

Something peculiar had happened. He loved Rasmus now. The flesh under his hands. It was just something human.

A nightingale could easily perch on one of these stems, he said. *There's plenty of space. I'll look out a nice one for you, maybe from Gould, or Audubon. Come back tomorrow night.*

"I *would* like a nightingale," Rasmus said to Matt. "I'll come back tomorrow."

LATE THAT NIGHT, looking up at the moon, Nico was wondering what the view was like from up there to down here.

RASMUS CAME IN the next day to find Matt confused. The nightingale was already drawn. Matt thought he must have had some kind of migraine or something the day before; his memory was shot. Maybe the painkiller didn't mix with—though he hadn't had a drink yesterday. Anyway, maybe he should take it easy. This work, he said, was like nothing he'd ever done before—wild, in a good way.

Tattooing the nightingale went well—his hands moving again with a kind of freedom he'd never had before.

Afterward, Rasmus, Matt, and Nico walked to a local bar for pastis and *moules*, to continue a conversation they'd started, about what music actually *means*. Matt told Rasmus that this was the best tattoo he'd ever done. The conversation was curiously disjointed, but Rasmus was elated.

Rasmus enjoyed Matt's company, and took to popping into town every few days, for coffee or a drink, as a head-clearer when the studio got too intense. It was great that this guy didn't know who he was.

36

❧

You in Your Condition

OCTOBER
En route

RÓISÍN ARRIVED ON time, vast, having been assisted by every gallant on the train, male and female. She was looking amazingly beautiful: her skin like an untouched magnolia petal and her curls growing through again, thick and silky and scruffy. She'd hardly had to wheel her own bag ten yards in the whole journey, which was just as well because the flesh was bulging around Nico's ring on her swollen hand and it bit into her with the handle of the suitcase. She couldn't have taken it off if she'd wanted to. Which she almost did.

There'd been such a lovely little girl opposite her. Róisín hadn't been able to take her eyes off her. She was maybe six, in a little tracksuit, her hair tied back. Stripy socks. *Am I really going to be in charge of one of these?* Such pleasure the girl took in everything! She smiled shyly at Róisín when she saw her looking. Sources of great joy to her included breathing on the window; drawing a little face in the steam; showing her mum how cold her cheek was after she'd been laying it against the glass—"Feel it, Mum! It's really cold!"; managing to wiggle on her own through the crowded train as far as the loo and back;

scratching her mum's head, and making faces with her about how disgusting the sweets they ate were: "You hate these ones, don't you, Mum?" "Yeah, they're horrible." "Yeah, I hate them too. Can I have another one?" Her cheeks were round and red like apples. The mum was plump and fake-tanned, with dyed black hair and pale turquoise nails and eyebrows like a crow's wings. "I never been on a train before today!" the little girl announced with real excitement. "It's lovely. Look, Mum, there's four buildings look exactly the same!"

"They're tower blocks," said her mum. "People live there."

Róisín so hoped she and her kid would be nice together, like them. She thought of her own mum. *The long, long conversations with all of us, while stirring a pot and running a tap and soothing a baby, and yelling to someone not to do this or that thing that shouldn't be done. My lovely family—and here I am running away from them all—because sometimes it's just too much.*

"Look at that big building. Look at that one. Look, there's a window open! There's a human, Mum! Two humans! And a human dog!" The girl knew that was funny and glanced at Róisín to see if she laughed.

My child who will be half Nico, Róisín was thinking. *My child who will grow and I will look after it and feed it and be amused by it. I'll be in charge of its socks and its lunch and its tea and its moral welfare. My boy or girl. Not just a baby. A lifetime.*

The woman looked across at her. "When's it due?" she asked, and the little girl stared as if trying to see right through to the baby inside the lady's belly.

Róisín's tears were right there, jewel-like, so close. If she'd moved too quickly, they'd have overflowed.

Nell and everyone thought she was mad to go racing off to France. They all agreed she should be nesting. "You should be up a ladder painting shelves and us telling you to get down from up there," Nell said.

"I *am* nesting," she'd said. "Only in a different way. If Nico were here it would be different . . ."

"Well, durr," said Nell.

Who is this Rasmus, they all wanted to know, after Nell put the news about. Who is this man you're off abroad to see, and you in your condition.

He's just a friend. It's work! Why, what do you think?

Several Aunties back home didn't know what to think, and made sure everyone knew it. Her mum and Nell took care of them with some firm slap-downs on the family WhatsApp groups. She's an adult. It's only France. The baby's not due for at least another month and no, of course she's not flying, she's going on the train. It's for work!

Róisín was not worried at all. She was restless restless restless. She couldn't sit still anyway, so she might as well not sit still doing something interesting and exciting and fun. She was glad not to be home. Thoughts and memories of Nico hung so strong around the flat . . . No, she would be glad to lie down in her new bed in a honey-gold French manor house surrounded by lavender and olives (she'd looked at the studio website—oh my God), and chat to Rasmus when he wasn't working, and be cooked for and have nobody telling her things and what to do and not to eat the cheese. To film, store up raw material. It was only a week, and then she'd come home and be mother for the rest of her life.

I'm the Virgin Mary, she thought. *Holy Mary Mother of God, I understand how you felt. Am I ever ready for my stable. Me and my swollen feet and swollen hands and massive overheated self.*

She emerged from the station into warm October sun and a marine twist to the air, and she drank it in as deeply as her squashed lungs would let her.

Now, which of these fine cars is my donkey?

◆   ◆   ◆

THE CAR WAS a low-slung leather-seated Citroën, with magazines and bottles of Perrier in holders in the back. The driver was a
young, hyper-relaxed, long-haired Chinese man of about twenty, in
jeans and an Iggy Pop T-shirt; terrible English, French accent. Eric.
The air smelled of woodsmoke and lavender; the car of polish and
air-con and money. The journey was short; the gates broad and automatic between golden stone gateposts, the grounds sweeping, the
trees poetic. The building lay low and prosperous, like a lazy cat in
the afternoon sun. When Eric turned off the engine, she could hear
the sea. *Fuck me, it's gorgeous.*

The arcade of windows, the huge pots with citrus trees, the red
mossy tiles, the last autumn roses lounging like starlets on their
boughs. The *openness* of everything. The *quiet.* The *warmth.* In England, any warmth there ever is is always showing off: *look, I'm here!
I'm special, be grateful!* This warmth didn't give a shit. It just lay around.
Her shoulder blades slipped down her back, and she shivered. The
journey, the days, the months, the worries, began to slide off her.
She hadn't even known she'd been tense. *Of course you've been tense.
Idiot.*

She glanced at the sun in the sky and thought, *there's time.* "I'm just
going to swim if that's okay?" she said. "Is Rasmus working, do you
know?"—and Eric thought he was, and took her up to her room, and
told her the beach was just at the bottom of the lawn, through the
gate, and dinner was at eight thirty, and Róisín wondered if she had
died and gone to heaven. She was thinking about that as she struggled into her pregnant-lady tankini with the expanding panels, and
flung her kimono round herself as best she could, and set off, bare
feet over the dark-wood floorboards, the worn stairs, the cool flagstones, the short short grass, and the prickly sand of the dunes, to
where the beach and the rocks and the setting sun lay spread out

before her, the bay and the horizon, as delicious and welcoming as an embrace.

Oh my God oh my God oh my God, as she stepped forward into the gentle evening waves, cold but not too cold, ankle, knee, splash, *ooh*, sliding up her thighs to her waist, which always gave her the giggles, and the weight left her as the sea took over. Her skin shivered, her legs rose, and she was in. She let her head fall back, limbs afloat, scalp a-tingle, as the water found its way into her scruffy, hot, travel-weary hair. *Oh my God oh my God oh my God*. Her belly suspended before her like a child's picture of a desert island. *Just needs a palm tree growing out of my belly button.* She closed her eyes. The water held her.

It was a good ten seconds before she thought of Nico, and how if she were a really amazing swimmer, or a whale, she could swim south and south round the foot of Italy and back up the other side, across the Ionian Sea, as far as Ithaca, and maybe he would be there off the rocks at the opening of the bay at Frikes, dolphining about in the wine-dark sea.

She'd pulled herself out and was perched on a black rock in the last spot of sunlight, wrapped in an assortment of cloths and robes, trying and failing to reach her toes to dry them, when Rasmus came out. Walking across to the bay, he saw her, this curious mermaid, newly arrived in these exceptional surroundings, taking to them with such ease and pleasure. A memory, suddenly: he'd managed to bring Jay out of the ward, and down into the stark ugly courtyard where the staff went to smoke. She'd sat there in her wheelchair looking at the spindly tree and the concrete and the gray Tupperware sky, saying, "Outside! Look at it! It's amazing! Never forget, Ras."

Róisín looked up and waved. He hadn't seen her for weeks. She had hair! Scrunched and trying to be curly, but not quite long enough yet. Sticking up from the salt. And she was massive. She looked like thick cream overflowing from a jug.

"Heya!" she called, her arm up in the air. Her smile was purely happy. It wasn't that the grief wasn't there. It's just that space had been made for happiness.

SHE WAS SITTING with Rasmus at a long table in a long dining room. Outside, the last of the roses dripped from the balustrade, and cypresses stood tall against fading blue skies. She felt the presence of the sea twinkling below. On the dark wooden table in front of them lay the detritus of a big meal: a wide dish of roast chicken, white linen napkins, green salads, and long green beans; empty plates and glasses where everyone else had already eaten. Brass candlesticks. Róisín was mopping up chicken juice and fresh livid green olive oil (pressed the day before, as the harvest was in full flow) with a piece of bread. Rasmus was waving a chicken drumstick about and asking her about her mother's childhood. A flask of yellow wine stood elegiacally among Duralex tumblers; some of the roses draped about in a rough blue jug. Woodsmoke and beeswax in the air.

"Well, she *is* kind," Róisín said. "And was when we were small. But she had a great many children."

"Whereas mine . . ." Ras said, and fell silent.

Róisín had suddenly remembered the meal outside the pub in February. Only eight months ago. Eight whole long enormous months. Forever, and no time at all. *And now here I am drowning in material perfection, in all the beautiful things the living get.*

Eric brought in a dish of raspberries and a jug of cream, and started quietly clearing away plates and remnants.

"You are ready for Pernille, in the Mill Room," he said.

"Fine." Rasmus smiled. "Sorry," he said to Róisín. "I won't be working every evening. But look, there's everything you'll need. Library, pool, hammocks, little cinema. Wurlitzer. I'm using all the Mellotrons, though. Go anywhere, unless there's a red light over the door. We can sort out the filming tomorrow. Will you be all right?"

Her room was west-facing and had a four-poster and a freestanding claw-foot bath in it. There were twelve books on the bedside table and a fire set, ready to light. She'd already made friends with the cook, Francine. She would be all right.

That night she gazed at the beautiful bath, but the idea of lying down in it, seductive as it was, also made her nervous. What if she couldn't get out again? A comical and embarrassing scene unrolled in her mind . . . French firemen called to hoist her out, a great pregnant wench lolling in a sling midair . . . No.

Instead she had a beautiful shower in the bathroom next door—well, a wet room really, at least she thought it was what was called a wet room, though she'd never actually seen one before. Anyway, there was no requirement to keep any part of it dry; it was lush as a waterfall, roomy, a strong massage as it drummed on her shoulders and her back, steaming her lightly, not too much. Someone had laid her bathrobe on the towel heater outside, so it was warm for her. She came back up the corridor like a massive movie star, and dried all of herself that she could reach before slipping between the posh sacking sheets. *Would you look at that, someone's been in and lit the fire.*

She pulled the plump pillows and bolsters around her to prop her on her side. She had half an idea of reading a few chapters. She didn't. She was out like a light.

37

And Where Does That Lead?

OCTOBER
France

RASMUS WOKE THINKING about the bass line on "83 Miles the Wrong Side of Birmingham." Whatever Pernille thought, it needed to be grittier. It needed to sound like tar. He actually had some samples of hot tar being extruded onto a road. But it didn't sound how he wanted tar to sound.

Róisín woke up needing to pee, again, and thinking about the film she really wanted to make, and the filming she was here to do, and the gap between the two of them, and how glad she was she hadn't sent that email.

Rasmus went directly into the main studio and started work.

Róisín went to her camera bags and unpacked the PXW-FS7 II 4K, which Ayesha had been good enough to let her bring, all eleven grand's worth of it. She was filming here "run-and-gun," as the more macho cameramen called it. A little bit Dogme 95. She was determined to be noninvasive. Perhaps one day she could make the film she dreamed of; these days would provide material. But was that not taking advantage of their friendship? Using him? *Because he was famous?*

She was very far from sure that she wasn't being a schmuck. That if Rasmus knew what was on her mind he wouldn't be disappointed or hurt or angry. *But he doesn't care about what I do, why would he care?*

Because you've become friends.

But I won't be doing anything wrong.

You're afraid to be honest with him because you like him.

Yes.

And where does that lead?

Evasiveness. Manipulativeness. Lack of trust.

Don't you trust him?

So far, yes—

So take your time—

But if you're honest with people and you start to trust them and then you like them, then . . .

Then what?

They die.

She went downstairs to the flagstone dining room, and ate a croissant with pure yellow butter and homemade jam, plus coffee. There was almost no room inside her for food now, so she put two muesli bars in her pocket knowing she'd be hungry again in an hour. Francine was bottling tomatoes at the table. "Just come and ask," she said. "Anything you need to eat, just tell me." They had the conversation: is it your first, when's it due. Francine had four children. Francine did not know Nico was dead, or why Róisín was here without a father for her enormous pregnancy, and she didn't ask. She said: "The kitchen is open, and there are always snacks over there—" gesturing to a table at the other end of the long room. "Eric can always help."

Róisín wanted to cry. She loved being helped. Turns out you can give up on pride and independence for a moment or two. You can accept a cup of tea, or a week in a place with staff.

She went outside, walked, sat, watched the beauty. Umbrella pines, silver olive leaves shimmering, people calling to each other as they clambered around in the trees, throwing olives down on the nets. Voices carrying. Smell of autumn and woodsmoke on the air. She set up the camera. Local color. Minute-long still shots. She had the spare battery.

That afternoon and the following morning she filmed Rasmus and Pernille in the main studio: a huge room, done up like a gentlemen's club, polished wood everywhere, massive sofas, bookshelves. Even the mixing desk—clearly twenty-first century—was built into a mahogany-and-leather frame with a nineteenth-century glow. Thank God for the space! Her size made her move very slowly. Rasmus, Pernille, and the musicians ignored her, but for the odd grin. She felt like something from a Japanese animation: a huge, slow, benevolent monster, silently gliding about, observing.

She liked the balance. Both of them working, separately, together. She had to remind herself not to film only him. Once or twice he glanced up into the camera and it was as if he'd caught her.

He offered her a line to the desk for the sound. Occasionally he came over and put headphones on her. "Here," he'd say, slipping the big puffles over her ears. *Snug.* He didn't ask her what she thought of anything, or tell her what it was. She closed her eyes and listened to disembodied webs of sound: frameworks and infills, isolated lines and vocals and solos, layers hanging alone in silence. It was like looking at a painting color by color; seeing random stills from a stop-motion. That afternoon the theremin player arrived and Róisín filmed her, hands plucking sound out of air. A Scottish Ghanaian arrived with a van full of African drums, rolling his shoulders and turning his face to the sun.

The concentration was tiring. When she went to lie down, images flew round behind her eyelids.

She longed to lie on her back, but was convinced that if she did so she would suffocate, and also squash the child. She wasn't looking up how big it was anymore. She knew how big it was. It was as big as a baby.

She wanted to be able to film all day, but her body wouldn't let her. She was afraid of being unprofessional. *It's unprofessional to be pregnant. Is that what you're saying?*

It's tiring *to be pregnant. I've got a full-time job going on right inside my body, manufacturing this miraculous item.*

Every time it kicked she heard the words "Heya. I'm here. I exist!"

In the evenings they all ate together, speaking English, French, Danish. Rasmus spoke Danish with Pernille. Róisín was surprised. *But why wouldn't he? His mother was Danish.* He seemed to be a different man, in the different language. *I hardly know him.*

38

❦

Enthralled

OCTOBER
France

JAY WAS WATCHING out for Róisín. She was surprised by the ferocity of her feelings. She envisaged a velvet cape of protection flung round her; a halo of blue and golden light. When they arrived, she'd handed over Róisín's well-being to Eric, to Francine, to Rasmus. She swam with her, circling her on the surface and below, a porpoise, a spiral, an intention. She sat by the wet-room door, listening for danger. She glided behind her up the stairs, and in front of her when she came down, an invisible cocoon. She lay at night in the chair by her bed, unless Nico came—then she moved on.

She was amused to see how the studio enthralled Nico. He'd never seen a theremin before, let alone Ashanti talking drums. He was craning over everybody's shoulder.

"Was this your life then?" he asked Jay. "Because bloody hell!"

"A bit," she said. "Long ago." She was grateful for having had choices, not regretful over the ones she'd made.

39

A Bench or a Grave

OCTOBER
France

EVERY NIGHT, OUT like a light.

All in the dark like the Protestant bishops, Nico thought—a phrase he'd got from Róisín, or from her granny, to be precise. It's what you say when you turn the lights out for a child.

He didn't go into the shower room with her. *That would be creepy. Why? We've had plenty of showers together before. But it would. Because she wouldn't know.* He didn't watch her undress, though that had been his privilege for years. It seemed different here, in this new place, which was for her, and not for him.

I don't belong here.

He sat now on the edge of the bed, recognizing her sleeping breath. He just wanted to look at her. *Sleeping Beauty,* he thought, not for the first time.

If I could tell her, without it giving her the shock of her life, I'd tell her this:

Róisín, my love.

I am so happy, so happy for you.

*You can talk to me anytime. I'm here. You don't need a bench or a grave.
I didn't go into the shower with you tonight. I'm going to respect that you
have a life to lead and I don't. I'm thinking this through. I don't know what
happens now.*

I feel . . . unfinished.

If I had my wish . . . Well.

It seemed safe to kiss her. She wouldn't wake. This wasn't a fairy
tale. He wasn't there. He could—

She shifted, and made a little noise.

He kissed her: her cheek, not her mouth.

*I could lie down. She won't wake. She's always been a deep kipper. I could
just lie down.*

He rested his hand on her belly. A ripple ran up his arm.

All in the dark.

He lay down behind her, resting his arm weightlessly across her
huge waist. Feeling the life inside.

Pulled himself away. *Stop it.*

JAY WAS GLIDING silently across the bay and back, swooping
under the water and bursting silently through the surface, when Nico
appeared.

"Look at those beautiful olive groves," she called, rolling onto her
back amid wavelets of silver on the black water. "The trees look like
brains against the night sky. And the nets spread around. It's so
magical."

He was pale and serious.

"I can't bring myself to swim out, though," she said. "I'm not sure
why. It's not like I'll drown."

"I kissed her," he called across the darkness.

"What do you mean?"

"While she was asleep. I kissed her."

Jay swam swiftly back to the shallows, and stood, water running through her. "Nico," she said, coming out.

"While she was asleep," he said again.

"Oh Nico . . ." she said.

"I can't be," he said helplessly. "I know I . . . and I want to . . . but I can't. It's too much. I put my hand on her tummy and she almost woke and I . . . It's so dreamy, like a miracle. Or a nightmare. I can't even tell."

Jay tried to speak but he shushed her. Carefully, respectfully. *Shh.*

She whispered: "I would put my arms around you."

He closed his eyes. After a while, he said: "I'd lean my head on yours."

She sat him down beside her on the rock where Róisín had sat before; lifted her arm as if to drape it over his shoulders.

"I'd stroke your hair," she said.

"Thank you," he murmured.

But for the sea, rustling irrevocably up and down the sands, all was silence and stillness.

40

Cheeky Sod

OCTOBER
France

IT BECAME A rowdy, restless night. Dreams and storms built up, a ragged moon set sail, and winds came up that promised rain, then fell away. As Róisín dreamed of Nico holding her, kissing her, lying down with her, so Rasmus dreamed that he was awake, and found himself again in that strange and lovely and slightly sinister frame of mind where you're aware of being unconscious and yet quite a lot is going on. Toward morning, Jay was there.

She sat on the bed, and curled up beside him. *So real. Half conscious. Hypnogogic. No, the other one.*

"Is this a dream?" he said, and she told him, "Kind of."

Hypnopompic?

"Is it like last time?" he said, and she laughed quietly and hugged him. "Because you said . . ."

"Never mind what I said," she murmured. "If there's one thing we learn, it's that things change."

Don't wake, he said to himself. *Don't be too alert. Just stay.*

After a while he sat up, and took his guitar, and sang her the new songs.

"Backing vocals?" he asked, and she closed her eyes and smiled, and the harmonies rose out of her, and she made a few comments on the lyrics that made him smile as wide as the southern sky. The wind was rattling the windows and shifting in the long curtains.

"How've you been?" she said.

"I can live on alcohol and marzipan," Rasmus sang to a simple tune in the chords they called James and Sebastian, still picking. *"Err . . . I can live on week-old vindaloo-ooo—"*

"Yeah, don't you do that again," she said, which made him snort. *". . . I can live on promises, you bet I can,"* he continued, jazzing it up with a minor seventh.

"Oh *nice*," she said. "Rhyme for marzipan. *Chapeau.*"

". . . But I—can't live—without you . . ."

Their eyes met.

"Your go," he said, still picking.

"Verse two," said Jay, counting in: *"Okay . . . I can live on hopes and dreams, um, and Mama's prayers . . . I can live on Jeee-sus too; I can live on—ha ha—coffee and gummy bears, but I—can't live—without you . . . "*

"Middle eight!" he cried, and whistled the melody, which wandered into Nelson.

She joined in: *"You're my . . . er . . . vitamins, my venial sins*—is it okay to say VI-tamins, not vit-tamins?—*ah, my poetry, my prose; my happiness that's deep within, my . . . er . . . butterfly? No—daffodil!—my rose . . .* Does that sound like she's deep within his daffodil? And does that not sound a little rude?"

"You *are* deep within my daffodil, my darling. Always. Chorus?"

"You're my everything," she sang. *"I can't live without you; you're my everything."*

He played on a few bars, noodling, thinking. Then:

"*I can live on oxygen and three-chord songs,*" he sang. "*I can live on grace out of the blue . . . I can live on nothing for however long it takes, but . . .*"

She joined in.

"*I—can't live—without you . . .*"

He ground to a halt.

"You can, you know," she said.

"Can I?"

"Yes," she said. "You're doing it."

There were tears in his eyes, on his face. *Don't open your eyes. Don't wake.*

He held on to her. The thought of her. *Don't go.*

"I can't believe a word you say," he said. "You said you wouldn't be back."

"Couldn't keep away, baby," she murmured.

He strummed and hummed: "*Couldn't keep away, baby* . . . nah. Bit clichéd."

"I'm pretty sure this was not the first ever use of 'I can't live without you,'" she said. "Or 'You're my everything.'"

"We bring our own special magic, though, don't we, babe?"

Jay sang it loud, kinda Motown-y: "*We bring our o-o-own special ma-agic, yeah don't we, babe . . .*"

"Very Sonny and Cher," he said.

"I love you," she said.

"I miss you," he said, and it was too much.

He jumped up. "Look!" he said, pulling his T-shirt off and showing her his astonishing new tattoo, still swollen and gleaming, scabbing over.

"Oh, wow," she said, tracing the tendrils. "It's going to be beautiful. Oh, look!"

"What?" he said,

"I'm there!" she said.

"Where?" he said, spiraling round and losing himself. Turning and turning: spinning and emerging. Her hands caught him. He'd forgotten it was a dream. Deep in it.

"There's a *J* behind your heart."

"Really?" he said, craning his head round trying to look at his back, but he couldn't see. "I didn't know about that!"

"The tattooist put it there without saying," she said.

"Must have! Cheeky sod, but how—?"

"Is his name Nico and does he have a rose on his wrist?"

Ras smiled. "Come here," he said.

His mind was full of leaves and nightingales and roses.

It's a dream after all . . .

He woke with his heart thumping: he'd let her go again, he'd lost her again, she'd slipped away while he was sleeping—

But she only came when he was sleeping—the images fled.

The emptiness was unbearable.

He thought about the tattoo, and her liking it. Closing his eyes again, he tried to think what it looked like, remembering it in the mirror. But of course he hadn't seen *it*. He'd never see it in life. Just images and reflections.

A new song was coming to him. *There goes the past again . . . you think it's yours but it's gone.*

He sat up. D minor seventh?

> *There goes the past again*
> *You think it's there but it's gone*
> *It slipped away while you weren't looking*
> *You didn't turn away for long*

"Jay," he said. "I like this woman. But I need time alone and so does she, and she has a baby and her own dead lover, and you are queen of my heart."

No answer.

41

Feathered Hat

OCTOBER
France

"RASMUS," RÓISÍN SAID over breakfast a couple of days in. "Feathered-hat moment."

He looked up.

"They still want me to follow up on the remaining questions from the interview . . ."

This produced a long silence. She sat with it. He didn't see any need to apologize for taking his time. Then he said: "Will it damage you if I say no?"

She'd picked up his habit: she, too, thought before she spoke. "It would help me if you said yes," she said.

"Feathered-hat-wise?" he said. "Would it be a feather in your cap?"

"Kinda."

He thought some more. Ignored his coffee, his toast, the peach on his plate. He ate peaches on toast.

"I don't want to," he said. "No."

"Oh," she said. "Okay. Um. Yes, of course." She felt slapped.

"It's not personal," he said. "It all grew rather. From no press to filming the show to the interview to your being here—"

"You *invited* me here!"

"Yes I did, and I want you here. I do want you here. But I don't want you to interview me anymore."

And that *was* a slap.

She didn't know what to say.

She'd fucked up. What had she done? Any or all of the following: *been unprofessional. Been absentminded. Taken him for granted. Been unable to control myself. Been insecure. Let him down. Let myself down, dreaming and scheming of intrusive projects I haven't talked to him about. Stealing his soul. Having ideas above my station. Getting in the way. STUPID pregnant woman. Too big. Milk for brains. Untrustworthy. Not worthy of his respect.*

"Oh," she said.

"It's not personal," he said. "I mean, it is personal. Don't you have enough footage to be doing with? For them? I mean—tell them I was being difficult. It's absolutely not your fault."

"Okay," she said, mortified.

Pernille popped her sleek little head round the door. "*Vi er klar,*" she said, and Rasmus stood up.

"I'm sorry if . . ." Róisín said. "I—if my pregnancy has intruded or affected anything."

He said, "Why shouldn't it? It should. It's real and important."

"Yes," she said.

"But it hasn't anyway," he said. "Let's talk about this later."

"Nothing to talk about," she said brightly, picking up her crois-sant. "Hardly going to come and interview you when you don't want me to! It's fine—I'll tell them you were an utter impossible bastard."

"Attagirl," he said, nodding, as he headed off.

Róisín put down her breakfast and lumbered upstairs. *Fuck fuck fuck.*

*Humiliating, to hang around. Like she was here for the jollies. For the
linen sheets and the fucking late-season peaches.*

Whenever things went wrong in her family, or with Nico, she just
rode it out. Withheld any response. That was her habit. Things pass,
after all. You don't even need to address them. Don't give them the
oxygen of your attention, someone had said. But for her that was just
a kind of fear, really. In a big family like hers there wasn't much point
fighting, because there was always someone who'd shout louder, or be
more invested. She was more likely to just go and read a book and
wait till it was all over. Deny it had mattered that much anyway. Lick
her wounds, maybe. Absolutely withhold what she felt about it.

Go home, get the footage sorted—she had plenty of studio
footage—maternity pay, concentrate on the baby. Never mind.

She checked the time: ten fifteen. Checked her ticket: open.
Texted Eric and asked would someone be able to take her to the station for two o'clock. No reason to be here after all.

Time for a last swim.

She texted her friend Ciarán in Paris before she walked down—
there was no reception on the beach. OMG he would love to see her
and yes, he'd meet her off the train but Jesus, Róisín, aren't you about
to have a baby? When's it due?

Not for a couple of weeks, she said, nothing to worry about.

"WHAT WAS THAT about?" Nico said. "That's no good."

"He can be very direct sometimes," said Jay.

They were drifting up the stairs behind her.

"Evidently," said Nico.

"He just says what he means. He doesn't always think about how
it might sound to someone else—things of theirs that he wouldn't
know about, that might hang unspoken on what he says."

"Uh-oh," said Nico.

"Like she'll think it's her, rather than interviewing, that he's saying no to."

"Yes."

"He needs to make these things clear. Rule out misinterpretations."

"You think she's misinterpreting?"

By now they were sitting on her bed.

"Yes. But she's pregnant. It's his fault. He knows better, but he's forgotten. He's engrossed in his work."

"So is that why he doesn't want her to interview him again? Because it's disturbing his work? Because that's not been apparent."

Jay smiled. "No. It's because he doesn't want to relate to her as a window through which other people will stare at him. He wants to feel safe with her. He's having to mind himself constantly because even though he trusts her, or wants to, he knows there will be footage, so he can't just throw himself open."

"He should have said that."

"He kind of did."

"Some things you have to say more than once."

"I think he's planning to."

"It may be too late," said Nico, as Róisín pulled out her suitcase and started collecting up her things.

"Then you get what you want," said Jay.

"I don't want it anymore," he said. "I want them to like each other and do their own fucking being-alive thing. As they wish."

42

~

Melty Like a Whale

OCTOBER
France

SHE WAS WAIST-DEEP, facing out to the mild sea, cradling her belly with her neoprene-gloved hands, crying. *Come on, sea, lift me up and comfort me—* She felt like a bloody maiden in a folk song. Abandoned. *When my heart you'd so beguiled, why did you skedaddle from me and the child, Johnny, I hardly knew ya . . .*

Clearly this was not about Rasmus. *Rasmus owes me nothing, it's not like I've put any . . . he's a passerby, I don't even know what I'm doing here, fuck's sake, why did they let me come?*

Obviously this is about Nico.

Who left.

When you're not good enough for them to stick around for.

JESUS FUCK, Róisín, as if Nico had a great big heart attack because you're not good enough! Stop that right now. You know everything isn't about you.

She couldn't stop crying, though. She let herself and why shouldn't she. It was fucking sad, after all. *What should have been the happiest time in his life and in mine. Nothing is guaranteed.*

The thing is I'm alone in this. I am alone. And I am responsible.
I alone am responsible.

She walked on out, swaying herself through the gentle waves, her fingertips dragging lightly on the surface, and softly launched herself out to swim. *And this is why I love it*, she thought. *Because water really and truly does take the weight off your shoulders, supports you and soothes you, lifts you up when you can no longer carry your own burdens.* The tension rippled off her, shivering off her shoulders and down her spine, she could nearly see it shaking the water as it went, shimmering out from her in concentric circles, her back now in the only comfortable position that existed in this world anymore, her whole self a great big AAAAAHHHHHHH—then she rolled over and dived down, underneath, not the jackknife she'd usually do, instead sheer strength, a stream of pearls behind her through the calm and steady water, from her strong kicking feet and her clear breath as she powered down. She rolled over onto her back down there like a seal, free in this other element, free of the weight, of the sheer corporeal mass of herself. She opened her eyes to the salt and the light, and saw herself reflected on the underside of the surface, as if she were in a different world, in the past foxed with mercury; or a future, beyond imagination. Her heartbeat roared in her ears; the sky and the sun beyond were so far away. In that moment she was happy. Strong. Melty. Like a whale. A sea mammal.

She twisted back up to the surface, and burst up wishing she could spout. *Imagine having your nose on the top of your head . . .* The movement in her torso didn't stop. Something carried on twisting, churning. Diving around inside her. A kind of gurgling sensation.

Oh.

Then a kick—not a baby's little heel, but a fucking donkey thwacking in the base of her belly.

Holy shit. Holy Mary Mother of God.
Swim in.

Swim in.

For a moment she thought of the *Birth of Venus*, of whales, they do this all the time. *I'm just an animal . . . starfishes! Unity with nature.*

Then *sand. Bacteria. Thirty-seven weeks. Placenta. Seaweed. Cold. Breathing. Tiny lungs. Nonsterile. Emergencies.*

Jellyfish.

To be honest, it was the jellyfish that did it. All the rest could be filed under "whales do this all the time."

Is this it?

At the appointment last week the baby had been head-down. "Ready when you are!" they'd said, cheerily. Nobody said, "Don't travel."

Well, maybe they did. She couldn't recall. She wouldn't have listened. Probably.

Her feet found the bottom and she paused for a moment. Nobody on the beach. Her phone rolled up in her kimono.

Phone who?

Home?

Hospital?

No reception!

Car coming—

Francine?

Water was streaming off her as she walked in. *Off me? Or out of me? Or both?*

She'd left the kimono on a high rock so she wouldn't need to bend to pick it up. She released herself from the top of her tankini. Too cold, too wet. Kept the bottoms on. Felt safer. Wrapped the big towel round her torso, and the kimono over that. Remembered that gorgeous photograph of Beyoncé so pregnant in a kimono. *Birth of Venus, that's me.* She glanced back out at the sea.

She dried her salty fingers and found her phone. Leaned gingerly against the rock.

She texted Nico. It's happening, darling. It's starting.

•   •   •

NICO READ IT over her shoulder. Laid his hand on her head, so gently. Sat beside her, his hand on the back of her naked neck.

"Her waters have broken," Jay said. "We must get her inside. Infection can get in, now the caul is punctured."

"I know," he said.

"'Course you do," said Jay kindly. "Now, who would she want? A woman? Shall I get that nice cook?"

Nico looked up and nodded.

Jay found Francine in the kitchen garden. She was getting in the last of the tomatoes, which lay jade and coral in the basket on the ground beside her. Jay stood in front of her and said, RÓISÍN RÓISÍN RÓISÍN RÓISÍN RÓISÍN RÓISÍN RÓISÍN RÓISÍN RÓISÍN, as loudly as she could, as clearly, as strongly. It had worked with Dougie; it had to work again. But Francine did not seem the sensitive type, ghost-wise.

So, as Francine was reaching into the depths of one of the big leggy tomato plants, Jay laid her hands on the largest, finest, glossiest tomato in the little basket. With concentrated effort, she felt for the solidity of it. *It's a living thing, it can help, I can help, come on . . .*

The veil is thin again, Jay thought, and she was right: she felt the smooth movement under her fingers, felt the momentum build, and grinned with relief as she tipped the tomato out of the basket and onto the dusty path that sloped through the ilexes down to the beach.

Francine glimpsed it as it rolled, scarlet against the dun. She huffed, *how did that happen? I must've tipped the basket, how odd*, and went after it. She bent to pick it up, and looked up as she rose, down toward the beach: Róisín on the rock, swaying gently, arduously arching her back, her head craning back as if she were about to howl at the moon.

Francine had grown up on a farm. She had seen that movement before. Sheep make just that arch. She hurried down.

•　•　•

WALKING UP TO the house with Francine, Róisín's legs felt as if they had come unscrewed. She sat on the wooden bench by the front door, propped up like some ungainly doll, unable to bend in the middle. Her stout ankles stuck out on the path. How she wanted her ankles back, her slender, well-turned ankles, so fine and pretty, so lost in a pudding of flesh, two puddings of flesh, packed so tight into the skin it was almost painful. *Pregnant all over, that's me. And coming to bits.*

Francine was on the phone to the hospital. Eric appeared, and actually said, "*Oh là là*," which made Róisín laugh and laugh.

"Bring her water to drink," Francine told him.

"Don't leave me," Róisín said, and Francine said that she would not.

"Is this it?" she asked.

"Yes," Francine said.

JAY LAID HER hand on Róisín's forehead.

Nico stood by. "I'm even less use than fathers usually are at this moment," he said.

"It's not about you, darling," Jay said with a smile. "But you've made yourself felt before. Just—do that."

"I don't know how we do it," he said.

"Me neither," said Jay. "Just do it."

Nico slipped behind Róisín and wrapped himself round her like a blessing.

RASMUS CAME OUT, white-faced. "Hey," he said, smiling. "Are you all right? What do you need?"

"A doctor," Róisín said. Her breath was short. "They're coming to take me away . . ." She smiled and then yelled—a hard wail she tried to curtail. "Sorry," she moaned. She looked amazed.

"No apologies," he said. "You yell. You do what you need to do." He sat by her. "Shall I come in with you?"

She laughed again. "They'll think you're the dad," she said.

"Can I call anyone for you?"

"Text Ciarán," she said, passing her phone to him. "With a *C*. Tell him I won't make it to Paris tonight."

Rasmus took the phone and held it out for her to unlock it with her fingertip.

"Were you going to Paris?" he asked.

"Never mind," she said. "And Nell. Tell Nell."

The ambulance was delayed.

"Come in and be comfortable," Francine said, so they helped her in, and she perched on a bench in the hall, and that was no good, all wood and flagstones and music industry magazines laid out on a table, so she walked around in circles, and around and around and around. Francine pursed her lips.

Rasmus lifted her phone. He opened texts, and saw the last one she'd sent. It's happening, darling. It's starting.

Such a sigh left him then.

He found Ciarán, saw the exchange, felt like a turd. Messaged: Ciarán, this is Rasmus, Róisín's friend. She's gone into labor early so won't be on the train. Call me if you like. And he put his number.

JAY SMILED. PERFECT punctuation, as ever. He was texting Nell now, giving her his number.

This baby is coming soon, she said.

RÓISÍN, YOU NEED a bedroom, said Nico.

"I think I need a bed," Róisín said. "I can get upstairs. Want to take some clothes off."

"Or we can get in the car and go," Rasmus said. "Which do you want?"

"Whales do it in the sea," she said. "And sheep on hillsides. Bring me to my linen sheets. If the cord's round its neck, loosen it and slip it off. Clamp it both sides and cut it if you can't get it off." She paused for breath. "Don't cut it otherwise. Don't pull it, whatever you do. Wash your hands," she threw over her shoulder as she started up the stairs, slowly and carefully, a galleon gliding up and out of sight.

Francine went with her. Nico and Jay, too.

"Me? Or Francine?" Rasmus called up after her.

"Francine, of *course*!" she shouted back. "You go and write a song or something!"

He stood in the hall, thinking. Then he went all round the house looking for the right cupboard: one full of clean towels. He brought piles of them up, and paused by her door before stepping in quickly, not looking, and plonking his pile on an armchair. "Good luck!" he cried, eyes averted, scurrying out, half a glimpse of her kneeling up in her kimono, her arms wide, her hands against the bedposts behind her, her back arching. She looked like a ship's figurehead in a crazy gale.

She laughed. "Get out of here, you monkey!" she cried.

Francine was taking instructions on the phone.

"You know where I am if you want me," Rasmus called from behind the door, his heart pounding. He laughed, feeling idiotic, and went down to the studio to write something.

NICO WAS IN front of her on the bed, gazing at her, eye to eye, close. "I'm here," he said. "Right here." Nico had delivered a lot of babies. Hardly ever in a bedroom, funnily enough. Lay-bys, mainly. Car parks. Once on a train.

"FECK!" Róisín yelled.

JAY STOOD BY Nico, clocking the length of time between contractions. Occasionally she went behind the bed and took Róisín's head between her hands. She kissed her clammy forehead. *You are doing this beautifully*, she said. *You are doing so well. You're a fucking heroine. Don't push between contractions.*

Róisín roared.

"You are doing so well," Francine said. "Don't push between contractions. Breathe and count. They'll be here soon."

Not soon enough, said Nico.

"Not soon enough," said Róisín, exhilarated, panting, terrified.

Then it kind of stopped.

And started up again and *oh my fucking God.*

NICO STOOD PROUD as a warrior king at the head of the bed. A girl. A daughter. His line continued after all.

Without thinking, he knelt, and leaned in, and spoke to her in Greek. *You little beauty*, he said. *You wonder.* Her eyes drifted open: looked right at him. *Κόρη μου. Σε αγαπώ*, he said. *I love you. My daughter.*

She heard him all right. He could tell. She blinked at him. Their souls, in transit. Arriving as he left.

TIRES ON THE gravel below; brakes, voices. Rasmus: "She's upstairs."

Francine calling out of the window, "*C'est arrivé! Vous êtes en retard!*"

Rasmus hurtled down the corridor, beating the footsteps pounding up the stairs. Róisín was laughing. Her hair still wet from her swim, sprawled on the yellow and gold brocade bed, pillows thrown all over the room, body battered and bleeding, holding on to this tiny thing, waxy, warm, and damp, so strange, so natural, so weird, so perfect, and the livid cord between them still throbbing.

"Rasmus, look!" she cried. "Look what I did!"

The cavalry swarmed in, and with one look at the situation decided to take her to the hospital.

"Oh, must you?" she said chattily. "It's so nice here," as someone carefully clamped the cord.

"*Voulez-vous le couper, Papa?*" said the paramedic to Rasmus.

Róisín laughed and laughed. "I told you so!" she cried. "Well, go on. D'you want to?"

"Do *you* want me to?" he said, borderline aghast.

"Someone has to," she said, so he did, and the squidgy crunch of it made him shiver.

"I'll get your things together," he said.

"*Félicitations, Papa!*" said the paramedic, as she wrapped Róisín in a blanket and rolled the two of them into a chair, down the stairs, into the ambulance.

Rasmus banged on the doors.

"I'm fine!" yelled Róisín. "Go away, I've no pants on."

"Sorry," he said. "Your phone . . ." and passed it in.

"*Tout va bien! Ne vous inquiétez pas,*" the paramedic called cheerfully.

And they drove off, and standing there on the drive Rasmus felt suddenly sick sick sick.

Jay was beside him, kind of leaning on him, as if she wanted to soak him up. She knew he didn't ever want to see a woman taken off in an ambulance again, not even for the best of reasons.

"I guess she does not want for two o'clock her car," said Eric.

Rasmus bit his lip and said, "Bring it now. Come on, Francine. What will she need in her bag?"

Francine passed Eric her apron, and put on her sunglasses.

43

Yellow Roses

OCTOBER
Marseille

RASMUS WAS IN the family room at the hospital, surrounded by luxurious shopping, writing on his phone. Francine had gone into town to the children's clothes shop, and returned. It had been a couple of hours. He didn't know what was happening.

"*Monsieur?*" A nurse was approaching him. "*Elle est prête,*" she said, and beckoned him to come.

Rasmus put away the phone and followed. Approaching the room, he stopped. "*Je ne suis pas Nico,*" he said.

The nurse was puzzled. "*D'accord,*" she said, and went back inside.

Rasmus turned away, and slid down the wall. Nurses and trolleys, gurneys and the beeping noises of lifesaving machines. Voices down hallways. Swing doors.

Everything is all right, he told himself. *It's gone well. Not everybody goes to hospital to die.*

Jay was sitting next to him on the floor. Her hand on his black denim thigh, her head on his tense shoulder. Tears running down her face.

◆ ◆ ◆

"*VOTRE MARI*, MADAME," said the nurse.

"Who?" Róisín said, not looking up.

"*Votre* . . . 'usband? *L'homme aux yeux d'argent.*"

"Is he here?" she said.

"*Oui.*"

Róisín closed her eyes. The tiny weight of the child on her was shockingly alien and yet already entirely familiar. They'd given her something for the pain, she didn't know what. That earlier hysterical energy had drained like a sluice.

The nurse was now rinsing something in the sink by the window. "Yes?" she said. "No?"

"Does he want to come in?" Róisín asked.

"I think so, yes," the nurse said.

Róisín was nodding. "Yes," she said. "He should come in."

The nurse straightened Róisín's sheets and wiped her face. "*Quel beau miracle,*" she said, patting Róisín's hair and smiling at her.

Moments later Rasmus put his head round the door. "Hello," he said. He had on one arm a bunch of yellow roses almost as long as himself, and on the other several white carrier bags. "How the hell are you?"

"Bit knackered," she said. "Thank you. But I've a feeling it was worth it."

"Let me have a proper look then," he said, putting things down. His voice was gentle. He remembered what she'd said about the chemicals dousing the infant brain, the adrenaline and the serotonin. *All that screaming.*

"It must be pretty traumatic being born," he said.

"Poor little blighter can't know what hit her," Róisín said.

"Her?" he said, and looked up with a smile.

"Her," said Róisín. "My little daughter."

He was kind of dumbstruck. "Can I?" he said, meaning could he peep in and take a look, but Róisín, misunderstanding, said, "Yeah, 'course you can," and wrapped her a little tighter in the hospital shawl and passed her up.

He took the bundle. She blinked up at him with delicious, unseeing, alien eyes. Made a little fish-mouth. *So delicate and new.* She was skinny and somehow kind of see-through. *Really, like a comic-book alien. Or a comic-book alien was like her.*

Well, she looked at him, and she took hold of his finger with her tiny, soft hand.

"Hello, little one," he said. *I've held babies before,* he thought, though he couldn't remember when. *I can hold a baby.* And indeed he could. He was breathing especially carefully in case adult breath was too much, too robust, for such a tiny new creature. His hand seemed so big and old and worldly next to her.

"Seven pounds three actually," said Róisín.

"That's big for an early baby, isn't it?"

"She's really not very early at all, apparently. The due date was off."

"Oh good," he said, sitting down. He couldn't take his eyes off her. "So she was really an aubergine all the time we thought she was a courgette . . ."

"Her pomegranate days were long behind her . . ."

"And here she is, the full pumpkin . . ."

"Funny-looking pumpkin," said Róisín. "She looks more like . . ."

Black-haired, brown-eyed, red. Stick limbs. Unbelievably clean and new. "Like a newborn human," he said, and she laughed. Laughed quite a lot, actually.

"Are you on drugs?" he asked.

"Yes! Finally."

"I had some leftover morphine of Jay's at home. Probably just as well I forgot."

"Lucky you didn't offer it to me," she said. "I'd've been at it like a ferret up a trouser leg . . ."

"Oh," Rasmus said. "Talking of drugs. Chocolates. Grapes." His long arm held the baby easily as he passed the small packages over.

"You're relaxed with her," Róisín said, mildly surprised.

"It's funny, isn't it?" he said. "I didn't think I would be. But look how nice she is!"

They both looked. She was squeaking, tiny little noises like a mouse at the back of a cupboard, little mouth movements.

There's a silence you get when staring in disbelief at a newborn. Not unlike the silence when food finally arrives at a table full of hungry people. An *at last* silence. An *ah, that's what we needed.*

Rasmus broke it.

"Don't race back to London," he said. "You are one hundred percent welcome at the studio. It might be nice, and you presumably shouldn't travel yet. You'll be fed and laundered and kept company. Clean sheets. Francine is very excited. Also Eric, who I learn is the eldest of five. He wants to babysit. Think of it as a recuperation. No rush. Oh, and . . ." He passed over the carrier bags. "Francine got her some things. Including many tiny pairs of bloomers, and a furry set of pilot's combinations, apparently, though my French may be letting me down here . . ."

They took it out. It was a smart little onesie, white and exquisite, side-fastening, with a little hood.

"Better get her a little airplane to fly, to go with it," he said.

"They're just waiting for some results," Róisín said. "Make sure she's properly ripe all over. We should be out tomorrow."

The baby's squeaking became insistent, and Róisín's arms came up. It was time to feed her.

Rasmus knew that breastfeeding was something you had to learn. *Who wants to learn with someone leaning over their shoulder? Someone who knows nothing about it.* He passed her back.

So he said, "Text me and I'll come and fetch you. And if there's anything you need, if you want me to tell anyone or anything . . ."

Róisín smiled at him. It was brief.

She's busy now. And will be for a while.

"*Au revoir, mademoiselle la capitaine*," he said with a grin, and he left.

As he walked down the corridor, he thought, *I could just open my arms.*

And, *What are you doing?*

I could.

I have music to make, the album, the tour—

I'm not a boy. I'm a grown man. I could.

Now is not the time. When is the time?

Jay stood in front of him.

He shivered as he walked through her.

44

∽

The Songs

OCTOBER
Marseille

NICO WAS IN the hospital car park, gazing across to where an umbrella pine stood so magnificently you had to think it meant something. A quick wind off the sea rattled it, sending a skittering of pine cones across the tarmac.

"Pine nuts," he said. "My mum would have had me after those in seconds. Koukounaria. Delicious."

"Mm, pesto," said Jay. She'd had an Italian friend in London who made it fresh, from basil and pine nuts and garlic and Parmesan. It was one of those foods where the stuff in the jar was *nothing* like the fresh and juicy real thing.

"Quite like," he said. "No cheese. Lemon juice. Not necessarily basil."

"I don't even think about food anymore," she said. "I've forgotten about it."

"Me too," he said. "What *do* you think about?"

"Big question," she said. "You?"

He folded over his legs, put his nebulous head in his discarnate hands.

"Sometimes ghosts are just envious," he said. "Of the living. They just can't let go."

"Is that us?"

Barely ten feet away, Rasmus was opening the door to the car, climbing in out of the wind, turning on the engine. Nico and Jay watched him.

Nico turned a bitter gaze from Rasmus to her. "Hell, yes," he said. "Isn't it?"

Am I envious? she thought, her eyes still on the car, and the man inside it. *No, because I am pragmatic. I don't waste time wanting what I can't have.*

Is that true? Was it true when I was alive?

Now, looking back—I gave up too easily. But I don't want to feel I wasted anything; I don't want the pain and trouble and regret of saying to myself: you did it wrong. You should've done it differently.

Are we going to get judged? Is someone going to say I should have done it differently?

"I don't think I envy the living," she said, as the car drew out. "I think I was ready to go."

Nico stared at her for a moment. "I never want to leave," he said. "My love will not die."

"That's sick and weird, though," she said. "You know the songs."

He didn't know the songs. Well, he knew some songs, but he didn't know what songs she meant. He thought of Róisín singing "Fhir a' Bháta" for Rasmus.

"'Sweet William's Ghost'?" she said. "Sweet William is dead in his grave but Lady Margaret still wants to marry him. Or, William marries another, Margaret dies of sorrow, and comes to stand at the foot of his bed. They kiss when they shouldn't. Their halls are full of kine, or wine, and their bed is full of blood. Reports vary."

"Hmm."

"Shall I sing one for you?"

"We've nothing else to do," he said.

So there in the car park she sang for him, in her full-throated, gospel-inflected voice:

> *There came a ghost to Margret's door*
> *With many a grievous groan*
> *And aye he twirléd at the pin*
> *But answer made she none.*

> *"Is that my father, Philip?*
> *Or is it my brother, John?*
> *Or is it my true love, Willie,*
> *From Scotland, new come home?"*

> *"Tis not thy father, Philip*
> *Nor yet thy brother, John*
> *But tis thy true love, Willie,*
> *From Scotland, new come home.*
> *Oh, sweet Margret, oh, dear Margret*
> *I pray thee speak to me,*
> *Give back my faith and troth, Margret*
> *As I gave it to thee."*

> *"Thy faith and troth thou'll never get*
> *Nor will I give it thee,*
> *Till that thou come within my bower*
> *Till that thou kisseth me."*

> *"If I should come within thy bower*
> *I am no earthly man*

And should I kiss thy earthly lips
Thy days would not be lang."

"Thy faith and troth thou'lt ne'er reclaim
Nor yet will I thee lend
Till you take me to yonder kirk
And wed me with a ring."

"My bones are dug in a far kirkyard
Afar beyond the sea
And it is but my ghost, Margret,
That's speaking now to thee."

She stretchéd out her lily-white hand
All for to do her best —
"Then here's your faith and troth, Willie
God send your soul good rest."

Now, she has kilted her robes of green
And a piece below her knee
And all the live-long winter night
The dead corpse followed she.

"Is there room at your head, Willie,
Or room there at your feet,
Or room there at your side, Willie,
Wherein that I may creep?"

"There's no room at my head, Margret,
There's no room at my feet,
There's no room at my side, Margret
My coffin's made so neat."

"Hmm," Nico said again.

> Then up and crew the red cockerel
> And up then crew the gray —
> "'Tis time, 'tis time, my dear Margret,
> That you were gone away."
>
> No more the ghost to Margret said
> But with such grievous groan
> He vanished then in a cloud of mist
> And left her all alone.
>
> "Oh stay, oh stay my own true love,"
> The constant Margret cried
> Wan grew her cheeks, she closed her eyes
> Stretched forth her limbs, and died.

She stopped.

"So what are you saying?" Nico asked.

"You know what I'm saying," she said. "I'm saying—if there's a ghost, there's something wrong. And you know, I feel it calling. Sometimes the living call louder, like now, today, the baby . . . and I feel strong again, and I can be with Rasmus, like these past days . . . but then that ebbs, and the living world fades out, and I fade from it—have you felt that?"

He had.

Jay extended her arms, rolled her neck, although there was no stiffness to stretch out. *There are times*, she thought, *when a person has to recognize that desire and truth are not reconcilable. They're just not.*

"What have you learned from the songs?" he said after a while. "If they're our main source of information."

"That a ghost being around on earth is an unnatural and undesirable state of affairs, and we won't get away with it."

"We *are* getting away with it."

"Nico," she said. "The people we love most in the world would be terrified if they saw us. We can only be with them sneakily. If we did that in life, would they not despise it? And wouldn't *we*?"

"We're *not* in life, though," he persisted.

"Exactly," she said. "We're not. Yet here we are. We're in the wrong place."

He was silent.

"Do you think we maybe feed off them?" she asked. This fear had come to her recently. It made her feel sick. "Like your Greek vampires?"

"No!" he said.

"Think about it."

"We'd know!"

"But would we? We know nothing! Where do we get our energy, to be? What *is* feeding us, if not that?"

"We don't feed off them," he said.

"Well."

"Are we in some cycle?"

"Exactly," she said. "Are we?"

"Just look at us," he said. "Two ghosts arguing about the nature of being, in a hospital car park. There should be a word for it."

The sun was going down, clouds moving and gathering, the wind shivering the trees. Jay sang again, her voice pure and low:

> "Cold blows the wind to my true love,
> And coldly drops the rain
> I've never had but one true love,
> In the green wood he lies slain.

I'll do as much for my true love
As any young girl may
I'll sit and mourn all on his grave
For twelve months and a day."

When twelve months and a day were gone,
The ghost arose to speak
"Why weep you now at my graveside
And will not let me sleep?"
"'Tis just one kiss of your lily-white lips,
One kiss is all I crave,
One kiss, one kiss, from your lily-white lips,
Then return back to your grave."

"My lips are cold as clay, my love,
My breath is earthy strong
And if you kiss my cold clay lips
Your days they won't be long."
"How oft on yonder grove, sweetheart,
Where we were wont to walk
The fairest flower that e'er I saw
Has withered to a stalk."

"Go dig a grave both wide and deep,
As quickly as you may
I'll lay down in it and take my sleep
For twelve months and a day."
"When will we meet again, sweetheart,
When will we meet again?"
"When the autumn leaves that fall from the trees
Are grown green and sprung up again."

A couple passed them, coming off shift, putting up their collars. The weather was turning.

He said, "So you're saying I shouldn't have kissed her and now she'll die?"

"I'm saying we can't go on kissing them," she said, "and that if we *are* wandering souls, what is there that we need to put right?"

"I'd like to apologize to Róisín for being a bit of a dick," he said.

"So do that. And I'll—but listen," she said. "Perhaps we're created by the living. We could be psychological. Hallucinations, or dreams, or delusions."

"And?" he said.

"Are we a figment of their grief?" she asked. "Is it them holding us here?"

"Hmm."

"Perhaps we need them to let us go?"

Oh, unbearable thought.

"Ah," he said.

A car drove through them, slowly, water arcing up from its swishing tires. Jay glanced down, and up to him, with a soft snort.

"Are you ready to go now?" he asked.

"Yes," she said. "We're just traces of ourselves, Nico. We don't belong here." Then, "Watching her contractions, you know—it's the same kind of rhythm. Pushing, and then not. Breathing through it. Knowing it must happen."

He laughed. "Anti-birth."

"Not so bloody," she said.

"Nor so rewarding."

"We don't know that."

"Are you expecting reward?" he asked.

She waved a hand. "Maybe when I was a child . . . but no. I only ever expected nothing, and I got—all this."

"A car park outside a hospital containing my daughter who will never know me," he said.

"Oh, Nico," she said.

They started moving, drifting along the road back toward La Ficelle, in the dusk.

"I tell you what I think," she said. "I think we have to break up with them. And them with us. Release each other from our promises. Give back our rings."

"Oh," he said.

"I think we should . . . talk to them," she said. "Next time I fade, I want to turn my face that way. Throw myself on that tide."

"But we don't know what's there," he said.

"Come on. We never knew. No one ever knows."

He nodded.

"You coming?"

He dropped his head again. "Love wants to happen. And it will," he said. "I can't stay here and watch."

45

Baby Baby Baby

OCTOBER
France

THAT NIGHT STORMY winds set in, and the day after dawned wet and dark and ferocious. Late in the morning Róisín scurried from the hospital exit like a maiden lost on the blowy moors, pulling her baby inside her coat as skeins of rain lashed the car park. Eric was waiting with the Citroën, and Rasmus was beside her with an umbrella blowing inside out in his hand.

"It's howling a fuckin' hooley!" she yelled, as she clambered in bum first, the child getting squashed as she bent, and the great confusion of trying to get everything in the right place. Eric had located a car seat, but Róisín didn't want to let go of the baby. *You have to,* she told herself. *You can keep your hand on her. I suppose this is how it is now: fuss, care, fear, forever.* Doors were slamming in the wind, bins rolling over, wet hair slapping on faces. The umbrella pine was tossing its head like a '70s heavy metal star and Róisín felt not dissimilar. Back inside she went straight upstairs and into the shower while Francine held the child in the corridor outside, with Róisín calling out "Is she okay?" every thirty seconds.

She sluiced everything, sluiced and sluiced and looked herself over. She was all still there. Just about. Dried herself off, bloodied the towels, felt embarrassed, felt fucking great, actually. She took a moment and gazed out of the window, at the storm over the sea. *I was in that so recently*, she thought. Froth was whipping up from the waves on the little beach. The rocks scarcely visible in the rioting water. *Baby*, she thought. And *food*. And *baby*. *Baby baby baby*.

Someone had prepared a cradle beside her bed. *Maybe visiting rock stars bring their babies with them*, she thought. *What excellent service. This place.*

Francine brought up four vast cabbage leaves. "For the tits," she said cheerfully. "When they are hot and red."

Everything is different now.

Róisín and the baby retired to the four-poster bed, overlooking the wild sea, comforted by the thickness of the walls and the flickering fire. In the depths of linen and gold brocade, peace came to her: they lay warm and still, each in her own way contemplating the mystery of life. When Francine brought up soup, steak, spinach, chips, béarnaise sauce, watercress, and a crème brûlée in a little copper pan, Róisín ate the lot with a glass of Malbec.

She dozed.

The baby woke. It was dusk out; the curtains were drawn and someone had slipped in and put the baby in the cot. Róisín rolled over cautiously, maneuvering around her tight, swollen breasts, to look at her. *What's your name, Captain Aphrodite Anto Pumpkin?* She picked her up and brought her into the bed. Changed her nappy. Kissed her, breathed her. Dozed again. Woke again. Her breasts were leaking: milk everywhere, great blue veins. Aphrodite was still asleep. Róisín took a photo of her and sent it to her mother. To Nell. And to Nico.

You want to watch that, she thought. *That's not a great idea.*

She desperately wanted now to be at home, with her mum and her sister.

And also not. Wanted to keep this distance from reality, from the everyday, *which, let's face it, is going to be along for you soon, with its bus stops and its drabness and its sole responsibility. Because you know this is all bonkers. Fairyland. I mean, why am I here with these people, in this country, in this house, with this baby? Where is my life? Where is Nico?*

So she sat for a while, leaking milk and bleeding and crying.

She picked up the child, to cry on.

Oh no. None of that. None of that.

Aphrodite was fish-mouthing again. *She's not called Aphrodite.* Carefully Róisín tried again to feed her. She'd lost weight since she was born. *This is normal. It is normal not to believe it is normal.* Róisín propped herself up, put a pillow across her lap and the baby on the pillow like she'd been shown. Tiny little pink frog. Moved her breast about, positioning the nipple. Tiny relentless mouth. *Jesus, but you're determined for something so extremely small.*

WHOA she latched on.

FUCK.

PAIN.

Tug like steel hawsers through your veins . . .

And then . . . not.

Seven minutes on one side; six minutes on the other. *Fucking brilliant!* The little belly was suddenly full like a bag; *you could almost see the milk inside, the skin is so fine.* Plus, tits relieved. She reached for the cabbage leaves and slipped one into each bra cup.

Oh joy. The chill.

It's all so extreme and now I'm lying here with a bra full of cabbage.

As she lay back, her phone pinged: something in the mysterious world of flying messages had shifted, and a bunch of texts and emails came in all at once. Mum, Nell, Ayesha—*bless 'em. All of 'em.*

She thought to check her emails. Smiled to see one from Rasmus. *When had he written that?*

Oh! A long one.

Dear Róisín,

You won't have time to read this for a bit, so pick it up in your own time. You are four doors down bringing a baby into the world; I'm sitting here feeling useless. But perhaps there will be some time in the middle of the night when the baby is asleep and you're not, and your mind is racing and maybe you'd like to have it taken somewhere else. If not, put it to one side and read it later. Weeks, months, years. Doesn't matter from my point of view.

Róisín glanced down. The baby's eyelids were fluttering. She was quiet.

I'm so sorry you wanted to leave. I think I must have been very thoughtless in how I expressed myself about not wanting to be interviewed. It genuinely isn't about you as a filmmaker. I think you're probably a good filmmaker, and could be a very successful one—creatively, I mean; professionally I know nothing about it so am not qualified to say. But the pieces I've seen of yours are beautifully shot and edited with wit and clarity. The way you move around, the way you look at things, the questions you ask, and the angles you find are indicative of a creative, original, and curious approach. As a filmmaker, of course all these are desirable and necessary qualities. In a friend, too. The problem for me is the overlap. I realized I wanted your eyes, not your camera, to see me. I wanted your ears, not your microphone, to hear me. I wanted to speak to you, now, not to the world and his wife at a later date via you. I want the

questions you ask and the answers I give, and the questions I
ask and the answers you give, to be between us. And I wanted
our entire conversation to include, to the exact same degree, as
a natural part of it, me asking *you*, hearing *you*, looking at *you*.
This is what made it difficult for me.

I want to tell you a few things. Things I wouldn't be able to say to
camera. I offer you this in apology, and as a confidence.

When that cab knocked me flying, and I was lying in the middle
of Atlantic Avenue with several too many broken bones, the
ambulance needed to know who was going to pay for my
treatment. I was unconscious, but they were put on to the record
company, who, as I lay in the ER at the hospital in Brooklyn, were
already, apparently, trying to dispute the responsibility. The
argument was along the lines that I wasn't on band business
when the accident happened. The facts being I wouldn't have
even been in New York if it weren't for band business . . . So far,
so distasteful; so threatening and frightening. I didn't know
anything about it. Meanwhile Jay got hold of her uncle—a
lawyer. He got hold of his pal—another lawyer, who had cut his
teeth on shyster record companies representing musicians in
Detroit in the '60s and '70s. These two took my case in hand. It
took forever and was hideous and boring at the same time. But
they rescued me.

The tour, of course, had to go on. The band and the company
whipped in a new guitarist, moved the parts around a bit, and
headed off without me. On the one hand, of course they did. On
the other, we were kids together, and I was not a part you could
just exchange. Again, I didn't know at the time because for six

months Jay only told me good things, but George had made
three separate visits to her, trying to persuade her not to leave
the tour. He was pissed off about her and me being together; I
knew that. I pretty much knew that he had at least partly invited
her on the tour in the first place because he, er, wanted her. I
hadn't told her though. A woman likes to believe that men are
better than that, and God knows her talent and disposition
meant she deserved her place in the band in every way. His
interest in her just muddied that. I don't know if she knew. If he
ever tried it on, as they say. All these years together and I never
asked her and she never told me.

George never acknowledged her as a member of the band.
To him she was an extra. Hired help. The traditional attitude of
rock 'n' roll! So revolutionary—and yet amazingly enough
the only woman, the only Black person, is the only one
not on the contract as a member. They thought I was mad to
suggest it.

You'll be wondering why I'm telling you all this now.

So you can understand me.

Yes, the timing is not great. I do know that. Now of all times it
isn't about me and my past, and it won't be for years. But I upset
you and I'm sorry.

So, George wanted her to go with the band, go with her career,
go with the music, go with her bright future, go with the double
wages he persuaded our manager to offer. To go with him, and
not to stay with me. She stayed with me.

I don't think I'm exaggerating if I say I never quite forgave myself for letting that happen. Something in my mind or heart still thinks I should have dissuaded her. Done something gallant—I couldn't have pretended I didn't love her. But anyway, it was about two years before I could do anything at all. She took me in hand. She worked, she really worked; she kept me—until her uncle's efforts paid off, the insurance finally took the debt off us, and the royalties started coming in on the songs. I would have been lost without her. Literally. No parents, no family, not a lot of friends, to be honest. The band had been my friends. So then I was able to pay for her medical training.

We both lost so much. Lost out. Or—look at it this way: we both didn't quite get the golden prizes that hovered *so* near. We didn't win.

But I look at George now, and I'm pretty sure that despite everything, if there's a competition going on (and maybe there still is, in his head) then I did win.

Jay, however, didn't win. She would have liked to go on singing. She wanted to be out there in the world. She wanted a baby. She could have pulled other rabbits out of other hats if my injuries and then her illness hadn't constrained our lives.

I'll tell you about the other rabbit. Her main rabbit. Jay understood that Western society and Western medicine fails Black people by persisting in using white people as the physical default. She very much wanted to work with and for Black people—Black women in particular, because society's other default is male. And medicine soon shows up the differences, and the overlaps, and the areas in between. So that was where she was aiming her ambitions, and

that is where she didn't go, because I was too needy, too
damaged, too depressed, and she chose instead to go with me to
the back of beyond and look after me. And then she got ill, which
happened in waves, and effectively prevented us from having a
child. And then it killed her.

So this is why I am telling you.

She had to wait to find out why he was telling her. The nappy
needed changing again and the nappy-change required a washdown
and hmm, Sudocrem. By the end of that, the baby was hungry again.
The hawsers were strung a little less tight this time, and Róisín found
she was able to balance the child on one pillow and her elbow on
another, to hold the phone at an angle she could read. It felt somehow
louche. *Check me, multitasking. In my four-poster bed.*
     She continued.

I've been thinking about what you were saying about your work,
your frustration, in your emails before you came out, and this is
what came to me. Don't laugh. The timing, as ever, is absurd.
But: have you thought about film school? As I understand it, it
would give you support and training and time to make films
unlike the ones you've been involved with and which haven't
satisfied you. Your professional experience could only be a
useful entrée. It will seem totally impracticable right now, as you
sit there with an entire new person depending entirely on you.
But everything is impracticable until you work out how to do it. If
you like the idea—yes, later, obviously—then I want to help you
do it. I have spent my entire life surrounded by women whose
lives are bruised and battered because of men or by men or
simply because men glide on by without even thinking about it.
My father did it to my mother, leaving her, a depressive with

self-medication issues, alone with a cranky baby. I did it to Jay. I did. Despite loving her and having no intention ever to limit or hurt her in any way, quite the opposite. I made up for it somewhat, but not enough. I am mad and sad about what she didn't get to have, that she so deserved.

So—in your own time.

Re the current project:

To whom it may concern—to the record company and to Ayesha, for example—I will support any desire you have to make exactly the film you want.

I'd like it if you wanted to use that as a calling card for film school. If you're not in a position to pay for film school, what with everything, which wouldn't be surprising, we could maybe talk about that. Fuck it, I'm rich and I'd like to be better at being rich. I gather being generous is an important part of it. So you'd be helping me out.

This offer is not time limited. Just something to think about, when you're ready. We're measuring out our lives in lifetimes now.

Listen, they died and we have to live. We have to go out and be alive and love this world and have adventures. This is just plain fact. I've been locked away too long; you've been thrown from one extreme to another. I'm doing this album, and I'll tour; you've got your baby, and an entire new life to set up. The biggest adventure of all.

I mean, perhaps you have your baby now. I'm not sure what's going on in there. Tell me all about it? Obviously correspondence is not number one on your list at the moment. When can I come? I feel a bit oddly shy about just turning up.

I'll turn up.

Rasmus.

PS It's now many hours later and I'm actually in the family room at the hospital, waiting while they do what they're doing. They say everything's OK.

PPS I'm really not expecting you to read this while you are just out of labor.

PPPS There is an entire new person. It's kind of unbelievable. This is such a totally inappropriate thing to write to you now. I'm sorry. Nerves! Not that it matters at all how I feel. But for the record—I am so impressed by you. I think you're great.

I'd better read this again, she thought. *And then again, probably.*
For all the detail and the delicacy, she wasn't sure what he was saying.
Does he fancy me?

46

❧

A Glass of Champagne

OCTOBER
France

IT WASN'T THE middle of the night; it was about six in the evening. Rasmus put his head round the door, with two glasses, and an ice bucket with a bottle of Ruinart in it. His hair was standing on end.

"Would you like some champagne?" he asked. "I looked it up and if you're feeding her around eight times a day that means every three hours, so if you had a glass now the alcohol would be out of your body in two to three hours for when she needs to feed again, if you've just fed her. That's if she's aware of her timetable and sticking to it. Which I imagine she might not be."

"I would like a glass of champagne, thank you," said Róisín. "Yes, I would. Do you want to hold her? I'm desperate for a pee."

Rasmus held out his arms, and squinted at the baby. "Take your time," he said, as he settled her into his scrawny elbow crook. Then when Róisín returned, he said, "Oh, she's okay here on me," so Róisín just got back in the bed, leaky, sore, and blessed, and stared at her baby from that angle instead.

"She looks nice on you," Róisín said.

"We're old pals now," he said. "That's about ten percent of her earthly existence we've just spent together. Are you cold? I could make up the fire."

"That'd be good," she said, quaking slightly as he stood up, holding the baby; went to the fireplace, holding the baby; and started rustling around for firelighters and laying logs, holding the baby. *You too will come to do everything, holding the baby. Holding the baby is what we do now.*

"You'll probably need, I don't know, a doctor or something?" he said, coming back, holding the baby. The fire started licking and taking behind him. "Should they be coming back?"

The baby stretched, yawned, and made a small noise. She couldn't have looked healthier.

"I suppose," Róisín said, enchanted. He was standing close enough for her to reach out and take the baby's little hand, count the wrinkled fingers. Several times.

"I read your email," she said, stroking a tiny forefinger. "It just came through today."

"I was wondering if it had disappeared," he said, "when you didn't mention it, but I know—bigger fish."

"It's quite a big fish," she said. "Kind of from a different shoal—oceans away."

"Mm," he said, and there was a knock on the door: Francine wanting to talk about dinner, then Pernille, Eric, the theremin player, and the drummer, in ones and twos, knocking shyly, to smile and wonder and say congratulations. Rasmus sat on the end of the bed, leaning on the post and ordering things on his phone: baby clothes, more nappies, a carrier, and a buggy. The fire settled, burning low and fragrant.

"What's her name?" everybody asked, but Róisín didn't know yet. Eric had already drawn up an astrological chart for her. After dinner, people came back with instruments, playing the lullabies and love songs of their youth. Champagne appeared again and the baby's head was wetted. Róisín was asleep by then, so Rasmus made everyone go away.

"You stay, though," she said, half waking, her face in the pillow.

"Are you sure you don't want to rest?" he asked.

"I am resting," she mumbled.

And later in the evening, supper trays on the floor and the baby back in her mother's arms, Rasmus and Róisín lay back on the piled cushions at either end of the bed. He'd opened the shutters: the storm had passed, and Róisín wanted to look at the sea.

"I'd you down as someone who couldn't trust people," she was saying.

"No, no," he said. "It could have been that, but it's not. Jay was an excellent model for trust. It's just that when fame and the attention of strangers start coming into it, I get edgy. It's so fickle that I have to not allow it any value. And the easiest way to do that was to turn my back on it entirely."

"Was?"

"Still is. But you know, there's maneuvering to be done. It depends who and what."

"It does," she said, and they didn't speak for a while, listening to the fire crackling.

"I thought," she said, "Nico is dead, I'm going to be sad forever. Nobody will compare to him or take his place, so how could I ever even think of getting close to someone else, and anyway who would want me when that's how I feel? And even if they did, how could I inflict myself on them, lying?"

"That is very much part of it, isn't it? But then: you and I both know what a good marriage is, a good partnership. We know what we want and need; we know how to love. It's not a competition. It's different."

Róisín would have liked to continue this conversation, but she fell asleep.

Rasmus too.

47

Big Ragged Moon

OCTOBER
France

Dear Róisín,

I was just dreaming. It was shockingly real: right here, in my face. Jay was here. She wanted to see the baby, and so I showed her, and she stroked her cheek, and had tears in her eyes. She said to congratulate you. So—that's for you. And she said she wants me to scatter her ashes. She said she's fed up. I told her how I'd tried to before and they'd blown back at me and I hadn't been able to; she said yes, she knew, but it was all right now. In fact I got the impression she had been there at the time. Then she said she had to go. I asked her, do you want me to take them back to Luskentyre? and she laughed and said the ocean is all one. She said, "There's no water between us." And she said that Nico was going to go too, that it was time.

It was quite disconcerting. I really felt as if she'd been waiting to make sure the baby was all right. Which is me projecting, of course. People often say "something has shifted" but in this case it really has, hasn't it? Right out of your body.

You're asleep at the other end of the bed as I write this. I can see your feet. It's very late, or early. I didn't mean to fall asleep on your bed but now I have.

The storm has completely cleared, and there's a big ragged moon out there. It's shining right at you. You look beautiful.

And restless. Perhaps you're dreaming too.

I'm going to go out now and do what she asked. Off the rocks, in the shining path of the moon, to the west. It seems right.

The timing of this is not going to improve, is it? Not for, what, a couple of years? I know you need to be in love with your girl now. But I'm not going anywhere.

Rasmus.

He slipped from the end of the bed, and out of the room. In the corridor he pressed send.

Done it.

Oh God.

Dear Róisín,

PS I mean obviously I am going out to the beach now. And I'm going back into the studio in the morning. And I'm going on tour in the new year. Do you want to come? You could film. Eric could be nanny.

Rasmus.

Róisín was restless in her sleep, her body slack where it had been taut, aching where it had been full, leaking and confusing. A different size, a different shape, a different texture. A new, older body. Nico was holding her, close but hardly touching, tender, his cheek resting on the top of her head, saying to her, *It's time, it's time, my dear . . .*

What is time? Time for what?

Set me free, he said. *Give back my ring, set me free.*

Nico?

And I will set you free, he was saying.

Oh . . .

She felt his hand leave her shoulder, and she woke with a start. The moon had moved across the window, and the night was filled with its light.

He's dead. He's really dead.

It was as if she simply hadn't really known before *at all*. The man is dead.

Well, that's it then.

Her phone pinged. She blinked at it, flashing intermittently on the bedside table, propped among tissues, a muslin square, and a champagne coupe, like a lighthouse at night on a pile of rocks and spray. And a rose, for some reason. Wet from rain.

There was a tune in her head: *give back my ring to me and I will set you free, go with him . . .*

She picked up the phone.

Rasmus again.

Sleepily she read the messages, and her eyes sprang open.

Dear Rasmus,

Are you awake?

Róisín

Dear Róisín,

Yes.

Rasmus.

Dear Rasmus,

Do you want me to come down with you?

Róisín

Dear Róisín,

No.

Rasmus.

Dear Rasmus,

Come over to me, will you, when you're done?

Róisín

She went and stood by the window, looking out into the night.

I would like to see two figures following him in the moonlight, she thought. *I'd like them to tell us it's all right.*

Maybe they already have.

The baby mewed, and she followed the tight cable of motherhood to the crib. "Hey, sweetie," she murmured, leaning over to pick her up. Both of them were yawning as they settled back against the pillows and Róisín opened her robe and lifted her breast. *Feels so usual, already. One and a half days old. Here I am. Mother.*

Ow.

The skull ring on her finger caught the moonlight. She spread her hand out to look at it.

"This is yours, darling," she murmured, and she reached over the child to pull it off her finger. It came easily—the swelling of her ankles and fingers had subsided overnight, and they were all her own again. *Unlike everything else, which is, for the foreseeable, devoted to you, my baby.* She held the ring up. "It belonged to your dad, who I will always love," she said, and she positioned it by the baby's starfish hand splayed on her breast. "It's yours now. I'm going to put it in a box for you, for when you're bigger." The brown eyes opened momentarily, gazed at her, drinking her in. The tiny determined face.

"Mm-hmm," Róisín said. "All yours. All yours."

She looked out toward the window, her burden so warm and sweet in her lap.

"Mostly."

WHEN RÓISÍN WOKE again, at some ungodly hour of the morning, Rasmus was there at the other end of the bed, collapsed like a giraffe, fast asleep.

She watched him for a while, and then she leaned over and said, quietly into his ear, "Listen, I'm no good at reading between the lines, but was that you saying you fancy me?"

He was laughing at this before he even had his eyes open. So she kissed him. Not a *deeply* carnal kiss, but enough to know.

"Don't wake up," she said, into the hollow of his neck.

"Wouldn't dream of it," he murmured.

"Not yet," she said.

"Aye aye, cap'n," he said, and rolled over.

48

What IS Your Name?

"I INSIST," RASMUS said.

"I couldn't possibly!"

"I insist."

"Oh, but I can't!"

"Why?"

"It's too generous," she said.

He observed her curiously. "That must sound absurd, even to you," he said.

"Yes, it does, but I can't help it," she said.

He put his elbows on the breakfast table and went into one of his diagonal thoughtful stares at the floor.

"Do I have to do something like persuade you you're doing me a favor to make you accept?"

"That's one thing people do, yes," she said.

"Okay. Okay, how about . . . one of the Mellotrons needs to go back, I don't trust Eric not to steal it, so would you and the lassie please accompany it? You'd be doing me a great favor, you really would!" His eyes grew large and frank.

She laughed. "I still can't believe you really brought two Mellotrons," she said. "When there was already one here."

"You can never have too many Mellotrons," he said. "Meanwhile, how about you just accept a favor?"

"It's too much—" she began to say, and he stood up and came round to her, and said: "No it's not. It's the least anyone would do for anyone. Including you. You'd do it. So accept the bloody help."

They hadn't kissed again. God, but they'd looked at each other.

THE RIDE HOME was lovely. Leisurely. Luxuriously sprung, in the back of the big Citroën. Eric stopped every few hours; they ate like kings, and spent a night at Tours. The baby (*What IS your name?* she thought) snoozed, woke, fed. France rolled out before them, wide.

On the ferry, she stood on deck, salt in her hair. She'd chosen the route: Cherbourg to Portsmouth. She wanted to look out, to the west. Have a little think. Hold the baby close. Her first visit to his grave. Her dead dad. A relationship to build there. Important to get it right.

Eric brought her a whiskey. She took a sip, before throwing it into the sea as they left the southern tip to port, to come up the Solent.

"OMG," SAID NELL. "You kissed him. In front of the baby!"

"My fanny not yet healed from giving birth to another man's child," said Róisín.

"You baggage."

"Indeed."

"So can I read his email?"

"You cannot."

"Oh, it's serious then?"

"What the fuck? Of course it's fucking serious."

"Has he got any tats?"

"I don't know."

"Ah so you haven't . . ."

"Nell, Jesus Christ, of course we haven't. Don't be disgusting."

49

Symbolic

NOVEMBER–DECEMBER

Dear Roisin,

I miss you.

Rasmus.

Dear Rasmus

You left out my accents! This has never happened before. Are you all right?

Róisín

Dear Róisín,

I am mortified. Forgive me.

Rasmus.

Dear Rasmus

OK.

Róisín

Dear Róisín,

Thank you.

Factual update time . . . (Does this need a new font? Or the curly one? I don't know. I would think about it, but things are racing ahead, hence the need for the factual update.)

Re band for the tour: I think I'm there. Markus Ofori the drummer, who you met. Katie the Scottish viola player, who I don't think you met. Sharon the violinist (the one working on the world's longest bow stroke) who you definitely didn't meet. On bass, Matt Gruenberg who I've known for twenty years. I've persuaded Dany, my Berlin tech producer pal, to take on keyboards and synths, about which I'm incredibly pleased. And a young Argentine accordionist who is obsessed with Dave Brubeck. They're all coming back to rehearse next week; we'll do some practice gigs, then the tour starts early February: Paris, Barcelona, Madrid, Milan, Rome, Athens, Belgrade, Budapest, Vienna, Salzburg, Prague, Berlin, Brussels, Amsterdam, Utrecht. Fifteen little theaters, fifteen hotels, eleven flights, some vans, some drives, thirty gigs, forty days. You, me, the baby, the travel cot, Eric, the PXW-FS7

ll 4K, and both the Mellotrons. You can leave whenever you
want. What do you say?

Love Rasmus.

Dear Rasmus,

It's ridiculous.

Love
Róisín

Dear Róisín,

Yes, I know. Equally, it's vital.

Love Rasmus.

Dear Róisín,

There is blossom. Francine tells me it is almond. There is sun.
Please think about this. You could film.

Love Rasmus.

Dear Rasmus,

I just don't think I can. I mean I would love to. But all I can think
about is nappies and sleep. What will I do about the nappies?
Will we just leave a trail of baby shit across Europe? What about

laundry? Literally she wears three or four or five outfits a day.
What about all those musicians who don't want to hear a baby
crying on the bus? What about the fact she and I spend the
whole time in bed, or in the bath, burbling?

Love Róisín

Dear Róisín,

Come for a few days. Nobody will mind for a few days.

Love Rasmus.

Dear Rasmus,

STOP PRESS I HAVE A NAME.

She's called Aoife. It's been hard, what with the surnames, what
a combination, and all the opinions there's been floating around
here, but what can you do, a Greek Irish girl needs her
Greek and Irish names or how will she know who she is? I was
actually and seriously tempted by Anto. Such a beautiful, simple
word and meaning. But in the end I just don't want to hang a
sorrow round the child's neck in perpetuity. She'll have her own
relationship with that sorrow. I'm not going to prescribe it. Or
describe it, or proscribe it, or anything. So, on the dotted
line, she's

*** Tarantara ***

AOIFE MARINA TRIANDAFILIDES KENNEDY

Which the moment her grandmother came round became
Evaki-mou, of course, instantly. BTW she now has her first
mataki eye necklace sewn on round her neck.

Re minding: Ayesha might. I'm going back to work in February—I
can't even think about it. It's not that I don't want to, you know
that. I would bloody love to. I have two projects in mind now—
well, three (maybe four, actually), none of which I've been able to
do a stroke of work on. Seriously, I hardly get dressed—it's not
worth it, when there'll be milk and shit and baby-sick and God
knows what all over me within minutes anytime I do. I just drift
around draped in muslin. But a girl can plan, while
breastfeeding, and plan I do. I'm filming all the moments Aoife
lets me: I have to, as babyhood is one of the things on my mind.
Time is boss for sure, for both that and for filming you. You're
right: if I can get raw footage now, I'll be set up for later. I've
been looking into the film schools! There's a lot that are clearly
outright scams looking for rich foreign students, but I've located
the respectable few. This coming September is too soon but
next, I mean the year after next, well, we'll see, but I think I
would like to have it lined up. There's nursery and relatives. The
grandmas can't keep their hands off her. She'd be turning two.

Love
Róisín

PS It's pronounced "Eefa."

Dear Róisín,

That is a beautiful name for her.

I had a dream: I was at the airport, I looked up and there you were, with the baby and the papoose and the luggage trolley piled up between us, and I said "Could it be any more symbolic?" and tried to stretch over and past to kiss you and I couldn't reach you, and you said "No." As in—I think—no, it couldn't be any more symbolic.

We've been having long discussions about the title for the album. I don't like their suggestions; they don't like mine. I'm glad you've found a good one for your project.

Love
Rasmus.

Dear Rasmus,

I'm feeling kind of teenage. I don't know how you lost your virginity. Mine should have been with the boy I'd been with since I was fourteen—i.e., too young—and we had a terrible time deciding when was the right time to do it. Because all around you'd see people meeting, falling for each other, getting on with it. But we'd been snogging for years and so it was a constant anxiety because I didn't want to yet obviously I did, and he really wanted to but also didn't, and to be honest it was exhausting. So in the end we—well, I—decided that we'd go by the law, i.e., hold off (people say wait but to me that just sounds like they're sitting there reading the paper and glancing at their phone, and that's actually not how we were spending our time) till I was seventeen. But to be honest by then I'd gone off him, and was thinking of ways of breaking up, but he was preparing this touching absurd kind of romantic date night for the occasion of

my seventeenth birthday, which I would've found embarrassing
even if I'd still loved him, involving a posh pub on the coast
with purple metallic patterned wallpaper and silver mirrors, and
him in an ironed viyella check shirt and a jacket. Which I
didn't know he was going to do. And I got terrified he was going
to ask me to marry him—WHICH HE DID. Something very
old-school Irish and respectable just leaped out in him, which I'd
never known was there, and I'd this image of me at thirty
married to him with five kids because he wouldn't want
contraception, and going to Mass and doing nothing strange
or new in my life at all, and so I broke up with him that very
night like a complete cow, and he went off crying and I
went out and got very drunk and slept with my friend's brother
instead which was quite the fiasco in itself. And after all that I
could hardly show my face as nobody was talking to me at all, so
I moved to London and went to college and became me.
Anyway, I'm not expecting you to come up with a pretentious
dinner and I'm not planning to dump you before we've even
started but I am . . . nervous. I know I kissed you while you were
asleep, but I think I was mad on mad birth hormones or
something. But . . .

Oh God, I don't know.

Love
Róisín

Dear Róisín,

Yes you do.

Love Rasmus.

Dear Rasmus,

Oh very funny.

Love
Róisín

Dear Róisín,

Thank you for telling me all that.

OK, this is my plan. One day I will look at you and you will look back, or perhaps you will look at me and I will look back, and we will both know that your period of physical and emotional delicacy following childbirth is over, and that our periods of mourning for those we loved (and will always love, only in the way you love the dead, not in the way you love the living) have silently and miraculously slipped over an invisible boundary, into a territory where we can love each other. We won't even need to talk about it. Though I daresay we will.

Love
Rasmus.

Dear Rasmus,

That sounds right.

Love
Róisín

Dear Róisín,

Among the things people do with which I'm not 100 percent
up-to-date is Christmas. It seems all the musicians, etc., want to
go home. Can I come to yours?

Love
Rasmus.

Dear Rasmus,

It depends. Are you ready for the full onslaught of mothers-in-
law? Extreme levels of Greek/Irish negotiation have been
going on about who gets Aoife for Christmas Day, and it turns
out that we, and Marina, and my mother, and plenty of the
rest of everybody, are all going to Nell's in Hastings. So it will
be quite a full-on hooley, I imagine. The drink will be plentiful,
the company mixed, the food excellent—avgolemono,
melomakarona, lahanodolmades, kleftiko, though fortunately
not the one where you've to clean out the lambs' intestines, as
well as all the turkey and stuff (the mams basically turn it into a
grand cultural competition: who can be the most persistent,
generous, and flagrant personification of food-based
national-identity mothering)—and I will leave by 5 p.m. when the
going will begin to get rough. You are very welcome. But be
aware there will be inquisition, maybe disapproval, and definitely
tears.

Love
Róisín

Dear Róisín,

Maybe next year, then. Inflicting myself on you is one thing; on Marina and so forth would be another. When the time comes, I want her to love me too.

Love
Rasmus.

Rasmus

You big soppy!

Róisín

Róisín,

Guilty as charged.

I mean, yes, I want to be loved (everyone in a band wants to be loved, it's symptom number one of any inclination toward stardom and performance) but also, and more importantly, I want to be all right in the eyes of your family. I can't be involved in a family that resents or rejects me. So not Christmas—too highly charged. Especially this one, the first with Aoife and the first without Nico.

Love
Rasmus.

Dear Rasmus,

Then let us fit in as we can.

Love
Róisín

Dear Róisín,

I can't leave here. The band is being created as we speak, and I am the glue, the gardener, the mother. For Christmas itself I'll go to Jay's brother in Ghana. Then we'll be back in the studio on the 29th.

Love
Rasmus.

Dear Rasmus,

That sounds right and good. It's all just dates in calendars but things can jump out, can't they?

In the new year, then. When does the tour actually start?

And do you have a band name and album title yet? It seems a little late . . .

Róisín

Dear Róisín,

First date is Paris on 14 Feb. Valentine's Day! Maybe there's a pub in Paris with purple metallic patterned wallpaper and silver mirrors. Come for the day, even. We could eat ice cream on the Île Saint-Louis.

Oh, I looked at the trains; last one leaves at 8 something. But the first in the morning leaves at 5:40. You could be back with her by 8?

Love
Rasmus.

PS Almost. The band don't need a name, apparently. We're just going out as Rasmus Sartorius. I refused to let it be Raz. Is *For Her* a good title for an album? *Songs for Her*? Or does that bring to mind a single long-stemmed red rose on a shiny black piano lid, and Julio Iglesias? I was tempted by *The Boatman*, actually— death but not death—but there was *The Boatman's Call*, so it's too close.

Dear Rasmus

We're on—Nell will come and stay.

Love
Róisín

Dear Rasmus,

Actually, do you know what? Our meeting can't be the night you open your tour of songs about her. And Valentine's. It just can't. And, coming soon: anniversaries. I don't know how they'll hit either of us, but they will. I just think—I realize I'm thinking this tour is for her. Your farewell tour for her, in a way. I think we should meet at the end. Not the final date or anything significant like that, just—afterward.

Love,
Róisín

PS Can I ask Carola for the list of your dates/hotels, etc.? I want to know where you are.

Dear Róisín,

You're right. Thank you.

How about *Unquiet*? Or does it sound like a horror film?

Rasmus.

PS Of course.

Dear Rasmus,

How about *Jay*? Or, the letter *J*?

Róisín

50

❧

Not So Far Away

FEBRUARY–MARCH

Dear Róisín,

There's a thing called mimosa, do you know about it? All these little lemon-fluff bobbles bouncing and swaying on every breath of breeze, and narrow gray leaves slowly opening like monkey paws to the sun. Smells nice.

I like it.

Rasmus.

Dear Rasmus,

I spent the anniversary of Nico's death in Hastings with Nell. We ate fish and chips and looked at the sea, and rootled in a vintage clothes shop. I didn't think for at least five minutes about how everybody who'd owned those clothes before would be dead now. I'd a long conversation with Aoife on the beach, and that was all right, then we just tucked up at Nell's and watched *Singing in the Rain*, which Nico loved, and lo and behold Aoife loved it too. She's musical! Waving her little hands around and laughing. She knows what sadness is, though.

We lit a candle for Nico, to be commemorative, and she stared at it for so long. Entranced by it. I kind of felt him, in a way I haven't for a while. It was so cold and blustery outside. I know, babies stare at lights. I'm telling her everything now, so she already knows, and never has to feel that there was a time she didn't. Nell sends her regards.

Rasmus, are we getting unbalanced, just writing to each other? Are we? Because I miss him, God knows I do, but I miss you, and you exist and we have hardly started.

Love
Róisín

Dear Róisín,

Something that surprises me is that I miss Aoife too. My theory has always been that you're unlikely to miss a person unless you're in circumstances where that person would normally be, and of course Aoife hasn't been any part of my life at all except those amazing days at La Ficelle, and as any fule kno, Berlin in February is not La Ficelle in October. Perhaps it's because she is just launching on belonging anywhere, at all, that the idea of her can be so pervading.

Thank you for the funny little old-school photo of you both. Where did you find a photo kiosk—is that what they're called? Photo booth? In a very old-school manner, I have put it in my wallet.

Love
Rasmus.

Dear Rasmus,

It was at a christening party of all things! Ayesha dragged us along because she wants me to know more mothers of babies. It was ridiculously glamorous and they had the photo booth, and a person whose job it was to hold a baby up straight while remaining invisible, if you wanted a picture of your baby alone. As Aoife hasn't been alone for a second of her life so far that seemed absurd, but there we go. I don't mind at all being in your wallet. Just don't take me out in bars and cry on me like a country song. I don't know how Aoife feels about it. Mostly all she cares about is milk, and a small woolly thing Mum knitted for her, which she likes to put up her nose. So I reckon it's safe.

Love Róisín

PS MOLESWORTH! I can't believe you're a Molesworth fan.

Dear Róisín,

And Jay's anniversary has passed now too. It's just gone midnight as I write.

I got up. I drank coffee. I remembered. I looked out of the window at Prague. I'm near the cathedral, which has fine old bells, with names. The biggest and oldest is called Zygmunt. I thought about her, but I didn't feel her near. I felt again the punch in the face; the tsunami. I knew what it was. It passed, and by the end of the day, it was you I was thinking about.

I've had those songs about twelve months and a day on my mind all week.

The venue tonight was a little velvet and gold theater that looked as if it had been built for light opera. Prague is beautiful; the people looking after us are unfailingly kind. The audience was the usual mixture of Capos fans, people who bought the album, and the idle curious. I told them it was the anniversary of Jay's death and even more of them than usual cried. Afterward, as we came out, a woman came up to me. (There's been a bit of that, but not too much. I've been avoiding the merch stall, and not signing—the others took it on after some Capos obsessives turned up on consecutive nights in Germany.) This person was American. She'd seen the Capos on the first tour. She remembered Jay. She wanted to talk about her; how fabulous her singing was. Other people have done this, and it's been OK. Or they've told me their heartbreak. I've heard quite a few stories of love and loss, by the stage door, in the rain. Anyway, this woman knew it was the anniversary. "That's why I came today," she said. She had a picture of Jay; an actual photograph, a black-and-white agency eight-by-ten. She wanted me to sign it, and she wanted a selfie of her, me, and it.

I know the songs kind of invite this, but I don't want it. I really don't.

Bear up. We're OK. It won't be long now.

Zygmunt is still clanging away like a ship in a storm. It's beautiful. Going to take a drop of whisky and go to bed now.

Rasmus.

Dear Rasmus,

Christ. I'd not thought of that. By being creative with your sorrow you open it up to public attention, and that includes public attention of any kind. What did you do? I wouldn't begin to know how to handle that.

Róisín

Dear Róisín,

I disentangled myself, and then beat myself up a little about what I owed her and what I didn't, whether I'd invited too much confidence, what responsibility I have here. I finished on the undoubted truth that I owed her nothing. My songs are a gift that I'm happy to give on my own terms, as people give their attention to me as a gift on *their* own terms. I give my performance; I don't give me. I learned that at sixteen when teenage girls first started making eyes at us and waiting outside. Even then I knew the difference, and I knew how I would handle it. It hasn't changed, just because we're all grown-ups now with grown-up sorrows and experiences.

Love
Rasmus.

Dear Róisín,

UPDATE.

Due to everything, the dates selling well, the nice reviews, the album being well received, and now the nomination, the company are quite determined that the tour must be extended. They're saying Japan, where we are apparently suddenly hot and the iron must therefore be struck. And perhaps Australia and New Zealand while we're over that way. The US will be ready to receive us in September, unless we want to hold off for SXSW next year. They're saying a month free at the end of what is now being called the European Leg, then all off to the other side of the world.

I am saying no, and here's the reason. I'm finding it harder to sing those songs. If those songs are what people want, they're not going to get them for much longer. It was at least partially to do with what happened on Jay's anniversary— when I told the audience the significance of the date, then seeing their reaction. I felt in the pit of me that it was some kind of manipulation or exploitation on my part. At least it seemed like that. It wasn't consciously, of course. But.

I talked to you before about how I didn't want these songs honed. And I don't want the performance honed. And it is becoming so, which means audiences are starting to get a version the integrity of which is honed, and thus lost. And I can't sing them without integrity. On one level this is unprofessional of me, yes, but the strength of what I do is that it means something, and these songs mean something else now. So if the tour is to support the album, which of course it is, then that's a problem.

And that woman did upset me. I don't want it to become the Jay 'n' Raz Tragedy Roadshow. Playing with grief too long can become necrophilia. And what you said stayed with me: the farewell tour. At previous gigs—at Bush Hall, and the Albert Hall, I felt that I really was singing for her, and she really was there. But she's not now. She's gone. The farewells have been said; my tabula is rasa.

So we're trying to work it out. My ideal would be to change the focus of the show, do new songs—I have a few and wouldn't need too long to work them up with the band. I could do some of my old Capos songs. And I wouldn't mind singing one or two from the album. It's having the album as the whole of the show that can't continue. If they can accept that—which they should— then yes, end of April off we go again.

In the meantime, the final dates are in two weeks. Amsterdam and Utrecht. Lovely towns. Not so far away. Closer than many places in the UK. Nice direct train. Please come. Please come. It's been too long.

Love,
Rasmus.

PS By the way I'm hoping our Hot Date applies to the end of this leg, whatever happens afterward tour-wise.

Dear Rasmus,

I wondered if you and I would have anything to talk about as grief moves on. I don't doubt that anymore. But I am doubting what use I can be to you. Forgive me, but I'm feeling small. I can't sing, I can't perfect lyrics, I can't save lives, I can't go on tour with you, I can't even film at the moment, I don't have posthumous fans—I'm just a lump, committed to someone else. I can't even go out at night. I haven't even been able to come to you.

Sorry.
Roísín

Róisín,

Hey.

I can't drive. I can't sail. I can't catch octopuses. I can't talk Greek or do tattoos. I can't restart hearts and give the kiss of life.

I don't want you to be her. I want you to be you.

Rasmus.

Dear Rasmus,

I want you to be you too.

Though I would dispute the idea that you can't restart hearts.

Róisín

51

◦~◦

Toward Home

FEBRUARY–MARCH
Hastings and Prague

JAY AND NICO hung together over the sea at Hastings, the wind whipping through them. There was less of them than there had been.

"Look," Jay said, lifting her slip of an arm to point at the figures moving across the beach, shuddering in the cold, the little pushchair piled high with blankets. Judging by the bulk, Aoife herself was tucked inside Róisín's coat, like a second pregnancy swathed in scarves and padding. Róisín's gloved hands lay on her tenderly, head bent in as if they were in conversation.

The wind snatched the end of Nell's scarf, and chucked the bright surf up over the shingle in rainbows of spray. She turned back up toward the old town, saying something, shouting slightly to be heard, though neither Nico nor Jay could make it out. Róisín's arms pulled tighter round the baby, and after a glance out across the Channel, a scan of the flurried milky sea and blurred horizon, she started to pick her way delicately up the beach. Soon after that the snow started: soft flurries, light and quick as a newly swirled snow globe. Shrieks and giggles rose as people noticed: some retreated inside and others came out to laugh and jump. A patch of early golden crocuses craned upward, gleaming and disbelieving, as silver ruffs of snow settled around them. Muddy grass turned magical; puddles slowly froze. Róisín moved between the black sheds and huts toward her sister's home.

Jay and Nico saw Nell come out of the Mermaid, raising the bag of fish and chips in triumph. Nico drifted up after them; Jay hung back. Before the blinds were drawn against the wintry evening, he saw the flicker of the TV screen, heard the muffled crackle of Hollywood music and wit, the settling of a family who had got cold, but were warming up now. Later, through the gap in the curtains, pressed against a window he could no longer pass through, he saw the lighting of a candle, and the baby's steady gaze.

He sat and watched for a while on the window ledge, before swinging his legs round in the falling, twisting snow.

At about four in the morning, when everyone was in bed and the snow had slowed to a thick, heavy fall that was not going to stop, the candle burned down and sputtered out. Nico dropped his head, holding his hand out to Jay. She draped over his shoulder, silently. They hadn't talked. He looked about inside himself for anything, but there was nothing. Even if anybody had been out that snowy night, and had looked up, they would only have seen a drift of pale snow, a skein of frost on a window, a drowsy swan.

When the sun came up, dripping gold onto the white world, he wasn't there. Jay slipped through into the house and curled for the morning at the end of Aoife's cot.

SIX WEEKS LATER, Jay sat alone on a velvet chair in a hotel room in Prague, the ceilings high above her and the ornate gray shutters closed. She had been to the gig. She had seen the woman with the photograph. She had come back alongside Rasmus; now she watched as he stood by the window in his T-shirt and boxers, a minibar whisky in his hand. The bells of St. Vitus Cathedral were ringing out for midnight, and he had creaked open the big window to stick his head out. He'd set up his little field recorder to catch it, and was smiling as the wonderful noise rolled round him.

He left the whisky on the sill, and fetched a hotel notepad. He started scribbling: *B flat, F below, then (40 secs?) sounds like ships horns, trawlers on Turnagain Sound, lonely blare of foghorns calling blindly through a sea fret across San Francisco Bay. E flat! Unexpected.*

He picked up his guitar. Strummed, moved to picking. B flat, F below, E flat. "*By the end of the day,*" he hummed, "*it was you I was thinking about.*" He leaned forward, made a note. "*By the end of the day I was thinking of you.* Yeah, maybe better."

He went over to his laptop, opened it, read a few emails, and started writing.

Jay had never felt so far from him. It felt right.

She lifted her hand. The window swung. He looked up, but Jay didn't look back.

As she stood on the ledge, looking across the great square and the cold night, she didn't see Nico. But he was there, his hand lifted toward her. He'd waited for her. She didn't need to speak.

The doors of the universe swung wide from the stone pavement below and the high cold sky above, from the dark bare trees and rippling strips of pale cloud, from the echoing river and the sound of bells. Before them lay everything: the vastness of eternity, glowing, reverberating, all its atoms shimmering, its darkness shining, its stars glittering, its quantums leaping, its planets swooping. Behind them, suddenly distant, spun the gorgeous little turquoise Earth, plump and round as a blue tit rolling in a birdbath.

They were not alive. They couldn't gasp. Their hearts could not beat faster with the joy of it. The bells fell silent and they were gone.

52

~

Let No One Say That Romance Is Dead

APRIL
London

HIS FINAL FLIGHT was delayed. The trains from the airport were delayed. The Tube was packed. The lifts were packed. He got a cab from the station; all the lights were red. Paying, he dropped his card.

The door to the flat was closed, squawks and squeaks coming from inside. He rested his head against it for a moment before ringing the bell.

A stranger opened, and looked him up and down with a disbelieving gaze. He slipped past her, jet-lagged, girded, dropped his bag in the hall, and found himself ankle-deep in tiny children and balloons. Babygros, bibs. Dungarees. Chocolate-mushed faces. Some were toddling about—*well, those ones aren't Aoife, she wouldn't be doing that.*

The final obstacle. Deep breath.

Róisín was on the other side of the sea of childhood. She raised her head, and her smile when she saw him was like the midmorning sun swiftly burning off a mist. He waved. He couldn't take his eyes off her. The pull was so strong—*can't step on babies, though . . .*

Hello, he mouthed, making gestures of despair with his hands, and Róisín began picking her way across the room. "Seems to me as big a day for the mother as for the child," he said, waving a package, as she drew near. "I've brought, um, well, it's giant plastic sushi. Do babies like giant plastic sushi? I hope it won't turn out to be single-use. Where is she?" *Please let me recognize her.*

"Over there on my brother Seán," Róisín said. He recognized her. Her black hair, which had been flat, was beginning to stand up in swirly little licks. Her expression and her eyes were all her. She was sitting on a man's lap and Rasmus felt a pang.

Róisín had stopped and was just gazing at him. "She's all right there for a mo," she said, and she reached him, and took his arm, drew him out of the room. In the hallway she looked him in the eye. And then laid her head on his chest and sighed like it was the longest breath she'd let out in months.

A gravelly female voice with a Greek accent carried from the room: "Who is that man. Clare? Nell? Who is he?"

Róisín slung herself upright, stared at him, and breathed in again. "Ready?" she said, and she led him back inside.

"Mum, Marina," she said. "This is Rasmus."

A second of desolate blankness. Maternal eyes flicking.

"He lost his wife at the same time as we lost Nico," she said.

Two seconds. Maternal minds ticking. And Marina said, "I take Evaki for the night. You go out and have some fun, my darling. Go and stay in hotel maybe. You look after her, you Rasmus, or we all kill you."

NEW BODIES. NEW territories. Narrower shoulders; a smaller bum. Dryer skin. A hairless chest. Old joys in new forms. Awkwardness. Hunger. Jokes. Surprise. Tears. A rising tide of rightness, making itself felt. Massive relief.

"Do you feel like you're being unfaithful to him?" he asked the curve of her throat, in the dark.

"Of course," she murmured. "Don't you?"

"No. She told me to."

"How literal you are ... Actually, he told me to as well."

"Really? How so?"

"At La Ficelle. The night after she was born. He asked for his ring back, and said I was free. I woke up humming that song: 'Go to Him.' Sounds mad too but I think he left me a rose."

"Hmm," said Rasmus. "Let no one say that romance is dead."

"Let's not talk about them when we're in bed," she said, and rolled back to him.

"And, um, the rose was me," he said.

"IT'S A J, I think," she said, the next morning, white sheets all over the place, bolsters and pillows littering the room. Her finger touched it. "Can you read it through your skin if I trace it?"

He could.

"Or maybe part of the plant. A curlicue. I don't know. Could be either."

"It's a J," he said.

"And there's a rose," she said, spotting it. "And a little rosebud!"

Spring light was bouncing round the room, reflected from the Thames, from the mirrors, moving and shimmering on the ceiling and, it seemed, through the leaves and tendrils.

"Strange," he said. "It's as if it were written . . ."

"Downright peculiar," she said.

SHE WAS CURLED in a chair by the window, a sun-trap, musing over breakfast, when he said, "Jay wrote you a letter."

"Did she now?" said Róisín. "For me?"

"For whoever turned out to be you," he said. "Do you want it?"

Róisín thought about it. Drank a little coffee, looked down toward where the river rippled and streamed. The tide was coming in.

"I'm not sure I do," she said, after a pause almost as long as one of his. "Would you mind if I said no?"

"I would not," he said.

"No disrespect," she said. "But I think we're on our own here."

"We are," he said, just as a knock came at the door. She laughed; he rolled his eyes.

"Oh God, give it here," she said. "I mean, what, would you keep it unread forever? Or read it yourself and not tell me what was in it? We'll both read it and we'll smile ruefully and then we'll—"

It was a waiter come to take away their tray. They sat in dignified silence till he was gone, and then she said, "No, keep it. Maybe one day."

"This time next year?" he said. "For our anniversary."

"You're very sure," she said, a mite saucily.

"I am," he said, and she beamed at him.

"Though to be honest, I'd like our anniversary to be just us, too," she said.

He nodded. Reached over into his bag, and pulled out an envelope.

"Take it then, and read it when you want," he said. "Your choice. Or not."

"Oh," she said, looking at it, feeling it giving off the intense magnetism of the unread. "You've been carrying it round with you?"

"No," he said. Then, "You'd rather not?"

"There's too much going on!" she cried, feeling suddenly helpless. And then suddenly and beautifully powerful. "Oh, there's always too much going on," she cried. "Give it here. I only wish I'd met her. Only then . . ."

"Likewise," he said.

"Weird," she said.

"Balanced."

"True."

"Oh," he said.

"What?" she said.

"And I've written you a song."

She smiled. "Well, go on then," she said, and he put the letter down, and got the guitar.

She said: "But I want to sit on you while you do it."

"Bit impractical," he said, on the side of the bed, tuning up.

She went and crawled round to sit behind him, spine to spine, legs out. Her head leaned back on his shoulder, her nose almost in his hair. "Will that work?" she asked.

"Mmm," he said, tuning, strumming, then beginning to pick, and beginning to sing.

A Note on the Songs

"Fhir a' Bháta" ("The Boatman") is a Scots Gaelic song from the late eighteenth century, written by Sìne NicFhionnlaigh (Jean Finlayson) of Tong, about her fiancé, Dòmhnall MacRath, a young fisherman from Uig. Róisín knows it in Irish, like the version by Niamh Parsons.

"Sweet William's Ghost" (Child 77, Roud 50) was known by 1740, and exists in many versions.

"The Unquiet Grave" (Child 78) dates from around 1400, and is sung to the same melody as "The Star of the County Down," though perhaps not so cheerfully. I commend the very different versions sung by Karliene and the Morrigan.

"The Parting Glass," so well-known from Irish funerals, is in fact Scots. The Dubliners do the business, but Declan with the good voice sounds more like Hozier. It dates from at least 1605.

The "song about I gave you rosewater" is "Se Potisa Rodostamo" by Mikis Theodorakis, from a poem by Nikos Gatsos. Maria Farantouri sings it beautifully.

"Tuwe Tuwe" is a traditional Ghanaian song, which again changes depending who's singing it. The cutest version on YouTube is listed as "Tuwe Tuwe dance performance."

Rasmus's songs "Love Ain't Listening," "One Goodbye Too Many," "Just Because You're Strong," "Blackbird," "There Goes the Past Again," and "Everything" are by me, Louisa Young. Some appear on the album *You Left Early* by Birds of Britain, and are locatable on iTunes, SoundCloud, YouTube, etc. They're not performed by the Capos, sadly; I couldn't get a fictional band to do that. I had to do it myself, with Alex Mackenzie. You can also hear them on the audiobook, sung by the reader Isabel Adomakoh Young.

The poems are "Ithaka," by Constantine Cavafy, and "Crossing the Bar," by Alfred Lord Tennyson.

Acknowledgments

My thanks to my agents Ariella Feiner and Yasmin McDonald at United Agents; my editor Suzie Dooré, Ann Bissell (even though she's leaving me), Amy Winchester, and the team at Borough Press; to Alex Mackenzie for making the music happen; to Boris Romanos for Greek music advice; to Susie Boyt for all those conversations about it; to Dr. Ciarán Rua for Irish expertise; Paul Green for the Royal Albert Hall camera plan; Charlotte Horton; Louis Yaw Adomakoh; Isabel Adomakoh Young for letting me use the song I wrote for her, and for continuing her unbroken record as the finest and most supportive offspring a writer could ever want. To Robert Lockhart and Eva Youren. And to my dear and most consistently unexpected Michel.

Twelve

Months

and a

Day

LOUISA YOUNG

A Conversation with Louisa Young

Discussion Guide

BOOK
ENDS

PUTNAM
— EST. 1838 —

A Conversation with Louisa Young

What inspired you to write *Twelve Months and a Day*?

Life! Death! Everything!

No, seriously, I'm a widow, and I wrote a pretty serious, dark, and strong memoir about him and me, our love, and his alcoholism—*You Left Early: A True Story of Love and Alcohol.* He died ten years ago; life goes on, I met someone new—also a writer, also a widow. We were able to communicate as widow friends with shared experience in a way which was profoundly harmonious and supportive. And, of course, we couldn't help but muse on what we would have made of each other's late partners, what they might make of us now. . . . And the novel grew out of that. I wanted to write a lighter, happier book about loss and recovery, and I wanted to play with the idea of the dead having feelings and opinions, of them being characters in the drama of life for a little bit longer than the living expect. People die; love doesn't. So what are we to do with that?

Rasmus, Jay, Róisín, and Nico are so dynamic. Were any of them inspired by real people?
The situation was inspired by real life, but no, the characters are all made up.

Between Rasmus's career as a musician and the songs that play on the radio throughout the novel, music plays a significant role in the story. What significance does music have for your story? What, if anything, can music teach us?
I'm not a musician as such, but I am a songwriter and I sing, so writing songs for Rasmus gave me a further in into his character. The scenes where he and ghostly Jay work together on music are some of my favorites. My late fiancé was a composer, and we did a few things together, but not enough (he was fifty-one when he died) so in a way that's about him, too. For me all books have a soundtrack, if only in our heads. But, I don't know if you know, quoting lyrics is a very complex and expensive thing to do. You need all kinds of permissions, so it seemed easier just to use my own songs. Plus the reader can look them up online and listen! They're available on CD and vinyl, as well as on the all the usual apps. The album is called *You Left Early*, by Birds of Britain (that's my little band) and I'm doing a Spotify playlist, too.

What was your favorite part of the writing process?
I like it when you fall asleep and wake up in your fictional world; when the story has swept you away into itself and you're just rocketing along with it. If it's doing that with you, it'll do it with the reader.

For a novel that is in many ways centrally about death and grief, *Twelve Months and a Day* is also cut through with so much hope and humor. Why was it important for you to include such lightness in this story of love and loss?

Really, because of my own experience. Living with terrible grief, you have to accept the dark humor, and the passage of time. You can't stay mired forever; you have to have moments of light and, in the end, a settling into your new normal.

What do you hope readers recovering from losses of their own might take away from your story?

That they're alive! Even if the one they lost isn't. And that the one they lost doesn't need them to be sad forever. It's not that grief goes away, but a little space can be made for happiness.

Who was your favorite character to write, and why?

Oh, all of them. I especially like Nico's mum though. She plays a small part but I love her.

Your characters have such interesting and diverse backgrounds. Why was it important for you to portray these cultures and heritages? Do they have significance to you?

Yes, they're all part of my everyday life. My daughter is Ghanaian-British; I have Greek blood, Irish blood. And in London, my city, everyone is from everywhere, so to me it's completely natural to have characters from everywhere. Books without a bit of diversity, if set in a modern city, seem kind of off-kilter, a bit limited.

Without giving anything away, did you always know how the story would end?

I did. The end was the whole point of the exercise. It's the obvious ending, but so what? The pleasure is in the journey, and this isn't a psycho-thriller, a detective novel, or a horror story. It's kind of a rom-com!

What's next for you?
I'm working on an opera of *Twelve Months and a Day*. And a musical—two different shows! This is new ground for me but pretty exciting. And thinking about the future, on a thousand levels. And about a dozen new novels.

Discussion Guide

1. If you were Róisín or Rasmus, how would you have responded to that type of heartbreak? Do you think you would find love again? Have you ever experienced a similar loss, and if so, how did you handle it?

2. Would you play matchmaker if you were Jay and Nico? Do you think they did the right thing by Róisín and Rasmus?

3. *Twelve Months and a Day* features different music throughout the novel, almost as if the songs are supporting characters in each of these characters' journeys. In what ways do you think the addition of music elevates this story, and what was your favorite song in the novel?

4. If you were Jay when she was alive, would you have prepared Rasmus for the future like she did? Why or why not?

5. What was your favorite scene in the novel, and why?

6. Discuss what true love means to you, and how this sentiment is portrayed in *Twelve Months and a Day*. Do you believe there is such a thing as a soulmate? Do you believe you can love more than one person? Why or why not?

7. Do you think there is an afterlife, or a place in between where loved ones go after they pass? Have you ever felt like a loved one was close to you even after they were no longer alive?

8. What would you have done if you were in Róisín's position after Nico's death? In what ways do you think her healing process was different from that of the other characters?

9. In what way do you think the author shows there is hope for each of these characters to find their happiness throughout the novel?

10. Were you surprised by the ending?

© Habie Schwarz

LOUISA YOUNG was born in London and studied history at Cambridge. She cowrote the *Lionboy* series with her daughter and is the author of nine other books, including the bestselling *My Dear I Wanted to Tell You*, which was shortlisted for the Costa Novel Award and was a Richard & Judy Book Club choice, and *Baby Love*, longlisted for the Orange Prize. Her work is published in thirty-six languages. She lives in London.

VISIT LOUISA YOUNG ONLINE

LouisaYoung.co.uk

 Louisa-Young-author-171807502876528

 RileyPurefoy

 LouisaLouisaYoung